From the Grave to the Cradle

A Cold Wind in East Anglia

The main events in this novel take
place in 2005 and 2006.

Keith Plummer

Grosvenor House
Publishing Limited

This book is published by
Grosvenor House Publishing Ltd
Link House
140 The Broadway, Tolworth, Surrey, KT6 7HT.
www.grosvenorhousepublishing.co.uk

A CIP record for this book
is available from the British Library

ISBN 978-1-83975-964-2

Dedication

For my daughter Leena who has always
believed me to be the real David Fairfax.

Also, for my two grandsons, Joshua and Oliver,
who simply want to see their names in print.

Preface

As the number of television channels has increased so the quality of most programmes has declined.

And it is the same in the world of books, particularly fiction, where ever increasing numbers of books are published but where, with a few notable exceptions, their content is mediocre at best.

It was while bemoaning this trend to my wife and daughter and suggesting that, perhaps, I could do better, that they issued this challenge. "If you think that you can do better, then do so. Write a novel that is highly original and keeps the reader guessing right up to the last page."

For someone who, in the past, had written only for a scientific publication and whose only entry into the world of fiction consisted of a collection of short stories, this was quite a challenge. But a challenge I relished and accepted and this novel is the result.

Each
and every one
of us has secrets, or
one particular secret, that we
would wish to remain undiscovered.
Sometimes, however, fate intervenes and
such a secret is revealed. When this happens
there is no way of knowing just what
the consequences may be;
revenge, retribution
and even
murder.

Chapter One

"I don't understand this," shouted Greg struggling to make himself heard above the roar of the wind and rain, "when you asked me out for a bit of fishing I thought it would be a nice way to spend a night, something to take my mind off my practice. But where on earth did this storm come from? I can't remember one like this for a long time. And to blow up so suddenly as well."

"Don't blame me! I checked with the local weather guys and the harbour master and none of them had any idea we were in for this. They forecast a calm clear night," replied Chris at the top of his voice, clearly agitated as he struggled to steer the small boat against the combined forces of the wind and waves, "If I'd known this lot was coming I certainly wouldn't have put to sea. The money's all very well but I want to live a bit longer. Nothing's worth taking this sort of risk."

As he spoke a huge bolt of lightning flashed across the sky and almost instantaneously a deafening crack of thunder exploded right over the boat. Chris fought to retain control and looked towards the cliffs that were approaching at a rapidly increasing pace.

"Did you see that? On top of the cliffs!" Chris bellowed in an attempt to make himself heard above the thunderous roar of the waves.

"See what?" replied Greg at the top of his voice desperately trying to maintain his balance as the boat was swamped by a wave and the wheel house became drenched in foaming water.

"There, on top of the cliffs! We're approaching Maiden's Point and I'm sure I saw someone or something up there."

"Up there! Well if there is anyone up there they're even more stupid than we are to be out on a night like this. On the other hand they are on dry land, if you can call it that at the moment."

"Look Greg, I'm sure I saw a couple of figures up there. I know it's hard to tell from here but it looked as if they were fighting or struggling."

"Your trouble is you've got too vivid an imagination. I bet there's no one up there at all. It's just a tree swaying in the wind silhouetted against the sky."

"Perhaps you're right. Anyway, I've more important things to worry about, like hanging onto the wheel to avoid the rocks as we come round the headland."

Suddenly there was another terrific flash of lightning. As both men looked towards the cliffs they saw what looked like a body plunging onto the rocks.

"There, I told you." Shouted Chris almost triumphantly, "Don't tell me you didn't see that!"

"Well something's certainly fallen off that cliff but whether it's a person, a body or a tree, I couldn't care less. The sooner we're on dry land the better."

"Come on Greg. You are supposed to be a doctor. There might be someone in the water who's hurt and needs your help."

"All right then. If you think you can get this old tub closer to the cliffs then I'm willing to take a look. But if this wind and rain don't die down we'll have one hell of a job. Even opening the wheelhouse door will be risky enough. I don't fancy hanging onto the side of the boat peering into the sea for something, or someone, who might not even be there."

Then after a moment's reflection Greg added, "Anyone falling on those rocks is a goner for sure."

Chapter Two

David Fairfax leaned forward towards his driver and snapped, "Can't you go any faster? I promised the family I'd be home for dinner. That meeting at Stansted Airport took much longer than planned and now all this blasted traffic!"

"Sorry Sir David, but *it is* market day today. At the best of times Epping High Street can be crowded and now we're caught up in the rush hour."

David settled once again into the back seat of the Mercedes and thought about the meeting. It had been tough but as always he had struck a hard bargain and he was happy to have settled some old scores in the process. He looked around and then helped himself to a drink from a small cabinet and gently stroked the leather seats. He was used to luxury but he quickly tired of things. Although the car was less than a year old he was already thinking of changing it for the latest model, "Must have leather seats, though," he mused to himself.

As the car slowly made its way along the High Street he glanced at the clock on St. John's Church and checked it against his Rolex, "Damn clock's never right! Never has been for as long as I can remember," he fumed to himself. His thoughts then turned to what he would tell his family. Unlike him who had worked his way up in life they had always had it easy. However, like him they were now used to living in luxury and were even more avaricious than him.

As the car negotiated the twin mini-roundabouts by St. John's Church he reflected on recent events, "Can I really become a minister in the government? And a senior minister at that?" He mused on the past, "I wonder if there are any old acquaintances who will have to be 'encouraged' to forget!"

The car left Epping and headed into the outskirts of Epping Forest. "Handy place a forest," he reflected with a chuckle to himself, "you can lose all sorts of things in there and they won't be found for years."

The car sped through the forest down a long winding and very bumpy road towards the village of Theydon Bois, "Hey, steady on Feb! I want to get home in one piece."

"Sorry sir," said his driver apologetically.

Suddenly, on the edge of the forest and in a prime location overlooking the historic village green Fairfax's Folly came into view. That wasn't its name, it was called Forest Glade, but the house had acquired this nickname from the villagers. Even after six or seven years they still couldn't understand how planning permission for such a large mansion had been granted in this prime green-belt land. David Fairfax could. He had bribed key members of the council. Not with money but by uncovering unsavoury things from their past that were better kept hidden. He smiled to himself as he thought about those councillors, those upright pillars of the community, who he had dancing for him like puppets on a string. When he clicked his fingers they came running. This was his way of doing business and it always achieved the desired results.

The Mercedes swept onto the drive and crunched the gravel. It approached the portico at the front of the building between two rows of neatly pruned cypress trees that partially obscured the extensive but well-stocked grounds.

The house itself was illuminated by coloured floodlights and looked magnificent. Built in the imposing style of a mock-Tudor mansion its deceptively low two-storey construction concealed the fact that it had 6 bedrooms, 4 bathrooms and 4 reception rooms in addition to an underground games room and swimming pool.

The electronic gates closed sealing the property from the outside world once again. All round the extensive grounds there was a six foot high perimeter wall made of quarried stone. This was topped with barbed wire and there were closed circuit television cameras at every vantage point.

Security was paramount for David Fairfax. He was well aware that in a business career spanning over 30 years he had made more than his fair share of enemies.

There were many people who wanted to "get even" with him. Some had tried – and quickly wished they hadn't. Still, he was taking no chances. In addition to his chauffeur Feb he employed a small number of bodyguards. One or two of these were occasionally billeted in his house and sometimes they travelled with him on his more risky ventures.

Most of the time David Fairfax was content to be accompanied by Feb. John February was an ex-SAS colonel who resembled a body builder, but who was as nimble as an Olympic athlete. He was also highly intelligent with an incisive mind and could quickly react to any situation. He had more than proved himself in the past. There was no questioning his loyalty but to make sure he was paid more than double the going rate. "Insurance" was David Fairfax's way of putting it.

Feb opened the car door. David Fairfax got out and strode quickly into the house as a female servant pulled apart the heavy double front doors. He entered the drawing room and immediately all the family members stopped talking and looked at him in anticipation.

Why had they been asked, or should that have been summoned, to be here on this fine autumn day? They all regarded him in awe. Although they wouldn't admit it deep down they were all more than a little scared of him. This was partly due to his stature. At 5 feet 10 inches in height he was not a tall person but he was fairly powerfully built and always had an air of authority about him. It was also partly due to his infamous bad temper or 'short fuse' as he preferred to put it.

Straight away David's daughter Callisto ran up and gave him a big hug. She was a very attractive 23 year-old. As usual she was dressed in the latest designer outfits that enhanced her more than ample figure. She clung to him until he could bear it no longer. "That's enough," he said in as tender a way as he could. He then thought to himself, "I do like this show of affection but unlike the boys who are almost transparent I never really know what she's thinking. One of these days I'm sure she'll stab me in the back to get her hands on this business. Then woe betide the boys, they won't stand a chance."

The twins Tom and Nick were lounging on one of the many settees tormenting the two Persian cats. Like their father and sister they had a good head of blonde hair. It was only David's wife Lucy who had dark hair. In the early days of their marriage as the children grew up she had often dyed it blonde but for the last few years she had reverted to her natural brunette.

Lucy looked up from her armchair and nodded to Katie, their servant. She promptly left the room and came back almost immediately with a large tray of tea and biscuits.

"Forget that stuff!" said David rather harshly, "Let's open a bottle of champagne."

"Champagne?" questioned Lucy.

"Yes, champagne. When you hear my news you'll want to celebrate in style."

All the family immediately sat upright and looked towards David. He ignored Nick kicking both cats off the settee and sat down in his favourite armchair. To heighten the tension he deliberately delayed the start of his announcement.

Katie poured the champagne and Sir David waited for her to leave. He then lifted his glass and looked slowly around the room at his assembled family and said very deliberately, "You will soon be looking at the new Minister for Trade and Industry. A Cabinet Minister with full departmental responsibilities."

There was silence for a few seconds then Lucy stood up and said, "Well done. More than deserved after all the time, effort and money you've lavished on that party. It's about time you got something in return. What exactly will it mean though? Will it involve time away from home? Oh, and what about clashes with your business?"

"Please! One question at a time. The Prime Minister hasn't formally asked me yet, but he will do so tomorrow – or so I'm reliably informed. Naturally I will appear surprised and humbled by the offer but will, of course, accept. There won't be any problem with the businesses. They'll be put into blind trusts. Officially I will have nothing to do with the day-to-day running of them. This will avoid any possible public conflicts of interest. Unofficially, however, I will still keep an eye on them as they will be divided amongst you, my family.

So far as official duties are concerned then I expect it will involve some time away from home. There will even be some foreign trips. These will be very useful, not just for industry and the government, but also for our own future business. This appointment could give me the sort of power I've dreamt about for years."

David sank into his armchair with a broad grin on his face and finished his champagne with a single gulp. The two cats seized the opportunity and jumped onto his lap.

"That's just great, dad," said Callisto between sips of champagne, "I can't wait to see you chauffeured about in one of those ministerial cars. True recognition at last."

"We'll need to be very careful about the businesses though," said Nick, "but what great potential. I have a feeling this ministerial thing is going to make us a lot of money."

"You bet!" exclaimed Tom, "This could be the chance of a lifetime. We're just going to have to take full advantage of it." And the entire family fell into laughter.

Chapter Three

The chauffeur-driven car turned into Downing Street through the now-open heavy security gates past the armed police and came to a halt outside the door of Number 10.

As Sir David got out of the car there was a series of blinding flashes. The assembled press corps unleashed its full fury in an attempt to capture the first photographs of someone they believed would soon be a new minister. There had been comings and goings all through the afternoon and the hacks were anxious to make sense of it all. Who would be getting the sack? And who would be in the next generation of ministerial appointments? Those were the questions on the lips of all those patiently waiting across the road. Here was a Back-Bench Member of Parliament so speculation was high that a new appointment was about to be made.

"Sir David," a roar went up from the press corps. They shouted in unison to try and get him to talk to them, "Rumour has it you're destined for trade and industry." "Have you a few words for our readers?" "Will you be joining the Cabinet?"

David Fairfax ignored them all. But he did turn and smile. "After all," he thought to himself, "best to keep on friendly terms with them. They may be useful in the future – particularly if things become difficult."

He strode briskly up to the door and acknowledged the salute from the solitary policeman. He disappeared inside as the door was opened by unseen hands as if by magic.

Sir David stepped into the hall and was met by the Prime Minister's private secretary. He was ushered upstairs to wait outside the PM's study. It seemed an eternity while he sat and waited in a rather plush armchair. He amused himself by looking around the room and thinking how dowdy and old-fashioned it all seemed.

"If I was Prime Minister," he thought to himself, "the first thing I'd do is have the place redecorated and bring in some modern comfortable furniture."

He would like to have been Prime Minister but Sir David was sufficiently realistic to know that was now out of the question. Besides his age being against him, it was now 2005 and he was 54 years old, there was his past. Yes, his past, "Just what does the Prime Minister know about that?" he wondered.

"You can go in now," said a rather energetic looking personal assistant. One of many no doubt vying for promotion or some other favour in the eyes of "The Establishment".

He strode confidently into the room and heard the heavy oak doors close firmly behind him. "Come in

David," said the Prime Minister with a beaming smile, "I think you may have some idea why I've called you here today. Take a seat over there. Let's not be too formal. Much more comfortable and relaxed to sit round the coffee table. Drink?" and the Prime Minister opened a small drinks cabinet. He poured two glasses of whisky, one of which he slid across the table towards David Fairfax.

Sir David remained silent. He wanted the Prime Minister to initiate the conversation in case his informants had been wrong.

"I won't beat around the bush. I've been aware of your talents for some time now. Although you became an MP only two years ago you've impressed me with your drive and enthusiasm. You get things done. I like that. Reminds me of myself when I first entered the House. I've also been keeping an eye on your outside interests and businesses. Again, what can I say? You seem to breed success; a business empire that spans top fashion shops, international freight, telecommunications, commercial farming and now the manufacture of consumer electronics goods – and right here in the UK as well.

As you are aware the party's fortunes have taken a dive over the last few months. Amazing how fickle the electorate is. What short memories people have. After only two years in office they're already saying our policies have become stale. Some are even calling for the opposition to return. We need to reinvigorate our current term, get people and industry moving again. That's where you come in. I need someone in my

Cabinet with the drive and energy to enthuse the country. I also need someone who will present a positive image of the UK abroad and attract inward investment. God knows we need all the outside help we can get if we're to reverse what is fast becoming a deep recession.

Whilst admiring your drive and business acumen I am more than aware of your colourful past. You're no stranger to courting publicity. There have been many rumours about unfair business tactics and underhand dealings. However, I have had these checked out by the, how can I put it, appropriate bodies. I am assured there's nothing in your past that can possibly be described as illegal or reflect badly on the government. I thought it only fair to tell you this."

Sir David listened intently trying desperately hard not to betray his inner thoughts. His informants had been right after all. He struggled to suppress a smile as he guessed what was to come next.

The Prime Minister continued, "It is with great pleasure, therefore, that I'm offering you the post of Minister for Trade and Industry. As you are aware this post has full Cabinet membership. In this position you will play a key part in the party's, no, the government's, policy and decision making."

David Fairfax sat silently holding the whisky glass in his hand. He slowly spun it around so the liquid inside swirled up and down the sides in a rhythmical pattern. "Better not keep him waiting too long," he thought to himself, "or he might think I don't want the job."

"This is most unexpected and a great honour Prime Minister. I will do my utmost to be worthy of such a position and trust my time in the post will enhance both the country and the party's fortunes. I will certainly bring all my business and organisational skills to bear on the ministry. I pledge that no stone will remain unturned in my quest to make this country great once again."

"I knew you would accept the post and I'd like to take this opportunity to welcome you to the government. As this is your first ministerial appointment, and a senior one at that, I will put you in the hands of one of my personal private secretaries. He'll go over the basic points with you before you actually set foot in the ministry. Glad to have you as part of the team.

Just one other matter, though," continued the Prime Minister with a concerned look on his face, "You've been married three times and it wouldn't do for a Minister of the Crown to be seen to be playing around. We've got our standards to maintain."

David Fairfax smiled inwardly to himself. He knew all about the Prime Minister's standards but best not to rock the boat at this early stage.

"You've got no worries there," he quickly replied. "I have been married three times but as you know this was not of my own choosing. My first wife died in a tragic accident and my second wife died by her own hand. It was only through the help and understanding of Lucy that I was able to pull myself through those difficult years. It's probably not common knowledge but we've known each other since our secondary school days. We've been married now for nearly 25 years. A very happy marriage I would add with three wonderful children that I think the world of. I certainly have no intention of spoiling my family life with any misconceived affair. You know me, I don't do anything rashly, everything is well thought out before I make a move."

"I guessed as much," smiled the Prime Minister. He got up from his chair, leaned over the coffee table and the two men shook hands warmly. He then contacted Philip Dobbs one of his private secretaries. He came into the room and escorted David Fairfax to a small office where the necessary formalities could be gone through.

"This is it," David thought to himself wryly, "a new career as a Minister of the Crown. Just think how much this is going to help me and my businesses. No point helping the party, helping the government, helping the country, helping the people even, if one can't help oneself in the process!"

Chapter Four

"A bit slower Feb," snapped David Fairfax as the car reached the heart of Canary Wharf and the Fairfax Building came into sight, "I want to appreciate the view. I won't be seeing it so often now that I'm a Minister of the Crown."

"Very good, Sir David," replied Feb with a rather resigned note to his voice, "I shall miss driving you. I hope it doesn't mean you'll no longer need me now that you're getting an official chauffeur."

"Quite the reverse. In fact I might need you much more in the future. Official cars and chauffeurs are all very well but there are times, and I don't think I need to spell them out, when I'll need to have someone I can trust. Someone to take me where, perhaps, I shouldn't be seen. Someone who can keep their mouth shut. Someone who can take care of themselves – and me too of course!"

As the car turned the futuristic steel and concrete structure that was the Fairfax Building slid into view. On this sunny autumn day it looked simply magnificent as its reflection shimmered in the water of this former dock area. David Fairfax's car came silently to a halt. Before Feb had an opportunity to open his door a uniformed commissionaire rushed out and opened the rear door for Sir David to alight.

"Thank you Wilson," he said and strode into the building and made his way towards his personal lift. Already a member of the security staff was opening the door in readiness and David acknowledged him as he always made a point of doing. His view was that you never knew when you might need these people in the future. He then pressed the button for the third floor. This was where the Board Rooms were located and he waited as the lift silently ascended.

In his dark Saville Row pin-striped suit he cut an impressive figure. He slowly and deliberately walked into the Board Room and glanced around the huge glass table. No dark mahogany wood tables for David Fairfax. He had said on more than one occasion to his trusted lieutenants that it does no harm to keep on the good side of the green lobby. You never knew when you might need their support.

Sir David entered the room and everybody went to rise to their feet. With a small gesture of his hand he motioned for them to continue sitting. He waited for a few seconds before starting to speak.

"First of all I'd like to thank each of you for making this meeting at what has been very short notice indeed. Things moved faster than even I had anticipated. I've called you all here today because now that I'm a Minister of the Crown I will have to relinquish my business responsibilities in the Fairfax Group. For the period of my Ministerial Office I will have nothing whatsoever to do with the running of these companies. My shares will be put into a blind trust in accordance with established government policy. That is why, in addition to the Managing Directors of my core businesses and my children, I have arranged for our auditors and legal people to be here. The necessary legal niceties and frameworks can be put into place and that way we all know where we stand.

Before letting the auditors and the legal boys have their say I would like to take this opportunity to congratulate you all on what has been a truly outstanding year. We have expanded into new areas and profits have continued to grow at a hitherto unprecedented rate. Needless to say, your hard work in this success will be more than adequately reflected in your end-of-year bonuses. Well done everybody!"

At that point David acknowledged the murmurs of appreciation from around the table and handed over to the auditors and lawyers. They spelled out the legal ramifications of what was to take place and put into being the formal legal procedures. When all the necessary paperwork had been signed the auditors took their leave and David turned to face the Managing Directors of his empire.

"Angela, shut and lock the doors. I don't want anyone disturbing us so all mobile phones off as well please."

There was a short period of rustling of papers and phones being taken out of bags and pockets. Becoming impatient David lightly tapped the table with his fingers to signal that he wished to proceed.

"Now, contrary to what has just been said in front of the auditors, I want to make it crystal clear that I have no intention whatsoever of relinquishing control over the DF International Group! And I want you all to remember that! Officially I have severed all my ties with the Group. Unofficially, however, I can't afford to do that for even the briefest of periods. There is just too much at stake.

Although I won't be in this building again officially make no mistake I will be popping in and out whenever it suits me. Furthermore I have charged Callisto, Tom and Nick to be my eyes and ears. They will report to me on all matters. Through them I will make sure that you're left in no doubt as to what my views and wishes are. It will be business as usual – for both you and me! Between them they have a presence on all four boards of the Group and that presence will ensure that I maintain total control."

He knew this decision would be received in silence so David leant slowly back in his chair. He observed his colleagues as the full weight of his statement sunk in and they began to reflect on the implications.

Immediately to his left sat Alan Box who was the Managing Director of the DesboroDenim Fashion Group. He was in his middle 50s and a slightly-built weasel-faced man. He was not liked by many of his colleagues or staff as he had a reputation for being ruthless when it came to getting things done. He also had a cruel and almost sadistic tendency when it came to exploiting third-world labour to remain competitive. David admired these traits. Because he had been with him for over 20 years Alan Box had his full confidence and support in every decision he took. His personality, however, was bland to the extreme and he would hardly be noticed in a room or a crowd of people. He was also very sensitive about his name and in correspondence he was always referred to as Mr Box or Alan Box, never as A Box! He was nicknamed 'Cardboard' by his fellow directors but never to his face.

On Alan Box's left sat Ken Winter the Managing Director of Fairfax Forwarding, the international freight and delivery arm of the Fairfax Empire. In terms of physical appearance he was the exact opposite of Alan Box. He was in his early 50s but was an imposing thick-set man who exuded authority everywhere he went. He quickly dominated any conversation or meeting and had a more than deserved reputation for being a ruthless businessman. He was also aggressive and had no hesitation in bending all the rules if it meant winning new business or obtaining new contracts. He had also been with David Fairfax for over 20 years. During that time he had been involved in numerous shady middle-eastern deals many of which, with the connivance of local politicians and governments, had given Fairfax Forwarding exclusive rights to the detriment of rival firms. David gave a wry smile as he looked at Ken Winter and thought about the less savoury types of freight that he had been instrumental in smuggling into the UK, illegal immigrants included!

Next to Ken Winter was Rahul Dixit. In contrast to the former two Board Members he was still only in his mid 20s. Although he had been with David Fairfax for just 8 or 9 years he was already the Managing Director of Fairfax Telecoms. Originally he had been in charge of Fairfax Telecoms' All India Division. He was dynamic, highly qualified, bright and intelligent and, with his very likeable personality, had quickly been promoted to overall Managing Director. The convenient disappearance of the previous Managing Director in a remote part of India about 18 months previously was still the subject of a police investigation.

Rahul Dixit was disliked by many on the Board. He was always snappily dressed but possibly because of his impeccable manners he tended to get on peoples' nerves. He was also a devout Hindu and made no secret about this. However, he was still deeply involved in the black market and the trafficking of people to the UK from India to work in other parts of the Fairfax Group.

The last of the four Managing Directors was Craig Bentley. He was in his early 40s and had been with David Fairfax for about 10 years and was now the head of Fairfax Farms. He had been in commercial farming for all his life and was an expert agronomist and shrewd businessman. He was most adept at maximising subsidies from the UK Government and the European Union, even when the activities or particular crops did not qualify! He was also in charge of a number of gang-masters and was famed for obtaining labour at absolute minimum cost employing cheap illegal workers whenever possible in preference to local labour.

Next to Craig Bentley sat Callisto who was on the board of the DesboroDenim Fashion Group. As befitted someone of her status she was very fashion conscious and always dressed in the latest designer fashions. Her father had long recognised her as being highly intelligent. Combined with her incisive mind and good business acumen he felt she would be a worthy successor. This was a view shared by Callisto herself even though she was still only 23 years old! She was also very cool and calculating and rarely showed her feelings as she regarded this as a weakness to be avoided. Although she had a number of boyfriends none of them was serious or long-term. She tended to use them and they were around only as long as they served her purposes.

Sitting next to Callisto were the twins Tom and Nick who were a year younger than their big sister. They were not as overtly ambitious as Callisto but both held positions on the boards of Fairfax Telecoms, Fairfax Forwarding and Fairfax Farms. Tom was the older by a few minutes. He was more dynamic and go-ahead than Nick but he had a cruel streak whereas Nick was more easygoing and prepared to take the easy option.

On the twins' left sat Susan Rumble the Chief Accountant of the Fairfax Group. Although only in her early 30s she was a highly qualified accountant who specialised in company tax law. Her skills had saved the Group many thousands of pounds in the 5 or 6 years she had been employed. She had a reputation for continued study and apparent lack of a social life. Combined with her bespectacled and rather dowdy appearance she was nicknamed 'the spinster'. But so far as her work was concerned she was acknowledged as being one of the best in the profession.

Finally going round the table and on David's right was Angela Hamilton his personal assistant. She was in her late 20s and had proved herself to be highly efficient in all aspects of her work and David had come increasingly to rely on her. She was a very beautiful woman who always dressed most professionally. She never wore anything that was too revealing although sometimes there were plenty of hints. David had often been tempted to 'try it on' but had always thought better of it. This was partly due to her very strong character and partly because of her value to his business. It was probably more to do with the latter reason as she had been instrumental in clinching some very profitable deals for him, including some 'shady' ones. She had a good knowledge of all areas of David Fairfax's business empire including the illegal ones. In just 2 years of employment Angela Hamilton had become a trusted and valued member of the top team. She was often referred to behind her back as 'Lady Hamilton'. This amused David who often imagined he saw some of his own character in her.

After a few minutes quiet musings on his fellow board members David Fairfax once again raised his voice.

"Now that we're on our own the real purpose of this meeting can commence. As I said, forget what I told the auditors. I've no intention whatsoever of giving up control of this business or any part of it. I've spent too long building it up to turn my back on it even for a moment. Besides, I know you would all miss me," he said rather cynically with a grin on his face. "Basically things will go on as before but because of my position in the Government I will have to be careful. No, we will all have to be careful, very careful indeed! Officially I have relinquished all control of the business but unofficially I will still retain control through Callisto, Tom and Nick. You will all report to me through them and they will give you my decisions and directions. That way nobody outside of this room will be any the wiser as to what is actually going on. So, Callisto will deal with the DesboroDenim Fashion Group, Nick will deal with Fairfax Telecoms and Tom will deal with both Fairfax Forwarding and Fairfax Farms. Any questions?"

There was a long pause as David Fairfax slowly looked around the table.

"Yes," said Alan Box reluctantly breaking the silence, "I don't like it. I don't like this idea of you being a minister at all. I think it's going to lay all our activities open to scrutiny. The press is always looking for ways to discredit you and your business activities. I think they will look upon this appointment as a means of delving ever more closely into your background. Why deliberately spoil something that is working so well?"

"I had already thought of that. To the world at large I will be a model minister. Already on my first day of office it's public knowledge that I have severed all connections with my business empire. And that is a notion we are all going to have to foster. There must be no room for complacency. No room for anyone to point an accusing finger. No prying eyes, particularly from the press."

"I still think you're making a mistake."

"Look, before accepting this appointment, before I first thought of even becoming a Member of Parliament, my primary concern was 'what's in this for me? What can I get out of it?' And I haven't deviated from that view. Becoming a minister, particularly Trade and Industry, is the best possible thing to come out of being in Parliament. I will be getting lots of inside information on what's going on with business in this country including our competitors. I shall also be making several official ministerial trips abroad and going on some important trade missions. And guess what? I'm not looking just to benefit the UK! I'm looking to benefit the Fairfax Group. To benefit you, every single one of you sitting around this table today."

"I'm beginning to like what I'm hearing," interjected Rahul Dixit, "I think you've already got a trade mission going to India in the New Year."

"That's correct. I've also got similar missions lined up that are going to Africa and South America. These are all areas in which we are actively expanding. Officially I will be promoting trade with the UK. Unofficially, of course, I will really be using these visits to promote our own interests. That's why, apart from the usual officials and civil servants, I will make sure I'm accompanied by my wife or by some of my children. There is also the possibility that I will just happen to bump into you or a local manager in the course of my travels."

In the general conversation that followed there was much praise for David Fairfax's cautious but sensible approach and the many benefits that should accrue to all. It was also agreed that there was to be the utmost secrecy surrounding any contact with him. That way it would be impossible for any outside party to suggest that there was even the slightest hint of any conflict between his official ministerial duties and his private companies.

"Don't forget the latest technology," said Rahul Dixit opening his briefcase, "we can also keep in touch with Sir David by email and the internet."

"Isn't that rather risky," suggested Ken Winter, "I've heard stories of people being convicted of all sorts of crimes because they couldn't wipe their computers clean. They erased the files but somehow they could still be read if you had the right software. And the police have that software."

"Ken is of course perfectly correct. But," continued Rahul, "it is now possible to erase all traces of those files if you have the right software. And we have that software."

He handed an impressive looking gold-cased CD ROM to all those seated round the table.

"Install this CD on all the PCs that you use including your laptops. When you logoff after each email or internet session it will automatically clean your hard disc of all emails, internet sites visited, cookies and temporary internet files stored offline. Even if you were in the middle of a compromising message or email the mere fact of switching off the machine would mean that all traces of it would be erased from the hard disc in the PC's logging off sequence. So you can communicate with Sir David if the need arises and be safe in the knowledge that no traces will remain whatsoever."

"Thanks Rahul," said David Fairfax approvingly, "but email communication should only be used as a last resort."

"There's a disc for you too Sir David. You might wish to install it on your ministerial PC as an added safeguard."

"Angela, the champagne!"

Angela Hamilton went over to a large cabinet at the far end of the room and opened the double stainless steel doors. She took out two bottles of expensive champagne and poured a glass for all those present.

"A toast ladies and gentlemen! A toast to our future prosperity!"

Chapter Five

Lucy Fairfax lay back on the chair-shaped lilo as it slowly drifted across the pool. She looked up as the reflections from the coloured lights on the pool bottom danced across the ceiling. She lazily took another sip of her drink.

"What a good idea of mine to have this pool built particularly as David and the boys insisted on having a games room and a snooker table."

She thought about the rest of her day. Meeting 'the girls' as she liked to call them. A group of like-minded middle-aged women who all had far too much time on their hands and, just as importantly, far too much money. A girlies day out was in prospect. They would meet up at Woodford at one o'clock, take the tube to London, spend the afternoon shopping in The King's Road and Sloane Street, and then round the day off with a meal and a drink. Sometimes they also took in a show but this time they had decided to concentrate purely on the shopping.

"Just time to have a sauna before I get ready," she thought to herself, "Now what shall I wear?" And she directed the lilo towards the side of the pool and pulled herself up on the steps and out of the water. She paused briefly at the top of the steps to look at herself in the wall of mirrors that lined one side of the pool. "Not bad for your age," she said out aloud as she walked briskly towards the sauna looking at herself in the mirrors from different angles.

About an hour later she had changed into a rather risqué outfit, at least for a woman in her fifties, and she walked out of the back of the house. There were always several cars parked there. Hers of course, the children's and sometimes those of visitors. Since David had become a Minister there were often even more cars as Government business frequently intruded into his home life.

Lucy looked at her gleaming red sports car. It was less than six months old and was in immaculate condition. Every weekend she had a couple of lads from the village wash and wax all the family's cars. They were under strict instructions to be very careful, very careful indeed, with her little number. As she walked towards the car she checked inside her handbag, mobile phone, keys, credit and debit cards and about three hundred pounds in cash, "That should be enough for today," she thought to herself.

She sat in the driver's seat and started the engine. With a mighty rev and a screech of gravel she raced towards the electronic gates. They opened barely in time to let her through. Now was the part of the journey she relished the most, the drive through the forest along the winding narrow roads in the midst of the trees. She had a reputation for driving very fast and had lost count of the number of speeding tickets she had picked up in the village. The speed cameras around the village green and the pond posed a particular nuisance for her.

"This is the life," she thought to herself as the car picked up speed and she left the main road to hurtle along the country lane. This was a slightly longer route than sticking to the main roads but for her it was much more fun. Besides at this time of day there wasn't much risk of meeting an oncoming vehicle on this narrow single track.

As she reached the brow of a small incline where the road forked into two she was vaguely aware of a large four-wheel-drive vehicle standing on the side of the track. She went to turn into the left-hand fork but without warning the vehicle suddenly pulled out right in front of her. She was forced to swerve violently to the right and take the right-hand fork. Unlike the road she was on this was even more of a country track. Not only was it narrower but it was also more uneven and windy.

Despite Lucy's best efforts to maintain control the car left the narrow track. She desperately tried to brake without skidding and attempted to steer between the trees that suddenly seemed to be closing in on all sides of her. They were becoming denser by the second as her car raced out of control. All of a sudden a tree loomed up in front of her and she was unable to avoid it. Her car hit the tree head on and buried its bonnet into the trunk. Lucy seldom bothered to wear a seat belt. She was flung forward and her head smashed into the windscreen before bouncing back onto her headrest and finally came to rest on the steering wheel. Her face was covered in blood and she remained motionless slumped over the steering wheel.

Slowly and very quietly the four-wheel-drive vehicle descended along the track and stopped adjacent to the wrecked sports car. After a short while a figure clad all in black from head to toe jumped out athletically and made its way to the sports car.

For a while the masked figure surveyed the scene then very deliberately lifted Lucy Fairfax out of the sports car and laid her on the ground with her hands folded across her chest in the manner of a medieval effigy. Then the contents of Lucy's handbag were examined and the bag placed beside her prone body after her mobile phone had been removed.

The masked figure dialled 999. In response to the question about which service was required replied in a rather rasping gravely voice "Ambulance. There's been an accident." The location of the crashed car was then given and the phone placed by Lucy's side. The masked figure walked back to the four-wheel-drive vehicle and returned with a small carrier bag which was placed on the passenger seat of the sports car on top of Lucy's jacket. After returning to the four-wheel-drive vehicle it was reversed back onto the narrow road and then sped off towards Loughton.

Chapter Six

"Sir David. I have the police on the line for you," his Private Personal Secretary said and transferred the call through to the Minister.

He put the receiver to his ear, "David Fairfax here. What can I do for you?"

"Sir David, it's the Assistant Chief Constable of Essex. I have some bad news for you. It's your wife, I'm afraid there's been an accident."

"What! An accident! Is she all right?" he blurted out most uncharacteristically.

"There's no need for you to worry. She's been involved in a car accident. She's still unconscious but the doctors tell me she should make a full recovery."

"Where is she? I must go and see her."

"She's in Princess Alexandra Hospital, Harlow. We can send a car for you if that would help."

"No, thank you. I'll quickly finish here at the ministry and get my driver to take me there." Sir David replaced the receiver and quickly finalised a few papers. He then strode into his outer office and handed them to one of his staff.

"I've got to leave straight away but I've finished with these. My wife's been involved in an accident. Not sure if I'll be in tomorrow but I'll let you know later today or tomorrow morning." He gestured to his official chauffeur who followed him out of the office and down to the underground car park.

It was a very worried David Fairfax who sat in the back of the limousine for the almost two-hour journey to the hospital.

When he arrived he was met by two uniformed police inspectors and taken inside the hospital by a side entrance so he could avoid a small group of reporters who had gathered outside the main entrance.

"Most sorry about this Sir David. I've no idea how they got hold of the story. If indeed there is a story."

"Never mind. I'm no stranger to the press. Anything to do with me and they seem to think it's worth having a dig. Any idea what happened?"

"No, not really. We've got the forensic boys over there at the moment. It looks like she was driving along one of those narrow roads through the forest and she simply run out of road."

"Really! She's usually such a good driver but," and he hesitated, "she does like to drive fast. Could be mechanical failure I suppose but the car's less than a year old, six months I think."

"Well, the forensics will tell us."

David Fairfax approached the private room and saw Callisto, Nick and Tom waiting in the corridor. At his appearance they all stood up and came to meet him.

"Thank God you're here," blurted out Nick, "mum hasn't come round yet. We're so worried about her."

"So am I, Nick. So am I. Do any of you know what happened? I know your mother was going to London so I assume this happened on the way to the station."

"The police think it was an accident but there's some mystery about who phoned for the ambulance," added Callisto, "somebody actually used mum's mobile phone."

"Was she on her own or was there somebody else in the car with her?"

"I spoke to Katie and she said mum left on her own. She turned out of the drive straight onto the road to Woodford where she was due to meet the others."

David was about to reply to Callisto when one of the doctors emerged from the room and said Lucy had regained consciousness.

All the family immediately went into the room and stood around the bed. Lucy appeared to be in a bad way but the doctor explained that it looked worse than it was. She had sustained a severe blow to the head and her nose was broken, she had two black eyes and her lips were cut and swollen but there would be no lasting damage. He then went on to lecture the family about the dangers of not wearing seat belts. This point was picked up by Chief Inspector Westwood of the local CID who had followed them into the private room.

"Lucy! Thank goodness you're all right. We're all so worried about you," said her husband. "How do you feel?"

"I feel bloody rough. My face hurts, my neck hurts and my whole body aches. And to top it all I have the worst headache I can ever remember."

"Given the circumstances I think you've been lucky."

"Luck's got nothing to do with it. I was forced off that road!"

"What! What do you mean forced off the road?"

"Exactly what I said. Somebody forced me off the road. I was approaching Robin Hood's Dell when a large four-wheel-drive Land Rover type thing pulled out right in front of me. I swerved and had to take the other road. The last thing I remember was leaving the road and trying to avoid the trees. I suppose my luck ran out and I hit one. Knowing me a bloody big one!"

"That's a serious allegation Lady Lucy," interjected Inspector Westwood. "So far my officers haven't found any trace of another vehicle. No tyre prints or evidence of anyone else having been at the scene."

"Then who made the phone call requesting an ambulance?" added Callisto rather cynically, obviously giving her mother the benefit of the doubt.

"You were alone in the car I take it? No passengers?"

"No, none." said Lucy most emphatically and she stared at the Inspector in sheer disbelief at his remarks.

"Well what motive would there be for someone to deliberately run you off the road? Nothing appears to have been stolen. Your handbag with your credit cards, money and mobile phone were all found by your side," pondered the Inspector. "Still there are a couple of odd things about this incident."

"And what are they?" enquired David Fairfax rather sarcastically.

"Somebody, and this may be the person you allege ran you off the road, lifted you out of the car and laid you on the ground and placed your belongings by your side. That person probably made the call summoning the ambulance. The motive, if there was one, was certainly not robbery. All calls to the emergency services are recorded. We've played that call back many times but it is difficult to come up with an accent or even if the caller was male or female. The voice seems to have been disguised using a voice modulator or some such thing. Our forensic guys are still working on it."

"I can assure you Inspector that I did not run out of road. I was forced off it! I know every inch of that road. I could do that journey blindfolded if I had to."

"We'll get to the bottom of this don't worry. By the way your jacket and the carrier bag on the passenger seat also appear to have been untouched."

My jacket and carrier bag! Yes," said Lucy thoughtfully, "Yes I did have a jacket in the car but I didn't have anything else with me, certainly not a carrier bag!"

Inspector Westwood left the room and returned after a couple of minutes with two large polythene bags containing the jacket and the carrier bag.

"Here," he said, "this is what was found on the passenger seat."

"My coat, right enough," acknowledged Lucy, "but the carrier bag's not mine. Looks like it could be one of ours. It's from the DesboroDenim Fashion Group but there's something odd about it. Is there anything in it?"

"Here, give it to me," said Callisto and snatched it out of the Inspector's hands.

"It does look like one of ours but it's obviously a fake. Look at that rather odd logo! The logo looks so old-fashioned! Look at this! There's some underwear in here. Now," and she pulled the items out, "we certainly don't make this sort of stuff. It's for wrinklies. Just look at it!"

David had remained silent up to this point. But without warning he suddenly stood up and tore the carrier bag from a surprised Callisto's grasp.

"I don't understand," he stammered, "this is a genuine DesboroDenim carrier bag and this is genuine DesboroDenim underwear." He held them both up so that all present could see them. "But what's most odd is that all the items are at least 30 years old. These are from the DesboroDenim range of the mid-1970s."

"Now let me get this straight," butted-in Inspector Westwood who sensed that all might not be as it seemed. "You are saying Lady Lucy that you did not put this carrier bag and its contents into your car when you left your house earlier today. And you Sir David are saying that these are genuine DesboroDenim items but that they date from the 1970s."

"That's correct!" responded both Sir David and Lady Lucy in unison.

"Could it be then that they were deliberately left there by the person you say forced you off the road? The same person who phoned the emergency services? Can you tell me why somebody would want to do such a thing? Why someone would go to so much trouble? Surely, if they had wanted to frighten you, or even kill you, then why this extra touch? Why bother to phone for an ambulance? Have you any enemies Lady Lucy? Can you think of anybody you've upset or offended? Someone who would be capable of doing this?"

"No, nobody at all."

"This DesboroDenim fashion label. You say it's been a part of your business for a long time?"

"Yes," answered David, "it was my first real venture into the business world. It's the oldest part of the Fairfax Group. I retain a great affection for it even to this day. It was what set me on the long and at times difficult road to success."

"Did you start this particular business on your own or did you have a partner?"

"On my own I suppose."

"You suppose. Surely you know."

"Well actually the business was started by my first wife's parents. They founded it soon after she was born and that's where the name comes from, a shortening of their surname, Desborough. Sadly both parents died when Dawn was still in her teens and by the time we married the business was in bit of a sorry state. Together we made a go of it and little by little it has grown into the world-wide fashion group of today. It's not just underwear, nowadays the group produces a whole range of clothes."

"And what happened to your first wife? Did you divorce her? Is she still alive?"

"No, I regret to say she died about two years after we were married. It was a tragic accident. We were on holiday in Suffolk. She went for a walk on her own along the cliffs on a particularly blustery evening and didn't return. Apparently she fell into the sea and was drowned. I was devastated but her death only made me more determined to make a success of the business. I've even kept the name unchanged in her memory."

"I'm sorry Sir David. I was just trying to make a connection. The motive for a crime, if that is indeed what took place in the forest, can often be rooted in the past. But as your first wife is dead that rather rules out that possibility."

"It certainly does. Her body was washed up along the coast a couple of days later. I identified the body myself in the mortuary. Often in my mind I can still see it even to this day. There's no doubt that she is dead."

"Well, that's all for now. I'll be going. We'll be making enquiries and will keep you informed of progress. The Chief Constable himself has expressed an interest in what has happened so we have more than sufficient resources. In the meantime, and just to be on the safe side, I'd be careful Lady Lucy if you are going anywhere on your own. For the immediate future at least I'd make sure you're accompanied."

"Don't worry inspector," said David Fairfax reassuringly, "I'll make sure one of my security team keeps an eye on her. She'll be safe enough."

"We'll need to keep Lady Lucy in overnight for tests to ensure that there is no concussion but I'm confident she should be able to return home by lunch time tomorrow," said one of the doctors. "If you wish you can spend the night here with her. There's an adjoining room that can be made ready for you."

"Fine!" said Callisto, "I'll stay with her. But I'm going to remain here in this room."

"As you wish," agreed David, "we'll go home now and check how things are with you in the morning."

* * * * *

The journey to Theydon Bois took a little over 20 minutes. Feb had arrived and took Sir David home in his Mercedes allowing the official chauffeur to return to London. The two boys followed in Tom's car.

When they had all arrived back at Forest Glade and had changed and had something to eat there was the sound of a car pulling up on the gravel drive.

"Inspector Westwood for you sir," announced Katie and ushered the detective into the drawing room where the family were gathered.

"We have a development. The four-wheel-drive vehicle that was involved in this regrettable incident has been found. It was stolen earlier today from Epping High Street and was found in the car park of Loughton Tube Station. The forensic boys are there now but the early indication is that it's clean. No fingerprints or anything else to shed light on the attacker. We're not sure if the station has any relevance but we're working on the theory that the attacker may have gone to London."

"Thank you inspector. Katie, please show the inspector out."

Chapter Seven

"Come on! Hurry it up!" urged a hooded shape just visible in the darkness.

"I'm almost there. I'll soon have this door open," reassured his colleague.

"Look out! There's a car coming. Might be the police! Let's get out of here!" and the two shapes quickly melted into the shadows as a dark-coloured car sped almost silently along the dimly-lit street. The driver glanced at the clock on the town hall and noted that it showed just before midnight. The car continued through the deserted town of Witham, past the Police Station closed for the night, and turned into the warren of roads that make up the industrial estate.

The car made its way to the end of a small cul-de-sac and parked between two lorries that were in a particularly dark secluded spot. After a short while a black-clad figure emerged carrying a small holdall and ran silently towards a chicken processing plant. After scaling a small perimeter wall the figure continued to an adjoining large warehouse and approached a small side door. The figure tried a number of keys and eventually gained entry. After about 15 minutes the figure emerged from the building still clutching the holdall and made its way back to the car which then left the industrial estate and took the road to Maldon.

Less than 10 minutes later the car had driven through Maldon High Street and was en-route to the nearby village of Latchingdon. Just before reaching the village the car turned into a deeply rutted track and silently approached a farm that boasted several large outbuildings and silos. The figure waited in the car for a few minutes then got out and approached the outbuildings again carrying a small holdall. After a short while the figure returned to the car and drove off silently into the night.

* * * * *

David Fairfax was awakened from a deep sleep by the sound of his mobile phone. He reached over to answer it and was surprised to see that his bedroom clock was showing five o'clock in the morning.

His natural inclination was to shout at the caller for disturbing his sleep. But now he was a minister of the crown he had to curb such instincts because it might just be some civil servant on government business. Or worse still it might be the Prime Minister or one of his advisers. It wouldn't do to upset any of them. So far his ministerial position had led to a number of very lucrative deals and he didn't want to jeopardise any future such opportunities.

"Hello David it's Alan, Alan Box. Sorry to disturb you but I've got some bad news. It's about the clothing warehouse in Witham. There's been a fire and almost all the stock has been destroyed."

"What do you mean almost all the stock destroyed?" he angrily cut in, "What about the sprinklers? How did the fire start anyway?"

"Well, that's just it. The fire brigade and the police are here now. They think it was started deliberately. They've got the place sealed off and aren't letting anyone in – and that includes me!"

"What about the night watchman? Don't we have someone there on site to keep an eye on things?"

"Yes, last night it was a guy called Andy Bennett. Good man, been with us for years. But there's something else you should know. The sprinkler system didn't go off. It should do so automatically when fire or smoke is detected but the fire brigade says it was turned off at the main switch. They've got some of their people looking at it now."

"Look! Stay there. Find out as much as you can. Get back to me with anything that the police or fire people come up with. I want to get to the bottom of this, do you understand?" David snapped angrily and went to turn off his phone but Alan Box interrupted him.

"There's something else you should know. On the wall by the sprinkler switch the fire brigade found a small carrier bag, a DesboroDenim carrier bag, but not one of our current ones. They've bagged it up and shown it to me and it looks similar to one of our older numbers. Matter of fact it looks very much like the one found in Lucy's car when she had that accident last month."

David Fairfax was silent for a while. Then very deliberately and very slowly he hissed into the phone, "I don't like the sound of this. I'll get back to you. Maybe we have to do a bit of digging ourselves. Let's see what the police come up with then we'll have our own investigation."

He placed the phone back on the bedside table and as he settled back under the covers looked at Lucy fast asleep beside him. Then, barely ten minutes later as he was drifting back to sleep, the phone rang again.

This time he was not so polite, "Who is it?" he shouted, "What do you want?"

"David, is that you? It's Craig here. Afraid I've got some bad news!"

"Bad news! Bad news! What sort of bad news?" he bellowed into the phone.

"It's the farm at Latchingdon. I'm afraid there's been a fire and we've lost most of the produce stored in the outbuildings."

"What!" he roared and sat up in bed so violently that Lucy woke up with a start.

"David, what's going on?"

"Shut up and go back to sleep!" he snapped.

"Look here," shouted David Fairfax into his phone, "just what is the damage?"

"Nearly all the buildings and their contents have been destroyed. The scene is like something out of a disaster movie. Almost everything apart from the farmhouse itself has been burnt to the ground."

"What about the fire brigade? Didn't they get there in time?"

"Afraid not. Apparently they were fighting a big warehouse fire in Witham. They also claimed it was hard to find us because we're in such an isolated spot."

David was incandescent with rage, "Fighting a fire in Witham. You bet they were. It was at my warehouse!"

Craig was silent for a moment then continued, "The police are also here and have got everything cordoned off. They think it was deliberate and are saying it was arson. Oh, and one more thing, they found a small DesboroDenim carrier bag with some underwear in it a short distance from the buildings. Most strange!"

"This is getting personal!" screeched David Fairfax, "Stay there until I get in touch with you!" And he slammed the phone hard down on the table.

"Trouble darling?" enquired Lucy who was not yet fully awake.

"Trouble! Trouble! It hasn't started yet! There's going to be trouble all right! Someone's started to play a very dangerous game and I'm going to finish it! Mark my words. I'm going to finish this good and proper!"

David continued to sit up in bed for a while pondering the situation then he jumped out of bed, "I'm getting up. I've got some serious thinking to do."

* * * * *

Breakfast came early to the Fairfax household next morning. All the family were sitting round the table rather gloomily digesting the news about the events of the previous night.

"Think dad! Who would want to do this to us?" asked Nick.

"Why would they want to do it?" added Tom, "Have we trodden on any particularly sensitive toes lately?"

"No, the real question that comes to my mind," said Callisto slowly turning to face her father, "is who *could* do this to us? Who is in a position to do it? Who has the information needed to do it?"

"Good thinking Callisto," agreed her father, "this could be an inside job. But who? Let me think. Why and who? Or who and why?"

"And those old DesboroDenim carrier bags and the ancient underwear. What is the significance of those?"

pondered Callisto out loud, "And anyway where are they coming from? If they are genuine who could possibly have kept them for all this time – and for what reason? Surely nobody harbours a grudge for 30 years or more before doing something about it? Do they?"

"I thought the bags and underwear may have had something to do with the DesboroDenim Fashion Group. Perhaps an ex-employee but the attack on the farm tends to suggest otherwise. Nonetheless I'll get 'Cardboard' over here today and have it out with him. Yes, and I'll also make sure that Craig comes over to the house so I can find out just what did happen on that farm."

There was silence while he sipped his coffee then David added, "We'll also speak to those *so-called* night watchmen who were supposed to be keeping an eye on things. I want to hear for myself what they have to say about the events of last night."

A leaden silence came over the breakfast table. Then just as Katie was clearing away the dishes David Fairfax's mobile phone rang again.

Chapter Eight

David Fairfax listened with increasing disbelief and growing anger to the voice on the other end of his mobile phone. He had been about to get up from the breakfast table but he immediately sat down again. "Leave it with me. I'll get back to you later. Just make sure we're in the clear!"

"Have you finished with these Sir?"

"Leave them! Get out! Do you hear me? Get out! I want to speak to my family in private! Leave us, now!"

A rather flustered Katie stopped collecting the dishes and hurried out of the dining room. She wasn't unduly concerned at David's attitude. He was renowned for losing his temper and she had seen him in far worse moods.

After Katie had left the room he looked around to make sure the family were alone. David then grabbed his mobile phone and dialled. After a few seconds there was a response, "Feb, get 'Laurel and Hardy' and meet me in 'The Shop' in about two hours' time."

He then phoned Alan Box and Craig Bentley and told them to meet him at 'The Shop' accompanied by the night watchmen who had been on duty at the farm and the warehouse the previous night.

Turning to his family David motioned to them to remain at the table. In a voice trembling with emotion he said, "We've got a problem all right, a serious problem. That was Ken Winter. You'll never guess what's happened now. One of our container lorries has been pulled over by police and immigration. Apparently it had cleared the docks at Felixstowe but after it left the A14 and joined the A12 it was stopped. It was taken to a lay-by where the immigration people found 24 illegal Chinese immigrants."

"I don't understand this. How can these things all be happening at once?" asked a puzzled Callisto.

"Well I'm going to get to the bottom of it and I'm making a start now. Ken says the lorry wasn't actually from our fleet. It was one we had hired so he thinks the police shouldn't be able to link it directly to us."

"All the same," said Tom, "we're going to make a loss on the deal aren't we?"

"In more ways than one. This time those workers weren't for our farms but a special 'consignment' we were bringing in for our Chinese friends in London. This is going to be tricky and costly. They're a vicious lot and will be demanding some form of recompense. I'll have Ken speak to them and sort it out."

At that moment as David was about to answer a question from Tom there was the sound of a car drawing up on the drive followed by the chimes of the door bell. A little later there was a tap rather than a knock at the dining room door and a rather hesitant Katie announced that Chief Inspector Westwood wished to speak to the family.

"Come in Inspector, we've been expecting you," said David Fairfax. He motioned the Chief Inspector to a vacant seat at the table, "Tea or coffee?"

"No thanks, I'm ok. I'll come straight to the point. You're already aware of the events of last night and the attacks on your business premises."

"Strictly speaking they're nothing to do with me now that I'm a minister of the crown," and then he thought to himself, "Thank goodness he hasn't mentioned the illegal immigrants. If he linked them to me then we're all in trouble."

The Inspector continued, "As I was saying, we think this is a warning to you, or to your family. We're confident that the forensic boys will come up with something but in the meantime you may be at risk. We think you should have some form of protection. Not just when you're on official business or travelling to and from work but also here at your home."

"That's very considerate of you Inspector but I must decline the offer. I agree this is a serious matter but I don't see what's happening as being directed at me or my family. If that was the case then the attackers could have struck here, at the family home, at me and my family. This sounds more like a business thing to me, somebody with a grudge. I can have people in the grounds here at night. And when I haven't got my official government chauffeur I've got Feb. I've every confidence in him being able to look after me."

"As you wish, Sir David. By the way have you thought any more about the significance of those DesboroDenim items? I suppose you know those found at the warehouse and the farm were similar to those left at the scene of Lady Lucy's accident. They're still at the lab but I hope to be able to show them to you soon."

"That would be appreciated but as I said before I've no idea what they mean. It's a complete mystery to me."

"Very good Sir David, I'll be off now. But take care," and the Inspector left the room.

When the sound of his car crunching the gravel on the drive could be heard David Fairfax looked at his watch and fumed, "I don't need the police to fight my battles. I'll find out who's doing this and when I do I won't need any police or court to tell me what to do with them!"

He thumped the table with his fist and walked out of the room without saying another word. He went upstairs and changed. Later after reassuring Lucy and the children that they had nothing to worry about David left in his car for 'The Shop'.

'The Shop' was situated in Epping High Street. At one time it had been a blacksmith's and then a tobacconist's, but now it was a hairdresser's, a unisex hairdresser's. Not the type of hairdresser's that David Fairfax approved of. In his view it was nothing better than a 'poof's paradise'. He favoured the traditional type of barber shop but had to admit that these had all now but disappeared. He had no time for homosexuals and when in his presence nobody ever used the word 'gay' when discussing sexuality.

Owned by one of his companies the hairdresser's was run as a going concern but it also had another more important use. Above it was a convenient local meeting place away from prying eyes that had the advantage of having a large back yard with an entrance door opening on to a side street. The employees there had long since learned to keep their mouths shut about any odd comings or goings and were well rewarded for their silence.

David Fairfax was the last to arrive and he went straight up to the suite of offices on the upper floor. His office was to one side and had been fitted with a one-way mirror looking onto what he jokingly called his interrogation room. After a few minutes he was joined by Alan Box and Craig Bentley. He gave a signal and Feb called in Andy Bennett from an adjoining room. Bennett entered the room looking around him rather sheepishly. This was his first time at 'The Shop' but he knew about its reputation.

Feb beckoned with his hands. Bennett walked forward and sat in a solitary chair positioned in the middle of the room. Feb came and stood immediately in front of him and looked down on this quite large and rotund figure.

"Tell me what happened last night!"

"Not much to tell really. I had finished one of my regular patrols and had just returned to my post at the main entrance. Suddenly I was aware of smoke seeping under the door so just as the emergency procedures state I phoned the fire brigade. That's it really. They arrived after about 10 minutes and started to put the fire out. I did think it odd though that the sprinklers hadn't come on."

"That's it is it? You've nothing further to add?"

"No. That's what happened. Just as I told the police and the firemen."

"Just as you told the police! Then how did someone get into that warehouse? Didn't you look at the alarms or the sensor panels? How were the sprinklers disabled? You must have seen something. Or were you asleep? Well we're not the police as you well know. You're going to tell us exactly what happened!"

Feb paused then quietly called, "Laurel! Hardy!"

As Feb backed away from the chair two figures emerged almost silently from the shadows around the door. One stood in front of Bennett and one stood behind him. Bennett was by now sweating profusely.

Viewing this from the safety of his office David Fairfax gave a wry smile and thought to himself, "Now for the part I like most. It'll be interesting to see the reactions of Cardboard and Craig once the fun starts."

The diminutive Laurel slowly tightened his arms around Bennett and the bulky frame of Hardy moved closer in front. Then without any warning Hardy punched Bennett hard in the stomach. "Anything to say now?" enquired Hardy sarcastically.

"No, everything was as I said."

Hardy leaned over Bennett and punched him squarely on the nose. There was a trickle of blood and Hardy repeated the process, only this time with more force. He was about to hit Bennett a third time in the face when Bennett shouted, "Enough! I'll tell you!"

From behind the mirror David Fairfax was most disappointed. He had hoped Bennett would have held out a bit longer and prolonged the fun. Alan Box was breathing a sigh of relief. He was glad the violence had stopped. He went along with it but really didn't have the courage or stomach for it when things began to turn nasty.

"I was asleep on a camp bed near main reception, just like I do most nights. I had patrolled the warehouse earlier but that was at about 10 o'clock. Everything had been in order and I did check the alarms. I swear they were all activated and the sprinkler system was switched on. Believe me!" he blurted out.

"Oh we believe you! We believe you all right, Mister Bennett! What else?" and with that Feb nodded to

Hardy who punched him in the face once again. Bennett let out a yell as the blood ran down from his nose and into his mouth. Feb looked over towards the mirror.

David Fairfax dimmed the lights. This was a signal to Feb that he believed nothing more could be gained from Bennett's interrogation.

Feb looked over at Bennett and snarled, "You're fired! Don't bother coming to collect your things. Laurel and Hardy will give you a lift home in the van."

Feb looked at Hardy and said, "Throw him in the back of the van and then we'll talk to our friend Tom Hunt. Let's see if he's got a better memory than Bennett."

Just as the two heavies were lifting Bennett to his feet Hunt seized his opportunity. He had been petrified watching Bennett being 'questioned'. With the two heavies occupied he ran out of the room and down the stairs so fast that he almost lost his footing on the well-worn treads.

"Get him!" shouted Feb.

Hunt reached the foot of the stairs and grasped the door handle. Locked! He shook the door violently but to no avail. It was a stout hardwood door with a good solid lock. He started to panic and turned to the side door that led into the hairdressing salon. This was more flimsy with a glass upper panel but once again as he grabbed the handle he realised that it too was locked. With sweat pouring from his forehead he banged on the door shouting at the top of his voice, "Help! Help! Let me out!"

But it was no use. Nobody came to his rescue. He cowered trembling in the corner as Hardy came slowly down the stairs and stood over him. With a broad grin on his face Hardy's large fist smashed into Hunt's face and he crumpled into a heap. Hardy grabbed him by his collar and dragged him roughly up the stairs.

Hunt was flung into the chair and subjected to a savage beating by Hardy.

"That's more like it," smiled David Fairfax as he relished every single blow directed onto the hapless Hunt, "I reward loyalty but I have no place for people who let me down." Turning to Alan Box and Craig Bentley he added "I'm sure you'll agree with that?"

"Certainly Sir David," they responded, both trying to suppress their fear.

"Now look here Hunt why don't you spare yourself a lot of, er, how can I put this, unpleasantness. Tell us what happened on the farm," snapped Feb.

"I was there all right but I admit I wasn't keeping a look out. I was spending the night with my girlfriend in the old caravan at the back of the farmhouse. Nothing ever happened at the farm. For months I've wandered round those barns and outhouses every night. I've never seen anything out of the ordinary. I thought for once it wouldn't matter."

"You thought for once it wouldn't matter! So, rather than do your job, rather than look after what you are paid to protect, you thought you would have a night to remember with your girlfriend. Well everything has a price and I can assure you it will be a night to remember. Hardy!"

Hardy stepped forward once more and directed a barrage of blows to Hunt's face. After a few minutes it was covered in blood and barely recognisable.

"Take them away," snapped Feb angrily. Laurel and Hardy pushed the moaning Bennett and Hunt down the stairs as Feb went into David Fairfax's office.

"Good work, Feb," enthused a smiling David Fairfax. He had enjoyed the whole spectacle immensely.

Alan Box and Craig Bentley remained silent. They had been with David long enough to know his methods but it wasn't often that they witnessed them at first hand. When they did they found it highly repugnant but they daren't tell him so.

"I didn't think we'd get much out of them but it was worth a try. What it does confirm though is that we are looking at an outside party. Someone is out to get us. Someone has it in for us. Possibly with inside help. Gentlemen we must remain vigilant. If you have any doubts about anybody, any one of your staff, then let me know. *I'll have a word with them.*" Then after a moment's pause he looked them directly in the eyes and added, "Even if they're at the very top of this organisation!"

A chill went through Alan Box and Craig Bentley. It was with some relief that they slowly left the room and made their way to their cars.

Feb thoroughly cleaned the office then drove David Fairfax back to his house in Theydon Bois. There he found Chief Inspector Westwood waiting for his return.

Chapter Nine

David Fairfax strode purposely into the dining room and greeted the Chief Inspector.

"Inspector Westwood. Nice to see you again. I hope you've come to report progress."

"Not exactly, but I thought you would like to know what we've discovered so far. We've found out that entry into the warehouse at Witham was gained by a small side door and that a key was used. There was no sign of a forced entry. Also the sprinkler system had quite simply been switched off."

"That's bad news. It may invalidate the insurance claim. But no matter. I want to know who did it."

"Well, we have got some clues. The devices used to start both the blaze in the warehouse and the fires at the farm were identical. From fragments found at both scenes it appears they were homemade. But having said that they were not crude devices. They were certainly not weed killer and sugar. No, whoever made them knew quite a bit about chemistry. The ingredients, if that is the right word for them, are not generally available but would not be too difficult to obtain for someone with the right connections in the chemical or pharmaceutical industry. Or even the academic world."

'The academic world? I don't follow you!"

'Well they're the type of substances that form the basis for a lot of post-grad type work at a number of universities."

"Interesting."

"The timers used were those that can be bought over the internet or at any electronics store. I don't think there's much chance of tracing the buyer."

After a few seconds' pause Chief Inspector Westwood continued, "Although the fires were started within minutes of each other it looks like both incidents were the work of one person. At that time of night as you might expect there aren't normally many people about. However, from what we have been able to gather, a dark coloured car was seen in the vicinity of both incidents and we believe it contained a single occupant. We have looked at CCTV footage from the Witham industrial estate but I'm afraid there's nothing usable."

At this point in the conversation Katie brought in a tray of tea and biscuits and poured a cup for the two men. As she left the room they were joined by Lucy who had been enjoying a swim when she learned of the Inspector's arrival.

"Come on in dear," beamed David, "Inspector Westwood is just bringing me up to date on the fires.

There's been some progress but I don't think any arrests are imminent."

"That's right, Lady Lucy, but we'll get there."

Lucy helped herself to a cup of tea but resisted the temptation of the biscuits.

"Sir David, your business empire. Sorry, I mean your former business empire," the inspector corrected himself, "spans several diverse areas. Have you any idea why the DesboroDenim Fashion Group and Fairfax Farms should be targeted in particular?"

"No, no idea at all!"

"What about Fairfax Forwarding or Fairfax Telecoms?"

"Inspector, you *have* been doing your homework!" retorted David Fairfax.

"All part of the job. Leave no stone unturned and all that. Good solid policing methods produce results in the end." After a few seconds in thought he continued, "Quite by chance I was talking to the immigration boys a little earlier. They told me a lorry full of illegal Chinese immigrants had been stopped this morning near Ipswich. Was that one of yours?"

"No, certainly not!" responded David Fairfax indignantly, "Fairfax Forwarding is a highly respected organisation and deals solely in legitimate freight. What exactly are you getting at? If that lorry had been anything to do with my companies then I would certainly have known about it. Fairfax Forwarding is not involved in anything underhand or illegal."

David was feeling decidedly uncomfortable at this line of questioning but he was able to resist his natural desire to challenge the Inspector.

"Tell me Sir David, how long have Fairfax Farms and Fairfax Forwarding been a part of the Fairfax Group?"

"Let me see now, Fairfax Farms has been a part of the group for about 15 years but Fairfax Forwarding has been with me for nearly 30 years. I suppose you could say it was the second area I expanded into after I'd got DesboroDenim onto its feet. It was quite a challenge moving into a completely new sphere of activity and turning the company around. Something I relished doing."

"How did you acquire this freight forwarding business? Was it as the result of a take-over?"

"No it was started by my father-in-law. Well, ex-father-in-law actually."

"I'm not following this," said the Inspector.

"Let me explain. Fairfax Forwarding, or Jenks Forwarding as it was originally known, was started by Leslie Jenks my second wife's father. Trouble was it was run as a small family concern and its potential was not fully appreciated. After I married Beverley Jenks I became a partner in the business. When her father died

I became co-owner with Beverley. Together we started to build the business up and it quickly became a successful going concern."

"I see. What happened to Beverley Jenks, *your second wife*?"

David Fairfax did not like the tone in Inspector Westwood's voice when he stressed '*your second wife*'.

"It was all quite sad really. Beverley was desperate to have a child right from day one of our marriage and she became pregnant about a year after we were married. She was a very keen horse rider and kept two horses in stables at our home. Most days she would go riding but on one fateful day she had an accident. She wasn't seriously hurt but she did lose the child. For any woman that would have been a severe blow. But when the doctors told her that as a result of the accident she couldn't have any more children she fell into a deep bout of depression. Naturally I ensured she saw the best doctors but there was precious little they could do. She was on a lot of medication after that. Although it mitigated the effects to a degree she was never the same person again.

In a bid to lift that depression I suggested we took a foreign holiday. This was something we had promised ourselves since we had married and so we went on a luxury cruise to the Far East.

All was well for a few days and she seemed to be getting back to her old self again. The warm weather, the pampering and the exotic places we had visited, appeared to be having the desired effect. However, at dinner one day she complained of a severe headache and went back to our suite to have a lie down. That was the last I saw of her. Well, the last time I saw her alive anyway.

She did go back to the cabin but for some inexplicable reason she later went up on deck and threw herself into the water. It was sometime before I realised she was missing and even longer before the ship could be searched. There was no way the ship could be turned round to look for her in the sea but a few days later her body was found by a local fishing boat. It was badly disfigured and bloated from being in the water. It had also been partially eaten by fish but there was no doubt it was her."

David Fairfax paused and took in breath. He appeared to be genuinely upset at recounting this series of tragic events.

"There was an inquest, of course, and in this country too. The Coroner recorded a verdict of suicide. Before you ask, Inspector, any suggestion of foul play was ruled out. 'Taking her life, while the balance of the mind was disturbed.' I think that was the official verdict but I'm sure you can check up on that."

"No need, Sir David, I believe what you tell me. Wouldn't do to have a Minister of the Crown who couldn't be trusted, would it?" and with that the Inspector went to take his leave.

"Inspector, you will keep me informed of any developments."

"Of course. By the way, are you planning any trips out of the country in the near future?"

"Yes, as a matter of fact I am. I leave in two days' time on a trade mission to a number of countries in Central Africa. The Government is anxious to increase trade in that area of the continent and I've been asked to lead a delegation of British companies with that aim in mind. I'll be away for about ten days."

"Fine, I'll be in touch on your return."

"If you should need to contact me for any reason while I'm away then I'm sure the ministry can arrange it. Or you can speak to Angela Hamilton my PA she'll be happy to oblige."

After the inspector had left the room, and the sound of his car was heard driving away from the house, Lucy glared angrily at her husband, "Why did you tell him about Beverley? That wasn't a very wise move at all!" she snapped.

"Don't worry!" replied David gently squeezing her hand, "Better he hears it from me than from somebody else. Relax, there's nothing to worry about. It's all too long ago."

"All the same," he added after a short pause, "I think we need someone to look into this matter. Someone to do some digging on our behalf. Someone with only our interests to consider. A name comes to mind. I'll get in contact with him when I get back from this blasted trip to Africa. In the meantime while I'm away I suggest you take Feb with you when you go out, just in case," and with that David left the room.

Chapter Ten

Following his ten-day official Government trip to central Africa David Fairfax decided to spend some time with his family. He arranged for them to take a flight to South Africa to join him at a friend's villa.

During the trip he had been accompanied by top civil servants from his ministry and a number of important businessmen and a great deal of business had been generated for British Industry.

In the four countries visited the delegation had been most warmly received but numerous projects and deals had had to be declined because of the widespread use of bribes and other incentives. This was most disconcerting for the civil servants and some of the businessmen. For David Fairfax, however, this represented opportunity. He had made a careful note of who the key players were in the countries visited. As soon as he got the chance he would be making contact with them. Bribery and the use of incentives were endemic in this part of the world. While it resulted in many deals being lost to the official delegation it meant more potential business for his companies.

His family arrived at the villa which overlooked its own private beach just outside of Cape Town some five days after David. This had been sufficient time for him to establish contacts in the countries previously visited and to set up a number of very lucrative deals. He had quickly primed senior figures in his business empire of what was taking place. Replies, all channelled through Angela Hamilton for security, were already being received confirming some very worth-while and high-earning contracts. All of them of course highly suspect or in contravention of various United Kingdom trade agreements.

David arranged for his family to be collected from the airport and driven straight to the villa.

"You've surpassed yourself this time!" exclaimed Lucy. She looked around the villa and out onto the golden sandy beach, "Luxury, sheer luxury! I'm certainly going to enjoy it here. This must have cost a fortune!"

She rushed forward and gave her husband a hug and a big kiss.

"No, not really. Matter of fact it didn't cost me a single penny. Let's just say an old acquaintance of mine owed me a favour."

"Very nice indeed dad." said Callisto, jumping up and down on one of the settees before settling down on it.

"You can say that again," joined in Tom, "I could feel very much at home here."

"By the way," said David pushing Callisto off the settee, "I've arranged for us all to go on a little fishing trip in a couple of days' time."

"A fishing trip?" questioned Tom.

"Yes, a fishing trip. But a fishing trip with a difference. We'll be hunting for sharks and the like. Proper deep-sea fishing."

"Marvellous," said the twins together.

"And that's not all. Next week we're all going on safari for three days. How about that then?"

"We've got the best and most thoughtful dad in the world," Callisto said picking herself up from the floor and hugging her father.

Then both boys grabbed hold of Callisto and dragged her out through the French doors and onto the sandy beach. They had thought of throwing her into the water but at the last moment had second thoughts. They decided to put her down and the three of them just stood paddling in the warm water and enjoying the hot sunshine.

"Just think," laughed Nick splashing the other two with his hands, "it's almost the end of November and back home it's freezing cold. Here it's lovely and warm."

"Yes," agreed Callisto, "I can't wait to top up my tan. We've got two whole weeks of nothing but sun, sand and sea."

"You won't have to cheat now will you and go down to that tanning studio when we get back to England," chipped in Tom.

"That's not cheating. That's preserving my tan. I can't bear to look pale and pasty. Come on. Let's unpack then go for a swim."

The three of them ran back to the villa, grabbed their cases and were shown to their rooms by one of the houseboys.

Downstairs David and Lucy were discussing business matters. They paused as the children rushed through the room and out towards the sea.

"You wouldn't think they were in their twenties would you?" remarked Lucy, "It's not as if they've never seen the sea before. Every year we take them somewhere nice and hot."

"Yes," replied David as the sound of the children splashing in the water wafted in on the light breeze, "it will do them good to have a few days to unwind and take their minds off what's been happening back home. I know they've been worried. Even Callisto, who rarely shows her true feelings is worried, or should I say puzzled? Never do know what that one is thinking."

"So, you're pleased with the way the trip went?"

"I certainly am. Lots of good contacts. Should make a packet out of this little trip. I'd say it's one of the most lucrative I've been on so far. Good thing this being a minister and helping one's country."

"Helping yourself more likely!"

"That's right. Helping the country but, more importantly, helping us. Angela has been in touch a few times and so far things are going really well."

"I think I'm going to like it here." Lucy said cuddling up to her husband on the settee, "One thing, though. I think you should take it easy. It's time for you to relax for a change. It worries me when you work so hard. I wouldn't want anything to happen to you. You know through over-work and that."

"Don't worry. I'm as strong as an ox. I've no intention whatsoever of letting anything happen to me."

* * * * *

One week later the family were having breakfast on the veranda enjoying the early morning African sunshine when the telephone rang. One of the maids answered it and brought it over to David at the dining table.

"Hello. Oh, hello Angela, everything ok?"

"No Sir David, it's not. I've got some rather disturbing news. In the last two days both DesboroDenim fashions and Fairfax Telecoms have lost tenders. I'm talking here about important large contracts. We've even been outbid on the contract for specialist army uniforms that we've retained for the last ten years or so. Can't say too much over the phone but I am reliably informed that the small differences in tender prices were the same on all the bids."

David Fairfax was silent while he pondered the full significance of what had happened. "I don't like this! I don't like it at all!" he shouted down the phone, "Heads are going to roll!"

He became visibly angrier and angrier the more he thought about the situation. "Look, get all the papers together and bring them over to the house tomorrow afternoon. Make sure that Susan Rumble and our other accountants are there with you. I'll make arrangements to come home on the first available flight."

"Oh dad!" said Callisto, Tom and Nick in unison, "Do we have to?"

"Are you sure darling?" Lucy added her voice to the chorus of disappointment.

"Yes! Get your things packed. We leave immediately!"

"But what about that safari? We were really looking forward to that," piped up Nick in a very sheepish fashion.

"Sod the safari! We're going home right now and that's that!"

None of the family had the courage to argue. They had all learned the hard way never to disagree with or question what David had decided. They had to accept the holiday was now over and they were resigned to the long journey back to the United Kingdom. It was a journey that was made all the more memorable by the atrocious mood swings and bad temper displayed by David to all and sundry. "Not the type of behaviour that was expected from a Minister of the Crown," commented many of the other passengers in the first class section of the aeroplane.

Chapter Eleven

David Fairfax and his family hurriedly left Heathrow Airport via the V.I.P. lounge. They went straight to his Mercedes where Feb was waiting to drive the family home.

"At least there's a few perks worth having when you're a minister," Callisto joked to the family. But they were in no mood for jokes and David motioned to her to be quiet.

The family sat silently in the car as it made its way towards Essex. There was heavy traffic and it soon became apparent that the journey, which normally took approximately 90 minutes, would take considerably longer. David gazed out of the window trying to think what had gone wrong while he had been away.

"Somebody's taken advantage of my absence," he thought to himself, "but who?"

As the car turned off the M25 and onto the M11 for the last leg of the journey he was awakened from his thoughts by the ringing of his mobile phone.

"Yes, what is it?" he asked angrily.

"It's me, Angela. I thought you should know there's a crowd of reporters camped outside your house. There's been a leak about the loss of the tenders and they've heard about your early return from South Africa. You're probably tired after your long journey so I've booked you all into the Kings Head in North Weald. Far enough to be away from the reporters but close enough to return home once the press realises that you're not coming straight back to Theydon Bois."

"Well done, Angela. I'll drop the family off there then I'll go on to 'The Shop' in Epping. Will everybody be there?"

"Yes, I've given them a three-line whip. They'll be there all right."

"Good," and with that he turned the phone off and returned to his thoughts.

"Pity they're not all like her. Must keep an eye on her though, make sure she's well rewarded and not snapped up by anybody else."

After seeing the family settled into The Kings Head David was driven to 'The Shop'. He entered discretely via the yard so he did not have to walk along the High Road.

In addition to Alan Box, Ken Winter, Rahul Dixit, Craig Bentley and Angela Hamilton, the Chief Accountant Susan Rumble and her two assistants were also present.

By the time David sat down at the head of the table he was visibly seething. He banged his fist hard on the table and looked angrily around the room. His mere presence was usually enough to instil fear in his senior lieutenants but this time he was shaking with rage and they all tried to avert their eyes from his gaze. He studied a wad of papers placed in front of him for a few minutes in complete silence. Those present sat in obvious discomfort waiting for the onslaught to begin.

He brushed his arm to one side and inadvertently knocked a cup of coffee onto the floor.

"Leave it!" he screamed at one of the accountants who went to clear it up, "I want answers! I want to know how this has happened. Yes, we occasionally lose the odd contract, but nothing like this. Why do we pay people to tip us off? Why do we pay them to give us information? Why? I'm asking you, why?" and he thumped his fist hard on the table once again.

There was an uncomfortable silence that was eventually broken by Ken Winter. His thick-set, rather imposing figure, usually brought some semblance of order to the proceedings but today he too seemed dwarfed by the towering presence of David Fairfax. He very calmly said what many seated round the table were thinking, "Somewhere in the organisation we must have a mole. Someone who, for whatever reason, wishes the organisation harm."

Again there was a long uncomfortable silence before Rahul Dixit added, "And it must be someone in a very senior position!"

"Are you suggesting it's one of us?" angrily cut in Ken Winter, "We'd all have too much to lose. Each of us round this table has just too much to lose. Any one of us would be cutting his own throat if we ...."

"No need," interrupted David, "I'll be doing the throat-cutting when I find out just who is behind this. Susan, what do you know? What have you managed to find out?"

Susan Rumble nervously shuffled her papers, "All the contracts were lost by a margin of only a few pounds. I've checked our figures against those of the winning bids and in each case it was a matter of just a few pounds. Oddly enough, it was the same margin in each case. This does, I'm afraid, lead me to the conclusion that someone had advance knowledge of our bids. It does point to an inside job and ...."

"Who got the contracts?" said David interrupting Susan Rumble's flow.

"That's the odd thing. They were all won by 'The Anne Harvey Group'. I'd never heard of them before. I had to look them up at Companies House."

"So, what did you find out about this group?"

"Not much. The group was founded by someone called Anne Harvey, as the name would suggest. Over the last ten or so years it has been pretty small fry in terms of both size and contracts tendered for. However, recently it has expanded in a number of areas directly in competition with us. We'll need to keep an eye on it."

"We'll do more than keep an eye on it! We'll destroy it!" screamed David, "I'm going to get someone to investigate this outfit. When I find out who's behind it I'm going to annihilate them; them and the whole damn group."

Just then Angela Hamilton's mobile phone rang.

"Sorry, Sir David," she apologised, "I'd better answer this, it's Robin Gladwin from Fairfax Farms. I'll take it outside," and she went to get up.

"No, take it here!" he snapped, "It might be important."

There was a hushed silence as Angela listened intently to what Robin Gladwin was saying. When he had finished she said, "Thank you. I'll let Sir David know," and she turned off the phone.

"Well, what did he want that was so urgent?"

"More bad news I'm afraid. One of our farms in Norfolk was raided by immigration officers earlier today and nearly 50 illegal migrants were found working there. They've been taken away for questioning and so have all our staff. Robin says he only just managed to slip away. He was on his way back to the farm when he saw the police and immigration people so he quickly turned back and phoned me."

At this revelation David turned red then purple and stood up kicking his chair over in the process.

"Heads are going to roll for this! I'm going to get someone in to get to the bottom of this mess. Find out once and for all what's going on," and with that he went to leave the room. But as he strode towards the door his mobile phone rang.

"Yes!" he screeched into the phone and listened with increasing incredulity to the voice on the other end.

After a few seconds he switched off the phone and turned back towards those sitting round the table.

"The Prime Minister wants to see me. He wants to see me now or as soon as I can get to Downing Street. And I think I know what he wants," and he stormed out of the room.

After David had left there was a short period of silence. It was eventually broken by Alan Box.

"Let's not panic. I suggest we go back to our respective businesses and make a few discreet inquiries of our own. It would be better for all of us, less painful too, if we could crack this one before any further damage is done."

There was a general murmur of agreement from around the table. Angela concluded the meeting by assuring all present that she would keep them updated on any developments.

Chapter Twelve

Feb drove as fast as he could through the evening rush-hour traffic. At the Trade and Industry Ministry David Fairfax quickly transferred to his official car for the short drive to Downing Street.

The door of No. 10 was opened as he approached and David was immediately ushered up to the Prime Minister's study. The Prime Minister purposely ignored him until he had finished reading a document, signed it and put his pen into his inside jacket pocket. He then motioned for David to sit down.

After a short period of silence the Prime Minister looked directly into his eyes and said, "I've only got a few minutes so I'll make this as brief as I can. You're a damn fine minister. You've achieved more in a few months than most ministers do in a year. I wouldn't want to lose you but I don't like what I'm hearing. This talk about your companies, or your former companies should I say, being involved in the smuggling of illegal immigrants and employing illegal foreign workers. Don't like it at all. To make matters worse the press have got hold of it. They smell blood."

"I know Prime Minister. I agree it looks very serious but I ...."

He was cut off abruptly in mid-sentence, "Sort it out! And sort it out now! I don't want to have to ask for your resignation but anything else, even the slightest hint of impropriety, and you'll be on your way. Understood?"

"Perfectly, Prime Minister!" and without further word David took his leave.

It was a relieved David Fairfax who left Number 10. He smiled at the waiting press corps but didn't reply to any of their questions. He knew better than to be drawn into their clutches. He did wonder, though, what would be in the papers, particularly the tabloids, the next day.

On the drive back to the Kings Head in North Weald David was in a pensive mood. After a long period of silence he leaned forward and said, "Feb, there's a pub up ahead. I need a drink. I need to unwind before facing the family. Pull over. There's something I want to run past you."

The two men went into the pub and Feb went straight up to the bar and ordered some drinks. He took them to a secluded corner of the room to chat with his boss.

"I've decided who I'm going to get to look into this matter and find our mole for us," said David in hushed tones, "You'll be surprised at my choice, and so will the family. I can't wait to see their faces when I tell them. I'll leave it, though, until we're all back home tomorrow morning. This is who I have in mind," and he grinned as he whispered a name into Feb's ear.

Chapter Thirteen

A late breakfast at The Kings Head proved to be a rather solemn affair for the Fairfax family. But at least they could relax safe in the knowledge that they were out of the media spotlight, for the time being anyway. Once breakfast was over and packing had been completed Feb drove the family back to their home in Theydon Bois. Thankfully the press had decided there wasn't a story to be had after all and were no longer camped out on the pavement outside Forest Glade.

David Fairfax glanced through the morning papers. None of them was calling for his resignation. Even the more sensational among the tabloids had relegated his past involvement with the companies under suspicion of employing illegal immigrants to a small paragraph on an inside page. He gained immense satisfaction from this and poured himself a drink by way of a small personal celebration. He was far from complacent, however, as he now knew he had to be particularly vigilant in future. Any hint whatsoever of any wrongdoing on the part of any company he had been involved with would lead to immediate dismissal from his ministerial position. It would also signal the end of what had, so far, proved to be a very lucrative appointment.

Over lunch David said he had something he wanted to tell the family and waited for Katie to leave the room before making his announcement. He briefly outlined the events of the past few months. Lucy being deliberately injured, the firebombing of the group's premises, the tip-off to police and immigration about the use of illegal immigrants, and the recent loss of some very important and valuable tenders.

"We do, of course, have the very capable Detective Chief Inspector Westwood investigating these matters. But I'm convinced he knows more about the Fairfax Group than what he lets on and we can't fully trust him. What we need is our own man, someone on our payroll whose sole allegiance is to us. Somebody who is not constrained by, how can I say this, the niceties of conventional policing. And I have just the person in mind."

He paused largely for dramatic effect and then continued, "I'm thinking of employing James Palmer."

There was a short pause before Lucy shook her head in sheer disbelief and exclaimed, "James Palmer! Are you mad or something? He nearly ruined you. And now you want to bring him in to find out who is trying to do exactly what he failed to do."

"Who's James Palmer?" said Tom between mouthfuls of food, "And why did he try to ruin you? Let us in on the secret."

"I thought you all knew this. It was in the spring of this year. We were in the process of taking over a large meat-packing business based in Chelmsford. We hadn't officially taken it into the group so it was still trading under its old name. At that time James Palmer was a Detective Inspector with Essex Police and he was investigating illegal imports of beef that were finding their way into the food chain. The meat-packing business we were acquiring operated country-wide so was ideally suited to this sort of scam. As far as the Fairfax Group was concerned this acquisition was a Godsend, it dovetailed nicely into our farming group's operation and would make us a lot of money."

"So what happened?" asked Nick tossing a piece of meat to one of the cats.

"Well James Palmer came very close, very close indeed to uncovering the racket and finding out that the Fairfax Group, and me in particular, was up to my neck in the scam."

"He had to go, then?" mused Callisto, "How did you manage it?"

"Easy, really. A number of employees at the meat-packing firm made allegations, all false of course, that Inspector Palmer had offered to drop criminal charges in return for money."

"Bribes!" exclaimed Callisto, "Never fails!"

"Yes, and at the same time some large deposits of money appeared in the good Inspector's bank accounts. There was an investigation but at the end of the day he couldn't offer any satisfactory explanation for the money. There was talk of a court case and I understand the Crown Prosecution Service actually prepared a file but in the end the Police allowed him to leave the force quietly. I believe he receives a small pension so it wasn't entirely bad news for him."

"What is he up to now? Retirement and looking after his garden?" asked Tom rather sarcastically.

"No, he's only in his mid to late fifties and I'm told he now runs a small private detective agency."

"How small?"

"Just him and his wife, Jenny. I have it on good authority that he still has connections with the Police, unofficial ones of course, but apparently his business isn't doing too well at the moment."

After a few seconds thought David continued, "I think he's ideal for what we want. Anybody got any objections?"

Tom and Nick stopped tormenting the cats with pieces of left-over food and looked at their father. Tom spoke first, "My view is that he could be dangerous. But if he didn't find out about our connection with the meat-packing firm then what have we got to worry about. After all, we do need someone who will be able to get to the bottom of this business. If he's still got connections where it matters that can only be to our advantage."

Nick endorsed this view, "We could have the best of both worlds here. A private detective at our beck and call but one who is still able to use the resources of the police when he needs a bit of help. Sounds good to me."

"I still don't like it," exclaimed Lucy, "I think we could be making a terrible mistake."

"I can appreciate your feelings but whoever we get could ultimately pose a threat to us. In this case, however, we do have something else in our favour. I went to school with James Palmer and I think I know what makes him tick. We haven't kept in touch over the last few years but we used to regularly get together for a drink. As the business grew larger I drifted apart from most of my old school friends including him. It should appear logical to him that at a time of difficulty, both in the family and in the business, I would turn to him. Someone I know, someone I have faith in, someone I can trust. Besides, what could be more natural than an old friend offering him a job to help him out at a time when he's in need of a helping hand."

"One other thing, dad," asked Callisto in a worried tone, "Who are we going to tell about Mr Palmer and why he might be snooping around. Are we going to tell our MDs? Angela? Feb? Are we certain we can trust them?"

"They all have far too much to lose both in terms of money and ending up behind bars to be behind these events," he joked. "Besides, most of them have been with us for years. We'll tell them once he's made a start."

There was some further brief discussion before David finally picked up his mobile phone and telephoned James Palmer.

Chapter Fourteen

Two days later Katie showed James Palmer into the drawing room and David Fairfax rose to greet him.

"James, it's nice to see you again after all this time. Come and take a seat. We can talk round the coffee table. It must be all of five years now."

"Nearer to ten actually," responded James before adding with little apparent enthusiasm, "but it is nice to see you. And that offer of a job sounds very tempting too. You've obviously heard that I'm no longer with the Police and working on my own now."

"Yes, a nasty business by all accounts."

"Certainly was. At one stage I thought I was going to go down for a long time. Whoever set me up knew what they were doing. I tried to find out who was behind it but drew a blank. I never took a bribe in the whole of my service. You know that. That's what makes it all so hard to accept. I didn't want to leave the force but it was made clear to me that it would be the best outcome for all concerned. So, reluctantly, I took the package offered and used the money to set myself up in business as a private detective. In competition to my old mates as it were."

"How is business then?"

"Not bad, but it's all pretty low-level stuff. Unfaithful husbands mainly, although we get just as many unfaithful wives nowadays, debt recovery, petty disputes, unpaid fines to chase up, that sort of thing. It just about pays the bills but I do miss the big stuff. It would be nice to get my hands on something big, something interesting. That's what intrigued me about your call. You didn't say much on the phone but it sounded like a proper job for a change."

"Without sounding dramatic I think someone is out to get me, to ruin me. Not just to ruin me but to destroy me, my businesses and my family."

"Really!"

David picked up two folders from the coffee table and handed them to James with a certain degree of hesitation.

"I've had my personal assistant Angela Hamilton and my Chief Accountant Susan Rumble prepare these briefing papers for you. And I mean for you. For your eyes only. They detail the main events to date."

"Very professional! I wish more of my clients were as efficient."

At this point Katie returned to the room with a tray of coffee and biscuits. As she entered the two cats squeezed past her and began chasing each other over the furniture. The two men had fallen silent while Katie served the coffee. As James casually thumbed through the folders one of the cats jumped onto David's lap.

"I suppose you want a treat," he said stroking the cat gently and broke a large chocolate biscuit into four pieces. He held the pieces high above the cat's head and tantalisingly slowly he fed them one by one to the cat who ate them voraciously as if it hadn't eaten for a week, "Now-now, not too much at one go, Vienna."

"Vienna, that's an odd name for a cat."

"No, not really. In the seventies and eighties I was a great fan of the late Leonard Rossiter. You may recall his cat in 'Rising Damp' was called Vienna."

"Oh yes. What about the other one then?" exclaimed James, "Dare I ask his name?"

"Her name! They're both female. I named her Ponsonby after Reggie Perrin's cat from that other great series starring Leonard Rossiter, 'The Fall and Rise of Reginald Perrin'."

"Ponsonby! What sort of a name is that? Aren't the family tempted to call her Ponce for short?"

"No, they wouldn't dare. I'd always wanted a couple of Persian Blues so I bought them, mainly for the family I suppose, a couple of years ago. Callisto isn't too fond of them but the boys like them. Well they like tormenting them anyway."

"What about Lucy, is she a cat lover? By the way, forgive me, how is she? I haven't seen her for ages."

"She's fine now but a recent incident in the forest unnerved her and it took her a while to get over it. No lasting damage though."

After Katie had left the room there was a short period of silence while the two men sipped their coffee and watched as the cats chased each other round the room.

David was the first to speak, "It all started a few months ago when Lucy was attacked driving over to Woodford. It was a curious incident. She was forced off the road and crashed her car into a tree. Then, whoever had done it, lifted her out of the car and laid her on the ground."

"Very strange indeed. No apparent motive, nothing taken, nothing stolen?"

"No, everything was left untouched. The attacker, if that is the right word, even phoned for an ambulance."

"And the carrier bag and the underwear?" enquired James looking in the folder.

"That adds to the mystery. I've no idea at all why that was left there." David paused for a moment and then continued, "Then there were the fires at our warehouse in Witham and on our farm at Latchingdon, all on the same night would you believe!"

"And more carrier bags and underwear left at the scene?"

"That's right. Since then we've lost some very important contracts. The police and immigration people have also been tipped off about illegal immigrants in our lorries and illegal migrants being employed on our farms. Even my ministerial career has been threatened by these incidents. Illegal immigrants and migrant workers are very sensitive issues with the public at the present time."

"Sounds like an inside job to me."

"*Well done!*" said David sarcastically, "It didn't take me long to figure that one out! But who? All those in a position to do this would have too much to lose, far too much to lose."

"I take it you were aware of the illegal workers?"

"Yes, I have to admit to that one. I've learned to turn a blind eye if it will help the business. But I can't admit that to anybody other than you, do you understand? And I'm quite prepared to buy your silence. What's your fee? What do you normally charge for your services?"

"£60 an hour plus expenses."

"Well you can forget that," and David opened a small drawer and took out a bundle of notes, "here's £15,000," and he tossed it onto the table in front of James. "Consider it a down payment. There's double that when the job's done. No, I'll give you £50,000 if you can crack this for me."

"Very generous indeed. Pity I don't have more clients like you. I'll certainly take the job. Not just for the money, which will come in very handy of course, but for the challenge. This seems to be a most peculiar case," James replied and then spent a few minutes looking through the folders before adding, "It's possible this is the work of someone you've upset in the past, someone with a grudge who has done a lot of planning, done his homework."

David then spent a short while acquainting James with the structure of the Fairfax Group and its history including how and when he had acquired each part of the business. He also outlined some key aspects of his family history including how his first wife had died in an accident and his second wife had committed suicide. He concluded by saying how he had then married Lucy Murray who both he and James had known from their secondary school days.

After digesting what David had told him James said, "I relish taking on this case. I admit it's a huge challenge but people make mistakes, they leave clues, they forget things, they're not always as clever as they think they are. There is certainly a lot of research to be done here. I need to look into the background to your businesses, your private life, your friends and work colleagues, your rivals and competitors, as well as 'The Anne Harvey Group'. You said you had never heard of them before. Well that might be a good place to start, see what I can find out about them."

"Whatever you want you just let me know. I've got to get to the bottom of this before any more serious damage is done. Any problems or people not cooperating you just say the word. I also want regular progress reports. I must know how your investigations are getting on."

While talking David had become visibly more and more irate and looked as if he was going to explode with anger. "I want this bastard. I want you to nail him. But, when you do find out who is behind this, you tell me. You tell me and you tell nobody else. Is that understood?" he screeched. "You tell me who the bastard is and your job is finished. I'll take care of the rest. I have my own ways of, how can I put this," and he paused, "getting even, getting my own back. No police or courts of law. Natural justice I call it."

"When I'm paid my involvement in the matter finishes completely. What you do then is entirely up to you. After what I've been through this year the last thing I'll be doing is expecting you to go to the police."

James calmly finished making his notes then put the files in his briefcase. He said goodbye to David and made his way to his car.

David Fairfax settled into his chair and helped himself to another coffee, "At last," he thought to himself, "I'll soon be getting somewhere."

Soon afterwards his train of thought was interrupted by Lucy coming into the room and asking about the meeting. Once he had gone over the main points Lucy reminded him that he had promised to take her Christmas shopping to Bluewater. This was not how David had envisaged spending the remainder of the day. With Christmas just about a week away, however, he resigned himself to being dragged reluctantly around the most expensive designer shops. Hopefully not too many people would recognise him. He hadn't been in the public eye that long and was not yet a familiar face in the press and media.

Chapter Fifteen

Jenny Palmer was in the kitchen preparing the evening meal when she heard the familiar sound of her husband's car pull up outside. She put her knife down, dried her hands and made her way to the hall. As her husband came through the door she gave him her customary kiss on the cheek.

Jenny had recently been made redundant. The residential centre for people with learning difficulties where she had worked as a carer had finally closed. A lengthy programme to house the residents in the community had at last been completed. Jenny had enjoyed working there and her bubbly personality had made her particularly popular with the residents.

She wasn't a person to sit around idly and, although she had left the centre with a small pension, she had actively been seeking some sort of part-time work. However, now in her mid-fifties this had not proved easy to obtain. She was more than delighted, therefore, when her husband had decided to become a private investigator and asked her to be his assistant. James had believed she would be content just to run the office side of the business but Jenny had other ideas. She was determined to play a full part in the investigations that came their way. She also wanted to make the most of her time now that the children were off her hands.

"How did it go, dear?" she asked most excitedly, "How was that old mate of yours and, more importantly, did we get the job? I've been thinking of nothing else all afternoon since you left."

James tried to calm her down, "It was nice to meet up with David again. I wouldn't exactly describe him as a mate of mine but we did get the job. And a strange sort of job it is too," he said looking at Jenny rather mysteriously and went straight into the lounge without uttering another word.

He sat down in his favourite armchair with a broad grin on his face. Then, after a brief pause, he produced the wad of notes from his pocket with a flourish that would have done any magician credit and casually tossed them onto a small occasional table.

Jenny was beside herself. She rushed to the table and threw the notes high into the air and waited while they fell to the ground and scattered all over the lounge floor.

"I take it this is a big job, then," she exclaimed sitting on the floor covering herself with the notes, "but such a large amount of cash, and upfront too. Something's not right is it?" and her mood visibly changed.

"No, it isn't, I detected a big change in my old mate. David is a worried man. More worried then I can ever remember him being in the past. He's also an angry man and in his present state of mind a very dangerous man indeed. Look, why don't you finish getting the meal ready and I'll get changed. We can then talk about this case over dinner. I think, as my new assistant, you're going to find this a very interesting case indeed."

"So," said Jenny pausing between mouthfuls of chocolate dessert, "tell me about this case. No, tell me first a bit about David Fairfax. What do you know about him? What can you remember from when you grew up together?"

"I've known David ever since our secondary school days. He never had any close mates at school but, at the same time, he wasn't unpopular or bullied. In modern parlance I suppose you would say he kept a low profile and never, so far as I can recall, got into any serious trouble. I don't know why but I actually rather admired him while we were at school.

It's the little things I remember about him. He would never buy tuck from the school shop and always brought sandwiches rather than have school meals. I took this to be because he came from a fairly poor family but then, in the late fifties and early sixties, most families including mine were poor – certainly in today's terms anyway. One thing I do remember though is that he always spent his pocket money at a local cash and carry, or warehouse, as they were known at the time. He would buy cans of drink and packets of crisps and sell them to his mates in the playground at a small profit. Perhaps that was the beginning of his entrepreneurial skills. He was also no stranger to hard work. He had a morning paper-round which meant he had to get up before six in the morning and I believe he also worked in a shop on Saturdays.

David certainly didn't have any burning academic ambitions although he was very bright in just about most subjects and very quick on the uptake. He was also one of those irritating people who could pass exams without having to do much revision. We all thought he would definitely go on to university but he surprised us all by saying he had no intention of undertaking any form of higher education whatsoever. He said he would rather spend those three or four years while we were away studying earning money. He even joked he would be running his own business by the time our studies were over. And he was right of course. We left university penniless and he was already in the money with his own business and a big flashy car. I think it was when I came back from university that I first noticed that ruthless streak of ambition in him that would drive him to be such a talented and successful businessman."

"What about Lucy? You must tell me about her. When did he meet her?"

"Now there is a bit of a mystery here. David had known Lucy for most of their secondary school days. They had always gone out together and didn't have eyes for anyone else at all. It took us all by surprise, therefore, when he married Dawn Desborough. We were even more surprised following her tragic death when he married Beverley Jenks. Unfortunately she committed suicide and it was only after that unhappy event that he got back with Lucy. Apparently they are very happily married and have been so for about 25 years now."

"A strange tale indeed," pondered Jenny putting on her stern detective voice, "Nothing suspicious about the deaths of those first two wives, I suppose?"

"I don't think so but it will be easy enough to look at the records. I seem to recall there were inquests into both deaths. Besides," he added with a grin, "if I need any further information there are still a few colleagues in the force who owe me a favour or two."

James then finished his dessert and poured himself another glass of wine. After dinner he and Jenny studied the folders and discussed the various aspects of the case in some detail. Jenny was lost in thought for a while before looking up at her husband and exclaiming, "What's really odd is that all those in a position to be causing this are the very ones that stand to lose the most!"

"Precisely! That's what makes this case all the more intriguing."

"And we mustn't forget the sudden appearance on the scene of the Anne Harvey Group. I haven't heard of them before. Perhaps a trip down the high street is called for. A little bit of retail therapy," and she paused before adding in a rather flippant manner, "all in the course of the investigation you understand."

"Would I think otherwise? But I do wonder where the Anne Harvey Group fits into all of this. Looks like one of us will be visiting Companies House before long."

"Sounds good to me. You take Companies House and I'll take the shops."

Chapter Sixteen

"I'm glad that's over for another year," sighed a weary Lucy as she sank back into her armchair.

"The party did seem to lack a certain sparkle this time," agreed Callisto, "the MDs hardly said a word all evening and both Angela and Susan left early."

"Well what do you expect!" retorted an angry David, "after all the problems the business has had recently. Someone out there is trying to destroy us and we've no idea who."

"Calm down, dad," implored Callisto, "it's Christmas tomorrow so let's try and relax. Let's forget about the business for once."

"Sis is right," added Tom, "try and unwind a little."

"I'll try," said David appearing to calm down, "but it's nearly eleven and I'm tired so let's have an early night," and without further word he got up and left the room closely followed by Lucy.

* * * * *

Christmas Day in the Fairfax household followed the same pattern every year. The family got up later than usual and had breakfast together at about 10 o'clock. They then opened what they called their 'tree' presents or small personal gifts to each other. Then they relaxed over a drink or two before Lucy and Callisto cooked the Christmas lunch. After lunch surprisingly it was David and the twins who did the washing up in time for the family to sit around the television to watch the Queen's Speech. It was only then that the main presents were opened.

First to delve into the presents at the foot of the Christmas tree was Lucy. She handed a small parcel to David and gave him a big kiss on the cheek. "Thank you," she said, "for another wonderful year. I do love you so very much."

David opened the present and took out a state-of-the-art digital camera. "*Thank you*," he replied, "not just for this camera, and I'm sure I know who tipped you off about it," he added looking across the room and smiling at Callisto, "but also for putting up with me during what has been a most difficult year. You've had a lot to contend with over the last few months. My absence on business, the burdens you've shouldered as a result of my ministerial duties and those dreary political functions that you organised so efficiently." He then went to the Christmas tree, carefully selected a parcel, and handed it to his wife.

"Here's for being a wonderful wife. For much more than I deserve."

Lucy opened the present and let slip a gasp as an exquisite diamond necklace fell into her hands. "This is gorgeous. You shouldn't have," she stuttered as Callisto rushed across to the settee and helped her mother fasten it around her neck.

"Nothing is too good for my wife. You deserve this and much more."

"Simply stunning!" exclaimed Callisto, "Now what other presents are under this tree?" She rooted amongst the heap of brightly coloured gifts and handed a present to each of the twins then picked one up that had her name on it.

"Great! The latest games console! And what super games to go with it! Thanks mum, thanks dad," said Tom and he went to leave the room.

"Oh no you don't, young man! You can play with that later. Some people never grow up do they?" snapped David with a playful glint in his eye.

Then there was a shriek from Callisto. "Wow! You got me the ring! I thought you'd forgotten all about it!"

"Well it just shows what thoughtful parents we are," said a smiling Lucy, "we knew you liked it as soon as you saw it so we went back to the jewellers and bought it for you. We don't like to disappoint our children."

"You can say that again," interjected Nick, "look what I've got!" and he proudly showed the family an all-in-one white leather motorcycle suit, "I thought you may have guessed my old biking suit was getting past it but I never imagined for a moment you'd get me anything like this. It's smashing!"

"We like to do our best," joked David, "but there are lots more presents to open so let's get cracking. I'll get another bottle of champagne. It looks like we're all going to get lots of lovely things this year."

"Yes," added Lucy, "as usual there are presents from our relatives and friends and, I dare say, there will be something from the group's managing directors. No guesses what they'll be giving us."

"Bottles of wine and boxes of chocolates," said Tom disparagingly.

"I think I can guess what each one of them will give," added Nick, "it's the same every year. No imagination."

"Now-now," said Callisto, "after all it's usually you two who eat most of the chocolates and drink the wine." She bent down and retrieved another present from beneath the tree.

"Cheers everyone!" toasted David as he returned to the lounge and poured a glass of champagne for himself and Lucy, "Anyone joining us?"

"Yes please," piped up Callisto handing a small parcel to Tom, "Don't know who this one's from there's just your name on the tag."

Tom took the parcel and opened it. He was silent for a moment. Then with rather an embarrassed look he blurted out, "Is this somebody's idea of a joke? If so then I don't think it's very funny at all."

"What is it?" queried Callisto. She examined the contents of the parcel and then silently handed it to her father.

David looked in total disbelief at what was in his hands. It was a paper bag from the DesboroDenim fashion group containing a pair of underpants. He remained speechless, seething in anger, while the other members of the family looked on too scared to say anything.

"This is impossible! This paper bag is at least 25 years old! And these pants, these pants must be of the same age. But why send them to you?" He looked up and stared directly at Tom.

"I don't know. Look at them, they're nylon. Imagine wearing them."

"That's not the point," retorted David. But as he threw the pants onto the floor in a fit of temper a small card fell out. He picked it up and read out aloud what was written on it.

'Picture yourself in these. Drop-dead gorgeous!'

The family looked nervously at each other. There was complete silence in the room for a couple of minutes before Callisto spoke up with what the others were thinking but were too scared to say out loud, "Let's look and see if there are any more of these under the tree. Is it just Tom or have we all got one? Maybe in the same type of wrapping paper."

After a short while delving around the tree Callisto retrieved another four parcels wrapped in the same distinctive paper, one addressed to each of the four remaining family members. As in the case of Tom's parcel there was no indication as to who the sender might be.

"Well," she said looking round at the family, "if you're not going to open yours then I'll open mine," and she carefully opened the parcel. Inside she found a DesboroDenim paper bag containing a bikini, once again both of 1970s style and vintage, together with a small card on which was written, 'You'll get a nice tan in this. But don't get your fingers burnt.'

"Is someone playing a rather sick practical joke or is there something more sinister here?" shouted David angrily, "Go on Lucy, open your one."

Lucy nervously opened the small parcel and took out a DesboroDenim paper bag. Inside she found a scarf with a small card bearing the words, 'This will look good around your neck. But don't go overboard. Don't get it wet'.

Lucy stared at the scarf for a moment then suddenly threw it down onto the carpet and ran sobbing from the room. Callisto dashed after her.

David started to get up but then changed his mind and turned his attention to his own parcel. He roughly tore it open and was confronted by a small DesboroDenim paper bag. He thrust his hand inside and pulled out a pair of women's knickers. A pair of knickers he instantly recognised as being one of the first items he had put into production after the death of his first wife. He read the card attached to the knickers, 'Just as betrayal comes before a fall so does pride'.

David leaned over towards Nick and grabbed his parcel. He attacked the wrapping getting angrier by the second as it came away in shreds rather than large pieces. Inside he found the usual DesboroDenim paper bag and a pair of old diamond-patterned DesboroDenim socks and a note that read 'Wear these and run out of time. Or should that be scramble out of time?'

By now David was in an uncontrollable rage and he shouted, "Tom, get my mobile phone! Get it now!"

Tom hurriedly disappeared into the study and came back a few seconds later. David immediately snatched the phone from his hands and punched in James Palmer's number. There was a lengthy pause before a voice was heard on the other end.

"James, something's happened. I need you over here now, and I mean, now! Can't tell you what it's about on the phone. Yes I do know it's Christmas Day. Yes I appreciate you've got your family there but I need you now!"

David stared at the ceiling trying to contain his anger while awaiting the reply. Once he had confirmation that James Palmer was on his way he turned off the phone and threw it onto a small occasional table. It bounced onto the floor and was eagerly pounced on by Vienna.

* * * * *

It took James Palmer about 20 minutes to drive from his home in North Weald to Theydon Bois. As he waited for the electronic gates of Forest Glade to open he began to muse on what might have happened on this day of all days. He had to admit that since being given this commission he hadn't made much progress. He had some lines of enquiry mapped out and had already accessed Companies House on-line but had decided that he couldn't really start work in earnest until the new year.

David Fairfax himself opened the front door and ushered James Palmer into the lounge. As he sat down Callisto entered the room. "Mum's lying down. She's crying and very upset but won't say what's wrong. It must be something to do with that scarf."

"I'll see to her later! Sit down! James is here now so perhaps we can begin to make some sense of all this."

David then recounted the events of the afternoon in some detail to James Palmer who closely examined the parcels, paper bags and articles of clothing they had contained.

"Pity," he mused, "that you didn't take more care when opening these. It might have given us some clues. As I understand it all the items are genuine DesboroDenim clothes from the 1970s. And these paper bags are those that shoppers would have been given when they bought DesboroDenim clothes in high street shops at that time."

"That's right. But what about those cards? What do you make of them?"

"Now they are interesting, very interesting indeed. Do they relate to things that have happened in the past? Or are they a warning about things that are going to happen in the future? Or," and he paused for maximum effect, "are they a combination of the two?"

There was an uncomfortable silence before James Palmer continued, "The scarf that was sent to Lucy obviously upset her. Is that why she's not here with us?"

"Don't you worry about Lucy, she'll be all right!"

"Of course the most intriguing question is how did the parcels get here? How did they get under your Christmas tree? Who put them there and when? Who was here yesterday at your party?"

"I wouldn't describe it as a party," said David.

"I'll second that," piped up Tom.

"Shut up Tom. This isn't a laughing matter," snapped David and continued, "it's just a gathering we have every year for senior executives of the Fairfax Group. Matter of fact the only people here were the four managing directors, Alan Box, Ken Winter, Rahul Dixit and Craig Bentley. Feb was here of course, as were Angela Hamilton and Susan Rumble. That's about it. Oh and the family, we were all here as well."

"What about the catering? Who did that?"

"A firm in Epping called Upper Crust Caterers. We use them every year at Christmas. They also do the catering for other functions we hold here during the year. Surely you don't think ...."

"I do think," cut in James Palmer quickly, "that's why I'm a good detective. We can't take anything for granted. I would suggest that those presents were placed under your tree sometime yesterday afternoon or evening. If not by one of the caterers then by one of your guests or," and he hesitated, "by one of your family!"

"How dare you!" roared David.

"We can't afford to rule out anybody at this stage, no matter how painful or incredible it may seem to you," continued James Palmer seemingly oblivious to David's outburst, "You would do well to heed a word of advice from an old friend of mine. His maxim was 'watch your friends because you know who your enemies are' and I've come to realise over the years just how much truth there is in those few words."

"Cut the philosophy! Stick to being a detective!"

"Could I hang onto the parcels and their contents for a few days? I might be able to come up with something. The cards, for instance, look like they were printed on an ink jet printer so were probably produced on a computer. Might be a lead there." He thought for a while and then added, "Have you told the Chief Inspector about what's happened today?"

"Inspector Westwood? No, I haven't! I don't pay Inspector Westwood but I do pay you and I'm beginning to wonder why. I pay you because I want results. Is that clear?"

"Crystal clear. All the same, I think you should tell him, and tell him now. Perhaps it's best if you give all this material to him. Does he know of my involvement in the case?"

"Yes, I made a point of telling him the day after we first spoke. He wasn't too keen but seemed to accept the situation when I told him it was you I had hired. He said he'd worked with you in the past. Although you're no longer in the force he's prepared to tolerate your presence so long as you don't get in his way."

"Very magnanimous of him I'm sure. It wouldn't do to fall out with him though. I know he's a bit of a plodder and always works by the book but he does get results and that's what counts."

"So, tell me, what have I got for my money so far?"

"It's early days yet but I've already made a start and been on-line to Companies House. The Anne Harvey

Group of companies has been in existence for a few years but it's only recently that it has started to expand. The Group's owner is actually someone called Anne Harvey and the Group itself is based in Ipswich. I plan a trip there in the New Year to find out more about the group and its founder.

I'll also be making enquiries into the early years of the DesboroDenim Fashion Group and other companies in your empire. I want to see if there is anything to shed light on what's been happening and who could be harbouring a grudge and want to see you ruined. Are these events connected to your business success? There's also the political side of things. Could your ministerial promotion have opened up an old wound or made someone jealous?"

"Just remember I want results. I'm paying you good money and don't you forget it. If you want access to company personnel or records just let me know. If anyone tries to hinder you in any way then you tell me and I'll sort them out."

"Fine! If that's all then I'll be going. Back to what's left of Christmas with my family. By the way, don't forget to contact Inspector Westwood."

After exchanging a few words with the rest of the family and reassuring them as much as he could James Palmer took his leave. He drove back to his home in North Weald deep in thought along deserted Christmas-Day roads, "My Christmas has been spoilt right enough but at least I'm returning to a happy home, which is more than I can say for David Fairfax and his family."

* * * * *

Back at Forest Glade David Fairfax was sitting next to his wife's bed.

"Somebody knows. Somebody knows." she repeated slowly.

"Nonsense! Nobody knows. Nobody can know. Still, just to be on the safe side, I'll get Feb to have a couple of the lads keep an eye on the grounds."

Chapter Seventeen

The Fairfax family spent the first few days after Christmas at home. Apart from Inspector Westwood they didn't receive any visitors at all. On Boxing Day Feb had arranged for two of his former SAS colleagues to take up residence in the grounds of Forest Glade. The following day Katie had returned to live-in with the family having cut short her Christmas break at David Fairfax's request. Soon after her arrival Inspector Westwood had called round to say that the articles taken away for forensic examination appeared to be genuine and from the 1970s. They did not appear to be fakes or modern replicas. However, he wished to retain them for further tests.

After the trauma of the mysterious, but rather sinister Christmas presents, life for the Fairfax family slowly began to settle down. Even Lucy appeared to regain her former composure. The children remained puzzled by the effect the scarf had had upon her but were even more intrigued by the fact that she refused outright to discuss the matter with any of them. Their father had also told them not to mention anything about it and when questioned refused to elaborate further.

On the morning of New Year's Eve the family were gathered in the dining room enjoying a late breakfast cooked for them by Katie and discussing their plans for celebrating the New Year.

"I tried my best darling," said a rather apologetic David, "but I'm afraid we have to go. The PM insisted. I must admit seeing the New Year in at Chequers with the Prime Minister and my Cabinet colleagues isn't my way of celebrating. But all the other wives will be there so it shouldn't be too boring for you. That reminds me, we're being picked up by my official chauffeur at about mid-day so we'll soon have to be getting ready."

"I'd much rather see in the New Year here, in the comfort of my own home," replied a despondent Lucy, "Besides, those other wives are so boring. All they talk about is politics and their husbands' careers. None of them seems to know what the inside of a shop or a good restaurant looks like!"

"Same for me really. But look on the bright side we'll be coming home after lunch tomorrow." He paused for a moment, looked up at the children, and asked, "What about you lot then? What are you doing to celebrate the New Year?"

Tom was the first to stop eating and respond, "Me and Nick are going up west to that new hotel and casino, you know, 'The London'."

"Yes, it's quite a plush place by all accounts. And very expensive too I believe!"

"It certainly is but it's worth it. We couldn't think of a better way to see out the old and see in the new."

"What's more we've booked a couple of suites so we don't have to worry about getting home in the early hours," chipped in Nick, "and we're going with John and Terry."

"John Burling and Terry Kingston!" exclaimed Callisto, "No need to ask what you'll all be getting up to then!"

"That's right," confirmed Tom, "what could be better. An evening at the tables followed by some good food and drink and all in the company of some pretty girls. There are always plenty of those in 'The London'. I remember the last time the four of us went there it was quite a ...."

"I can imagine," grinned Callisto as she interrupted him, "but mark my words, one of these days women will be the death of you Tom."

"No, I don't think so but what a way to go. Have fun while you can that's my motto. So, big sis, what have you got planned for this evening. Don't tell me you're not going out to have a bit of fun yourself."

"As a matter of fact I am going out but not gambling or ending up in an orgy like some people I know. I'm driving down to 'The Retreat'. It's a very exclusive health farm near a small village called Playford. I'm going to spend the last evening of the old year indulging in absolute luxury."

"Playford! With a name like that it sounds like my sort of place. Where is it? I've never heard of it."

"It's just the other side of Ipswich. I've never been there before but apparently 'The Retreat' is a health farm and spa in a converted Tudor mansion. I can't wait to get there. I'll be leaving during the afternoon as it will take me a good hour or so to drive down."

"So who are you going with then? Or are you seeing in the New Year on your own?" retorted Tom.

"I'm going on my own."

"I knew it," smiled Tom smugly, pulling a face at Callisto.

"*I'm going on my own* but I'm meeting an old friend there from my school days. You remember Maureen don't you? Maureen Bennett, she's been here a few times. I admit I was at a loss what to do this year. Then quite out of the blue a few days before Christmas Maureen phoned and suggested we do something different for a change. So while you and Nick are losing all your money at the tables I'll be spending an evening relaxing and being pampered in the lap of luxury. After a refreshing night's sleep in a four-poster bed I'll come home and sober you two up."

David finished his breakfast in silence. He looked round the table at his children and was pleased they had at last managed to put the events of Christmas Day behind them. For the first time they were actually looking forward to going out somewhere again. He hoped that Lucy too would snap out of her sombre mood and enjoy herself once she had left the house and was in the company of other people. Not the best of company he had to admit but company all the same. The very fact of being in a different environment should help to ease her present forebodings.

David and Lucy were the first to leave the house. A couple of hours or so after the ministerial car had left the grounds of Forest Glade Callisto threw her overnight bag onto the front passenger seat of her BMW Z4 sports car and drove out of the gates. She roared at a breakneck pace through the village. Tom and Nick had ordered a taxi which arrived soon after four o'clock to take them on the hour's drive to 'The London'. Katie watched from inside the house as the two security men ensured the gates were closed and then resumed their patrols around the grounds. She relished the prospect of a day to herself and the chance to relax before the family members began to return home.

* * * * *

The four lads arrived at 'The London' and made their way to the reception desk. It was then that Tom and Nick discovered that John and Terry had reserved them a suite each.

"It was a struggle to get four rooms," admitted John, "and very expensive. But based on the last time we were here when we just couldn't get rid of all that lovely talent I thought I should look on the positive side and plan ahead a bit."

"Well done John, I knew we could rely on you. There's bound to be lots of girls hanging around the tables. Especially later tonight in the casino with it being New Year's Eve and all."

"Don't heap too much praise on me Tom. I forgot to mention that I told the hotel you'd be settling the bill for all four rooms!"

Tom looked straight at John and was silent for a while. He then burst into laughter and patted him on the back and shook his hand vigorously, "Had you there for a minute, didn't I? Go on admit it."

The lads then booked into the hotel and went to their rooms to freshen up and change for dinner. They had decided to have dinner at 7 o'clock. This meant they would have time afterwards to go to the bar for a few drinks and still be in the casino by 10 o'clock at the latest. All went according to plan and they were in the casino soon after 10 o'clock. Immaculately groomed and dressed in black dinner jackets with contrasting white shirts they looked the epitome of young successful men about town.

Although all four lads enjoyed frequenting casinos they each had their own favourite games and usually separated once they were inside. Nick made his way to the blackjack tables, John and Terry went over to the chemin de fer table, and Tom went to play roulette.

As the lads had predicted the room was full of young and very attractive girls. Most of them were obviously after a good time. The festive atmosphere was enhanced by the waiters who continually moved around the room offering free drinks to all those sitting at the tables whether or not they were actually playing. Any player winning large amounts of money or who just happened to have lots of chips by his side soon found himself surrounded by beautiful girls offering advice and encouragement. Tom, Nick, John and Terry were soon spotted as falling into this category. They attracted more than their fair share of lovely ladies anxious to share in their luck at the tables.

Of the four lads it was Tom who was having the most success. He had a system for roulette which involved simultaneously placing three or four single-number bets and three or four double-numbers and lines of three. It was an expensive way to play but experience had taught him that the more such bets he placed the more chances he had of winning. By eleven o'clock he had amassed a formidable pile of chips by his side and was having to fend off an ever-increasing number of young ladies who were more than willing to spend his winnings for him.

Sitting watching the ball race around the inside of the roulette wheel Tom was suddenly made aware of two young ladies standing either side of him. They each pushed one of their breasts into the side of his face. He looked up. They were both most elegantly dressed in designer clothes and very expensive jewellery.

"Sorry!" giggled one of the young ladies, "Hope you don't mind but we got carried away with the excitement of the game."

"That's all right," said Tom taking full advantage of the situation, "rather liked it actually."

"Well, who knows what's in store for the rest of your evening. You've been lucky on the tables so who knows where that luck will take you. Perhaps we can share in your luck."

"You sure can. My name's Tom by the way," and he offered his hand to the girls who shook it in turn before grabbing another drink from a passing waiter.

"I'm Amber," said the girl on Tom's left, "And I'm Bamber," giggled the girl on his right.

"Amber and Bamber! I don't believe you. What sort of names are those? Are they your professional names? Are you models, actresses, that sort of thing?"

"You could say they're our professional names. We're not actresses but we do like pretending," said Amber, "And dressing up! Don't forget that," added Bamber with a smile and she pushed her left breast into Tom's face once again.

"Do you know, girls? This New Year's Eve has suddenly got a lot better. Here, put a few bets on for me."

"If you insist," agreed Amber enthusiastically and both she and Bamber squeezed onto a single seat next to Tom and placed a few bets on the table.

It soon became obvious that they were more interested in Tom than playing roulette. After 30 minutes or so when Tom had won even more money he decided that he couldn't resist the lure of these two beautiful creatures any more. He cashed in his chips and gave a sizeable part of his winnings to the girls. They laughingly pushed the notes down the front of their low-cut dresses and challenged him to retrieve the money.

"Not here," he said in a hushed voice, "how about my room?"

"Your room! What sort of girls do you think we are?"

"Now that would be telling. Are you up for it? Do you want to see in the New Year with a bang?"

"Why not! Lead the way!" and both girls wrapped themselves around him as they made their way out of the casino. Tom collected his room key from the reception desk and the three of them staggered towards the lifts. John and Terry were engrossed in their game and it was only Nick who saw the three of them leave. He gave a broad wink to Tom who smiled and carried on talking to the girls.

The three of them fell out of the lift and staggered towards Tom's suite as he fumbled for the key. After a bit of difficulty he managed to open the door and they all went inside with Tom only just remembering to close the door behind them.

Once inside the girls were anxious to leave the lounge and go into the bedroom but Tom persuaded them to sit down and have a drink with him. This gave him time to think about what bizarre types of sexual perversion he would like to indulge in with these two most nubile of young ladies. He certainly believed he was on a roll as he liked to put it. He couldn't believe his luck in having bagged a pair of obvious nymphomaniacs.

Suddenly Amber stood up and in the space of a few seconds removed her dress revealing the briefest of underwear.

"Who likes playing games?" she enquired.

"I do!" replied Bamber and she removed her dress in a most provocative manner and threw it over Tom.

"What are we waiting for then?" Tom agreed enthusiastically throwing the dress to one side, "I'm all yours!"

The girls grabbed hold of Tom's arms and dragged him into the bedroom. He pretended to struggle as they threw him on the bed and slowly began removing his clothes one by one but he was enjoying every minute of it. It was common knowledge amongst his friends that he indulged in a variety of sexual practices. He was also into bondage in a big way so he was very pleased when Amber produced some leather thongs.

"Must get all those nasty clothes off first," she pouted as she took down his trousers.

"What about you two? Aren't you going to reveal a bit more? Show me what you're made of. Show me what I'm about to enjoy."

"Later," both girls giggled in unison as they sat Tom up on the bed and with Amber in front and Bamber behind they squashed him between their almost-naked bodies. "You must learn to be patient," they teased, "all things come to he who waits." And then after rolling on the bed together Amber pushed Tom down forcefully and sat astride him and slowly spread-eagled him on the bed.

"This is more like it!" Tom enthused eagerly as Amber grabbed his left wrist and Bamber his right wrist and began to tie his hands to the bed using the leather thongs. They quickly removed his briefs and before he knew what was happening had also secured his legs. He lay spread-eagled on the bed naked and helpless. The two girls slowly lowered their bodies on top of him.

"That's enough girls!" a strange voice suddenly barked, and Amber and Bamber immediately jumped up off the bed.

Tom was speechless. Standing at the foot of the bed was a figure dressed all in black and wearing a face mask. He looked the figure up and down. From the contours of the tight fitting all-in-one body suit it was obviously a woman and a very well-endowed woman at that. He quickly realised the potential of the situation. "Girls, what can I say? You've brought one of your playmates. How thoughtful of you!"

He was silent for a moment then added, "No it's Nick and the lads isn't it. They've sent you. A foursome! I must remember to thank them. I've never done a foursome before."

The masked figure walked round the bed in silence.

"Okay you can go now," and without a further word both Amber and Bamber quickly put their clothes back on. Tom looked up with a feeling of disbelief and disappointment. "Do you have to be going? So soon? When things are just getting interesting?"

"Here," said the masked figure handing a package to Amber, "your money and your tickets. I've heard the weather in Rio is simply wonderful at this time of year. Have a good long holiday. Remember, I don't want to hear you're back in this country until the summer at the earliest. Is that understood?"

"Perfectly," said the girls who turned and left the room hand in hand.

The masked figure then approached the bed once more and focussed her attention on Tom who had witnessed the departure of Amber and Bamber in sheer disbelief.

"You'd better be good," he said with a tinge of menace in his voice, "I don't like to be disappointed!"

"You won't be disappointed I can promise you that," and the figure picked up Tom's glass from the small bed-side table and held it above his head.

"Whisky on the rocks. Whisky on ice," mused the figure who spun the glass in her hand so that the drink swirled around inside. Then without any warning she suddenly poured it onto Tom's forehead. The liquid slowly trickled into his eyes.

"Hey! What the hell did you do that for?" he shouted as the whisky burnt into his eyes forcing him to screw them up as the pain became almost unbearable.

The masked figure remained silent and still until Tom could at last partially open his eyes.

"Whisky on the rocks!" the masked figure repeated, "Dangerous things rocks. Sometimes rocks can be smooth like these," and she took a handful of ice cubes from an ice bucket on the table and rubbed them in a circular motion into Tom's body. She slowly made her way up to his chest and then onto his face all the time rubbing the ice into his flesh. For Tom this was now beginning to show potential.

"On the other hand," the figure continued, "rocks can also be jagged and sharp, like these!" and she deftly produced two short pencil-shaped pieces of ice from the ice bucket. "Got to be careful with these. Don't want anybody getting hurt do we?" she continued. But this time Tom detected a tone of malice in her voice. This made him feel uneasy and very vulnerable as he was still securely tied to the bed and unable to free himself.

The figure sat on the bed and then jumped astride an increasingly panicking Tom. She waved one of the pieces of ice in front of him and quite casually stuck it into his cheek. He let out a yell.

"You bitch! What did you do that for?"

Without any answer the figure continued to wave the piece of ice over Tom's face gradually getting closer and closer to his skin. Then to Tom's horror she suddenly thrust it with full force up his right nostril and left it embedded there. He let out a scream as he struggled to comprehend what was going on and he felt blood begin to trickle down the inside of his throat. After a few seconds he began to cough and choke as the warm blood flowed into his throat and blocked up his airways.

"As I said, dangerous things rocks!" taunted the masked figure, "Can do no end of harm. Could even kill!"

By now Tom was sweating profusely and struggling desperately to free himself but to no avail. Amber and Bamber were obviously experts in their field. He could only watch in horror as the figure picked up the second piece of sharp pointed ice and once again sat astride him. He struggled to unseat the figure but his movements were restricted by the thongs securing him to the bed. The figure stroked his cheeks gently with the ice playing with him like a cat plays with a mouse. Then just as quickly and expertly as before she thrust it fully up his left nostril and left it there.

Again Tom let out a muffled cry but he was now much more concerned about trying to breathe as the increasing flow of blood down his throat gradually began to choke him. He was just about able to breathe through his now open mouth but it was a struggle between bouts of coughing and choking.

"Who are you? What do you want?" he blurted out as he coughed and gasped for air.

The figure remained seated astride him and slowly and deliberately removed the face mask. She stared at him for a moment and laughed out aloud.

"You! It can't be. Here?"

Then to Tom's utter amazement the figure removed a wig. He stared at the face grinning before him and managed to blurt out a few words between fits of choking, "It can't be. I don't understand. Callisto? No!"

"You asked me what I wanted? I think you know the answer to that by now. I want revenge. And I'm starting with your death. Your time is past."

Tom looked on in horror as the female figure got up and emptied the contents of the ice box into her gloved hand. He watched in growing fear and realisation as she slowly came closer and closer to him and stood silently looking down into his eyes. He was now struggling to see clearly and he was also having real difficulties in breathing.

"If it's money," he blurted out, "I can give you all you want. Look in my jacket. There's a few thousand pounds there. You can have it. You can have it all!"

The female figure made no reply. With one hand she grabbed hold of Tom's open mouth and with the other she rammed the ice cubes deep into his mouth with as much force as she could muster. She held the ice there for about five minutes until all signs of movement had ceased.

"I told you," she said surveying his body, "rocks no matter how small can be dangerous, very dangerous indeed."

She then quickly untied Tom's feet and with a degree of difficulty pulled a pair of underpants over his legs and onto his body. Before leaving the bedroom she ensured that Tom's feet were tied and placed in exactly the same position as previously. It took only a few minutes for her to put some party clothes over her one piece cat-suit so she could blend in effortlessly with the revellers below. She then returned to the bedroom and produced a small digital camera from her handbag. After ensuring the room was arranged just as she wanted she took a photograph of Tom lying spread-eagled on the bed and put the camera back into her handbag. Before leaving the room she placed a small card on top of Tom's lifeless body.

She closed the door to the suite and before walking down the corridor towards the stairs turned the card hanging on the doorknob to read 'do not disturb'.

The fine figure of a young woman walked casually down the stairs past the reception area and out through the main entrance of the hotel attracting no attention whatsoever. She smiled to herself as she heard the chimes of Big Ben striking midnight and ushering in the

New Year. The strains of 'Auld Lang Syne' were being sung by the partygoers in the hotel's ballroom, "Very apt, very apt indeed," she thought to herself, "it was all a long time ago but the past has now returned to haunt the future, to take revenge!"

Chapter Eighteen

It was almost midday when Nick and Lisa Watson made their way down to the buffet restaurant for breakfast. They restricted themselves to a light meal of cereal and toast. They looked around for a vacant table and Nick saw John Burling and Terry Kingston sitting at a table by a large window overlooking the street below.

"You managed to get up then?" said Terry with a knowing smile on his face as Nick and Lisa sat down, "No sign of Tom yet though. Knowing him it was a wild night. Those two girls he took off with looked like a right pair of goers."

"Yes," acknowledged Nick, "still, it's a bit late even for him. This is Lisa by the way."

"Pleased to meet you, Lisa," responded Terry, "I'm Terry and this is John. And this is Emma and this is Laura," he continued pointing to the two girls who were sitting eating with them."

"We helped them to commiserate last night," said Emma, "They lost a lot of money so we helped them take their minds off it."

"That's right," said John, "we were really doing very well. We had the golden touch and then all of a sudden 'Lady Luck' deserted us. Nothing seemed to go right so we decided to cut our losses and leave the casino and join the party. We had a great time and didn't leave until about four this morning."

"I rather lost track of you two in the crowd anyway," Nick admitted, "We did spend a bit of time at the party but after a while we decided to get an early night," and he winked at Lisa, "We did stay and see the New Year in though. Can't miss that and Auld Lang Syne. It wouldn't be New Year."

When the six of them had finished their breakfast there was still no sign of Tom so Nick suggested they go up to his room.

"What a good idea," agreed Terry, "we'll surprise him, get the lazy so and so out of bed. He must be dead tired to be still up there."

"Or," added John, "he's still being entertained by those two nymphomaniacs."

"So what are we waiting for?" said Nick and they all left the restaurant and made their way to the lifts.

"Would you believe it?" exclaimed John as the six of them left the lift, "He's still at it! Look at that 'do not disturb' sign on the door. Who says we go in anyway? There must be a maid or someone on this floor who can let us in. Let's have a look around."

After a few minutes they saw a maid carrying a bundle of linen. They told her they were surprising an old friend so she unlocked the door and accompanied them into the suite.

The room itself was in near darkness. The curtains in the lounge were still closed but there was a shaft of light coming from the bedroom door which was slightly ajar.

"Come on let's see what he's up to," whispered Nick, "let's creep up on him."

"Is that wise?" asked Lisa in a hushed voice, "We could be interrupting."

"Serves him right," retorted Nick and they all made their way silently towards the bedroom door.

With a shout of "Got you!" the door was flung open. But instead of catching Tom in the act with the two girls all they saw was his prone lifeless body lying tied up on the bed. The maid let out a piercing scream and Lisa turned away and began to retch. Emma and Laura collapsed into each other's arms and staggered back into the lounge.

The three young lads stood rooted to the spot, speechless, surveying the scene in sheer disbelief. It was obvious from the colour of the body and the blood around his nose and mouth that Tom was dead.

Nick moved towards the bed but Terry grabbed his arm and pulled him back. "No, don't go near that bed.

Don't touch anything. We need to get the police," and he turned to the maid, "Phone reception, get them to call the police, now! Tell them there's been a murder."

"Murder!" exclaimed Nick, "You don't know that. It might have been a bit of fun that went wrong!"

"No, this is more just than a bit of fun. We need the police."

* * * * *

At Chequers lunch had finished. The Prime Minister was chatting to his guests seated round the table when one of his personal assistants came and whispered a few words in his ear. He immediately left the room. After a few minutes he returned with a grave expression on his face. He indicated to David and Lucy Fairfax that they should leave the room with him. He took them to a small study and closed the door once they were inside.

"I don't know how to tell you this," he hesitated, "it's about your son, Tom. I'm very sorry to have to tell you but he's been found dead."

"Dead!" exclaimed David in total disbelief, "Dead! Are you sure?"

"I'm afraid there's no doubt about it. I've just had the Metropolitan Police Commissioner himself on the phone. Tom was found dead earlier this afternoon in a room at 'The London'. I really am most sorry."

Lucy started sobbing uncontrollably then broke down in a fit of crying and had to be helped onto a chair.

"Why Tom?" she blurted out and began to hit the wall behind the chair with her clenched fists, "And what about Nick, is he all right?"

The Prime Minister looked on in silence and then took David to one side.

"Nasty business this. I suggest you get Lucy back home as soon as you can. There's nothing to be gained by staying here or going to 'The London'. You wouldn't be allowed to see him anyway. I'm told it will be several hours before the Scene of Crime officers are finished and the body can be moved."

"Do you know how he died?"

"No I don't, but the police are treating the death as suspicious. I'm sure they'll leave no stone unturned. But right now I really do think you should get Lucy home. If there's anything I can do just let me know."

* * * * *

The journey home to Forest Glade in the official ministerial car seemed to take an age. For most of the time Lucy was sobbing and crying uncontrollably but David, despite feeling the loss of Tom intensely, was putting on a brave face for Lucy's sake. He was also thinking about what could have happened. As the car approached Theydon Bois he pulled out his mobile phone and dialled James Palmer.

"Is that you James? Listen!" he said in hushed tones so Lucy couldn't hear him clearly, "Get over to 'The London'. Tom's been found dead and the police are treating it as suspicious. I want you to find out what's going on. I can't talk now but use your old contacts if you have to. Get back to me on my mobile as soon as you find out anything. No, better still, come over to Forest Glade so you can tell me personally."

And without waiting for James to reply he disconnected the call.

* * * * *

James Palmer was none too pleased to have his New Year's Day spoiled by the call from David Fairfax but he felt he had no alternative but to go to 'The London'. His natural instinct was to wait and see what the police came up with but before he could suggest this to David he had hung up. He was also displeased because it was a Public Holiday and there was a restricted service on the tube so he had to drive into London.

Despite there being not much traffic it was nearly two hours later that James reached 'The London'. Although the hotel remained open the floor where Tom's body had been found had been cordoned off by the police.

James approached the cordon and bent down to cross under the police tapes as he had done on numerous occasions in his police career.

"Sorry sir," barked a burly police sergeant, "but you can't cross that line."

"Sorry, force of habit. But I must see Inspector Westwood," responded James reluctantly replacing the tape.

"Inspector Westwood? Do you mean Detective Chief Inspector Westwood by any chance sir?" the sergeant asked sarcastically.

"Yes, that's right. Please tell him James Palmer is here at David Fairfax's request."

"And why should I do that, sir?"

"Because I'm asking you to. Asking you politely."

The sergeant thought for a moment then motioned to a nearby constable, "Tell Inspector Westwood that a James Palmer is here and wants to see him."

A few minutes later the constable returned and spoke briefly to the sergeant.

"Seems it's your lucky day sir. The Chief Inspector will see you. Here, put these on," and after holding up the tape for him to duck under he handed James a white all-in-one disposable boiler suit and a paper face mask.

James was escorted to the suite and told to wait outside until Inspector Westwood was ready for him. There was a lot of activity on the part of the forensics team but Inspector Westwood emerged from the bedroom after a few minutes. He motioned to James to join him.

"Well, there you are, Tom Fairfax," he said pointing to the body.

James looked at the body prostrated on the bed. Tom's eyes were open looking skyward in an expression of pure terror and there was blood around the nose and mouth.

"What can you tell me?"

"It's very early you understand so the pathologist won't confirm it at this stage but he thinks death occurred sometime between half past eleven and midnight. At the moment the exact cause of death is unknown but look at that expression on his face. He looks terrified. And although Tom is almost naked and tied to the bed there's no evidence that any form of sexual activity actually took place. Robbery is also ruled out as his wallet, containing a considerable amount of money and his credit cards, is still in his jacket pocket."

"He certainly does look terrified," observed James looking at the body closely.

"There's no sign of a weapon but it's possible that he was suffocated or he choked. We won't know for sure until after the post-mortem."

"Do we know his movements last night? Was he with anyone?"

"He came here with his brother Nick and two other lads from Theydon Bois, Terry Kingston and John Burling. We've got them all downstairs now. From what they say they were all here to have a good time. A bit of gambling then see in the New Year with some of the 'local talent' as they put it."

"So what happened last night?"

"It appears Tom was lucky on the roulette table and attracted the attention of two girls. The hotel staff say they go by the unlikely names of Amber and Bamber. Apparently they're well known here and all three of them left together for Tom's suite soon after eleven o'clock."

"So you're looking for these two girls."

"We certainly are but we don't think they killed Tom. No, we think they lured him to his room on the pretence of some kinky sex but there was somebody else lying in wait for him. We've checked the CCTV cameras and they clearly show Amber and Bamber leaving the hotel before eleven thirty."

"Are there any prints in the suite?"

"None, the whole suite has been wiped clean. But we did find this on the body," and Inspector Westwood handed James Palmer a small card on which was written 'Wearing these you really are drop-dead gorgeous!'

"It looks like our murderer has a sense of humour."

"Or .." hesitated the Inspector, "he or she is trying to tell us something. I'll see if the lab boys can come up with anything on the card and let you know."

"Thanks Ben, I really do appreciate this. You know of course that some weeks ago David Fairfax asked me to do a bit of private sleuthing on his behalf. He was worried about what was happening to him and the business. I have no intention of treading on your toes and I made a point of telling him that. I told him he couldn't have a better person on the case than you."

"I'm very glad to hear it. As you know it's most irregular to have, how can I put this, 'outsiders' at a crime scene. But I made an exception in your case for two reasons. First because you were a damn good copper who in my view should still be in the force and, secondly, because I need someone on the inside of the Fairfax empire I can trust. You help me by tipping me off about anything you find out and I'll keep you up to date with the investigation. Agreed?"

"Agreed!"

"Well, I can't tell you anymore at the moment. Suggest you report back to Sir David and let me know his reaction."

"Will do. And thanks, much appreciated."

James Palmer made his way back past the burly sergeant but wasn't allowed to speak to Nick or the others being held for questioning. He then retrieved his car from the hotel's car park and drove over to Forest Glade.

* * * * *

It was a sombre Katie who showed James Palmer into the drawing room where a very worried-looking David Fairfax was deep in conversation with Feb.

"Come in James, won't keep you a minute. Help yourself to a drink," and turning to Feb he continued, "That's settled then, we'll keep the two men in the grounds at all times and you or one of your men will accompany family members on all occasions when they're away from the house."

"I'll see to it straight away, Sir David," and Feb strode quickly out of the room with just the briefest of acknowledgements to James.

"Tell me James, what did you find out at 'The London'? And don't spare me any of the detail."

James then described the scene in the hotel suite and recounted his conversation with Inspector Westwood.

After he had finished his account the two men heard a car drawing up outside and soon afterwards Katie showed Inspector Westwood and Nick into the drawing room. Nick looked drained and his eyes were red and it was obvious that he had been crying.

"Nick! Thank goodness you're ok," said a relieved-looking David and he got up and hugged his son warmly, "Sit down and make yourself comfortable. You too inspector."

In her bedroom Lucy heard the arrival of the car. She got up and made her way to the drawing room in the hope that it might be Nick.

"Nick," Lucy sobbed, and took him in her arms, "you're home," and she broke down crying.

David sat next to her and attempted to comfort her but it was no use and in the end he left her to sob to herself.

Suddenly David looked up and exclaimed, "What about Callisto! Where has she got to? She should be home by now. She doesn't know about Tom. I don't want her to find out from somebody else or from news bulletins."

"Don't worry about Callisto, Sir David," replied Inspector Westwood almost immediately, "she's in custody."

"In custody!" barked David in sheer disbelief, "What the hell do you mean, in custody?"

"She's being held by the Suffolk police."

"Why would they be doing that? Who ordered her to be arrested anyway?"

"I did!" said Inspector Westwood, "I did!"

Chapter Nineteen

"What the hell do you mean you had Callisto arrested?" snapped an incredulous David Fairfax.

"Purely for her own protection," replied Inspector Westwood calmly. "Actually she's not been arrested. Simply taken into protective custody for her own safety."

"For her own safety!"

"Precisely. She should be here soon. I asked my colleagues in Suffolk to bring her over."

"Is she a suspect?" asked Nick. But before the Inspector could reply the sound of a vehicle was heard outside on the driveway.

A rather distraught Callisto was led into the drawing room by two constables. After exchanging brief words with Inspector Westwood they left. Callisto immediately ran sobbing to her father and hugged him very tightly, clinging to him as if she was still a child.

"Who did this to Tom?" she sobbed, "Why Tom?"

"That's what we're trying to find out, miss," responded Inspector Westwood, "Now I know where

Nick and his friends were last night but do you mind telling me where you were between the hours of eleven and midnight? Where did you see in the New Year?"

At this Lucy sat up and blurted out, "She was at The Retreat, a health resort in Playdon, near Ipswich."

"I beg to differ, Lady Lucy. I can assure you she wasn't," retorted the Inspector.

Nick suddenly became animated. He pointed an accusing finger at Callisto and shouted, "You killed him! You killed Tom!"

"Don't be ridiculous," protested Callisto, "I was miles away."

"You put a curse on him. Last night you said that women would be the death of him. And now he's dead!"

"This will get us nowhere," interjected Inspector Westwood, "Tell us Callisto where were you last night."

"It's all a bit strange really. I had arranged to meet an old friend, Maureen Bennett, at The Retreat for a New Year's Eve celebration with a difference. She phoned me out of the blue a week or so ago and invited me there all expenses paid. So naturally I thought I'd go. It would be a good opportunity to catch up on old times.

To cut a long story short it was a very difficult place to find. When at last I did manage to find the place it was closed. Yes, closed. I was fuming particularly as by now it was getting quite late. Luckily however there was an old couple in the gatehouse who said they would put me up for the night."

"So what happened then," enquired James Palmer pre-empting the Inspector's next question as he gently stroked one of the purring cats.

"I took my bags in and they sat me down and offered me a drink. The next thing I remember is being woken up in my car by the police. I was parked in a lay-by on the A12."

"And you've no idea how you got there?" asked James who appeared to have taken over the questioning.

"None at all. As I said the last thing I remember was sitting in an armchair having a well-deserved drink."

"An alcoholic drink?"

"Of course. It was New Year's Eve!"

"It could have been spiked I suppose," mused Inspector Westwood.

"Well it must have been. One minute I was having a drink and the next I was being woken up and carted off to a police station by your lot."

Inspector Westwood paced slowly around the room, "If you did have anything to do with Tom's death

I would have expected you to have had a decent alibi." Then he added casually, "Let me have Maureen Bennett's address and telephone number and I'll get someone to speak to her."

"I tried to telephone her last night but got no reply."

"Don't worry we'll go round and have a word with her," and then he added after a pause, "We'll also speak to this old couple at The Retreat."

Inspector Westwood noted down the details and then took his leave of the family.

James Palmer was deep in thought. He knew Callisto to be a highly intelligent young lady. If she was implicated in Tom's death then he too would have expected her to have had a cast-iron alibi. "On the other hand," he pondered to himself, "perhaps she's playing the 'double bluff'. The very fact that she hasn't got an alibi is an alibi in itself! Sufficient to put the police off the scent."

Chapter Twenty

Two days into the New Year and Inspector Westwood once again arrived at Forest Glade to speak to Callisto.

"Please take a seat, Inspector, I'll get Miss Callisto for you," and Katie left the room.

After a couple of minutes Callisto and her father entered the drawing room closely followed by the two cats.

"Good morning, Inspector. What can we do for you?" asked a worried-looking David brushing one of the cats off his favourite armchair.

"I've come to update you on the progress of our enquiries. We've been to Ipswich and the address given by Callisto. Maureen Bennett does indeed live there but she's away on holiday. According to her neighbours she's spending Christmas and the New Year with her brother in Australia. She's not expected back for another week."

"That's right, I remember her saying that her brother moved to New South Wales soon after finishing secondary school," Callisto said eagerly. After a moment's hesitation she added, "That means it couldn't have been her who phoned me. But the voice sounded just like hers."

"Possibly," continued the Inspector. "We also checked The Retreat. Its owners confirmed that it was indeed closed over the entire holiday period. Apparently this is when they take their annual holidays as it's a time when business is very slack. They also confirmed that the gatehouse, or small cottage to use their words, was also locked up for the closure period."

"Are you saying that Callisto was deliberately lured there? Lured there to place suspicion on her?" David enquired with an apprehensive look on his face.

"It looks very much like it. With the right connections and for the right price it would be easy to 'hire' a couple who would undertake a little 'sleeper' job such as this with no questions asked," replied the Inspector, "but we're keeping an open mind at the moment. One thing, though, Miss Callisto, you will tell us if you plan to leave the country won't you?"

"So you still think Tom's death had something to do with me?"

"Right now I don't know what to think but I'm not ruling anything out."

Suddenly Lucy came running into the room sobbing and babbling incoherently.

"Turn on the telly! Look at the news!"

David Fairfax picked up the remote control and switched on the television set and all present focussed their attention on what the newsreader was saying.

"Earlier today we learnt that a picture of Tom Fairfax, the son of the Trade and Industry Minister David Fairfax, had been posted on the internet. The police are currently treating Tom Fairfax's death as suspicious and it is understood that this picture shows the deceased participating in some form of risqué sexual activity. This is a breaking story and we hope to have comments later in this bulletin from the police and Downing Street. Now onto today's other news ...."

David angrily switched off the television set. He tried to comfort Lucy who was now in a state of utter bewilderment and sobbing bitterly on the floor.

"The Christmas presents!" exclaimed Inspector Westwood, "Yes, the Christmas presents. They could be a warning. What was the present sent to Tom and what did it say on the card?"

He thought for a moment and then took out his notebook and flipped open a page, "Tom's card read 'Picture yourself in these. Drop-dead gorgeous' and it was attached to the same sort of underpants found on the body!"

"You didn't mention that before," stammered David Fairfax in disbelief, "You didn't mention anything about underpants."

"Didn't I now? It must have slipped my mind," the inspector said thoughtfully and then continued, "I think this adds a new dimension to the case. I think you may all be in danger. I think you should all be very careful from now on, very careful indeed."

"Thank you inspector, we'll heed your warning."

Inspector Westwood then said a few words of reassurance to Lucy and took his leave.

* * * * *

The day after Tom's death the headlines in the newspapers had generally been kind to the family and had read, 'Tragic death of Minister's son', 'New Year tragedy for Minister', 'Minister grieves over lost son', 'Minister devastated at untimely death of son'. However, the morning after Tom's picture was posted on the internet, those same newspapers had completely different headlines that were far less sympathetic to David Fairfax and his family, 'Minister's son dies in sex orgy', 'Sex shame of Minister's son', 'Kinky sex led to death of Minister's son', 'Minister shocked by revelations of son's sordid sex secrets'.

David Fairfax sat alone in his study. He looked in total disbelief at the newspaper headlines and listened without comment to the speculation on the radio and television. He knew this spelt the end of his ministerial career. He knew he had no alternative but to resign. There had been an ominous silence on the part of the Prime Minister but David realised what was expected of him. He picked up his mobile phone and dialled Downing Street.

The evening news bulletins were the first to carry the announcement, 'Minister resigns following death of son. Sir David Fairfax resigned this afternoon from his post of Trade and Industry Minister. In a brief statement he said he had tendered his resignation and it had been accepted by the Prime Minister. After the recent tragic death of his son he wanted more time to spend with his family and to rebuild his life. A spokesman for the Prime Minister's office confirmed that the resignation had been accepted with great regret. Sir David was a very able minister who would be sorely missed. Sir David has also made it known that he will be stepping down as a Member of Parliament at the next General Election'.

Chapter Twenty-one

James Palmer drove the three miles into Epping and parked his car in the public car park behind St. John's Church. He walked back towards the High Street and reflected on how this small town had changed since his first memories of it in the late 1950s. Outwardly the buildings seemed little different to all those years ago. There were still a large number of independent shops and businesses but Epping was beginning to resemble so many other towns in this part of south-eastern England.

He crossed the road and walked towards the Upper Crust restaurant and bar. At ten o'clock in the morning it had a closed sign on the door which he ignored. He entered the restaurant and was immediately impressed with the décor, "Wouldn't like to foot the bill for a meal in here," he thought as he surveyed the luxurious furnishings and almost tripped over as his feet sank into the deep pile of a most expensive carpet.

"Can't you read!" a voice suddenly barked out, "We're closed!"

"I can read perfectly well thank you. I'm well aware what the sign on the door says."

"Then I suggest you leave!"

"I want to speak to the owner, Colin Rust."

"Well he may not want to speak to you."

"Then give him my card and see what he says," and James Palmer handed his card to a rather bemused barman. After reading that James was a private detective he hurriedly disappeared through a curtain into the back of the restaurant.

After a few minutes a well-dressed middle-aged man appeared holding James' card. "What do you want?" he said, "I'm Colin Rust the owner of this restaurant."

"Pleased to meet you Mr Rust," and James proffered his hand. "I'm here to ask you a few questions about the meal you provided for David Fairfax and his guests on Christmas Eve."

Colin Rust shook hands with James, "Nasty business. I mean Tom Fairfax being murdered. Is that what you've really come to see me about? I've already had an Inspector Westwood round here asking questions about that Christmas Eve job. I suspected there was something more to it. Why should I answer your questions?"

"Because I'm asking you politely and because Sir David himself has asked me to make enquiries on his behalf. If you don't want to co-operate with me then fine and I'll let him know. I'm sure he can make arrangements to take his business elsewhere in the future."

"No, no, please don't get me wrong. I wouldn't want to do anything that would upset Sir David particularly in view of his son's death. Besides, Sir David is one of my best customers. Tom too, he often used to come and eat here."

"So, do you provide the catering for many of Sir David's functions?"

"You've already mentioned his Christmas Eve do. We've done that one for several years now. We also cater for five or six dinner parties a year at his house as well as his annual summer bash as I like to call it. That's when he has a marquee erected in the grounds of his house and invites a lot of very important people over. That's usually held in July or August and is a very big job for us. Most years I have to bring in extra staff."

"So what does the Christmas Eve function entail?"

"That's a nice little number. Basically it's to cater for about a dozen or so people. A buffet consisting of traditional Christmas fayre and, of course, lots of booze. That lot like their booze in Forest Glade."

"Who was actually at the house helping with the arrangements?"

"As it's Sir David I always go myself and I take two of my more experienced staff with me. It wouldn't do for anything to go wrong. He doesn't cut any corners. Everything has to be just so and just as he wants it. He's a good tipper too!"

"Who went with you this year?"

"I took Susan Beattie and Linda Foster. They've been there several times before and Sir David has always been very pleased with their work. In answer to the question on the tip of your tongue I'll tell you what I told the Inspector, Susan has been with me since I started the restaurant ten or eleven years ago and Linda joined me about five years ago when I expanded into outside catering and started Upper Crust Caterers. I can vouch for them both. I've no doubting their honesty."

"I take it the Inspector didn't say why he wanted to know which of your staff were at Forest Glade?"

"No, and I don't suppose you will either?"

"Afraid not. Tell me, do you have the run of the house or are you restricted to certain rooms?"

"The meal is always cooked in Sir David's kitchen. He insists on everything being fresh and doesn't like anything frozen or heated up. Once cooked, we serve the food in the dining room. Afterwards Susan and Linda clear up while I accompany the guests into the drawing room and act, I suppose, as a sort of barman. Once everyone is settled with a drink and I'm happy that there's sufficient food laid out for later in the evening all three of us take our leave."

"So would there be any opportunity for you or your staff to wander around the house?"

"Not really. Apart from the family and guests there is the maid Katie Blanding. She keeps a very close eye on things on Sir David's behalf."

"Thank you Colin, you've been most helpful. I'll try not to trouble you again," and James turned and left the restaurant.

"Next stop 'The London'," thought James to himself as he contemplated the six or seven minute walk to the Central Line station at the bottom of the hill. "I don't think Colin or his staff were behind those rather odd Christmas presents. Admittedly they had the opportunity but what would be the motive. No, I'm fast coming to the conclusion that it must have been one of the guests," and his thoughts paused for a second before he added, "or one of the family!"

Sitting on the train looking through the window at the Essex countryside rolling past James let his mind wander. He suddenly thought of Colin Rust, "Colin Rust," he mused, "yes, C Rust. What parents would make that mistake when naming their child? Perhaps that's how he came up with the idea for the name of his restaurant. Or did his parents have a premonition that he would find a career in the catering trade?"

* * * * *

James had made an appointment to see the manager of 'The London' together with the receptionist who was on duty on New Year's Eve. He didn't want to risk coming into London and finding that one or other of them wasn't available. He walked up to reception and introduced himself.

"Oh yes Mr Palmer, Mr Ferdenzi is expecting you. I'll tell him you've arrived."

After a few minutes Mr Ferdenzi appeared and introduced himself, "Good afternoon Mr Palmer, my name's Ferdenzi and I'm the manager of 'The London'. A bad business this murder of Tom Fairfax. Very upsetting for my staff too. If I can do anything to find out who did it then I'll be pleased to help. Please come through to my office."

James followed Mr Ferdenzi to a rather large office where a petite young lady was seated at a small circular table. "With a name like Ferdenzi he must be Italian," James thought to himself, "but no trace of an accent."

"Mr Palmer, let me introduce you to Maria Lopez who was on reception on New Year's Eve." He pointed to a tray of refreshments on the table and added, "What would you like to drink, tea or coffee?"

"Tea will be fine please," and as Mr Ferdenzi poured he added, "no milk and no sugar."

"Ah, a true connoisseur of tea! A man after my own heart."

"No not really, I just don't like dairy products."

"How can we help you?" said Ferdenzi handing a cup of black tea to James, "Maria will be pleased to answer your questions and we also now have our CCTV pictures returned from the police."

"Maria, can you tell me if you noticed anything unusual or suspicious about any of the guests."

"Although it was New Year's Eve and the hotel was almost full reception was quite quiet. Most of our guests were in the casino or the ballroom," Maria explained in good English but with a heavy Spanish accent. "I've already told the police that I remember Tom Fairfax going up to his room with those two girls, Amber and Bamber. They were larking around and when I gave him his key he dropped it on the floor. Very few guests went up to their rooms until well after midnight."

"What about people coming down from their rooms. Were there many of them?" asked James, "Was there anyone who came down who you didn't see go up? Anyone who went straight out of the hotel rather than go into the casino or ballroom?"

"I didn't recall anybody at the time but afterwards when I looked at the CCTV footage there was one person."

"I'd like to see that footage," said James.

"Certainly," replied Ferdenzi, "the police returned it once they had made a copy," and he inserted a video into his player.

James Palmer watched fascinated as Tom Fairfax in the company of Amber and Bamber came along to reception, took his key and made his way to the lifts. A little while later he saw Amber and Bamber hand in hand walk jauntily past reception and out of the hotel as if they hadn't a care in the world. In the next half hour or so there were just a few people who came down from their rooms but with just one exception they were all couples and they all stayed in the hotel. Only one person walked straight out of the building and into the street.

James watched the CCTV footage several times. He didn't know what he had been expecting to find but on the evidence of this footage he could be looking for a woman. "Could a woman really have done this?" he thought to himself, "Pity the pictures aren't clearer and in colour."

He then took out from his jacket pocket photographs of Lucy, Callisto, Angela Hamilton and Susan Rumble and placed them on the table. "Maria, do you recognise any of these people? Could any of these have been here on New Year's Eve? Was that woman you saw leaving the hotel just after midnight one of these?"

Maria picked up the photographs one by one and looked at them closely. She hesitated and then slowly pointed to one of the pictures.

"I can't be sure but the woman who walked past my desk and out of the hotel looked a bit like this person," and she pointed again to one of the photographs. "I couldn't say it was definitely her. I couldn't swear to it. She looked a bit like the woman in the photograph but there is something, how can I put it, something different about her."

James Palmer tried his utmost to hide his feelings over this possible lead. He thanked both Mr Ferdenzi and Maria for their help and made his way out of the hotel and walked briskly to the nearest tube station.

Sitting on the train reflecting on the day's events James thought to himself, "It's very early days yet so I'd better not mention any of this to David Fairfax. Don't want him jumping to the wrong conclusion."

Chapter Twenty-two

Craig Bentley put his hand out of the car window and swiped his security card. The barrier lifted and he drove out of the underground car park. As he left the Fairfax Building he reflected on the meeting he had just attended. David Fairfax was back in charge and everybody round the table had been made very much aware of that fact. He had been in a particularly foul mood demanding to know why business and profits were down and who he could blame. He had humiliated the four directors and made no secret of the fact that he was instituting an internal inquiry into what was going wrong. They could all soon expect a visit from Angela and Susan who had been charged with looking at the books.

Normally Craig would travel down to Canary Wharf by train. It was a long journey and took nearly three hours but he liked the chance to relax and catch up on some reading or paperwork. He also found it easier than driving around London in his Toyota Land Cruiser. This vehicle was ideal for the East Anglian countryside and the rough terrain on the farms but wasn't really suited for town driving.

After he had been travelling for about an hour he left the M11 at Junction 7 and made his way to

The Blacksmith's Arms, a small pub and hotel in the village of Thornwood, a few miles north of Epping. He had already made a reservation and after collecting his key went immediately to his room. No sooner had he began to look over some papers when there was a loud knock at the door.

He opened the door and two men pushed roughly past him. A third quickly closed the door and stood in front of it. The two men who had barged past him were both about six foot six tall and powerfully built. They swiftly looked round the room and the en-suite and then returned and stood by the door. The third man who was shorter and of a more stocky build walked into the room and motioned to Craig to sit down. He then joined him round the small table.

"Dimitri!" exclaimed Craig in a voice that attempted to hide his uneasiness, "Good to see you again."

"I never turn down the chance of a good deal and the chance to make some money. You know that my friend," replied Dimitri with an accent that betrayed his Russian or east-European origins, "Our little enterprises have done very nicely in the past, very nicely indeed."

"Well we now have a good opportunity to make a lot more money. Sir David is preoccupied with the notion that someone is out to get him and bring him down. After that incident when those illegal Chinese immigrants were found in a lorry hired by Fairfax Forwarding he's called a temporary halt to the smuggling of any more illegal workers."

"I heard about that."

"He was very lucky to get away with it and has decided to cool things down a little. That means for the next few months we have a free hand. There are three or four of his drivers who can be trusted to smuggle in any cargo of our choosing including people. It's just a question of giving them some money."

"And what about the farms?"

"No problem. Because we haven't been bringing in any people we have lots of spare capacity at our factories and in the accommodation blocks at the farms. We could take up to a couple of hundred people right now. Our gang masters can make very good use of this, how can I put it, people bonus."

"That is indeed very good news my friend. Leave it with me. I'll contact our colleagues on the continent and let you know when to collect the first shipment. You can then organise the drivers."

"The usual arrangement. You speak only to me. If Sir David finds out then I'm finished – in more ways than one!"

"My friend, don't worry. How can he find out? This little arrangement is just between you and me. And the money! Don't forget the money. You'll get your share as always, in cash."

"Then it's agreed. We're in business."

"Korosho!" laughed Dimitri and produced a bottle of vodka from an inside pocket of his long black leather coat, "Let's drink to our renewed partnership."

Craig fetched a couple of glasses from the mini-bar. He was not overly fond of vodka thinking it to be the drink of eastern barbarians and fashionable silly young girls. But he couldn't afford to upset Dimitri Komarov. He could be even more ruthless and cruel than David Fairfax.

Dimitri poured them both a large drink.

"You should down it in one, like this," and he drained the glass with one large gulp. "Na starovya!" he shouted out excitedly.

"Cheers," echoed Craig and downed his drink in a similar manner.

Then without further word, Dimitri got up and left the room closely followed by his two minders. Craig was very relieved at his departure. Unbeknown to David Fairfax he often did business with Dimitri but he never felt completely comfortable or at ease in his presence. He helped himself to a whisky from the mini-bar, "A proper drink this time," he thought to himself.

A few minutes after Dimitri and his minders had left the room there was a muffled knock. Craig opened the door and there stood Susan Rumble.

"I thought they were never going," she said and stepped forward and kissed Craig lightly on the cheek.

"Quickly, come in and close the door before we're spotted. It's convenient to meet here but far too close to Sir David's territory for my liking."

"Don't worry, he'll still be ranting and raving at the Fairfax Building. I left soon after you did and poor Angela was getting a right earful. I don't know why she stays and puts up with it. If I were her I'd have left that job before now. With her talents she could easily get another top PA job."

"That's true, but I suppose you could say that of all of us. In a way we're almost too scared to leave. We're almost Sir David's prisoners. Still you're here now and that's all that matters."

Susan sat down on the settee and untied her hair. As her loose hair tumbled onto her shoulders she looked a completely different person. Gone was the austere and rather hard look that everyone in the office was familiar with and in its place was a very attractive woman.

"If they could only see you now," Craig said stroking her cheek, "what would the office think?"

"They would wonder what had happened to 'the spinster'. I know that's what they call me behind my back but it suits me. It suits me if people have that image of me. It gives me a certain satisfaction in knowing that I know them but they know so very little about me."

"In a way no-one is really what they seem. We all have secrets."

"Speaking of secrets, how did it go with Dimitri?"

"Very well, very well indeed. He'll soon be in touch and we'll be in business once again. This time we should be able to make a small fortune especially if Sir David sticks to his word and suspends the illegal immigrant racket for a few months. That'll allow us to clean up. As usual I suppose I can rely upon you to straighten out the books."

"Nobody will be any the wiser. Those books will fool even the best of auditors."

"That's what I like to hear."

"So changing the subject, can you stay the night?"

"I certainly can. I've been looking forward to this for a long time."

"I know but we have to be so careful. It wouldn't do if anyone in the organisation found out about our, how can I put this, little arrangement!"

"No," replied Craig as he pulled Susan towards him.

"What about your wife? Where does she think you are?"

"She thinks I'm spending the night away with Sir David on business. Just to be on the safe side I've told her that we're doing a bit of wheeler-dealing and can't be contacted. She's fine about it. She accepts it all as being a part of the job."

"Good," whispered Susan, "then let's make the most of our time here," and she cuddled up towards Craig.

Chapter Twenty-three

James and Jenny Palmer were having breakfast discussing their plans for the day. On the table in front of them were the four photographs James had taken with him to 'The London'.

"And the receptionist said that this could have been the woman who left the hotel shortly after Tom Fairfax was murdered?" Jenny said thoughtfully pointing to a photograph of Callisto.

"That's right," replied James, "but she wasn't certain. She said it could be but there were differences. In particular she said the woman looked somewhat older than this photograph. That's strange because this is a photograph of Callisto taken just a few weeks ago and is a very good likeness. It's a great pity the CCTV images weren't a lot clearer," and he looked closely at some stills of the footage given to him by Mr Ferdenzi.

"A shame these aren't better quality. That would settle it one way or the other. I'm still not convinced that this woman is Callisto though," added James.

"So," said Jenny enthusiastically, "we'll soon have to be going. I take it you'll want to take the Focus and I'll be lumbered with the Fiesta."

"Don't knock that little car. It may be seven or eight years old but it's never let us down. Besides, you're only going to Chelmsford and I've got to go all the way to Ipswich."

"Big deal, it's only 40 miles further and another hour's drive at the most." Then after a moment's reflection Jenny added, "It's a pity you won't actually get to meet Anne Harvey. I'd like to know what she's like. She must be a pretty formidable business woman to be able to get the better of David Fairfax, even if she is relying on a mole for inside information."

"But I will get the chance to meet her number two, Martin Travers. I'll try to find out a bit about Anne from him. I'll be thinking of you, though, trawling through all those old files at the Records Office."

After breakfast they quickly got changed and were soon into their respective cars. Jenny led the way in the Fiesta and James followed in the Focus as the cars turned off the short driveway and onto the main road to Chelmsford. After 20 minutes or so they arrived on the outskirts of the county town of Essex. Jenny turned left to drive into the town itself and James turned right towards the A12 and what he hoped would be a nice easy drive to Ipswich.

* * * * *

Jenny parked her car in one of the long-stay car parks and walked the ten or twelve minutes it took to reach the County Records Office. She much preferred this recently-built modern structure on the banks of the River Chelmer to the very cramped former premises. As a regular visitor the staff had issued her with a pass. Unlike most other visitors to the records office Jenny was not interested in researching a family tree or compiling a family history. She was usually looking at old court records and verdicts in connection with some investigation she and her husband were involved in.

On this occasion however she was after something a little different, she was searching for the records of a couple of inquests. One inquest had taken place in Essex and the other, although not held in Essex, should be in the archives as it involved an Essex person.

She was quickly spotted by one of the staff who knew her well and directed to a vacant microfiche viewer.

"You should find what you want in here," said the archivist handing Jenny a stack of reels before returning to her work.

Jenny soon found the reels containing the verdicts of inquests held in 1976 and eagerly started to scan the fiches. Unlike sifting through actual papers the fiches were all in black and white so the danger was that the eye could miss something. Suddenly, as she sped through the second reel there it was, the inquest into the death of Dawn Fairfax, David Fairfax's first wife. Jenny read the account of the incident avidly and then took paper copies of the relevant pages. She then loaded a reel for inquests that took place in 1980. Within half an hour she had found what she was looking for, the inquest into the death of Beverley Fairfax.

After taking paper copies of relevant documents from Beverley Fairfax's inquest Jenny paid the small charge and left the Records Office. She was feeling very pleased with herself and as she reached the town centre thought she would partake in what she liked to call a bit of 'retail therapy'. She had found what she was looking for in under an hour and a half so thought she would make the most of her time in Chelmsford and indulge herself. "Besides," she reasoned, "I've got plenty of time before James returns from Ipswich. I wonder how he's getting on at the Anne Harvey Group?"

* * * * *

James did not have the most pleasant of journeys to Ipswich. As usual the A12 was very busy with many large container lorries on the road, "Guess I'm stuck with this lot all the way to Ipswich. They're all probably going to the port at Felixstowe," he thought to himself, "Still I've got plenty of time. Pity they don't make this road three lanes all the way. The way it goes from two to three and then three to two makes it very dangerous, especially when lorries have this habit of pulling out without warning."

The Anne Harvey building was one of a group of fairly new buildings on a business park to the east of Ipswich. James was thankful he did not have to drive into the town centre itself. He parked in a nearby car park and walked the couple of hundred yards to the main entrance. After signing in at reception he was shown up to Martin Travers' office.

Martin Travers was all that James Palmer thought a Chief Executive should be. He was in his late thirties, extremely confident, well dressed in a most expensive suit and very affable and easy to talk to.

After introductions Martin motioned to James to take a seat at a small table in a corner of his office and he poured them each a cup of tea.

"Naturally the death of Tom Fairfax came as a blow to all of us here. Admittedly we're in direct competition with Tom's father but we do have feelings. Our thoughts are with him particularly after that recent bad publicity in the tabloids. However, I am at a loss to know how I can be of help in your enquiries. As far as I am aware no-one here at the Anne Harvey Group, at least any of the senior staff, have met Tom. So I was surprised when you wished to speak to Anne or myself about his death."

"It's not just about Tom's demise. I was hoping you could tell me a bit about the group and its history and how it is organised. I know you have recently outbid David Fairfax and won some important contracts but I have no intention of trying to find out anything that you consider to be commercially sensitive."

"I'm glad to hear it. There's not much to tell really. Most of what I'm about to tell you can be found in the Group's promotional literature. The Group itself was founded by Anne's father. In the early days it was one of many small family businesses in the fish processing industry. Gradually, however, it was able to buy-out its rivals and eventually achieved a near-monopoly in this part of the country.

With the death of her father two or three years ago Anne became a very wealthy woman. She took over the business and decided to expand and diversify into other areas. Some of those areas, such as fashion, transport and telecoms, are in direct competition with the Fairfax Group. Although we put in competitive bids in the past it's only recently that we have had some success against our rivals. What I can tell you, however, is that having now won those contracts we do not intend to lose them in the future."

After further brief discussion James took his leave of Martin Travers and walked down the corridor towards the lift. The lift soon arrived and as its doors opened a most attractive woman of about 30 years of age almost walked straight into him.

"I'm sorry," said James and stepped back to allow her to pass.

"That's all right Mr Palmer," replied the woman, "I'm Anne Harvey. Pleased to meet you. Sorry I couldn't spare you any time today but I'm sure Martin has answered all your questions."

James remained silent as he surveyed Anne Harvey from head to toe. Not quite what he was expecting. She was very attractive with lovely brown eyes and hair and very tastefully dressed in a smart two-piece business suit. But there was something almost familiar about her which he couldn't quite put his finger on.

"You're wondering how I know your name," said Anne breaking the rather embarrassing silence, "That's an easy one, it's on your visitor's pass."

"Of course," replied a rather flustered James, "You took me by surprise that's all. Nice to have met you," and he went into the lift without saying another word. He did, however, delay pressing the ground floor button until he had watched Anne Harvey disappear along the corridor.

"I'm sure I've seen her somewhere before or she reminds me of somebody, but who?" he thought to himself as the lift swiftly descended to the ground floor.

It was a cloudy afternoon and beginning to get dark as James drove home along the A12. Rather unwisely as he was driving he began to lose himself in thoughts about the case. It was as he was passing a Little Chef restaurant that he suddenly had a flash of inspiration, "The tea! That cup of tea! Martin Travers poured the tea right up to the brim of the cup. He didn't ask me if I took milk, somehow he knew I didn't take it." He thought for a little while before thinking out aloud, "Perhaps it's not just me that's doing the investigating. Perhaps somebody at the Anne Harvey Group is investigating me!"

* * * * *

James returned home and walked into his entrance hall. He was immediately confronted by Jenny wearing a new dress.

"What do you think?" she asked smiling most provocatively and giving her husband a big hug and a kiss on both cheeks, "It was ten percent day at Debenhams. I couldn't resist it!"

"Very nice but I thought the purpose of today's little trip out was to get information from the Records Office?" responded James in a rather sarcastic tone of voice.

"It was but this was such a bargain. I knew you'd like it."

"Just as I thought. You got it for me and not yourself."

"That's right. Now you've seen it I'll get changed and then we can have dinner and swap notes about how we got on today."

Over dinner James gave full details of his conversation with Martin Travers and also his chance meeting with Anne Harvey.

"An unexpected bonus," said Jenny, "What did you think of her?"

"It's hard to tell. From what Martin said she's obviously got a head for business and she certainly looks the part, very smart indeed. But there's something about her. There's something that's gnawing away at the back of my mind. I can't quite put my finger on it at the moment. Anyway, how did your day go? What did you find out from the inquest papers?"

"Quite a lot, actually. It appears that David Fairfax married Dawn Desborough in 1974. She was the heiress to the Desborough Design Fashion Group."

"That's where the name 'DesboroDenim' comes from," interjected James.

"Precisely! The group was founded by her father and was renowned for its 'DesboroDenim' range of underwear and other fashionable clothes.

It appears that about two years after they were married David and Dawn Fairfax went on holiday to East Deben for a few days. One night after dinner Dawn went for a walk along the cliffs by herself. Whether it was due to the wind and rain that blew up suddenly, or whether she lost her footing in the dark, she fell onto the rocks below and was drowned. By all accounts it was a very stormy night and her body wasn't found until it was washed up on the shore two or three days later. There was a post-mortem of course but her injuries were consistent with a fall onto rocks and drowning. The Coroner's report also says that Dawn Fairfax was pregnant but the unborn baby died in the womb. The body was formally identified by David Fairfax and the coroner's verdict was one of accidental death."

"Very interesting indeed," pondered James out aloud, "What about the inquest into Beverley Fairfax's death?"

"That again appears to be very straight forward. About two years after Dawn's death David Fairfax married Beverley Jenks. She was the only daughter of Leslie Jenks who owned a freight forwarding business. She was also a most accomplished horsewoman and stabled a couple of horses in the grounds of their house so most days she could go riding. However, 18 months after their marriage when Beverley was almost six months pregnant she took a bad fall from one of her horses and she lost the baby. To make matters worse she was told by her doctors that she couldn't have any more children. This was a terrible blow because she absolutely adored children and made no secret that she wanted to have three or four of her own. It is after this that she begins to suffer from bouts of severe depression and there is mention of an attempted drugs overdose.

In an attempt to get Beverley out of this cycle of depression David took her on a three-week luxury cruise to the far-east. Apparently things went well and Beverley did begin to lift herself out of this mood of deep depression. But one night at dinner she complained of a very severe headache and went to her suite. When David returned to the cabin after dinner he discovered that Beverley wasn't there. He searched the ship but was unable to find any trace of her. He informed the purser but despite an exhaustive search there was no sign of her. The conclusion was reached that she must have fallen overboard.

The ship was unable to turn back to look for her and it wasn't until some days later that her body was found by local fishermen. By all accounts it was in a pretty bad way from being in the sea and partially eaten by fish. There was no doubt it was Beverley as the body was identified by David Fairfax himself. The verdict of the coroner was that Beverley Fairfax took her own life while the balance of her mind was disturbed. Quite a tragic tale really."

"Yes, very tragic. But look at the similarities between these two incidents. There are certainly a few things we need to look into."

"I agree. There are nearly as many questions as answers stemming from this lot," added Jenny.

After pausing for a while James concluded, "In both cases David Fairfax married into families where his wife would inherit a profitable business. After their deaths those businesses passed to him. All very convenient. Also in both cases there are no witnesses to the actual deaths. Again in both cases there were pregnancies but no actual children from the marriages. That could be significant because after marrying Lucy, Lucy Murray as I knew her during our school days, they had three children. As I mentioned before, David Fairfax and Lucy Murray were almost inseparable at school. I and many others found it hard to believe that he would ever marry anybody else."

"So before I get us another bottle of wine what's your plan of action?"

"Two things spring immediately to mind. First, one of us needs to go to East Deben and find out what we can from local papers at the time. There may even be people still living there who can recall Dawn Fairfax falling off those cliffs. Secondly, I need to call in a favour and find out who was on that cruise ship when Beverley Fairfax went to a watery grave. It's annoying when certain facts are ordered to remain confidential for fifty years but I'm certain I can pull a few strings and get hold of that passenger list."

"The more we begin to delve beneath the glossy veneer of the Fairfax Empire the more we begin to uncover. Let's hope we can root out who is responsible and collect that fat bonus from your old school chum," said Jenny as she poured another glass of wine and she and James relaxed on the settee.

Chapter Twenty-four

Throughout most of January an air of deep gloom had descended upon the Fairfax household. There had been an inquest into Tom's death but this was adjourned by the coroner on the day it had been opened. The police had also refused to release Tom's body as they were not entirely satisfied about the cause of death. However towards the end of January Inspector Westwood called at Forest Glade and announced that the body would be released in the first week of February. It had been concluded that death was due to a combination of asphyxia caused by a blockage to the airways and to internal bleeding. A weapon was still being sought but the Inspector had to admit he had no idea what type of weapon could have caused Tom's injuries.

Arrangements were eventually made for Tom's cremation to take place at Harlow Crematorium during the second week of February. Both David and Lucy Fairfax were not particularly religious. They professed to be Church of England but neither of them had ever attended church in Theydon Bois since moving to the village. Nevertheless, they arranged for the local vicar to conduct the service, and both Callisto and Terry Kingston volunteered to give readings and speak about Tom's life.

The funeral itself was a rather grand affair and the roads surrounding the crematorium were sealed off about 30 minutes before the cortege arrived. Uniformed police officers checked the identities of those attempting to gain entry and kept the press at bay as there was intense media interest in the funeral. Inspector Westwood and a number of his plain-clothed colleagues were on duty in the grounds and the chapel itself. This level of security was deemed necessary not so much for the family's protection but more for the safeguarding of the various government ministers who had expressed a wish to attend.

The Fairfax group of companies was represented by the four managing directors, Alan Box, Ken Winter, Rahul Dixit and Craig Bentley, together with Angela Hamilton and Susan Rumble. A few employees from the group who had been close to Tom also attended. Katie Blanding and Feb were present as were John Burling and Terry Kingston and a number of other close friends of the children. James and Jenny Palmer were there at the specific invitation of David Fairfax.

The service itself passed off without incident. It was only when the guests were filing out of the chapel and looking at the mountain of floral tributes that some of them noticed one of the bouquets had a rather strange message attached to it. The card sported an old DesboroDenim motif and simply read 'Gone, and now soon to be forgotten in the troubles of the future', but there was no indication as to who sent it. Luckily this particular tribute was not spotted by any members of the Fairfax family. But when all the mourners had departed the bouquet and its message were quickly removed by Inspector Westwood. He mentioned the finding to James Palmer as they strolled back to their cars.

Back at Forest Glade a buffet lunch had been arranged for those mourners who wished to return to the house and many of them chose to do so. James and Jenny Palmer and Inspector Westwood circulated amongst the guests. They listened intently to the various conversations taking place in the rather forlorn hope that somebody might make mention of the floral tributes but none did so.

The catering for the buffet was provided by Upper Crust Caterers and Colin Rust was very much in evidence keeping a strict eye on events in the company of Susan Beattie and Linda Foster. His style was to be very visible but not overly intrusive. James Palmer watched how the occasion progressed as one by one the numbers diminished. In the end there were only close family members remaining but he did not see anything untoward.

The main surprise at the funeral had been Nick's state of mind during the service. Following Tom's death he had become very introspective and nervous of almost everything and everybody almost to the point of paranoia. And when Terry Kingston delivered his speech chronicling Tom's eventful life and outgoing personality Nick had broken down in uncontrollable sobbing. Later, as Tom's coffin disappeared behind the curtains, he broke down in a bout of crying. This was very much in keeping with his behaviour over the past few weeks.

Whereas Callisto had immersed herself in her work Nick had more or less stopped going to the office and had begun to spend increasing amounts of time alone in his darkened room.

David Fairfax had spoken to the family's doctor about Nick's behaviour. His advice was for Nick to have a complete change of scenery and to go somewhere where he could put the events surrounding Tom's death behind him. If he remained in his present state of mind then there was the potential for long-term mental harm and instability. David had discussed this matter with the family. He had also mentioned it to the four managing directors at the end of a board meeting where questions about Nick's increasingly erratic performance and fitness to continue in his job were being asked.

Surprisingly, Rahul Dixit immediately offered to take Nick to India. He was returning home at the end of February for a few weeks and said he would be happy to have Nick go with him. He believed if he showed Nick the sights and sounds of India and how people there lived then it would help to clear his mind of current events. It might also lead him to appreciate better his own state of affairs and put Tom's death into context.

David had reservations about this proposal and the reaction it might provoke but when he put it to Nick he readily agreed. Nick even said he was looking forward to the visit.

Chapter Twenty-five

After a non-stop flight of nearly eight hours the Air India Boeing 747 Jumbo Jet touched down at New Delhi's Indira Gandhi International Airport. Nick Fairfax and Rahul Dixit cleared immigration and customs and walked out onto the concourse of this most modern of airports.

"Not what I expected," said a rather disbelieving Nick as he looked around the vast hall before him, "From what I know about India I was expecting something not quite so ...."

"Modern?" interjected Rahul, "India's like that, full of surprises. On the one hand we have our ancient monuments and plenty of them. But we also have some very modern buildings indeed and they all blend effortlessly together, the ancient with the modern. Now, where is my driver?" he said staring into the sea of humanity that filled the arrivals hall, "Ah, there he is! Vinod's over there by the exit, come on."

The time was just after five o'clock in the morning and still dark so Nick was only barely able to glimpse the unfamiliar world outside as it rushed past the car. In less than an hour they arrived at Rahul's house and his servant Simran hurried out to greet them. It was as if she was celebrating the return of a long-lost family member.

Nick was impressed. The house was vast and spacious and very tastefully decorated. It benefited from a fusion of western and eastern furniture, art and decoration. It was readily apparent that Rahul liked to be surrounded by beauty and elegance. He was obviously very proud of his home as he showed Nick around and directed him to his room.

"Best if you try to get some sleep. I'll make sure you're woken by mid-day then we can go and explore. I'll take you for a walk and then you can tell me what you think of my little town. Tomorrow we'll go to Delhi. You'll need two or three days to look round the city properly. But I'll give you a small taste of India this afternoon so you know what to expect."

Nick quickly unpacked his pyjamas and was soon in bed sound asleep. It seemed he had no sooner put his head on the pillow than he was gently awakened by Simran.

"Malik said to wake you and give you tea," she said in good English, "then join him for lunch on the terrace."

Nick sat up in bed and drank the tea. He let his eyes wander around the bedroom and he marvelled at the expensive hard-wood furniture and exquisite decoration. He then made his way to the en-suite bathroom and was most surprised to find a room about half the size of his bedroom boasting a wash-basin, toilet, bath and a separate shower, all finished in expensive black marble.

Nick quickly showered and dressed and made his way to the terrace where Rahul was leaning back on a wicker chair sipping tea.

"I hope you're feeling refreshed. Was the bed to your liking?"

"Not just the bed but the whole room. As soon as I hit the pillow I was out like a light." Then after a short pause Nick added, "I had no idea you lived in a place like this. It's lovely, most impressive."

"As good as Forest Glade do you think?"

"From what I've seen I'd say it's better and certainly more tastefully decorated."

"I like to be surrounded by things of beauty," responded Rahul. He stood up and took Nick to the side of the terrace that overlooked the small town. As he walked across the terrace Nick was suddenly aware of the bright sunny weather and thought about the cold grey late-February he had left far behind in England.

"As you can see there are a number of houses, or bungalows as we call them, along this road. Over there in the distance to the right you can see some traditional Indian houses. To the left by the railway tracks you can see some high rise apartments or colonies as we refer to them. The colony buildings are fairly new and mainly house people who commute into Delhi. It's only about 45 minutes from here on the train."

Nick looked around and began to take in the sights that greeted his eyes. What a contrast! From his vantage point he could see a dozen or so houses of a similar size and splendour to Rahul's, but the traditional Indian houses looked nothing more than run-down shacks. The concrete colony buildings were also rather austere and drab. Although fairly new they looked old and seedy. The town itself was obscured from direct view and Nick could only see the roofs of the small shops.

After a light lunch Rahul and Nick walked through the grounds of 'Shanti Bhavan', as Rahul's house was called, towards the main gates. These were usually kept closed and were guarded by two watchmen. As soon as they saw the two men approaching they leapt up and immediately opened one of the gates. They saluted as Rahul and Nick slowly walked past their small cabin and out into the lane. Rahul acknowledged the salutes in silence.

"Is it necessary to have guards out here?" enquired a puzzled-looking Nick, "Is India a violent country?"

"No, in the main India's not a very violent place at all. We've never had any real trouble here but all the larger houses employ one or two men to keep an eye on the gate and look after security generally. Amrish and Shakti have been with me ever since I had this bungalow built."

"What about your servants? Aren't they terribly expensive?"

"No, not at all. If there's one thing that India's got it's an abundance of labour. And what's more it's cheap. I employ these two watchmen, my chauffeur Vinod who drove us here last night, and three maids. You've met Simran but later this evening you'll meet Juhi and Smriti. While I was in Britain I said they could spend time with their families but they'll be returning later by an evening train. Do you know it's cheaper for me to employ these six servants than it is for you to run a car in Britain. And what's more they're totally loyal. In common with other large houses in India we built a small block for the servants to live in at the rear of the property."

Nick was totally unprepared for what awaited him when he and Rahul rounded a corner and entered the main street of the town. The street itself was quite wide and lined with lots of small shops that opened out directly onto the pavement. Customers had to ask for what they wanted rather than go inside and choose themselves.

Everywhere there was colour. Colourful shops displaying colourful wares and people dressed in all colours imaginable. What's more there were lots of them, people were everywhere. So was the traffic. A multitude of cars, lorries, buses, bicycles and rickshaws, indulging in that peculiar Indian practice of sounding the horn at the slightest provocation. Nick was struck by the array of sounds but what really got to him was the smell of animal dung and urine that pervaded the air.

"You'll get used to it," said Rahul, "it's the cattle. Cows are free to wander around anywhere. Even in parts of Delhi and other large cities you'll see them wandering around the streets. Many traders believe they're lucky so they feed them and guess what? They come back for more everyday. Nobody would ever think of harming them. Although it looks like they wander at will they all have owners they return to at night."

"I suppose I'll get used to the cattle but what about the men urinating in the street. That isn't exactly what I expected to find. And spitting! Everyone here seems to spit all the time."

"I'm afraid that's a part of our way of life."

Nick enjoyed his introduction to India. He liked the little town but he was relieved when the hustle and bustle was left behind and Rahul's bungalow came into view. He hadn't been in any danger but somehow he had felt a little uneasy amid the turmoil of the town.

Rahul and Nick freshened up and relaxed in the drawing room while Simran prepared dinner. Suddenly Amrish appeared at the door and beckoned to Rahul who got up and went over to him. The two men exchanged a few words in Hindi so Nick was unable to make out what was being said. Then to Nick's surprise Rahul gave some money to Amrish who returned to his cabin.

CHAPTER TWENTY-FIVE

"What was that all about?" enquired Nick.

"Nothing really. There was a young man at the gate asking for money. He told Amrish he had an idea for a business venture but he needed some money to get it started."

"And you gave him some money! Just like that!"

"That's right. I gave him a few hundred Rupees."

"A few hundred Rupees! Are you mad?"

"No, far from it. That could well have been me at the gate. When I first started out in life I had plenty of ideas but no money. My family lived in a small town not unlike this one on the other side of Delhi but we were poor. I had plenty of ideas but no way of actually starting up a business. I needed a small amount of money to get me going. So what to do? Almost every day when I was looking for work I walked past the big house of a man I knew to have a little money. He wasn't really all that wealthy but he had a bit more money than most in the area. So one day I plucked up the courage and knocked on his door. His servants weren't too pleased and were in the process of throwing me out just as he returned home. Fortunately he took the time to listen to my proposal and to think about my plans. Then much to my surprise he gave me 500 Rupees."

"500 Rupees! That was sufficient for you to set up your own business?"

"More or less, but the story doesn't end there. About a year later I had really started making my mark in the telecoms industry and the business was doing well so I went back to see him. I offered to return his 500 Rupees and to give him a little extra as an appreciation of his kindness and faith in me. Do you know what he said?"

"No, what?"

"He refused to take the money. He said that in future if someone should knock on my door seeking money for what I considered a worthwhile enterprise then I should give that person some Rupees. And that is what I have done ever since. If I think there is merit in a proposal then I give the money. Who knows, perhaps I will be the cause of someone becoming a millionaire one day."

Nick was silent. Here was a side of Rahul that was new and which surprised him. A ruthless businessman but also someone prepared to help others in the way he had once been helped himself.

"In reality I am simply practising my religion. We Hindus believe that the more good deeds we do, and the more merit we build up in this life, then the better the next life will be." He seemed to be lost in thought for a while and then added, "I think dinner's ready, let's eat."

After dinner Nick and Rahul were in the drawing room watching satellite television when Juhi and Smriti arrived. Nick could hardly believe his eyes. Here were two extremely beautiful women in their early twenties dressed in very fine clothes indeed. Nick had thought Simran to be good looking but she was outclassed by these two beauties.

"Are you sure they're just servants?" enquired Nick after the girls had left the room and gone to their quarters.

"That's all they are to me. I promised their parents I would look after them and that's what I do. It's very common in India for young women to do this kind of work and live away from home. Their parents live in a small village and rely almost totally on their wages to survive."

"But don't people talk? You living alone here with three very attractive and unattached women?"

"No they don't! Why should they?" said a melodious voice in hushed tones from outside the room. Nick looked round and was astonished to see one of the most beautiful women he had ever set eyes on standing in the doorway. He gazed in almost disbelief at her sparkling brown eyes, her long flowing chestnut-brown hair and light complexion that gave her a most striking appearance. For a moment he appeared to be mesmerised by the sheer beauty of this figure dressed in a most expensive-looking gold sari and wearing some very heavy gold necklaces and bracelets.

"Meet my wife, Sunaina," laughed Rahul and he beckoned to her to join them in the drawing room.

Nick was completely overwhelmed by Sunaina's beauty. After a few seconds he regained his composure and said, "I didn't realise you were married, you never mentioned it."

"I don't tell your father and those managing directors everything about my private life. I'll get round to it one of these days, if you don't tell him first."

"No, no," blurted out Nick, "I won't tell him if you don't want me to," and he and Rahul once again turned their attention to the television while Sunaina went to her bedroom to get changed.

Chapter Twenty-six

James and Jenny Palmer had decided to make a day of it and they travelled down to East Deben together. Although late February it was a bright cloudless day and, with an absence of that on-shore easterly breeze that can be so cold at this time of the year, the weather felt quite pleasant in the warm winter sunshine. The journey took them almost two hours so they were glad they had decided to leave early.

Their first port of call was The Bull Hotel where Dawn and David Fairfax had stayed almost 29 years earlier. Before going to the hotel for lunch they took the path that wound its way along the cliff top and walked about a mile in either direction from the hotel.

"It's certainly a long way down. A sheer drop onto those rocks and they look very sharp and jagged indeed," said an anxious-looking Jenny. She stood as close to the edge as she dared and clung firmly onto her husband, "it must be terrible plummeting towards the sea with those rocks looming up in front of you."

"Yes, it doesn't bear thinking about," said James squeezing her tightly, and then after peering once more over the edge added, "I don't suppose this path has changed much over the years. There's little evidence of any substantial erosion along this stretch of the coast so I guess things are pretty much as they would have been when David Fairfax was here in 1976."

"It really is amazing just how close this path is in parts to the edge of the cliffs. There are no barriers whatsoever," a worried looking Jenny observed.

"I suppose that's what makes places like this so popular with ramblers. They can appreciate the beauty of the area in its natural state without any modern-day intrusions and constraints. Civilisation is a wonderful thing, but this preoccupation with health and safety by the powers that be has taken the joy out of much of what was once considered to be harmless everyday pursuits."

Just then, an elderly man exercising his dog appeared as if from nowhere and approached the Palmers. It was obvious he had spotted some people he believed to be like-minded souls and wanted to speak to them.

"We don't get many visitors up here this time of the year," he said struggling to catch his breath as he fought to get his dog back onto its lead, "but to my mind this is the best time to appreciate these cliffs and the wonderful views this particular vantage point affords. My name is John Harwood by the way."

"Pleased to meet you John, I'm James Palmer and this is my wife, Jenny."

"I saw you two standing close to the edge and looking down at the sea. You should be careful you know a lot of people have fallen off these cliffs. Most falls are accidental but we do get the odd suicide and, dare I say it," his voice quivered as he looked around as if checking to see if anyone had crept up on them, "the occasional murder too."

"Well we're here just for the day, but we'll take care," said James as he and Jenny turned to walk back to the hotel.

"If you're going back to The Bull then I'll come with you. I only walk the dog as an excuse to get away from the wife for a little while and have a pint in peace. This time of the year it's a pleasure to stroll along these cliffs but in the summertime you can't move because of the trippers and hikers. The pub gets crowded too so I tend to go somewhere else to have a quiet drink once the better weather is here."

John reflected for a moment and then continued, "Of course it's not always nice and peaceful up here like today. Often during February and March we have some really terrible storms with strong winds and driving rain. They come out of nowhere and can trap the unwary especially if they're not familiar with the area. That's when people fall off or get blown off the edge and come to a grisly end down there," and he pointed down to the rocks with an outstretched crooked finger.

The three of them continued to talk as they strolled along. In what seemed no time at all they had reached the pub.

"Would you like to join us for a drink?" enquired James as they went inside and he and Jenny quickly made for a table by a window overlooking the sea. There really was no need for them to have rushed as all the tables were vacant. There were only two other people in the bar and they were in conversation with the barman.

"That would be very nice," replied John enthusiastically and he tied his dog to a chair. The dog immediately curled up under a neighbouring table and went to sleep. "I don't often get the chance to meet anybody up here let alone have a chat to them."

James had driven down to East Deben so, while he and John could have a couple of pints, Jenny had to be content with tonic water as she was driving home. This was their attempt at sharing the driving and the drinking equally between them. One of them drives on the outward journey and can have a drink and the other drives home so has to avoid alcohol.

John proved to be a mine of local knowledge. He had lived in this area all his life and he obviously enjoyed telling visitors over a drink or two all about its past and how it had changed over the years. It wasn't long before the subject of the cliffs came back into the conversation and John began to recount some of the more unusual deaths that had occurred. In the course of recalling some of the more suspicious deaths John touched on the death of Dawn Fairfax.

"Now that was a rum old do," he mused in his broad Suffolk accent and sat in deep thought for almost a minute before continuing, "At the time we thought there was something a bit odd about that one. Nobody in their right mind would have gone out on a night like that. What sort of a man lets his wife go out alone in that sort of weather? It was blowing up into an almighty storm. I was here you know, when it happened, sitting in this very bar with Doug one of my old mates. He's been dead a few years now but I remember it as if it was yesterday," and he paused while he emptied his glass.

"Another one?" enquired James as he picked up both their glasses and turned towards the bar.

"Yes please," replied John and he remained silent, as if in deep reflection, until James returned.

"Doug was a reporter on the local rag, the Deben Echo, so it was a case of him being in the right place at the right time. That death made the front page if I recall correctly. It was a nasty business and although the inquest cleared David Fairfax of any blame there were many around here who thought otherwise."

"Why's that?" interjected Jenny looking intently at John.

"He said he was in his room when his wife fell off the cliffs but one of the maids said she saw him and Dawn going out of the hotel together. It was just as the storm was blowing up and they appeared to be arguing most violently."

"That's interesting," said a thoughtful James, "I've read the inquest papers and there's no mention at all of any maid giving evidence. According to the papers Dawn went out on her own against her husband's advice and left him alone in their room."

"So you're not here just to appreciate the scenery and the views? You think there's something suspicious about that death don't you? Isn't it a bit late now to be raking over this matter? Who are you working for?"

"I'll not try to hide the fact but I'm a private detective," and James produced his card.

"*We're* private detectives!" said an indignant Jenny.

"Quite so. We're private detectives," admitted James attempting to placate his irate wife, "and we're investigating the death of David Fairfax's son, Tom."

"I read about that in the papers. Last month I think it was. A terrible business and it brought back memories about the untimely death of Dawn Fairfax. That's why I could recall the events to you so clearly. They've been going over and over in my mind during the past few weeks."

"As I said, there was no mention of any maid's statement at the inquest. Very odd that!" pondered James.

"Look at the time! I must be getting back to the wife. It wouldn't do to be late for my dinner, never hear the last of it," and John woke the dog and much to its displeasure began to drag it towards the door, "Nice to have met you and best of luck with the investigation. Why don't you try the Echo, they keep back numbers going right back to the early nineteen hundreds."

* * * * *

James and Jenny decided to take John's advice. After having a traditional pub lunch they made their way to the town centre and easily found the offices of the Echo.

They introduced themselves and after presenting their cards said they were investigating events that took place in March 1976. They were pleasantly surprised when they were taken to a very small dusty room stacked high with large binders and handed two large hand-bound volumes containing copies of the Echo for the first six months of that year.

"In those days," said an enthusiastic young man who looked to be no more than 17 years of age, "the Echo was a broad-sheet but for the last seven or eight years it has been a tabloid. It's now much easier to handle and more popular with our readers. We're in the process of digitising back numbers but it's early days and we've only gone back a couple of years. Hope you find what you're looking for."

Jenny eagerly turned the pages of the first very heavy and unwieldy volume. And after just a few minutes there it was, on the front page of the very last issue for March 1976, an account of Dawn Fairfax's plunge to her death. It didn't give any more information about the death than she knew already so she turned to the second volume and looked through the first few issues. There were a few small articles and speculation but it quickly lost its news appeal and disappeared altogether by the end of April.

It was when Jenny was closing this volume that a copy of the Echo published in early April fell open on the 'births, marriages and deaths' page.

"Look at this!" she exclaimed loudly, "Look here in the births section! There's an entry you'll never believe," and she handed the paper to James.

James was visibly shocked. There was a small announcement saying a baby girl had been born to well-known local fisherman and businessman Chris Harvey and his wife Elaine.

"Well what do you know?" said a disbelieving James as he noted down the announcement word for word in his pocket book, "What a small world! This could be Anne Harvey's birth."

They then flicked through the next few issues of the Echo and found a small article a couple of weeks later. This described how Elaine Harvey, the wife of local fisherman and businessman Chris Harvey, had given birth unexpectedly at home to a girl named Anne two weeks before her baby had been due. Both mother and daughter were doing well and Elaine said she would like to thank publicly Dr Greg Smith. He was visiting her husband at the time and his prompt actions ensured a normal delivery and a healthy baby.

"It may just be co-incidence but perhaps there's more to this than first meets the eye," said James as he closed the volume and returned it to the rack, "I think we need to find out a bit more about the elusive Anne Harvey."

"Yes, we'll also need to take another look at those inquest papers. I'm sure Dr Smith and Chris Harvey figure in there somewhere," added Jenny, "There may just be a connection somewhere between the Fairfax and the Harvey families."

Chapter Twenty-seven

It took Rahul three days to show Nick the sights and sounds of Delhi. They had wanted Sunaina to go with them but she declined saying that the two men would be able to see more without her.

In New Delhi Nick was particularly impressed by the imperial grandeur of the President's palace, the Parliament building and the Rajpath, the wide road flanked by open parkland that leads down to India Gate. He also liked Connaught Place, the commercial hub of New Delhi, and felt at home wandering around this large circular arcade which is surrounded by a bustling roundabout. Here there were cinemas, banks, restaurants and the better class of craft emporia. In many ways while strolling around here Nick could almost imagine he was back home in England.

Nick spent a most enjoyable morning exploring the Red Fort. He was most impressed by the sandstone and marble pavilions, and the sheer scale of the structure, as well as the view over the Yamuna River. He was totally unprepared, therefore, for what awaited him when Rahul took him out of the Red Fort's Lahore Gate and into Chandni Chowk.

Chandni Chowk is the main thoroughfare linking Old Delhi's bazaars and shops. It's a complete contrast to the spaciousness and cleanliness of New Delhi. With numerous very narrow and dirty side streets it is a vast sea of people and seemingly uncontrolled traffic and Nick immediately felt the contrast between the two very different parts of the city. Here it was possible to buy almost anything, jewellery, clothes, traditional sweetmeats and just about any sort of household item. He admitted to Rahul later that he had felt a little uneasy when he was in this area and had been glad he was not alone.

After leaving Chandni Chowk it was a short walk to the Jama Masjid, the largest mosque in India. Although a practising Hindu Rahul accompanied Nick into the mosque. He said he had no problem with visiting mosques or churches as he had deep respect for the beliefs and traditions of others.

After visiting the Jama Masjid Rahul took Nick to see some Hindu temples or mandirs as they are known in Hindi. The most splendid of these was the Lakshmi Narain Mandir, or Birla Mandir as it is known locally after the family of rich industrialists who had it built. This was a large Hindu temple complex and Nick was fascinated by the many statues of the gods there. Although Rahul did an excellent job in explaining who the various deities were there were lots of questions he meant to ask. But because of the sheer beauty of the place and the numbers of worshippers there he didn't get an opportunity and decided to ask him later when a suitable moment arose.

On the final day of their sightseeing in the Delhi area Rahul took Nick to see the Raj Ghat, the simple memorial to Mahatma Gandhi that overlooks the Yamuna River, Humayun's tomb a splendid monument in the centre of some beautiful gardens, the Qutab Minaar said to be the tallest brick-built tower in the world, and the Jantar Mantar, an early type of astronomical observatory. Nick was impressed by the sheer scale of the monuments and the pageant of history that unfolded before his eyes. He had never imagined that India could be so interesting. He was in the midst of splendour but, at the same time, he was very much aware that he was in the midst of abject poverty.

When they arrived home in the evening of the final day of their sightseeing they found Sunaina praying in the house's small mandir.

"When we're at home we try to pray at least twice a day, early in the morning and later in the evening," Rahul explained, "Please excuse me," and he joined his wife in her devotions. Nick watched intently as they bowed before a statue and made a number of offerings and recited a prayer together from memory.

After the short ceremony was over Nick plucked up the courage to ask Rahul about the statues. Having visited a number of Hindu temples in Delhi he was anxious to know a bit more about this religion that he had so often heard about but which he knew so very little.

"How many gods are there in Hinduism and what are the ones you worship?" he blurted out a little uneasily.

"This may surprise you but Hindus believe in only one God who is known as Bhagvaan. You do see lots of statues in Hindu temples depicting a multitude of gods but they are just different aspects of that one God," and he paused before continuing, "Some people worship Lord Shiva or Lord Vishnu, others worship Lord Krishna or Ganesha, all of whom I am sure you're familiar with but in reality they are worshipping different aspects of the one God. People tend to have a favourite deity and worship that deity. They are all Hindus but have different ways of seeing or of approaching God. A difficult concept I know and one that is often totally misunderstood by people outside of the Hindu religion. In many ways Hinduism is not just a religion but a complete way of life.

Just as Hindus believe in the cycle of life and death, that one should do one's best in this life to try and have a better life next time around, so this pattern is reflected by the gods. Lord Brahma creates the universe, Lord Vishnu sustains it, and Lord Shiva destroys it so the cycle can begin all over again. That is why I try to do the best I can in everything I do and build up merit in this life to take forward to the next."

"That reminds me," interjected Sunaina, "tomorrow's Holi. Nick you must celebrate it with us. Come and take part in a very colourful Hindu festival that's also a lot of fun. Better not wear any expensive clothes though."

The next day Rahul, Sunaina and Nick left the house soon after lunch. Nick had taken Sunaina's advice and was wearing an old tee shirt and a pair of old jeans. Rahul and Sunaina were wearing simple two-piece white cotton suits resembling pyjamas. As they strolled towards the town Sunaina took the opportunity to explain to Nick what the festival of Holi was all about.

"Festivals are very important to the people of India. They are not only a part of the traditional way of life here but also a time when ordinary people can enjoy themselves and forget about the drudge of everyday life. Holi is the most colourful festival celebrated by Hindus. You're fortunate to be here for it as it occurs on the first full moon day of March. This year it's near the beginning of the month and luckily coincides with your stay.

There are many different origins to this festival. One of them has the fourth incarnation of Lord Vishnu killing the demon Harnaksha and another legend links the festival to Lord Krishna. As a boy he was very mischievous and used to spray the young girls of Varindaban, the village where he grew up, with coloured water. In some parts of India this festival can last up to 14 days but here it lasts for just one day."

By this time they had nearly reached the centre of the town. There were people everywhere running around in groups and Rahul suddenly left the path and went into a shop and came out with a large number of bags of coloured powder. "Here," he said to Nick and Sunaina, "we'll soon need these."

As they slowly walked on they watched as people began to shower each other with coloured powder and soon their white clothes were smeared with all the colours of the rainbow. It wasn't until they neared the centre of the town that the crowd turned its attention to Rahul and his companions. All of a sudden they were surrounded and pelted with a barrage of coloured powder.

"What are you waiting for?" exclaimed Rahul, "Let them have it!" And he opened up one of the packets and started throwing the coloured powder at the crowd.

Nick was somewhat reluctant to join in at first but after he had been the target of a particularly heavy bombardment of red powder he started to retaliate. It wasn't long before he was really enjoying himself and entering into the spirit of the occasion. Everywhere people were running and dancing and throwing powder at each other and Nick didn't realise that he was gradually becoming separated from the others. Rahul and Sunaina were also having fun and failed to see that they had left Nick behind.

Nick chased a small group of revellers around a corner and was suddenly confronted by a group of young men. They didn't have any powder but they did have water sprayers and they fired a barrage of coloured water at Nick soaking him to the skin. He was about to throw some powder at them when they stopped spraying the water and formed a semi-circle in front of him. They squared up and slowly moved towards him in a rather menacing way. In a moment of terror Nick realised he was on his own as Rahul and Sunaina were nowhere to be seen.

Nick edged backwards towards the main street trying not to take his eyes off the men but they were slowly coming ever closer towards him. He was now beginning to regret coming into town and was starting to sweat profusely. He continued to move backwards when all at once he felt a hand fall heavily on his shoulder. He froze in terror.

"There you are," said Rahul removing his hand, "we wondered where you had wandered off to. Having fun by the looks of it," and he threw some powder at the group of lads who responded by squirting him with coloured water before running off to find someone else to soak.

"Thank goodness you're here," Nick blurted out somewhat confused, "I thought they were going to attack me. I didn't know what to do. I felt all alone and lost."

"Lost," replied Rahul quietly, "You're only lost until someone finds you or," and he paused, "you find yourself."

"This is a festival and a happy time, a time for fun when people enjoy themselves," added Sunaina, "you had nothing to fear here, nothing to worry about at all."

"That's right," agreed Rahul, "you were perfectly safe."

The three of them made their way around the town and back to 'Shanti Bhavan' joining in the merriment and having fun with the crowds of people on the streets until their stock of coloured powder had been exhausted.

Even Nick soon forgot about his earlier experience and was happy to join in.

Back at the bungalow Rahul and Sunaina had a surprise for Nick.

"Tomorrow," said Sunaina, "we're off on a little trip. We're going to show you a bit more of India. We have to go to Varanasi to perform a religious rite but before that we're going to spend two or three days in Jaipur and Agra. So pack a few things and have an early night because tomorrow morning we make an early start. Vinod will be driving us to Jaipur and Agra and then back here but we'll need to take a plane to Varanasi."

Nick took a long time to get to sleep as he reflected on his experiences of the past few days. He was enjoying his stay in India but there were some aspects of the country, or perhaps it was its people, that made him feel a little uneasy.

Chapter Twenty-eight

Back at home James and Jenny Palmer were relaxing in the lounge with a glass of wine discussing the results of their visit to East Deben. Jenny was curled up in front of the fire thumbing through the inquest into Dawn Fairfax's death and James was sitting in an armchair looking through the papers of Beverley Fairfax's inquest.

Suddenly Jenny looked up and asked in a very excited tone, "Who do you think found Dawn Fairfax's body?"

"I've no idea. Go on tell me!" teased James.

"Dawn Fairfax's body was found washed up on the beach at North Deben two days after her fall from those cliffs by," and she paused to achieve maximum effect, causing great annoyance to her husband who playfully threw a paperclip at her, "none other than Dr Smith and Chris Harvey."

"Now that is interesting," responded James snatching the bundle of papers out of Jenny's hands, "very interesting."

"Hey, give them back to me!"

"In a minute, this is intriguing stuff," and after a brief pause he added, "Looks like we'll be going back to East Deben to make a few enquiries about Chris Harvey. We need to find out more about the family and the business, and Anne Harvey too of course. Could there really be some sort of connection there to David Fairfax? Don't think I can raise it with him at the moment until we get something more definite to go on."

* * * * *

The next morning in the post a large plain-brown A4 envelope arrived addressed to James Palmer. He opened it while eating his breakfast. Inside was the passenger list for the cruise liner that Beverley Fairfax was sailing on when she committed suicide. There was no indication as to who had sent the list but James was pleased that one of his former colleagues had repaid a favour.

He left his toast on the plate half-eaten and looked through the sheets. As he turned over a page he couldn't believe the name that was there in black and white and staring him in the eyes.

"Jenny, you'll never believe this! Who do you think was on that cruise with David and Beverley Fairfax? Who do you think was in a single cabin on one of the lower decks while the Fairfaxes were living it up in an expensive upper-deck suite?"

Jenny looked at her husband in silence. She didn't want to spoil his moment of glory so she just leant over the breakfast table and gently took hold of his arm, "Go on, surprise me!"

"It was Lucy Murray! *Lucy Murray* or as you know her today, Lucy Fairfax!"

"Are you sure? Let me see," and Jenny quickly pulled the papers from her husband's grasp, "You're right, Lucy Murray. Now what are the odds of that happening by chance? David Fairfax's first love who will later be his third wife, on the same boat as his second wife, *his soon to be deceased* second wife! There's something very strange, very strange indeed about all of this."

"You're right and it adds a totally new dimension to our enquiries," said a very thoughtful and worried-looking James, "but I'd better not confront David Fairfax with it at the moment. We need time to think this through. It could be dangerous if he knew we'd found this out. There may be a perfectly innocent explanation for Lucy's presence on that ship, but the very fact that David has never admitted to me that she was there means he could have something to hide. Knowing him and how he operates we need to keep this bit of information to ourselves for the time being or we may find we end up in big trouble ourselves!"

Chapter Twenty-nine

The condition of the road to Jaipur took Nick completely by surprise. It was a very busy road used mainly by lorries but it was in a very sorry state of repair. Everywhere there were potholes. Even though it was mostly a single carriageway vehicles would swerve into the opposite lane to avoid the gaping holes. Some attempt at repair was being made but filling the holes with tar and covering them with large leaves didn't really solve the problem. As soon as a heavy vehicle went over it the hole opened up again. Vinod drove as if there was no tomorrow and by the time they arrived in Jaipur Nick was feeling quite sick.

Nick soon recovered and spent a very relaxing two days exploring the renowned pink city of Jaipur and the many forts and old palaces in this area of Rajasthan. Of all the places he had seen in India this was, in his view, the best. He could almost imagine himself living in this part of the country.

On the third day the party drove to Agra and once again it was a nightmare journey Nick would not wish to repeat. Foolishly he had agreed to sit in the front seat and he had been appalled at the general standard of driving and had lost count of the times the car had almost been forced off the road. "In future," he thought to himself, "I'll sit in the back!"

The Taj Mahal was magnificent and Nick marvelled at the sheer size and beauty of this monument to love. He sat on a seat by one of the fountains and watched for a long time as the sun's rays contrasted the pure white marble of the building against the cloudless blue sky. And even better was to come. Rahul had connections in high places and as a treat for Sunaina had obtained permission to visit the monument after dark. The three of them joined a small select party in the evening that was let into the grounds amid tight security. They were completely overwhelmed by the breathtaking beauty as the Taj Mahal was illuminated by the near-full moon. It was a sight all three said would remain with them for the rest of their lives.

Nick enjoyed his stay in Agra visiting the Taj Mahal and the Red Fort but once again he was struck by the contrasts of this country. The town that boasted the Taj Mahal was very lively and colourful but was incredibly dirty and run down. As magnificent as the Red Fort was, the moat outside was nothing more than an open sewer.

All too soon the first part of the trip was over and Nick was back at the bungalow with Rahul and Sunaina. The following day Rahul promised Nick a new experience when he would be visiting Varanasi, one of the most holy places for Hindus, and one which every Hindu should visit at least once in his lifetime. Varanasi was formerly known, particularly in the West, as

Banares and, said Rahul, "Just as some people are holy, so are some places and Varanasi is one of those places."

It was just before dawn in Varanasi. Rahul, Sunaina and Nick were in a taxi weaving its way through crowds of people towards the banks of the Ganges River where Rahul had arranged for a small rowing boat to be waiting for them. They climbed aboard this most ancient-looking of vessels and the single oarsman rowed them along the full length of the waterfront, or ghats as they are called, just as the sun began to rise over the River Ganges.

During this hour-long experience Nick marvelled at the sheer numbers of people who were on the ghats and performing many different rituals. Some were simply standing on one leg looking into the rising sun and others were totally immersing themselves in what was, for them, the holiest river in the world.

"It is here," explained Rahul, "that Hindus believe Lord Shiva poured the holy Ganges River onto the plains from the Himalayas."

Rahul and Sunaina had taken some small offerings with them and these they launched into the water as they recited a verse from Hindu scriptures.

Before returning to the river bank the oarsman took them to view the cremation ghats where, even at this early hour, funerals were taking place. "Just think," said Rahul in hushed tones, "as we now look upon those being cremated so, one day, others will look upon us as we too make that journey, that none of us can avoid, back to infinity – from whence we came."

Nick was struck by Rahul's words and immediately cast his mind back to Tom's funeral. He could still picture the scene inside the crematorium and how upset he had felt when Tom's coffin had disappeared behind the curtains. He had imagined Tom lying still and lifeless and ever since couldn't get that thought, that image, out of his mind. A shudder had rippled through his whole body as he realised that he would never see his brother again. Now here, amidst scenes of death and public grieving, those memories once again flowed back over him.

Nick was visibly moved by the whole experience on the Ganges and didn't regret at all having to get up well before five in the morning.

Rahul and Sunaina then took Nick on a tour of Varanasi. Whatever he was expecting from this most famed of cities Nick was in for a surprise. This city, one of the world's most ancient and a renowned seat of learning and Hindu study, was an enigma. On the one hand there was the university, the splendour of the many Hindu temples and the mosque of the Moghul Emperor Aurangazeb, and on the other hand there was absolute filth and squalor. This was typified by the temple where Rahul and Sunaina went to make their offerings.

The Temple of Durga was a most magnificent structure with intricate carvings and exquisite statues but its courtyard was filthy and everywhere was covered in flies. This was all too much for Nick and he elected to wait outside and watch the sea of humanity that was Varanasi pass by in all its colours while Rahul and Sunaina went inside to pray and make their offerings.

"Before we return to the hotel we must take you to the Bharat Mata Temple," said Rahul, "there's someone there we'd like you to meet, someone who has guided us in the past, helped us when we've been in a time of need."

They arrived at the temple and all three of them removed their footwear and went inside. Nick followed the lead of Rahul and Sunaina as they made an offering to the deity and proceeded to a small ante-chamber to the side of the temple.

"This is Rahi," exclaimed Sunaina, and pointed to the figure of a small wizened old man sitting motionless with his eyes closed in the corner of a darkened room, "he can tell the future."

"His name means 'traveller' and he hasn't moved from this spot in over thirty years," chipped in Rahul.

Nick looked round the small room, or cell, as he would later describe it to friends back in England. The only items in the room were a small stool, a dirty bedroll and a few battered metal pots containing what looked like cold food. Rahi himself was sitting motionless cross-legged on the bare earthen floor. He looked totally emaciated, little more than a skeleton with skin stretched over the bones, and was wearing nothing more than a very dirty loin cloth.

"Why is he called 'traveller' if he never goes out of this room. And if he never leaves here how can he tell what is going to happen in the future?" enquired a very puzzled Nick.

"Simple!" exclaimed Rahul and whispered into Nick's ear, "His body remains here but he projects his mind out of his body and travels around the world at will. That's why he's nicknamed 'Rahi' or 'Traveller'. You should understand that here in India many people believe there is no need to travel at all. Travelling is simply a means of finding a home, and Rahi's home is here, in this temple."

"What rubbish!" retorted Nick, "I don't believe a word of it. He's nothing more than a fraud preying on gullible pilgrims and worshippers."

"Then why not put him to the test," Sunaina said gently and she took Nick's arm and sat him in front of Rahi, "He never asks, or indeed expects, any payment for his services. It is sufficient to leave him nothing more than a little food."

Rahi remained motionless for what seemed an age before opening his eyes and asking, in Hindi, why the three of them had come before him.

Rahul explained, again in Hindi, that Nick had come to India partly on holiday and partly to get over the untimely death of his brother but gave no other details about Nick or his family. Rahi was again silent and Rahul explained to Nick that his mind had now left his body. After about fifteen minutes, during which time Nick was beginning to get very uncomfortable and bored sitting cross-legged on the ground, Rahi opened his eyes and asked Rahul for Nick's date and place of birth. He was then silent for another lengthy period. Nick was fast losing patience.

Finally Rahi opened his eyes and spoke in Hindi for about two minutes before once again closing his eyes. Rahul and Sunaina looked at each other in apparent disbelief and turning to Nick said, "That's it. That's all he has to say."

"But what did he say?" asked an anxious-looking Nick, "If it's something about me or the family then I want to know."

"Outside," Rahul reassured him, "outside, where we can get a bit of fresh air."

The three of them stood looking at each other uneasily in the late afternoon sunshine and eventually Rahul spoke, "This may be difficult for you but Rahi said you do not have a future. He said your time remaining in this life was short. He also said that ...."

"Said what?" stammered an anxious and worried Nick who was visibly annoyed at Rahul's reluctance to continue, "What else did he say. I've a right to know!"

"Yes, I suppose you do have a right to know," continued Rahul, "but are you sure you want to know?"

"Positive!"

"All right, then. Rahi said you would meet an untimely death at the hands of your older sister."

"He said what?" roared a disbelieving but very distraught Nick, "He said Callisto would kill me."

"Not exactly. He said you would meet an untimely death at the hands of your sister. The two aren't necessarily the same thing."

"Well they are in my book," and he paused for breath, "I knew it was her all along. She killed Tom and now she's got it in for me. Well I'm going to sort her out once and for all. Come on! Let's get back to the hotel. We're leaving here tomorrow and I, for one, can't wait to get out of this place."

The holy man's prophecy cast a long shadow over that evening's dinner in the hotel. Little was said at the dining table and very little conversation took place during the flight back to Delhi the next day. During the drive back to 'Shanti Bhavan' Rahul tried to convince Nick that not all prophecies are fulfilled and he had nothing to fear from Callisto. He was sure she would soon be cleared by the police of any involvement in Tom's death. Nick, however, had made up his mind that Callisto was somehow involved.

After dinner when Simran had served them tea in the drawing room Nick put his cup down and turned to face Rahul and Sunaina, "I've decided to go back to

England on the next available flight. I've had a really good time here and I'd like to thank you both very much for making me feel so welcome and for showing me around, but the events in Varanasi have made me think. I've seen places and sights I could only dream about before. But the time has come for me to return to England."

"We quite understand," responded a sympathetic Sunaina, "we'd probably do the same if we were in your shoes."

"There's nothing here for me now," he concluded, "the secret, or should I say the motive, behind Tom's murder lies in England and that's where I should be," and he got up and left the room.

Chapter Thirty

On the flight back to the United Kingdom Nick had plenty of time to think about his visit to India. He thought about all the wonderful places he had visited and the splendid sights he had seen. But no matter how hard he tried he found it impossible to get Rahi's prediction out of his mind. His immediate reaction had been to believe the old man's words, particularly in view of there being some doubt as to where Callisto had been at the time of Tom's death, and the anger boiled up inside him. But as the flight progressed and he had time to reflect on what Rahul had said he began to question just how someone could possibly have any notion of future events in a country many thousands of miles away. By the time the plane landed Nick had managed to find a degree of inner calm inspired by Rahul's relaxed attitude to life. He was feeling much less agitated and was prepared to give Callisto the benefit of the doubt.

Feb met Nick at Heathrow Airport and drove him back to Forest Glade. Unlike his father, Nick preferred to sit in the front seat next to Feb so he could have a conversation with him. During the course of the two-hour journey home he told Feb all about his trip and the places he had visited. He also described how lovely

Rahul's house was but he didn't mention Sunaina or Rahi's prediction. He also said he felt in a much better frame of mind than before he went to India.

All the family were pleased when Nick arrived home. In the course of telling them about his adventures in India it was soon apparent that he was a changed person. He had returned home full of confidence and eager to start back at work and seemed to have put Tom's death to the back of his mind. He also greeted Callisto warmly and surprised her with a silk sari he had bought having remembered she was shortly to attend the wedding of an Indian friend of hers.

That night lying in bed discussing Tom's almost miraculous transformation David and Lucy Fairfax agreed that the trip to India had been a great success and David said he would telephone Rahul to thank him.

Nick returned to the office the very next day after returning from India and amazed everybody with his changed outlook on life. Gone was the morose introvert of recent weeks who had rarely bothered to come into work. In his place was an altogether different person who exuded dynamism and was keen to get things done. Nick's social life also blossomed and his first day in the office was marked by him taking his personal staff out for lunch. This was something he hadn't done for many weeks. He also telephoned John Burling and Terry Kingston and the three of them arranged to meet up for a drink that night in a pub in Theydon Bois. All thoughts of Tom were not entirely banished as Feb had arranged for one of his minders to accompany Nick whenever he ventured out of the house. This meant that while Nick and his friends were sitting in the pub talking amongst themselves, Vic Bolton one of Feb's former SAS colleagues, was sitting quietly nearby keeping a watchful eye on them.

Nick, John and Terry were all keen motorcyclists. They were also expert motocross riders who whenever they could went into the forest to practice their off-road skills. That night in the pub Terry reminded Nick that all three of them were due to take part in a motocross event that coming weekend in Ongar Park Woods. Nick admitted he had forgotten all about it and suggested they go for a practice run in Epping Forest the day before. The other two lads readily agreed. With Vic keeping a discreet eye on them the three lads spent most of Friday afternoon in the forest between The Wakes Arms and High Beech roaring along the many dirt tracks that criss-cross that part of Epping Forest.

* * * * *

John Burling's large white van pulled into the grounds of Forest Glade and Vic loaded Nick's motorcycle into the back alongside the two already secured there and then sat in the back himself.

"It's been sometime since you last competed at motocross," said a rather nervous Lucy, "but I'm sure you'll do just fine."

"Of course he will," beamed David patting Nick on the back, "I have high hopes of him. After all, unlike most of the competitors out there today you know those woods like the back of your hand."

"That's right," agreed Nick, "and with the rain we've had over the last few days it'll be muddy and very slippery. Hopefully my knowledge of the terrain should give me a good advantage."

"It should do that all right," interrupted Callisto.

"Well be careful. Make sure you get back home safe and sound and no broken bones," added Lucy.

"That's right. Make sure you don't fall off and dirty that nice new leather suit of yours," said Callisto making fun of Nick's new all-in-one white leather suit.

"Jealousy will get you nowhere," retorted Nick pulling a face, "you can have it when I'm finished with it."

"I don't want your cast-offs," snapped Callisto.

"Must be going," and Nick turned and left the lounge.

"Best of luck!" said Lucy sadly as she looked out of the window and saw Nick climb into the cab next to his two mates.

"Don't fall off!" shouted Callisto as Nick closed the van door.

"Don't fret, darling," said David in a vain attempt to reassure his wife, "he'll be all right. Nothing will happen to him. Vic's there to keep an eye on things."

* * * * *

When the lads arrived at Ongar Park Woods there were lots of competitors already there making last minute adjustments to their machines and revving them up incessantly. A large number of spectators were also present. Most of these tended to stand at the starting and finishing lines but a few braved the mud and prickly bushes to stand at vantage points in the woods. Vic was not a lover of motocross and chose to stay close to the starting line where he could keep Nick clearly in view.

The morning trials went well for the lads with all three of them making it through to the final heats in the afternoon. Apart from the actual races there were also time trials where competitors raced around the course singularly to see who could clock up the fastest times. Generally it took about 20 minutes to complete the course. Because of the conditions it had been decided that competitors would not set off at 5 minute intervals as they normally did but would only set off when the previous competitor was in sight of the finishing line.

John and Terry clocked up faster times than Nick in the morning events so they went before him and both completed the course in less than 20 minutes. This left Nick with a lot of time to make up if he wanted to be in the finals the next day.

As soon as the starter's flag was lowered Nick roared away and made a good start. He was in no doubt that he could get round in well under 20 minutes. This would give him an edge over those competitors who did not know the subtleties of the course.

Nick sped along the winding muddy track at a breakneck speed. He drove deeper into the woods past a few spectators who had made it a little way into the forest and began to descend into a basin renowned for its treacherous ruts and bumps that could so easily unseat the unwary. It was then he was most surprised to see another motorcycle going up the side of a rather steep bank to his left that was not part of the official course. As he watched the motorcycle approach the top of the bank it appeared to hit an object on the ground and the front wheel turned in on itself and unseated the rider.

He looked on in sheer disbelief as both machine and rider tumbled over the brow of the bank locked together. Nick was in a dilemma. What should he do? Should he continue the time trial and report the incident to the meeting officials after he had crossed the line? Or should he sacrifice his own attempt and see if he could provide some assistance to this unfortunate rider?

Nick's conscience won the day and he decided to see if the rider was hurt or if he had managed to pick himself up. With a huge skid he turned his bike off the track and weaved the machine through the bushes and small trees and reached the top of the bank. As he looked down he could see the motor cycle lying on its side with its engine still running and the rider lying a few feet away face down in the mud, lifeless.

Nick immediately revved up his machine and half skidded and half slid down the slope which was much steeper on this side of the bank than the other side. He was now not visible to the riders who would be taking part in the trials and following the official course.

He reached the fallen motorcycle, jumped off his machine and flung it roughly to the ground. He then removed his helmet and in a matter of seconds had made his way to the apparently lifeless figure. He stared briefly at the figure before going down on one knee and gently turning the body over. He was surprised to find that he was looking at a woman. She was dressed entirely in a one-piece black leather motorcycle suit with a black helmet sporting a tinted visor so he couldn't make out her face.

Nick bent down to get closer and, as he did so, the figure suddenly sprang to life and punched him full in the face with a gloved hand that was clasping a heavy wrench. Nick fell backwards and as he struggled to maintain his balance the figure followed up the initial blow with another to the head. Nick crumpled to the ground as he lost consciousness.

The figure immediately leapt on top of Nick and quickly tied his feet together. She then dragged him to a tree and fastened his hands together behind the trunk. She then retrieved Nick's motorcycle and tied his feet to the back of it.

After a few seconds Nick regained consciousness and looked up. It was then he realised that his feet were tied to the motorcycle and his arms were tied together behind a tree trunk.

"What do you want?" he blurted out in disbelief as he comprehended the situation he was in, "I came here to help you."

But there was no reply, the figure just stood above him in silence without moving. Then without warning the figure walked slowly round the tree and checked that Nick's hands were securely tied kicking him a few times in the body in the process.

"What the hell's going on? Who are you? Why are you doing this? I've done nothing to you! Let me go!"

"Let you go! Don't be silly. You're not going anywhere, you're finished," the figure snarled and she returned to Nick's motorcycle and revved it up and slowly began to let out the clutch. The motorbike inched forward and Nick quickly became aware that his body was now at full stretch.

Nick began to panic. He thought about how Tom had been cruelly murdered, he thought about Rahi's prediction and he realised that it was coming true, it was now his turn. He winced in pain as the joints in his shoulders, elbows and tops of his legs began to be forced apart. He was now sweating profusely and he let out a desperate yell as he could hear and feel his joints beginning to crack. He was also only too well aware that in his state of abject fear and dread he had defecated and relieved himself uncontrollably and this realisation added to his misery.

Nick lay on the ground in increasing agony as the motorcycle crept forward almost imperceptibly and his joints gradually reached breaking point. All of a sudden it happened. There was a loud crack as the joints in his shoulders were wrenched out of their sockets. Nick passed out and the figure quickly brought the motorcycle to a halt and returned to stand over him. Satisfied that he was not conscious the figure untied his arms and watched over him until he regained his senses.

Nick came round in absolute agony with his body wracked by pain. He struggled to say a few words but the pain was too much.

"Does it hurt? Never mind it'll soon be all over for you but let's have some fun first shall we? Let's go for a little ride!" and the figure looked around at the track that wound through the hollow, "Unlike the official course this track is full of boulders and stones, small rocks if you like. Dangerous things rocks, they can do all sorts of damage," and the figure roughly turned Nick's almost lifeless body onto its face.

With a roar the motorcycle leapt forward and Nick was dragged face-down over the stones with his useless arms flailing about wildly on either side of his body. The motorcycle made two passes in each direction along the track and then stopped. The figure walked back to Nick and casually turned him over with her boots. Nick's face was badly lacerated and covered in blood and he was barely recognisable. He struggled to make himself heard but his words were barely audible.

"I told you, dangerous things rocks!" and the figure stood astride Nick mocking his predicament, "Time to clean you up," and the figure once again jumped onto the motorcycle and roared up the bank to the official track. Nick's almost-lifeless body was thrown violently over the rough terrain but despite the almost unbearable pain he managed to keep conscious until the motorcycle came to a halt. Nick lay exhausted in a pool of deep mud and looked up in horror and sheer disbelief as the female figure stood over him and removed her helmet.

"You!" he exclaimed, "But that's impossible!"

The figure smiled and replaced her helmet. Then without another word she put her boot to Nick's head and forced it face-down into the mud. Nick struggled to get his face clear of the mud but couldn't shift the boot from the back of his head. He fought for breath as he began to inhale the mud which slowly filled up his mouth and airways until he began to choke and suffocate.

After a few minutes when all movement had ceased the figure pulled Nick's head from the mud. She made sure he wasn't breathing then thrust it back into the mud again. The figure then produced a pair of socks from within her one-piece suit and placed them together with a small card on Nick's lifeless body. With a leap over the body the figure ran up the bank and over the top of the ridge to retrieve her motorcycle and roared off deeper into the woods.

* * * * *

Back at the finishing line John and Terry were beginning to wonder why Nick had not returned. It was now nearly half an hour since he had began his time trial and they were worried that he may have had an accident or fallen off his machine. Vic also realised that something may be amiss and grabbed John's motorcycle and raced off along the track into the woods. It didn't take him long to find Nick's body lying face-down in the mud alongside his machine. From the ropes attached to the body Vic realised straight away that this was no accident and immediately telephoned the police on his mobile phone.

Chapter Thirty-one

Inspector Westwood was far from pleased. This was his first weekend off duty since Christmas and here he was, on a Saturday afternoon, on his way to Ongar Park Woods to the scene of a murder. His sergeant had been unable to give many details on the phone as he had only just reached the scene himself but from what information he had it sounded a most unusual case.

It was a difficult journey driving over very rough terrain to where the motocross had been staged and Inspector Westwood's annoyance was further increased when he realised just how muddy the whole area was. He stepped out of his car and walked gingerly to the boot trying to avoid the worst of the mud and he took out a pair of well-worn Wellington boots which he carefully put on. He then donned an all-in-one boiler suit and spoke to one of the constables who was explaining to the riders and spectators why they couldn't leave the scene until they had been interviewed and statements taken.

"If you're in charge here can you tell us when we can go home?" shouted an angry rider struggling to break through the police line and get to the inspector.

"All in good time! Once you've given your statements you'll be free to go but not before," retorted Inspector

Westwood rather abruptly as he turned and spoke to the constable, "Where's Sergeant Benson? He said he'd meet me here."

"He's in the woods, sir. Go through that gap in the bushes and follow the track through the trees into the forest. It's about half a mile but be careful it's very slippery."

Inspector Westwood left the moaning crowd and entered the forest. It was a most difficult track to negotiate as it was very uneven and slippery and several times the inspector struggled to stop himself falling as he stumbled along. After about ten minutes he could see in a hollow ahead of him the all-too familiar sight of a white tent covering a crime scene and he hurried on.

"Sir!" said Sergeant Benson as Inspector Westwood approached the tent, "The body's in here," and he held up the side of the tent and ushered the Inspector inside.

"Do we know who it is ..." and the Inspector's voice tailed off as he looked at the body lying in front of him in disbelief. Despite all the mud and cuts to the face he realised straight away that it was Nick Fairfax.

"Nick Fairfax!" exclaimed the inspector gazing down at the body.

"You know him, sir?" enquired a puzzled Sergeant Benson.

"I certainly do," replied the inspector, "but I had no idea when you called me that it would be him. But what on earth's happened to his face? It looks like it's been dragged over some stones or rocks to get in that state. And that mud! I dread to think how the poor lad died, he must have been in agony."

"So far," interrupted the police surgeon who had remained silent while crouching down and closely examining the body, "it looks like he was alive when the injuries were inflicted to his face and they certainly wouldn't have killed him. I would say he died from suffocation. He was probably held face-down in the mud until he stopped breathing. You'll notice that it's very muddy along here so it's probable he was dragged along over some rough ground nearby then brought to this spot to finish him off – if you'll forgive the expression. By the way, his arms have been wrenched out of their sockets and it looks like that was done while he was still alive as well."

"Thank you doctor," and turning to his sergeant Inspector Westwood asked, "Who found the body? And what was Nick Fairfax doing here anyway?"

"Apparently he was very keen on motocross and was taking part in some time trials through the woods with some of his mates. It was only when he was late in returning that they realised something was wrong. He was found by a chap called Vic Bolton who rang 999. He's over there outside the tent with one of the uniform boys. From his appearance and build he looks like an ex-army type to me. I thought you would wish to speak to him yourself. He says he didn't touch the body or get close to it but telephoned the police as soon as he realised what had happened."

"I'll speak to him in a moment. Let him stew for a bit. Have you been able to piece together what happened?"

"I think so and it helps that the ground is so wet and muddy."

"At least some good has come of this filth," said a rather sarcastic inspector as he tried to shake some of the heavy mud off his boots.

"The forensic boys have done a thorough search along this path and have found some motorcycle tracks leading over that bank to the left. On the other side there's a path that's strewn with rocks and in places they're covered with blood and bits of skin. There's evidence that another motorcycle was down there and left the woods along a track that leads towards Ongar. There are also footprints leading from here to the bank so it looks like the killer drove here on Nick's bike dragging him along behind before holding his face down in the mud and suffocating him."

"Let's have a look," and Inspector Westwood led the way out of the tent. The two men followed the footprints to the top of the bank and looked down at the forensic team working below.

Inspector Westwood bent down and studied the footprints, "What size would you say the boots or shoes were?"

Sergeant Benson crouched down on all fours and after a moment's thought said, "I'd say they're only a size five or six."

"Precisely!" agreed the inspector with a certain degree of enthusiasm in his voice, "Size five or six. A bit small for a man don't you think, but not for a woman."

"A woman! Do you think a woman could possibly have done this? She'd have to be very strong. Seems very unlikely to me."

"I'm not ruling anything out at this stage. I'm thinking back to Tom Fairfax's death. You weren't involved in that one but the only person caught on CCTV who didn't go to the party at that hotel but who went straight out into the street was a woman. Why leave a hotel at midnight on New Year's Eve? It doesn't make sense, everyone would be going to the party. Unless they wanted to get away from something!"

Just then Inspector Westwood's mobile phone began to ring. "Hello, yes it is. Oh is he! Here now? Well let him through but make sure he's suited up," and he put the phone back into his inside pocket.

"Now that's interesting. James Palmer is here. How did he know about this? I want a word with him but no harm in letting him up here. Let's see what he knows, see what he may have found out."

"Who's James Palmer?" asked Sergeant Benson, "Should I know him?"

"Well you might remember him. He's one of us – or at least he was until he had to leave the force. He's now working as a private investigator and David Fairfax has hired him to look into some instances of sabotage to his businesses. As events have taken a more sinister turn he's also been drawn into the murder investigation."

In a few minutes a breathless and very muddy James Palmer joined Inspector Westwood and Sergeant Benson at the top of the bank. It was obvious that in his haste he had fallen into the mud at least once. Inspector Westwood put James in the picture before confronting him, "How did you know it was Nick Fairfax who had been murdered?"

"Vic Bolton. He telephoned me immediately after he had contacted the police so I came over here as soon as I could. He was also going to telephone Feb, I mean John February David Fairfax's driver, so I suppose the family will know about Nick by now."

"Damn!" exclaimed Inspector Westwood, "I wanted to tell David Fairfax myself to gauge his reaction. There's something he's not telling us I'm sure of it. Come and take a look at the body."

The three of them slipped down the bank and entered the tent where the police surgeon was finishing his work and the forensic team were taking photographs of the body and the surrounding ground.

"I almost forgot," said the police surgeon as he picked up his medical bag, "these were found on top of the body," and he handed the inspector a pair of diamond-patterned socks and a small card that had been placed in separate clear polythene evidence bags.

"What do you make of these?" said Inspector Westwood after examining the socks and the card and handing them to James Palmer, "Why deliberately place a pair of socks at the scene? And this card, all it says is 'Scrambled out of time', what sort of a message is that?"

James held the bag up and silently stared at the socks as his mind drifted back to Christmas Day and the anonymous presents that each member of the Fairfax family had received.

"Think about Tom and the card found on his body. Those Christmas cards were a warning, a warning that we ignored and now two people are dead. The Christmas presents and those cards are the key to this. Think! What present did Nick get and what was written on his card!"

Inspector Westwood immediately reached into his inside pocket. He took out his notebook and leafed through the pages, "He received a pair of old-fashioned diamond-patterned socks and a card that read 'Wear these and run out of time, or should that be scramble out of time?' Very cryptic indeed."

"Scramble out of time. Scramble out of time!" repeated James Palmer out aloud almost shouting, "Why didn't I think of that?" and he punched the palm of his left hand with his right fist in sheer frustration, "Scrambling or motorcycle scrambling is the old name for motocross. I remember during the 1950s and 60s it was very popular and took place in these very woods. As a boy I often used to come up here at weekends and watch it myself."

"Someone knows an awful lot about this family and their interests. I think we should..." but before Inspector Westwood could finish his sentence he was again interrupted by his mobile phone, "Yes, Westwood speaking," and he put the phone to his ear, "Ok, get forensics over there and let me know what they find."

"What was that all about?" asked James.

"They've found a burnt-out motorcycle and some burnt clothes on the other side of the woods. Looks like our murderer made his way out of the woods and destroyed the evidence before making his getaway."

"Or *her* getaway," stressed James.

"Quite!" agreed Inspector Westwood, "Let's see what our friend Vic here has to say about all this," and the two of them made their way out of the tent to where Vic Bolton was being held.

"So," said Inspector Westwood, "do you mind telling us what you were doing here today?"

"Not at all," volunteered Vic, "I was employed to keep an eye on Nick Fairfax and to be his bodyguard or minder. Since his return from India I've been everywhere with him. I've been his shadow. Up to today it's been money for old rope, like, best job I've had for a long time."

"So what went wrong today? Why *did* you let him out of your sight?"

"Well there seemed no reason to follow him through the woods. I didn't think anything could happen out here, like, with all the people out and about on the course. I thought it would be safe for him as nothing suspicious had happened at all since I started the job."

"I'm going to need a full statement from you. Not just about today, I want details of all Nick Fairfax's movements since you've been minding him and I want it yesterday! Do you understand? Accompany Sergeant Benson to Epping Police Station and see to it. Until I'm satisfied with what you have to say you're not going anywhere."

As Vic was led away down the track towards the starting line by Sergeant Benson, Inspector Westwood turned to face James Palmer, "I suppose we'll have to get over to Theydon Bois and have a word with David Fairfax. Can't say I'm looking forward to it but I would appreciate you being there as well. He might open up more to you. He might trust you a bit more than me."

"I was rather hoping you'd invite me. It'll be interesting to see where David and Lucy were this afternoon and, of course, where Callisto was. I wonder what size shoes she takes?"

Chapter Thirty-two

Inspector Westwood's car drove slowly through the gates of Forest Glade closely followed by that of James Palmer. One of Feb's men immediately closed the gates and then resumed his patrolling of the grounds.

The two men walked towards the portico. They were about to ring the bell when the heavy wooden door was opened by Katie. Without uttering a word she quickly ushered them into the drawing room. David Fairfax was sitting alone in an armchair sipping a black coffee and staring blankly in front of him. The two cats appeared to be asleep on a settee but when the door was opened they immediately seized the opportunity to escape to another room.

There was a long uncomfortable silence before Inspector Westwood said in hushed tones, "Please accept our condolences. I'm terribly sorry Sir David but we will do all we can to catch who did this and put them behind bars. I really hate to intrude at this time but I do need to ask you some questions that just can't wait."

"Go on, then," responded Sir David rather wearily, "but I don't know if I can be of much help. I've been here all day and haven't left the house."

"What time did Nick leave this morning and was he on his own?"

"He left sometime between 9:30 and 10:00. He went with John Burling and Terry Kingston in John's van as they always do when the three of them go to motocross events. Oh, and don't forget Vic, Vic Bolton, he also went with them in the van."

"Tell me about Vic Bolton. Why was he with them?"

"As you know since Tom's murder we've been very worried about Nick and Callisto's safety. Whenever they go out anywhere on their own we've arranged for them to be accompanied, discreetly of course, by someone who could intervene if anything untoward was to happen. Feb contacted his former SAS colleagues and hired a couple of lads and Vic was one of them. Since Nick's return from India Vic's been everywhere with him. Not too close but, if the lads were in the pub or at a disco or something like that, Vic would be there in the background keeping a watchful eye on things."

"I see. Tell me how you learned of Nick's death?"

"From Feb. He said he'd received a call from Vic who had just informed the police. Oh, and I asked Feb to let James know. I suppose that's how he came to be here with you." Then after a pause, he asked, "Can you tell me how Nick died?"

"It's still very early and Nick's body hasn't yet been removed from the scene, but all indications are that he was attacked as he went round the motocross course through Ongar Park Woods. We haven't pieced together the events yet but it appears he was suffocated in the mud and ..."

The Inspector's words were interrupted by a loud cry from David Fairfax. He put his coffee cup down on the table with some force and buried his face in his hands, "Why?" he shrieked, "Why?" and he started to sob.

Inspector Westwood and James Palmer looked at each other in surprise. This was most unusual and uncharacteristic behaviour on the part of Sir David. When told of the death of Tom he had expressed an almost total lack of emotion.

"There's something else you should know," said the inspector, "We could keep it from you until later but you'd find out soon enough from the post mortem report. It looks like Nick was tortured before he was killed. It's still to be confirmed but it appears his arms were wrenched out of their sockets and it looks like he was dragged face-down over some stony ground before he was suffocated."

"Nick was always my favourite," responded Sir David who had now composed himself somewhat but didn't appear to have fully grasped the significance of what the inspector had said, "he wasn't as brainy or as confident as Callisto and Tom and I knew he would never be my successor in taking over the business. But I felt we had a bond between us, not just in business but in a father and son sort of way. I was closer to him than ever I was with Tom or could ever be with Callisto. I can't believe someone would actually kill him let alone do these other unspeakable things to him."

"That's something that's been worrying me a lot since Tom's murder," interjected James, "We're not simply talking about murder here but about very sadistic methods of killing. This is more than just about taking revenge, it's about a deeply held grudge and retribution that is now being exacted at a terrible price. Do you have any idea who could be behind this? Any idea who could be capable of doing this?"

"Don't you think I've wracked my brains ever since poor Tom was killed? I'll admit I've made more than my fair share of enemies over the years but I doubt if any of them would stoop to this. Believe me, if I knew who was behind this there'd be no need to involve the police!" and turning to James he snapped, "That's why I'm paying you, to get to the bottom of all of this!"

After another uncomfortable pause Inspector Westwood rather unwisely asked, "Where was Lucy today?"

"What are you suggesting!" roared David Fairfax becoming agitated and visibly red in the face, "I hope you're not accusing my wife of being involved in this! For your information she was here with me all day. She didn't leave the house once. She wasn't keen on Nick having a motorbike and couldn't bear to see him ride. She worried about him falling off and injuring himself so she remained here with me. I was tied up with business matters at odd times during the day but I can categorically state that she didn't leave this house."

"Thank you," said the Inspector rather relieved and then added, "What about Callisto? Was she here all the time?"

"You're beginning to push your luck and try my patience, Inspector, especially after nearly accusing her of murdering Tom," Sir David said menacingly, "but I'm sorry to disappoint you, she was here all day too and," with a heavy hint of sarcasm he paused before continuing, "what's more there are half a dozen of her friends who can vouch for her. Callisto was here hosting a swimming party downstairs in the pool. I think one of them had a birthday or something to celebrate. I'm sure Katie can give you a list of those who were here."

"That would be useful. By the way where's Callisto now?"

"When the news came about Nick we had to tell her and the party obviously stopped straight away. Most of the girls knew Nick and everyone was so shocked and stunned that they just went home. Callisto has taken this very badly and is in her room. She doesn't want to speak to anybody, not even Lucy or me. I'm worried about her and have called the doctor."

"That's all right. I'll speak to her in a day or two," mused the inspector before adding, "Are you sure you can't think of a motive why someone would want to murder two of your children?"

"What about your two previous wives?" James Palmer asked before Sir David had a chance to reply to the inspector, "Are you sure they're both dead? Could one of them have survived and have some sort of a grudge now that you've become successful and well-known?"

"No, that's impossible. I regret to say they're both dead. I identified the bodies myself and there's no doubt whatsoever that they are dead."

Inspector Westwood and James Palmer then went to leave the room but Sir David had a question for them.

"One thing before you go inspector, where's Vic Bolton?"

"He's at Epping Police Station helping us with our enquiries but he should be released later tonight or tomorrow morning once we're satisfied with his account of the events."

"Fine, I'll be having a word with him myself sometime," David Fairfax said threateningly.

Chapter Thirty-three

David Fairfax stood and watched from the drawing room window as the two cars drove through the large gates and then went their separate ways. He was angry! Angry that Nick was dead, angry with Inspector Westwood for insinuating that he or Lucy or even Callisto might be involved, and angry with James Palmer for bringing up the deaths of his first two wives. But he was most angry at Vic Bolton for not doing what he was paid very good money to do, look after Nick and make sure nothing happened to him. The more he thought about Vic the more he began to boil inside, "Damn the man! If he'd done his job Nick would be alive here and now. Damn the man!" he repeated out aloud and reached for his mobile phone.

"Is that you Feb? Listen, I've got a little job for you and the boys. Get over to Epping Police Station, Vic's being questioned there about Nick's death. I'm not sure if he'll be released this evening or tomorrow morning but make sure someone's there to meet him. I don't want him coming back here or taking off somewhere. Understand?"

"I certainly do, Sir David. Do you want him to, er, how can I say this?" and he hesitated, "Disappear?"

"No, certainly not! I want him to suffer, and I mean suffer! When you have him take him to 'The Shop' and let me know when you get there. And in case I forget have 'Laurel and Hardy' join us and the boys. We'll have a bit of fun with our Vic and teach him a lesson about not doing the job he's paid to do."

"Very good, Sir David," and Feb hung up.

David Fairfax sat down in his favourite armchair once again and started to think, "Who?" he thought to himself, "Who could be doing this? I need to speak to James in a few days time to see how he's getting on but if he thinks it could be Dawn or Beverley then he really is barking up the wrong tree. They're both dead and buried! There's no doubt about that!"

* * * * *

The next morning breakfast at Forest Glade was a most sombre affair. Hardly a word was said and both Lucy and Callisto occasionally broke down in tears. Even Katie seemed very troubled by Nick's death and more than once spilled coffee on the tablecloth. As Katie was bringing in the Sunday papers on a silver tray and placing it on the centre of the table David Fairfax's mobile phone began to sound. Immediately he grabbed it off the table stood up and walked towards the door out of earshot of the family. He put the phone to his ear, it was Feb.

"We have him! We're on our way to 'The Shop', should be there in a couple of minutes."

"Fine! I'll join you there in about half an hour."

David then turned to Lucy and Callisto and said in as sad a voice as he could manage, "I've got to go out. It's business but it shouldn't take long. I'll be back in plenty of time for lunch." He returned to the breakfast table and gently kissed Lucy on the cheek, "I don't like leaving you but promise I won't be long," and he turned and left the room. A short time later the sound of his car could be heard crunching over the gravel as he drove out of the gates and took the road to Epping.

* * * * *

It wasn't often that David drove himself and he found the short journey to Epping through the forest in his Mercedes most exhilarating and it allowed him the freedom to focus his mind on past events. "I mustn't forget to have a word with James sometime next week," he thought to himself, "see what he's come up with so far. However, there's more pressing business to attend to right now," and his thoughts turned to Vic and the punishment that awaited him.

David Fairfax parked his car at the rear of 'The Shop' and made his way up the back stairs to his office. As he walked across the floor to the suite of offices he saw Feb and some of the boys in conversation with Vic Bolton. Feb looked towards him and David nodded his head. Immediately Feb grabbed hold of Vic and with the help of a couple of the boys dragged him into the interrogation room and tied him tightly to a chair in the centre of the room.

Both Feb and Vic were veterans of the SAS and at one time Feb had been Vic's commanding officer. Feb knew very well that Vic could stand a fair degree of interrogation and torture and had been surprised when David had told him what he had in mind for Vic as suitable punishment.

"You've neglected your duty, soldier!" shouted Feb, "You've not only let me down but you've let down the regiment. Most important of all, you've let down your employer and that's unforgivable."

"Sorry sir, it won't happen again," replied a confident-sounding Vic.

"You're right, it won't happen again. You're lucky! My immediate reaction was that you should disappear somewhere in that lovely big forest out there, somewhere where you'd never be found. But you're fortunate to have a most benevolent employer, an employer who will have to remember for the rest of his life that you let him down, that you were responsible for the death of his son. It's only fair, therefore, that you remember for the rest of your life exactly what you've done."

Feb was silent for a while then he shouted, "Laurel, Hardy, there's work for you here!"

Out of the shadows stepped the diminutive form of Laurel closely followed by the massive frame of Hardy. In his office looking through the one-way mirror David Fairfax forced a smile as he anticipated what was to come, "Revenge," he thought to himself, "there's nothing quite so sweet. It won't bring back poor Nick but it'll make me feel much better. If I've got to suffer for the rest of my life then so will Vic," and he settled back to watch and relish in the spectacle.

Vic looked on nervously as Laurel walked behind him and Hardy towered in front of him. He had been in tight situations before. He had dished out the punishment and he had also been on the receiving end of it, but somehow today was a very different situation. For the first time in his life he felt afraid and this showed in the sweat that began to glisten on his forehead.

Suddenly Laurel grabbed hold of Vic's head and held it steady in a vice-like grip. Hardy stepped forward and smashed one of his huge fists into Vic's nose. Vic remained silent as a river of blood flowed from his nose and into his half-open mouth. This initial blow was followed by one more to the nose and then by a hail of blows to the stomach and chest areas. Vic tried to remain silent but couldn't suppress a few moans as the blows rained down on him.

"Very good!" exclaimed Feb, "That's what I like to see, discipline, not cracking under pressure. I'm glad all that training at the taxpayers' expense wasn't in vain. You're a credit to the regiment."

Vic looked up and breathed a sigh of relief as Hardy left the room, "Perhaps that's it," he thought to himself, "not too bad really, I've experienced worse." But his relief was short-lived. He looked on in horror and disbelief as Hardy returned carrying a heavy baseball bat in his hand.

Once again Hardy stood in front of Vic and began taunting him. He swung the bat a few times very close to his face and then deliberately aimed it at Vic's head but stopped short at the last minute. He carried on in this way for a few minutes and then, just as Vic began to think it was all bluff, Hardy smashed the bat into Vic's left knee with full force and to the sound of crunching bone. This time Vic couldn't stop himself from crying out in pain and pleaded for Hardy to stop.

Watching from the comfort of his office David was delighted and stood up so he could get close to the one-way mirror. He was even more delighted as Hardy aimed a further two blows at Vic's left knee and Vic immediately shouted out in agony for the beating to stop. The knee joint was completely smashed and Vic's left leg hung lifeless swinging to and fro. This was what David was after, retribution and a punishment that Vic would remember for the rest of his life.

"Does it hurt?" enquired an apologetic looking Hardy who, on getting no reply from Vic, prodded the knee and made him writhe in agony. David Fairfax was now thoroughly enjoying the spectacle and his heart was beating fast in anticipation. He made a mental note to give Hardy a bonus for his good work. David admired people who were craftsmen in their chosen fields and who really excelled at and enjoyed their profession.

"Shame about the knee," said a cynical Hardy who without warning aimed a mighty blow at Vic's right knee smashing the joint in a single blow. He stood back to admire his handiwork and then approached closer to

Vic. "Tell me," he added getting very close to his face, "are you right or left handed?"

There was no reply from Vic who looked straight at Hardy and, after a pause, uttered a string of swear words and spat into his face. Hardy stumbled backwards but quickly regained his composure.

"My friend asked you a question," grimaced Laurel who tightened his grip on Vic's neck and began to twist it violently from one side to the other. After a few minutes of this treatment Vic broke his silence and said he was right handed.

"Very good," said Hardy, "that's what we want to know. We're not without pity," and with lightning speed he smashed the baseball bat into Vic's right elbow breaking the joint with a sickening thud. "We want you to have something to do when you're sitting indoors unable to walk to the pub or go out with your mates. And now you have, you can learn to write and do other things with your left hand such as wipe your backside," and he laughed out loud and left the room casually tossing the baseball bat from hand to hand. Laurel loosened his grip on Vic's neck and followed Hardy down the stairs and out of the building whistling a tune as he went.

Feb returned to the room and untied Vic who immediately slumped to the floor. Feb motioned to a couple of the boys and they picked him up and began to carry him roughly down the stairs.

"Take him back to his lodgings and then call an ambulance. He must have slipped on the stairs, they're responsible for so many accidents around the home nowadays!"

Once the boys had gone David emerged from his office, "Well done Feb that went well. I'm still worried though that we're no nearer to finding out who killed Tom and Nick. We need to keep the boys visible at all times in the grounds of Forest Glade and make sure that whenever Lucy or Callisto go out they're accompanied. And I mean accompanied by someone reliable who won't let them out of their sight no matter what they're doing."

"Very good, Sir David, I'll see to it straight away. Let me drive you home."

Chapter Thirty-four

A few days after Nick's body was found James Palmer received a summons from David Fairfax and decided to take Jenny along with him.

"Most impressive," exclaimed Jenny as the gates to Forest Glade were reluctantly opened for them by one of Feb's men and James drove the car along the tree-lined drive towards the house, "Who says crime doesn't pay?"

"Careful darling, we don't know that for sure."

"Admit it you have doubts about where so much wealth could have come from but, for the time-being, let's give him the benefit of the doubt. Actually, I can't wait to meet him. He sounds a most fascinating character."

"Fascinating yes, enigmatic yes, but also dangerous if what I've heard is to be believed so be on your guard."

Katie opened the heavy oak front door and immediately showed them into the drawing room. James sat down on the settee and Jenny played with the cats until Katie returned with a tray of coffee and biscuits.

"Sir David sends his apologies," said Katie as she put the tray down on a small side table, "but he should be with you in a few minutes."

As the maid left the room the cats ran to the door as if to follow but then had second thoughts as they remembered the biscuits. Jenny looked a soft touch so they jumped onto the armchair and nestled in her lap looking longingly up into her eyes.

James poured the coffees and handed the plate of biscuits to Jenny who couldn't resist the temptation of the chocolate ones.

"How sweet," she said struggling to keep the cats from jumping up and grabbing the biscuits, "what lovely cats, I bet they don't have to go out hunting for birds and mice."

"They certainly do not. In fact they're not allowed to go out of the house at all, even if they wanted to."

"David!" exclaimed James, "You wanted to see me?"

Jenny turned round to face the figure that had silently entered the room by a second door, "So this is the fabled David Fairfax in the flesh," she thought to herself, "looks better than he did on the telly, actually quite an imposing presence."

"Yes I did, but I didn't realise you'd be bringing your charming wife, a most unexpected pleasure."

"Jenny, this is Sir David and David, this is my wife Jenny," and after a moment's thought continued, "My partner in crime or should I say my partner in solving crime."

"Pleased to meet you," said Jenny extending her hand.

"Very pleased to meet you," replied Sir David shaking her hand warmly and then taking a seat opposite the husband and wife team, "but it's David, just David, let's not be too formal."

Sir David helped himself to a cup of coffee, took a sip and then added, "Being absolutely blunt, as you well know, things are going from bad to worse. Just what have you found out since I hired you?"

"On the face of it," replied James rather hesitantly, "not much, but we do have some questions that might shed some light on the matter," and he paused before continuing, "We firmly believe the key to all this lies somewhere in your past. Someone is bearing a grudge no, it's more than just a grudge, it's almost as if someone's got an absolute hatred for you and your family."

"Big deal!" shrugged David, "You don't need to be a detective to work that one out. But who? I've wracked my brains and can't come up with anyone at all."

"I must apologise for mentioning the deaths of your first two wives the other day when Inspector Westwood was here. I know it probably brought back sad memories but I really did think there might be a possibility that one of them could be alive. Why, though, would they want to harm you and your family after all this time? It just doesn't make sense?"

"I'll tell you once again, for the last time," said David most forcefully, "they're both dead. Just let that matter rest. There's no mileage there at all."

"We've been investigating Anne Harvey and her group of companies. Do you know her or her family from the past?"

"No, I'd never heard of her, her family or her company, until we lost those tenders last year. As you know we lost those contracts by the slimmest of margins and it appears we have a mole – who you've been unable to unearth so far! A mole that could inflict further damage."

"What if I was to say that one of the two people who found Dawn's body was none other than Anne Harvey's father?"

David Fairfax looked stunned. He drained his cup of coffee and stared silently into the empty cup slowly spinning it between his hands. "Could be co-incidence," he volunteered after a while, "I didn't actually meet either of them. I think they were at the inquest but I don't recall seeing them there."

"Nonetheless we think it might be significant and we'll be making more enquiries in East Deben. You can't think of any connection between you and the Harvey family?"

"No, none whatsoever."

"Changing the subject," continued James, "we've also been looking into the inquest on Beverley's death."

"What about it?" enquired an increasingly irritated David.

"For a start," jumped in Jenny, "we've got a passenger list for that cruise and guess who's name appears on it? Lucy Murray, or should I say Lucy Fairfax!"

James wasn't at all sure if it was a good idea to broach this subject but before he could intervene David sprang to the defensive.

"My, my, my, you have been busy little bees!" he sneered sarcastically and Jenny started to see a side of David Fairfax that began to worry her, "Perhaps I should congratulate you. I'm sure if the good Inspector Westwood had that information he'd have hauled me down to the police station by now. Yes, I'll admit it, Lucy was on that cruise but don't get the wrong idea."

"And what would that be?" enquired Jenny staring straight into David's eyes.

"That there was something going on between me and Lucy! As James has no doubt told you I've known Lucy as far back as our secondary school days. She has always been more than just a good friend, she's been a rock and a support I could turn to in times of crisis. And that's what that cruise was, a time of great personal crisis for me and Beverley. Beverley was getting over a very bad patch mentally and I was worried that during one of her bouts of depression she might try to take her own life.

After a lot of effort I persuaded Lucy to come on the cruise and keep a discreet eye on Beverley at times when I might not be around. That's all there is to it, nothing sinister or any ulterior motive. Lucy was as shocked as I was when Beverley threw herself off that ship and drowned. All that was found on deck was the scarf she was wearing at dinner before she suddenly left the restaurant and ran back to our suite."

David appeared genuinely sad as he paused and looked up at James.

"I'd appreciate it though if you could keep this to yourself and not tell the good inspector. I wouldn't want to put any false thoughts into his already overburdened mind."

"Of course," agreed James, "we've no reason to tell him. We work for you, remember."

As James and Jenny were about to take their leave the sound of a car pulling up sharply on the gravel outside was heard. Sir David went to the window and saw Inspector Westwood getting out of his car, "Damn! Speak of the devil and all that! Inspector Westwood has arrived. Don't go, stay and see what he has to say."

After a few seconds the door opened and Katie showed the Inspector into the drawing room.

"Sorry to trouble you Sir David but I thought I would update you on ..." and he stopped briefly as his eyes alighted on James and Jenny Palmer before continuing, "update you on progress with Nick's murder."

"Please inspector, take a seat," said a very polite Sir David.

"Thank you. Although the burnt out motorcycle was almost destroyed we have managed to confirm that it was the one used by the killer as there was just enough tyre treads left to make a match. The killer got away in a car or on another motorbike but there weren't any tyre tracks there to enable us to pinpoint a make or a model. The killer's clothes were burnt almost beyond recognition but the forensic boys have enough evidence to suggest they were an expensive designer brand that was almost new. They're making enquiries and hope to come up with who purchased them and when. The boots too look to be expensive ones so we might get a lead there. By the way it's possible we may be looking for a woman, footprints found at the scene suggest a small shoe size, but I expect James has already told you that."

"No, as a matter of fact he hasn't. Perhaps I should be paying you and not him, inspector," David responded sarcastically.

"The forensic boys have also had a good look at those socks found on Nick's body and they've confirmed that they do in fact date from the 1970s." Then, after briefly pausing he added, "Well I won't take up any more of your time, I'm sure you've got important things to discuss with James,"

But as the inspector walked towards the door he suddenly stopped and turned to face Sir David, "By the way, did you know that Vic Bolton is in hospital? He says he had an accident on Sunday afternoon soon after leaving the police station. He fell down the stairs at his lodgings and will be lucky to walk again."

"Really! Thanks for telling me inspector. I'll send him a get-well soon card."

Chapter Thirty-five

James and Jenny Palmer spent the fifteen or so minutes it took to drive back to North Weald in almost total silence. They were both thinking about the meeting with David Fairfax and whether or not it had got them any further forward.

A few minutes after arriving home they settled down in the lounge over a cup of tea and James was the first to speak, "So, what did you think of David Fairfax? Was he as you imagined him?"

"Yes," replied Jenny after a moment's hesitation, "and no. I thought he was remarkably well composed for someone who had recently lost two sons and managed very well to keep his cool. But there were times when I felt I could see that thin veneer of civility begin to crack and a different side of him was bursting to get out. I'd say our David Fairfax is a very complex character and someone I would definitely not like to get on the wrong side of, there's something frightening about him."

"Yes," agreed James, "a classic case of the iron fist in the velvet glove."

"There's certainly a degree of malice bubbling beneath the surface. I felt I hit on a raw nerve when

I mentioned Lucy being on that cruise ship with him and Beverley but after an initial lapse he quickly regained his composure and was then Mister Charming himself."

"So, let's see what we've got out of today's meeting," James proposed, "We have an admission from David himself that Lucy was on that cruise ship and for the best of reasons. But if that's the case why doesn't he want Inspector Westwood to know?"

"Interesting," responded Jenny, "and don't forget the scarf that was found on deck where Beverley is thought to have thrown herself into the sea. I hadn't realised the significance of that before. We should have picked it up from the inquest papers. Maybe we need to have another look at them. Perhaps we're not the only ones to have obtained a list of who was onboard that boat."

"Ship, dear, it was a ship not a boat."

Jenny immediately stood up and threw a cushion playfully at James, "When I need lessons in English *you know-all* I'll ask."

"Sorry, couldn't resist it. But you are correct you know, someone has found out about Lucy being on that ship and has also read the inquest papers. Think about those Christmas presents," and James got up and went into the study to retrieve his notes from a filing cabinet.

"Here it is," he said sitting down in the lounge again and thumbing through his notebook, "the present Lucy

Fairfax received was a scarf and one made by the DesboroDenim fashion group no less."

"The very same fashion group David Fairfax inherited when his first wife Dawn fell off the cliffs," interrupted Jenny taking the wind out of James' sails.

"Yes, it's all getting very cosy isn't it?"

"And the card," queried an excited Jenny almost unable to contain herself, "what did the card say?"

James decided to tease Jenny and deliberately took his time before replying, "The card said 'This will look good around your neck. But don't go overboard. Don't get it wet'."

"Precisely!" said a jubilant Jenny jumping up and down in her seat. "Don't you see, whoever wrote that card knew about Lucy being on board that boat, I mean ship," she said correcting herself, "and a scarf being found on deck, it's almost a kind of warning."

"You're right. Think back to Tom's present and card. He received a pair of old-fashioned underpants and a card which read," and James paused while he looked once more in his notebook, "it read, 'Picture yourself in these. Drop-dead gorgeous!' Lots of clues there to what eventually happened to poor old Tom."

"That's right, he was found wearing a pair of identical underpants and a photo of his body dressed only in those pants was posted on the internet. So let me get this straight. Are we saying that each of those presents and the cards that came with them were, in some way, references to the past but, at the same time, a warning as to what may happen in the future?"

"Exactly! I think you've got it, Jenny. Look at Nick for example. He was found with a pair of old-fashioned DesboroDenim socks draped across his body, the same type of socks he received at Christmas, and the note with them made reference to scrambling – the old name for motocross. What all this tells us is that we're not only dealing with a cold-blooded sadistic murderer, but a murderer who knows an awful lot about the Fairfax household."

"We need to think carefully about the other presents and cards then," said a pensive looking Jenny, "they could be clues as to what may happen to other members of the Fairfax family in the future."

"Good point. We mustn't forget to study all those Christmas presents and accompanying cards. It's possible we may be able to second-guess the murderer's next move. What did you make about Inspector Westwood's news?" asked James changing the subject.

"What, about the burnt-out motorbike and clothes?"

"No, they were a smokescreen, if you'll forgive the pun. No, the real reason the inspector called round to see David Fairfax was to gauge his reaction to the news about Vic Bolton."

"Vic Bolton! You don't think his falling down the stairs was an accident then?" queried a puzzled looking Jenny.

"No, far from it! I'd put money on it that poor old Vic Bolton was picked up and taken away and given a thorough working-over."

"By David Fairfax?"

"By his minders more likely. Just look who works for him at that house of his. They're all ex-military types, the sort who wouldn't think twice about 'evening up the score' or doing a 'little job for the boss'," said James and he closed his notebook.

"So," said Jenny, "where do we go from here?"

"We do a number of things. First, we find out all we can about Anne Harvey and her life before she came to prominence as head of the Anne Harvey group and that may involve another trip down to East Deben. Secondly, I've also got my doubts about the relationship between Chris Harvey and that doctor, what was his name? Greg Smith, that's it, Greg Smith. Is he still alive? I doubt it but it's worth trying to find out. Also, what was the relationship between those two and David Fairfax? David says he didn't know them but I think it's worth doing a bit of digging."

"Sounds like some more trips to the seaside," responded Jenny as she got up from her seat and left the room.

Chapter Thirty-six

Craig Bentley and Susan Rumble were on one of their routine visits to farms in Norfolk owned by the Fairfax Group. Officially they were conducting audits on behalf of David Fairfax, but unofficially they were checking on illegal foreign workers employed there that David Fairfax was completely unaware of.

Business had been good during the winter months and as spring approached the opportunities to make even more money loomed large. There were contracts in place with a number of local supermarkets and traders for the supply and packing of vegetables, and the operation had expanded to cover not only Norfolk, but large parts of Suffolk and Cambridgeshire as well. At a farm a few miles from the north-Norfolk coast the pair were joined by Robin Gladwin, one of the farm managers. He brought them up to date on building work to house the workers who were expected to arrive in time for the summer harvest. The hostels were basic but considered good enough to house migrant workers.

"David Fairfax's preoccupation with his family bereavements and his fear of illegal immigrants being found in his company's trucks has given us a golden opportunity," smiled Robin, "I don't know what his problem is. He's never been worried in the past about things going wrong. The lawyers he's got could get him out of any scrape. Still, it's good news for us. We've got plenty of work and with the paltry wages we pay these people we'll make a mint. People from eastern-Europe work hard for their money and don't complain. The small amount of cash they send home is worth a fortune out there so everyone's happy. I must say we've had no real trouble so far."

"You're doing a fine job, Robin," responded Craig, "I wish we had more in the firm like you but we have to be so careful nowadays who we can trust. If this were to leak out we'd be finished, David Fairfax would soon see to that."

"That's right," added Susan, "I've heard about his methods and they're not pleasant, believe me."

"I've seen them," Craig said sadly, "at first hand and they sicken me. Sometimes I think I'd like to get out of this business altogether but I'm not sure David would agree to it. We all know too much for his liking. He wouldn't sleep at nights worrying about whether we'd keep our mouths shut."

"That's true for all of us," said a thoughtful Susan, "none of us could leave and lead a normal life now. We'd always be looking over our shoulder in case of, how can I put it, we had an accident."

"We'd better be going. See you in a couple of weeks Robin but if anything crops up give me a call on my mobile," said Craig as he walked towards his Land Cruiser.

Craig and Susan left the farm buildings and began to drive along the narrow single track lane that led away from the farm. They headed towards the main road to Great Yarmouth where they had already booked a hotel room for the night. The lane was lined with high hedges that even at this time of year with no leaves made visibility difficult. Suddenly, from a field to their left, a large black four-by-four vehicle with dark tinted windows pulled out right behind them and signalled to them to pull-over. Craig and Susan looked at each other and immediately had the same thought, "Was this David Fairfax or some of his men? Had their little scheme been discovered?"

Craig carried on driving despite the continual sound of the horn and flashing of lights from the following vehicle until he was able to turn into the entrance to a field. He brought the Land Cruiser to a halt and both he and Susan got out as the other vehicle drew up close behind them.

The vehicle came to a stop. After what seemed an age the front doors opened in unison and two tall burly men dressed in long black leather coats and sporting dark glasses stepped out. The driver opened one of the rear doors and after a few seconds a smiling Dimitri Komarov eased himself out of the car and walked over to a five-bar gate on the edge of the field.

"Dimitri!" exclaimed Craig with a relieved tone to his voice as he walked over towards the gate to join him, "This is an unexpected pleasure!"

"My friend!" responded Dimitri in his heavy eastern-European accent looking at Susan and giving her a wry smile, "And Susan Rumble, a double pleasure, I'm sure, da?"

"I didn't know you'd met Susan before," stammered Craig.

"I haven't," acknowledged Dimitri, "but I know all about you two. Not just about our little arrangement of course but about your, how can I put it, outside activities and nights away from home. And," he paused for effect, "if I know then perhaps David Fairfax knows or that super efficient personal assistant of his Angela Hamilton. She knows everything so I'm reliably told."

"I don't think so. If David Fairfax knew about Susan and me he'd have done something about it by now."

"That's right," chipped in Susan, "but if Angela knows then she might well keep it to herself in case she can profit from it in the future. Very deep that one and I don't really trust her. On the surface she's the totally loyal and committed personal assistant but there's more to her than meets the eye. Hard to put my finger on it but call it a woman's intuition if you like."

"This is all very pleasant Dimitri but I'm sure you had a good reason for meeting up like this. I'm sure you weren't just passing and decided to drop in for a chat."

"You're right my friend. I've come to warn you that we have a rival."

"A rival?"

"Yes, and it could be very bad news for us," said a sombre looking Dimitri, "it's Ken Winter."

"Ken Winter! What's he been up to?"

"He's also going into business on his own and taking full advantage of David Fairfax's reluctance to sanction the smuggling of illegal immigrants. My contacts tell me he's gone into partnership with the Albanian mafia to smuggle people into the country in a big way. It's mainly women for the sex trade in some of the inner cities where there are large eastern-European and Asian populations."

"I see, but how does that affect us? We're quite small scale and only bring in people when we need them. Compared to when we regularly used to bring in all those Chinese immigrants we really have wound down."

"It's not the scale of the operation that worries me my friend, although the larger the operation the more chances there are of getting caught, da? It's the people he's dealing with, they're ruthless. I know, I've come up against them in the past and lost some good men, they are always armed and have no regard for life at all. I thought I should put you in the picture, put you on your guard. After all, if you go under then I do as well, da?"

"My thanks, Dimitri, I had no idea. How did you get wind of this?"

"My friend, let's just say I keep my, how do you say, eye to the ground!"

"Ears, Dimitri, ears to the ground."

"As you wish," and Dimitri paused for breath before continuing, "Well my friend I must be going. Business as usual but take care and watch out for Ken Winter and his new friends, you wouldn't want to cross them. Let's hope he doesn't either."

One of the heavies opened the rear door and Dimitri disappeared inside the vehicle. Craig and Susan watched in silence as it drove down the narrow lane and vanished into the distance.

"Things must be bad for Dimitri to risk meeting us in the open," a worried looking Craig said when he and Susan were alone again, "perhaps we should call a halt to all of this."

"And upset Dimitri? It doesn't matter which way we turn we're going to get on the wrong side of someone," mused a pensive Susan.

"Let's talk about it when we get to the hotel. Things will look better once we've had time to reflect on the situation."

The day had started on a high when they had realised just how successful the illegal worker racket was and how much money it was bringing in. But the meeting with Dimitri had soured things somewhat and both

CHAPTER THIRTY-SIX

Craig and Susan were in thoughtful mood as they drove towards Great Yarmouth.

Later that evening as they had dinner in the hotel's restaurant, Craig and Susan decided they would run with things as they were but at the end of the year they would take the money and run. Craig would go ahead with his plan to leave his wife and start a new life with Susan in Spain. They had talked about this for a long time but had both been somewhat reluctant to take this rather radical step. They each had active social lives and the present arrangement suited them fine but, if things were going to get dangerous, then this may be the opportune moment both needed to spur them into action.

"That villa in Spain looks more attractive the more I think about it," said Susan as she and Craig raised their wine glasses in a toast before leaving the restaurant and making their way to their room.

Chapter Thirty-seven

Rahul Dixit arrived at Heathrow Airport after a non-stop flight from Delhi and made his way through the arrivals hall to the waiting taxis outside. He got into a black cab and gave the driver directions to his penthouse flat in London's Docklands. He had spent most of the flight to England finalising a major tender and was looking forward to a relaxing evening before what he knew would be a most difficult meeting the following day with David Fairfax and his senior accountants. Sometimes he regretted his base in England was so close to the Fairfax Building in Canary Wharf but at other times he acknowledged that it did make his life easier.

* * * * *

It was a few minutes after midnight on a combined industrial estate and science park on the outskirts of Cambridge and a figure in black was dragging what looked like a body out of the emergency exit of a large factory complex. The figure placed the body in the back of a parked van and returned to the factory. Twenty minutes later the figure emerged from the building, made its way to a dark-coloured car parked in a secluded spot nearby, and drove off almost silently into the night.

Suddenly, about an hour later, there was a series of small explosions followed by a large fireball that rocketed into the air and lit up the pitch-black night sky.

* * * * *

Rahul Dixit woke at six thirty and opened the curtains. He looked down at the Thames stretched out below him. As the first of the sun's rays played on the almost still waters hinting at the colour and warmth to come he was reminded for a brief moment of the River Ganges, the river that was most holy to all Hindus. He quickly regained his thoughts and went over the tender papers once more before having a quick breakfast of cereal and toast. He was a frugal eater at the best of times and tried hard when he was away from India not to over-indulge. He was a firm believer in moderation and self-control, not just in eating but in all aspects of life.

But Rahul was troubled, not so much by the tender but by another matter. He had been unhappy for sometime at the direction the business was taking and he was becoming increasingly unhappy with David Fairfax's behaviour and attitude. He was considering resigning as the Managing Director of Fairfax Telecoms.

Rahul was the first to admit that in the past he had not exactly been a saint but felt that over the last few years he had atoned for his previous conduct and he now wanted to lead a more reflective life. He had calculated that he could give up working for the Fairfax Group and still be able to support his current lifestyle in

India by drawing on the considerable savings he had managed to accumulate from his eight or nine years of very profitable working for David Fairfax. This would give him the opportunity to lead a more contemplative life with his wife Sunaina away from the hustle and bustle of everyday cares and worries.

* * * * *

When Rahul arrived at the Fairfax Building he met Susan Rumble in the reception area and they went up to David Fairfax's office on the third floor together. David was already there sitting at his large circular meeting table poring over some papers. Angela Hamilton and three of Susan's chief accountants were also seated at the table.

"You two are late!" snapped David, "No wonder standards are slipping everywhere I look nowadays."

"Didn't even bother to ask if I had a good flight," thought Rahul to himself as he took a seat between David and Angela, "He gets ruder by the minute."

"So, let's see what you've got to tell us," enquired David, "We need to be very careful with this tender. Even for us this is a major contract and if we can secure this one there'll be plenty more to follow. Orders have been down over the last six months and we've got capacity at the factory to start work immediately. I think we can afford to just about break even on this one and look to future spin-offs to make the really big money."

"My thinking exactly," said Rahul eagerly, "I've priced this as low as we can go without making a loss."

"Excellent," replied a smiling David, "a small sacrifice to enable us to reel in the big fish later."

Just then one of Angela's staff opened the door and peered in rather nervously before catching her attention. Angela appeared most displeased at this interruption and reluctantly got out of her seat and left the office.

David caught a trace of her perfume as she brushed past him and immediately thought to himself that he must resume his attempts to get closer to her. In the past she had dropped hints but whenever he responded nothing had resulted as she always changed the subject. As he was thinking about how he could try and seduce her Angela returned to the room looking very worried.

"What is it?" he asked.

"This talk about tenders may be academic. That was the police on the phone. There's been a fire and an explosion at our electronics factory on the Cambridge science park."

"What!" roared David standing up so violently that his chair tipped over and his papers spilled onto the floor, "Fire, an explosion? I thought those days were over. So our saboteur is back in business is he? And at the very moment we're due to submit our tender!"

There was complete silence in the room. Nobody dared say a single word or move a muscle. They were scared of provoking a reaction from David. They had seen him in this mood before and knew just how dangerous he could be.

Angela broke the uneasy silence, "Inspector Westwood has been liaising with the local police and is on his way here now. He should be here shortly."

"Out!" shouted David at the top of his voice, "Get out now! Not you Angela, not you Susan and certainly not you Rahul. You others, out now!"

The three accountants were glad to be given their marching orders and almost ran out of the room in their haste not to incur David Fairfax's wrath.

"I thought we had seen the last of our fire-bomber. This could ruin our electronics and telecoms business. It could spell the end for Fairfax Telecoms. I've got to find out who's behind this." and David was silent for a while before continuing, "Susan, when those tenders go forward tomorrow let me know if there's one from the Anne Harvey Group, James Palmer seems to think there may be some connection there," he then turned to Angela, "Get James Palmer over here right now, I want a word with him."

Angela left the room and was about to make the call from her office when she saw Inspector Westwood with James Palmer emerging from the lift.

"Inspector," she said quietly, "and James, you're here sooner than we expected. Please follow me, Sir David is expecting you," and she led the way to David Fairfax's office.

David looked up in surprise when he saw James enter the office behind the inspector, "Good morning Inspector," but before he could say another word Inspector Westwood answered the anticipated question.

"I thought it would be beneficial to bring James along as he's closely involved with your affairs. Besides, it was on my way here."

David Fairfax knew James' house wasn't on the inspector's route to Canary Wharf at all but he remained silent before asking, "What happened at Cambridge? Do you think it's the work of the same person who attacked my premises in Witham and the farm at Latchingdon?"

"Undoubtedly," replied the inspector without any hesitation, "the forensic boys have already found fragments of the incendiary devices and they're identical to the ones used to start the other fires. I'm afraid there's not much left of the factory complex, it's been almost completely razed to the ground."

The inspector paused before adding, "Oh, and one more thing that clinches it. We found these placed outside the entrance to the factory," and he produced a sealed evidence bag containing a DesboroDenim carrier bag and some underwear and placed it on the table in front of David Fairfax.

"Don't open it!" Inspector Westwood said sternly as David held the bag up, "The boys at the lab will want to have a close look at that just in case there are any prints or other clues."

"What about the night watchman?" enquired David as he remembered security had been increased at all his properties after the previous incidents, "Surely somebody was there keeping an eye on the factory?"

"There was, but he was chloroformed. We found him unconscious in the back of his van in the factory's car park. He's been taken to hospital but is expected to be discharged later today."

David's immediate thoughts were that the man would have to be punished but he soon changed his mind as he realised he had been attacked while doing his duty and hadn't neglected it as had been the case with the fires at Witham and Latchingdon.

"Oh," responded David, "I'm glad he'll be all right. Are there any clues as to who may have done this?"

"As I said the forensic boys are still at the scene so they might turn up something but at the moment it looks like we're out of luck. Once again we have the underwear and the old DesboroDenim carrier bag left at the scene – you've no idea what the significance of these might be? Could it be some sort of message?"

"I've no idea what that underwear is supposed to signify. If I knew that I'd know who was behind this.

James thinks it's to do with my past but I've thought long and hard about this and I can't come up with any ideas at all."

"I take it you were at home all last night?"

"Yes I was," replied an indignant David Fairfax, "and before you ask so were Lucy and Callisto!"

"Just routine," said the inspector before adding, "I'll let you know if we come up with any leads," and without further word he plucked the evidence bag from David's grasp and left the room.

"I'll keep an eye on the police investigation and let you know if anything comes up," James added and turned to leave the room.

"Just a minute! Where do you think you're going?" snarled an angry David, "It's not just the fire it's the contracts. You and that inspector don't realise that today is the deadline for submitting tenders for some large contracts we expected to win. We can't bid now because we've no longer got the manufacturing capacity. I think the Anne Harvey group may be behind this in some way. Susan is going to let me know tomorrow if they submit a bid and, if they do, whether or not it's successful. If they do get that contract then it will confirm your suspicions. You told me you were going to find out more about Anne Harvey and that empire of hers. Well see to it that you do, and quickly! You can go now. There's no better time to make a start than right now!"

James Palmer left the room without responding or looking back and hurried to catch up with Inspector Westwood.

David Fairfax sat thinking for a while as Rahul, Susan and Angela sat in silence fearing what was to happen next. Suddenly he looked up and said in a high-pitched voice, "You can all go now. I want time to think in peace."

Susan and Angela got up and walked towards the door. David stared at Rahul as he made no attempt whatsoever to get up from his chair, "What's the matter with you? Didn't you hear what I said?"

"I heard you," replied Rahul quietly once the women had left the room, "but there's something I must tell you. I want to resign from my position as Managing Director of Fairfax Telecoms. I've no intention of setting up in business against you. My aim is simply to retire so that I can spend my time in contemplation and religious study."

This took David by complete surprise. He had always considered Rahul to be one of his most loyal lieutenants but he managed to suppress his shock, "This is all a bit sudden. I need time to think, time to think about you and time to think about rebuilding the business. That fire has to all intents and purposes ruined the UK side of the business. There's really only the India subdivision left and it would make sense for you to run that – from India if that would help, you wouldn't have to make frequent trips to England as you do now."

Rahul thought for a moment before stressing, "There really is no way you can make me change my decision. My mind is made up."

"Look, at least think about it. Take a couple of days to think it over. Return to India if that would be better for you but I really do want you to continue to run things over there."

"Ok," replied Rahul, "I'll go back to India and let you know my decision in a few days time."

When Rahul had gone David buzzed the intercom, "Angela, can you come in my office for a moment please."

Angela returned and sat opposite him with her notebook at the ready. David smiled and said, "Angela, have a word with Alan Box. I want him to get someone to go through the archives and see if there are any records of DesboroDenim stock being sold off or disposed of in the past to individuals or charity shops or that sort of thing. Also see if any old stock has been sold off to anybody in the last three or four years. Tell him if he finds anything of interest to let James Palmer know – and me as well, of course."

"Very good, Sir David."

"And there's one other thing you should know. Rahul has told me he wants to resign, not just as Managing Director of Fairfax Telecoms, but also from the India side of the business. He wants nothing more to do with the telecoms industry. I think you know I can't allow that to happen."

"What do you want me to do?"

"Nothing, well nothing at the moment, let's see how things turn out. But there is something you should know about him and his past, something that may enable us to get him to change his mind. After all, everyone has secrets, secrets they would prefer to leave *buried* in the past," and David stressed the word 'buried'.

David Fairfax then leaned forward in his chair and spoke to Angela in almost hushed tones as if he was frightened someone would hear what he had to say, "So," he said finally, "you may well have to go to India to do a little 'arm-twisting' on my behalf."

Chapter Thirty-eight

"At last," sighed a relieved James Palmer, "I've finished ploughing through all that literature we got from Martin Travers about the Anne Harvey Group. What's surprising is that there's quite a lot about Anne Harvey herself. As we know she was born in that little town of East Deben, went to primary school there and won a scholarship to Ipswich Grammar School. It looks like she was a bright pupil and passed three 'A' Levels in Chemistry, Physics and Mathematics. What's surprising is that she then went to Cambridge and obtained degrees in two totally different subjects, one in Economics and one in Business Management. Then for reasons known only to her she stayed there and got post-grad qualifications in Global Business Management, Macro Economics and World Trade."

"A very mixed bag indeed," replied Jenny thoughtfully, "but very handy now she's heading an international group of companies."

"Yes, and she looks the part too, a very confident young lady. How's it going then? Have you logged onto that website?"

"It's just coming up now, Friends Reunited. Here we are, now let's see," said Jenny as she paused to do a mental calculation, "Anne Harvey would have left Ipswich Grammar in the summer of 1994 when she was 18 years old."

"Left school in 1994! Makes me feel old," joked James.

"Looking down the list of leavers for that year there's no mention of Anne Harvey. Perhaps she can't be bothered to keep in touch with her old school friends or is just too busy."

"Are there any photographs that she might be in?"

"Just looking now," and after a minute or so Jenny added, "No, none at all but there is a photograph of her headmistress, a Mrs. Goodenough. It says she retired from the school about two years ago."

"It might be worth going to see her. She might remember Anne and be able to shed some light on her background. Does it say where she retired to?"

"Yes, and we're in luck, she lives in Kirton and seems to encourage her former pupils to keep in touch with her. She's quite open about her address and telephone number and welcomes contact from them."

"Where's Kirton?"

"Surely you remember, it's a little village a couple of miles outside Felixstowe on the road from Ipswich. We passed through it when we went to Woodbridge a few years ago."

"Ah yes, I remember it now. Looks like another trip out for one of us then."

"I'd like to do this one," said Jenny enthusiastically, "I could pose as a journalist doing an article on Anne Harvey as part of a series on successful businesswomen."

"And use one of those fake IDs my mate on 'Business Today' magazine had made up for us? I've always wanted to be the first to do that!"

"Well you won't be," said Jenny playfully, "this is one time where I can be the trail blazer for a change. I'm going to phone Mrs Goodenough and see if it would be convenient to go and see her tomorrow. What will you be doing? Have you got any plans?"

"As a matter of fact I have," James smiled rather mysteriously, "I'm going back to East Deben to see if I can find out anything more about Dawn Fairfax's death or any information about Anne Harvey's parents and her childhood. I think I'll start off in that pub. What was it called now? The Bull Hotel, that's it!"

"Any excuse for a drink!"

"No, I'm really hoping to meet John Harwood again. I wish we'd got his address or telephone number when we met him. He's lived in that town all his life so he's bound to have known the Harveys or known of them. He might even know the illusive Doctor Greg Smith."

"Still seems a long way to go for a drink to me. Never mind let's see what tomorrow brings. Let's see who can find out the most and get us closer to solving this case and getting that nice fat bonus from the charming David Fairfax," concluded Jenny, and then with a broad smile added, "The loser cooks dinner."

"You're on," agreed James with an equally broad smile on his face.

Chapter Thirty-nine

Jenny Palmer had arranged to meet Mrs Goodenough at her home in Kirton at eleven o'clock so she and James had to leave their house in North Weald by nine-thirty. This time it was Jenny's turn to have the Focus forcing James to take the Fiesta.

James followed Jenny along the A12 until just before reaching Ipswich when Jenny turned right and he turned left. Once again the drive to Ipswich had been characterised by lots of lorries on the road and also by poor visibility. Although it was late March the weather was cold and very overcast and there was a strengthening wind blowing up from the east. James looked ahead to the car in front of him and Jenny put a hand up and waved him goodbye as she continued round the roundabout and he turned left. He acknowledged with a flash of his headlights and took the slip road onto the A14.

Jenny soon reached the village of Kirton and found Rectory Lane without too much trouble. She had reasoned correctly that it must be near the church and had used that ancient focal point of many small communities as a landmark. Mrs Goodenough lived in a small detached bungalow surrounded by tall poplar trees and Jenny parked her car in the road and walked up the short drive. She approached the front door and as she went to ring the bell the door opened as if of its own accord.

"Mrs Palmer?" enquired a rather rotund and jolly-looking woman in her sixties, "I'm Nancy Goodenough, please come in."

"Jenny Palmer," responded Jenny with a smile, and went into the bungalow showing her ID card, "very pleased to meet you."

Mrs Goodenough showed Jenny into a room that had walls covered in photographs and other memorabilia from Mrs Goodenough's days as a teacher and beckoned to her to sit down.

"This room is simply amazing," said Jenny looking around, "most impressive."

"The academic world was my life, I knew no other. I like to be reminded of all the happy years I spent in education trying to impart a grain of knowledge into all those unwilling souls that came my way. That's why I surround myself in memories, memories of pupils and the happy times they conjure up for me," and she paused briefly and added, "Before we start can I get you something to drink, tea or coffee?"

"Tea will be fine, thank you."

Jenny busied herself looking at the collection of photographs, some old and some modern, until Mrs Goodenough returned to the room.

"By the way," volunteered Mrs Goodenough, "please call me Nancy, let's not be too formal."

"Fine," replied Jenny, "Nancy it is, and I'm Jenny."

"Well, how can I help you?"

"As I said on the phone my magazine is running a series of articles on successful business women. How did they get to be where they are today, what makes them tick, what are their hobbies and interests. But we're also trying to add a bit of depth and character and in addition to interviewing them in person we're also speaking to people who influenced them at key times in their lives or who had some impact on how they developed. And you are one such person. As Anne Harvey's headmistress throughout the time she was at secondary school you are in a unique position to give us an insight into what she was like at school, what subjects she excelled in and anything else that you think might be relevant."

"I remember Anne very well. She was a very bright pupil, some would say almost gifted until that term was considered not to be politically correct. She was at Ipswich Grammar for seven years from the age of eleven right up to eighteen when she left to go to Cambridge. I never had any doubts about her abilities and it's no surprise to me that she's done so very well since leaving university. She wasn't just academically bright you know she was also good at games. She represented the school at a number of field sports but she also held black belts in judo and karate and for a time was the school captain at those events. For a slightly-built girl she had plenty of stamina and could certainly pack a punch."

Nancy paused to sip a few mouthfuls of tea and handed a plate of biscuits to Jenny who politely declined.

"I don't think I ever remember Anne getting into any serious trouble. She worked hard but I suppose she had her moments like anybody else. Oh yes, she did have one particular hang-up, she insisted on her name being spelled correctly. Woe betide anyone, teachers included, who forgot to put an 'e' on her name. I think that's why for a time in her first and second years she was nicknamed 'Anne with an e', but it did the trick everyone quickly knew how to spell her name."

"Apart from her academic work and sports activities is there anything else that you can remember about her?"

"She became a prefect in the fifth year and during her time in the lower and upper sixth forms she was Deputy Head Girl. I must say she carried out her duties representing the school at outside events very well indeed."

Nancy thought for a while as she held a biscuit a couple of inches in front of her mouth before adding, "Acting, she liked to act. We used to put on a lot of plays for the parents and she really enjoyed taking part in those. Never had any trouble learning her lines either, not like some of them did. Just before Anne joined the school I lost my husband to cancer and it was a particularly difficult time for me. So I involved myself in a lot of extra-curricular activities, including the school drama society, as a way of escaping from reality I suppose," and Nancy stared longingly at a photograph of her and her husband on a facing wall.

"I'm sorry," said Jenny.

"It's many years ago now but I still miss him," and she paused, "but where were we? Ah yes, the drama society. Anne absolutely excelled in a range of parts and at one time I thought she might go on to become an actress but I think her parents discouraged her from pursuing that career. She did like dressing up though and at times it was difficult to recognise her. She had a very close friend, I can't recall her name, but when they dressed up for a part and put makeup on you couldn't tell them apart. Strange, because they didn't really look alike in real life. Now what was that girl's name?" and Nancy sat silently staring at the photographs that filled the walls.

"I'm sure it'll come to you," encouraged Jenny as she finished her tea.

"Got it!" exclaimed Nancy, "That other girl, that great friend of Anne Harvey, her name was Angela Hamilton."

* * * * *

James Palmer was relieved when he arrived at East Deben. The final few miles had been along rather tortuous roads and there was now a fine drizzle in the air which was being blown inland on the very strong easterly winds. He drove up to The Bull Hotel and decided to have a quick pint before embarking on his walk along the cliffs. He had hoped John Harwood would have been there but the bar was empty.

Half an hour later James left the pub. He buttoned up his coat, raised the hood, put his gloves on and strode along to where the cliff-top path began. He walked purposely for about a mile along the cliff tops and began to regret his decision to come to East Deben as the wind was both strong and bitterly cold and the fine drizzle was fast turning to rain. He looked down at the waves breaking on the rocks far below with an incessant roar and thought about the night Dawn Fairfax had died. How much more frightening must it have been to be up here in the dark with a raging gale all around. He turned to make his way back to the pub and in the distance could just make out the figure of a man and a little dog coming towards him.

As the figure came closer he was pleased to see that it was indeed John Harwood.

"Nice to see you again James," said a very breathless John who, despite the heavy winter clothes he was wearing, recognised James from their previous meeting, "You're the last person I'd have expected to meet up here on a day like today. Must be something important."

"Not really. Jenny's in Kirton today so I thought I'd come back to East Deben and see if I could shed any light on Dawn Fairfax's death."

"Glad you did," replied John struggling to get the lead on his dog, "I enjoyed our conversation last time but never imagined you'd come back here again especially in this weather. I almost didn't come up on the cliffs myself today because of the look of the weather. Let's go to the pub. It's nice and cosy there and we can have another little chat about old times."

"I was rather hoping you'd say that," agreed James, and the two of them made their way to The Bull Hotel through the now very strong almost gale-force winds and driving rain.

James bought the first round of drinks, "After this one it's nothing but shandy for me. Mustn't forget I've got a long drive back home. If the weather doesn't improve then I certainly won't leave it too late."

"Very sensible. Even though it's the end of March the weather here can be quite treacherous. So," John said after making sure his dog was comfortable under an adjoining table, "how can I help you?"

"Since we last met I've been looking at Dawn Fairfax's inquest papers and there are one or two people I'd like some information on, if you can recall them that is."

"I'll do my best. East Deben is still a small place so I should be able to help you. Who do you want to know about?"

"Doctor Smith, Doctor Greg Smith, what can you tell me about him?"

"Doctor Smith? He was one of the best doctors this town ever had. He was my family GP and I was very sad when he died. About twelve or thirteen years ago now just after he reached 65 years of age. He worked hard all his life and then a few months after he officially retired he died of a heart attack. Most of his patients simply couldn't believe it."

"Did he have a family? A wife or children?"

"No he didn't. He came here in the mid-1970s I think it was. Before that he'd been a medical officer in the armed forces. He never said which branch of the services but I got the impression it was the Royal Marines or something similar. He was certainly a very fit and active person and liked going on all sorts of activity and adventure holidays. He often admitted he'd liked to have had a family but his early life in the forces just didn't give him the opportunity to meet someone and settle down. Sad really, because I think he'd have made a very good family man."

"Did he have any hobbies that got him out in the wider community or was there anyone he was particularly on good terms with?"

"I'm not sure what hobbies he had but I do know he liked to go fishing. Not angling on the river or anything like that but sea fishing. He liked to be out on the waves and as he often used to put it, get closer to nature. There was a time in the latter part of the 1970s I think it was when he would often go out with Chris Harvey on his fishing boat. Sometimes they'd be gone for days at a time until they had a full catch."

CHAPTER THIRTY-NINE

"Chris Harvey? Would that be Anne Harvey's father by any chance?"

"That's right. At that time he was one of many small fishermen in the town trying to earn a living in the midst of the so-called 'Cod War' with Iceland and increasing restrictions or quotas imposed by successive governments. Your glass is empty," said John suddenly changing the subject, "let me get you another drink."

"A shandy mind, nothing stronger."

John's dog looked up nervously as its owner went towards the bar but settled down again when it realised they weren't going out to brave the elements just yet. James sat at the table and looked around the deserted bar. He could hardly wait for John to return and resume his account of Doctor Smith and Chris Harvey.

"Where was I?" said John as he returned to his seat opposite James, "Ah yes, Doctor Smith and Chris Harvey. Doctor Smith enjoyed his fishing trips and whenever he could he would join Chris Harvey on his fishing boat. It was also rumoured, and I have no way of knowing if this is true or not, that in order to get round government restrictions on the amount of fish that could be landed legally Chris Harvey would often go out after dark and indulge in a bit of illegal fishing. There would have been plenty of opportunities around here at that time for offloading any such contraband fish. Knowing Doctor Smith as I did I have no doubt he joined Chris Harvey on these illicit nocturnal activities.

It would be just the sort of thing that would appeal to his adventurous nature."

"Did you know it was Doctor Smith and Chris Harvey who found Dawn Fairfax's body washed up on the shore?"

"Yes, I remember it well. Her body was found on the beach at North Deben a small village a few miles up the coast from here. It was big news at the time. Doctor Smith was in the papers a lot over that incident as he was also the local police surgeon and it was he, I believe, who conducted the post-mortem on Dawn Fairfax."

"Really!" exclaimed James Palmer in astonishment.

* * * * *

"Angela Hamilton!" said Jenny struggling to contain her excitement at the possibility of establishing a tentative link between the Fairfax Empire and the Anne Harvey Group, "Angela Hamilton!"

"Are you all right, Jenny?" asked a concerned Nancy Goodenough trying to fathom out why the mention of Angela Hamilton's name should have provoked this surprised reaction."

Jenny immediately realised that she had to regain her composure and suppress her feelings or she might give away her real reason for coming to see Mrs Goodenough.

"Sorry, Nancy," she replied with a smile on her face while attempting to regain control of her emotions, "It's just that it's a co-incidence that's all. Would you believe that I'm also researching a high-flier in the David Fairfax Group and her name is Angela Hamilton. What are the chances of that happening?" and she paused before continuing, "Can you tell me anything about her?"

"Not much to tell really. She was in the same year as Anne Harvey and although they went around together she was nowhere near as bright or as academically able as Anne. I can't recall much more about her so I must reluctantly conclude she wasn't one of my better pupils or one of my, how can I say it, lesser achievers. It's a sad fact but for most teachers the majority of pupils simply pass you by. It's only the very good or the very bad that you remember with any clarity."

"Well, Nancy, you've been very helpful and I'd like to say how much I've enjoyed our little chat today. It's not often a journalist says that."

"But before you go I have to ask you about Angela Hamilton," said a rather confused-looking Nancy, "I think you must have made a mistake. Angela Hamilton is dead!"

"Dead! What do you mean, dead? I've seen her! She's alive and well, and working as a top-flight personal assistant."

"Then it must be a different Angela Hamilton. The Angela Hamilton who went to school with Anne Harvey was killed in a car crash soon after she passed her driving test. I remember it as if it were yesterday, a tragedy and a sad loss of life."

Jenny was stunned by this revelation and struggled not to show it in front of Mrs Goodenough, "You're right, of course," she responded hesitantly, "it must be a different Angela Hamilton. Simply a matter of co-incidence, nothing more than that."

"If that's all," and Mrs Goodenough showed Jenny to the door. She watched from behind lace curtains as Jenny walked down the driveway and was soon lost behind the trees. After a few minutes she heard the sound of a car as Jenny drove out of Rectory Lane and onto the road to Ipswich.

* * * * *

"So you're telling me that Doctor Smith was the police surgeon here as well as a local GP?"

"That's right," acknowledged John Harwood, "he was a very active person in the community, both in terms of his professional work and his voluntary work."

"What can you tell me about Chris Harvey?" enquired James Palmer.

"As I said before, Chris was one of many local fishermen based here in East Deben but, as the fishing quotas became ever-more severe, most of his rivals accepted the compensation offered by the government and left the industry. Chris was different and determined to carry on fishing. He said it was his life and as others left he gradually built up his business, not just fishing but he seized the opportunity to expand into processing and canning as well. Coupled with his undoubted illegal night fishing his business took off and he became very rich indeed."

"Very interesting. Did he have a large family? I know he had one daughter, Anne, but were there any other children?"

"That's the sad part of it. For many years Chris and his wife Elaine made no secret of the fact that they wanted to have a large family but somehow Elaine was unable to conceive. They sought help from Doctor Smith and he referred them to a clinic in Ipswich. I forget the name but it's the one that's attached to the hospital there. About two years later Anne was born but that was the only child they had. They wanted more but it wasn't to be."

"And Elaine, Chris Harvey's wife, is she still alive?"

"I'm afraid not. She died when Anne was in her early teens I think it was, so Anne was brought up by her father."

"Do you recall much about Anne?"

"No, not really, she went to the local school here until she was eleven but then I think she passed the eleven-plus or some-such examination and went to

Ipswich Grammar School. I remember on my way to work often seeing her and some of the other pupils at the bus-stop in the mornings. Now of course I hear she's done very well for herself."

John sat staring at his beer glass for a while and then added, "It was only when her father became seriously ill that she came back to live here. Before that she hardly ever visited the place. When he died, of course, she took over the business and since then it has gone from strength to strength. Poor old Chris would hardly recognise it now."

"By all accounts," responded James, "Anne Harvey is not only a successful businesswoman but also very rich."

"That's all right for some but I don't think I would want to change my lifestyle just now, I wouldn't know what to do with all that money."

"Quite," agreed James glancing at his watch, "Look at the time, I really must be going. Looks like it's still blowing up very nasty out there. Can I give you a lift?"

"That would be very kind of you, but it would take you a bit out of your way as I don't live on the main road back to Ipswich."

"Don't worry about that. A lift home is the least I can do. I've enjoyed our little chat and you've been most helpful. Here," said James remembering what he should have done the last time he met John, "take my card. If you remember anything else about the night Dawn Fairfax plunged to her death or anything more about the Harvey family or Doctor Smith, then please call me. And I mean anything, no matter how unimportant or trivial it may seem to you, please call me."

James Palmer dropped John Harwood and his dog outside his house. He declined John's offer of going inside to meet his wife and have a cup of tea with them and drove back through East Deben and headed towards the A14 and the road to Ipswich.

It seemed a very long drive back to North Weald in the strong wind and rain and the poor visibility but it meant James had more than enough time to reflect on what John had told him and what it may mean in terms of getting to the bottom of this case.

"I've definitely made some progress here," he thought to himself, "I wonder how Jenny got on. And just as importantly," he mused, "who will end up cooking the dinner tonight?"

Chapter Forty

It took James Palmer over two hours to drive home from East Deben in the rain and near gale-force winds. With very poor visibility and many lorries on the A12 that leg of his journey was a nightmare. It was with some relief when he turned onto his driveway and saw Jenny's car already parked there. "Thank goodness," he thought to himself, "Jenny has got home safely."

James let himself in the front door and hung up his still-wet coat on a hook in the hall as Jenny leapt out of the lounge to greet him, "You're back," she said with great enthusiasm, "and have I got some news for you. I think you'll be cooking the dinner tonight. And before you do anything else you can take that coat and put it in the utility room to dry. I don't want it dripping all over the carpet."

"Very good, dear," he replied sarcastically, "but I think it's you who'll be doing the cooking."

James reluctantly took his coat to the utility room and returned to the lounge where Jenny had made a cup of tea for him.

"Here," she said, "get this inside you, it'll warm you up a bit. So, who's going to go first?"

"You," replied James immediately, "did you find out anything interesting from Mrs Goodenough?"

"You'll be surprised," exclaimed Jenny with a hint of mystery and hardly able to contain herself as she continued, "but the most interesting thing wasn't about Anne Harvey at all," and she related to James in some detail the information she had learnt about Anne Harvey's school days. She highlighted her academic achievements and her prowess at sports and games and her penchant for acting and dressing up.

"Well that's hardly earth-shattering," responded James, "what else did you find out?"

"You'll never believe this but who do you think was at Ipswich Grammar School with Anne Harvey and acted regularly with her in the plays. Someone who, according to Mrs Goodenough, when they were both in costume and had make-up on you couldn't tell them apart?"

James pretended to think for a little while and then said with a wry smile on his face, "I don't know, who?"

"Angela Hamilton!"

"Angela Hamilton!" repeated James in almost sheer disbelief, "Are you sure?"

"There's no doubt about it but here's the catch. Mrs Goodenough says Angela Hamilton is dead. She was killed shortly after passing her driving test. She didn't say this but I think it was after Anne and Angela had left school."

"That's most interesting," agreed James, "we'll have to do some research into our Angela Hamilton. There could be more than meets the eye with 'Miss Super-efficient' as I'm beginning to call her. The name could just be a co-incidence of course but there might be something more to it."

"So, do I win and you cook the dinner?"

"Certainly not! You haven't heard how I got on yet. Guess who I met on the cliffs near East Deben?"

"John Harwood!" exclaimed Jenny playfully, taking the opportunity to pull a face at her husband, "And his dog of course."

"You've spoiled it now," he moaned, "but I didn't brave all that wind and rain for nothing because he did have some very interesting things to say," and James then outlined the main points to have emerged from his discussion with John Harwood.

"Very interesting I'm sure," said Jenny, "so we've established that Doctor Smith and Chris Harvey were close friends and often went fishing together on Chris Harvey's boat. It was they who found Dawn Fairfax's body on the beach at North Deben a couple of days after she went over the cliffs at East Deben and it was Doctor Smith who conducted the official post-mortem examination. This is all very cosy indeed. But there's still no sign of a link to David Fairfax. If you'd established that then I would willingly cook dinner but as you haven't then I think it's your turn."

"Just wait a minute," implored James, "you've overlooked one small fact that goes almost unnoticed. It's only after the illness and subsequent death of her father that Anne Harvey returns full-time to the family home. It's only then that she expands the business into other areas and goes into direct competition against the Fairfax Group. Why does she do that? Why pit yourself against a much bigger rival with all the potential that gives for failure and bankruptcy? I think her father told her something about David Fairfax. I don't know what it was but I'm sure it was something so significant that it set Anne on her quest to outbid the Fairfax Group at all costs and ruin them."

"Well done! Perhaps there is a tenuous link there. It's certainly worth trying to find out what it is. Tell you what let's call it a truce," said Jenny cuddling up to her husband, "I'll do the cooking and you can do the washing up!"

"It's a deal," agreed James, "I must say I'm feeling rather peckish after all this exertion today," and he and Jenny made their way to the kitchen hand in hand.

Chapter Forty-one

Nick's death affected the Fairfax household in different ways. David quickly appeared to get over the initial shock, especially after Vic Bolton met with his 'accident', by totally immersing himself in the business. His director colleagues did notice though that he showed more caution than previously and was unwilling to take any risks that could bring him into conflict with the law.

On the other hand Lucy turned into a virtual recluse and seldom left the house although after a little while she began to have a few close friends come round to visit her.

Callisto, always the most enigmatic of the family, was at first visibly shocked by Nick's death but regained her normal composure after a few weeks and appeared to shrug it off. So much so that she even gave her minder the slip on a couple of occasions to go out with her friends. For this behaviour she was severely taken to task by both her father and Feb.

About three weeks after Nick's death the coroner released the body and arrangements were made for the funeral to take place at Harlow Crematorium. This was altogether a different funeral to his brother Tom's. Gone were David Fairfax's former parliamentary and ministerial colleagues as it was now too risky politically to be associated with a family caught up in two gruesome murders. In their place were large numbers of people who had known Nick and who wanted to say a last farewell to him. So many that they couldn't all be accommodated inside the building and the service had to be relayed outside by loudspeaker.

The Fairfax Group was represented by Alan Box, Ken Winter and Craig Bentley but Rahul Dixit chose to stay away and did not return from India, a decision that greatly angered David Fairfax. Susan Rumble and Angela Hamilton were also there as were Inspector Westwood and James and Jenny Palmer.

Sergeant Benson was on duty at the entrance to the crematorium checking the identity of all those wishing to attend and both plain clothes and uniformed officers were present in the grounds. As before all wreaths and floral tributes were carefully examined and as anticipated by Inspector Westwood and James Palmer once again there was an anonymous wreath. This time the card had two old-style 'DesboroDenim' motifs printed on it rather than the single motif found on the card at Tom's funeral but the message was the same.

During the service readings were made by John Burling and Terry Kingston and, surprisingly, a very touching and humorous account of Nick's life and times was given by Callisto. It was then the turn of the vicar of Theydon Bois and he chose to speak about faith.

"We are gathered here today to mark the passing of Nick Fairfax who was cut down in the prime of his life. A young man who we have just heard from his family and friends enjoyed life to the full. A young man who was very popular and who had everything to live for. A young man who was still mourning for his brother Tom but, above all, a young man who was a son and a brother to David, Lucy and Callisto."

The vicar paused before continuing, "These two deaths, most unexpected in both their timing and ferocity, are a test to each and every one of us here today, a test of our faith. At times such as these it is easy to lose faith and claim that there is no God because, if there is a God, surely he would not let such things happen. So, what is faith? What do we mean by faith? Well, faith, faith as a schoolboy once said, faith is believing in something when you know it isn't true. But is religion really like that, just a fairytale to cheer us all up? Listen to these words from …"

But David Fairfax was no longer listening to the vicar's words. His mind was wandering as he thought, "What does that silly old fool think he's bumbling on about? Faith as far as I'm concerned is trusting and believing in yourself and nobody else," and he looked up as a shaft of sunlight suddenly streamed in through the stained glass window and shone directly on him, as if picking him out deliberately, "I'll show him and everyone else what I think faith is when I find out who's doing all this," and he forced himself back to reality and the vicar's words once again.

"So finally I would like to say a few words about the future and what may await us all," and the vicar paused for maximum effect before continuing, "because nobody knows when the future or fate is set to intervene. Today those who are strong can become weak so easily tomorrow, and those who are weak today can in turn become strong tomorrow. Those who are rich today can just as easily become penniless tomorrow, and those who are in poverty today can become rich tomorrow. Therefore, my friends, don't boast about your future prospects, your wealth, strength and even your intellect or take them for granted, because who knows what tomorrow may bring. Always be on your guard and always be wary of the future. You never know when fate will take you in its vice-like embrace and twist your very life into a wholly new and unanticipated direction."

All those present thought the vicar's closing remarks to be very strange indeed and in some way aimed at David Fairfax personally. For David Fairfax himself this was just further confirmation that the vicar had lost the plot and didn't know what he was talking about.

At the conclusion of the service David was the first to stand up and quickly led Lucy outside into the early-April sunshine. As if to pass judgement on the service he pointedly refused to shake hands with the vicar.

As James and Jenny Palmer were walking back to their car Inspector Westwood made a point of catching them up.

"Sergeant Benson has just returned from doing the rounds of the florists' shops in Epping. He's found out that the anonymous wreath with the two DesboroDenim logos was ordered yesterday by a girl who the shop assistant thinks was no older that twelve or thirteen and paid for in cash."

"A young girl?" said a puzzled Jenny.

"Yes," replied Inspector Westwood, "it's a pretty standard method in cases where someone wants to send something and not reveal their identity. They wait outside the shop and give a passing youngster a few quid to go inside and do the ordering for them. That way there's no chance of getting a description of the person from the shop assistant and the chances of tracking down the youngster involved are almost zero. I'm afraid we won't get any leads there to the identity of our murderer."

"Very clever! Well it was worth a try," said James as he and Jenny got into their car for the drive to Forest Glade.

James and Jenny didn't really want to go back to Forest Glade but as Inspector Westwood was going James felt he should be there in case of any developments.

Once again the catering for the wake was provided by Colin Rust and as usual he was accompanied by Susan Beattie and Linda Foster. Most of those present were friends of Nick and Tom and, despite their relatively young ages, the whole affair was very subdued. David Fairfax put in an appearance but Lucy complained of a headache and went to lie down in her room.

The representatives of the Fairfax Group all came back to the house but none of them stayed for longer than an hour, just sufficient time to ingratiate themselves with David Fairfax and prevent them from incurring his wrath. James and Jenny Palmer left soon afterwards.

Just as Angela Hamilton was departing David drew her to one side and said in a most unpleasant tone, "Did you notice how Rahul Dixit couldn't even be bothered to come to the funeral? Damn cheek! He's going to pay for this. Besides, he hasn't come back to me yet to rescind his resignation. Fairfax Telecoms in this country is finished the fire bomber saw to that, but there's still plenty of money to be made in India. I'll be speaking to Rahul in the next day or so and if he doesn't change his mind you may have to go on that little trip to India we spoke about."

"Very good, Sir David," Angela replied with a smile, and left the room without further word.

Chapter Forty-two

The day following Nick's funeral James and Jenny Palmer were having a late breakfast when the telephone rang. James got up and went into the hall.

"Hello, James Palmer."

"Hello Mr Palmer, it's Alan Box here. I hope I'm not calling at an inconvenient moment."

"No, not at all. What can I do for you?"

"Sir David asked me to give you a call. A few days ago he asked me to check our records to see if the company had ever sold off any old 'DesboroDenim' stock in bulk, particularly old 1970s' stock that could be used by whoever is committing these murders and sabotage against the group. Even though I didn't recall it we did sell off a lot of outdated stuff in the early 1990s. There were three organisations that purchased the stock, The Tom Collier Retailing Group, First Fashions of Farnborough, and East Anglian Designs."

"Do you have inventories of what exactly was sold to these firms?"

"Unfortunately we don't. All I can tell you is that each consignment was fairly large and came to several thousand pounds."

"That's a pity because if we knew which firms had bought which garments it would narrow the search considerably."

"That may be academic anyway. I've had Susan Rumble's people check with Companies House and there are no records of any of these companies still trading, at least under those names."

"That is a shame. Still, hang on a minute while I get a pencil and paper and take down the last known addresses you have for those firms."

James put the phone down and as he turned round there was Jenny sporting a wide grin and holding a pencil and paper in her outstretched hand. James mouthed a silent thank you to her as he picked up the phone again, "Right, fire away, let me have those addresses," and he carefully wrote down the information from Alan Box.

"If I come across any other information that may be of use to you then I'll get in contact."

"That would be much appreciated. Thank you," and James replaced the receiver.

James and Jenny looked at the list of names and addresses, "I've not heard of any of them," said Jenny.

"I didn't think you would have. They were most probably wholesalers who sold the clothes on to cut-price shops or market traders as small lots. It's easier and faster I would imagine to off-load them that way."

"So it doesn't help us much then?"

"Not immediately, but you never know we may just come across one of the names," and after a pause James added, "Now what was our plan of action for the day before breakfast was so rudely interrupted?"

"If you remember we hadn't actually got as far as agreeing a plan," Jenny said with a sarcastic look on her face, "but did you want to follow up that revelation from Mrs Goodenough about Angela Hamilton, or should I say, *an Angela Hamilton*, having been killed in a car accident?"

"I most certainly do, that's got to be high on our list of priorities. I also want to do some digging into the business empire of Anne Harvey's father and just what areas it covered. There may be something significant there. And we mustn't forget Beverley Jenks, David Fairfax's second wife, I want to know more about her too."

"Quite a bit there to keep us occupied then."

"Certainly is! Oh, and before I forget, we must try and find out more about Chris Harvey and that doctor friend of his, Greg Smith. There must be a connection there somewhere to David Fairfax."

Chapter Forty-three

David Fairfax often thought he could see a little of himself in Angela Hamilton and freely admitted that he had become increasingly reliant on her. In the two or three years she had been his personal assistant she had proved instrumental on several occasions in clinching some very profitable deals. It also didn't seem to trouble her that some of those deals were, how did she phrase it? 'Not entirely legal.' In his view, therefore, she was uniquely qualified for the task of persuading Rahul Dixit to withdraw his resignation or, if that proved impossible, to warn him of the consequences!

* * * * *

For someone approaching thirty years of age Angela Hamilton very much looked the part of the successful business woman as she took her seat in the business class cabin of the aircraft. She was dressed in a very smart two-piece navy-blue pin-striped suit over a white blouse. As she walked slowly along the aisle carrying her briefcase and a small handbag she was conscious of many heads turning and following her progress all the way to her seat.

"If Sir David wants me to go to India to speak to Rahul then he's going to have to make it worth my while," she thought to herself soon after takeoff as she pressed the button on her armrest to call the flight attendant, "It's going to be no expense spared and champagne all the way on this flight. After all, if I'm going to do his dirty work, then it's only fair that he pays in full," and after thinking to herself for a few moments she added, "and he will, in time he most certainly will!"

* * * * *

David Fairfax had told Rahul in no uncertain terms over the telephone what he thought of him for not attending Nick's funeral. He had tried to bully and threaten him into not resigning but when it was obvious that he couldn't persuade him to change his mind he told him he was sending Angela out to discuss the matter with him. This worked in Angela's favour. When she got to Delhi she found Vinod, Rahul's driver, waiting to take her to Rahul's house. Initially she had thought of staying in a hotel in Delhi but, having debated with herself on the flight over, decided she would take up Rahul's offer and stay with him in 'Shanti Bhavan'.

Soon after she joined the Fairfax Group Angela had gone on a tour of India and had stayed at Rahul's house for nearly a week. She had proved to Rahul that she could keep a secret by not mentioning to David Fairfax or anyone else that he was married.

By the time Angela arrived at Rahul's house it was already evening and it was beginning to get dark and she was feeling very tired after nearly a day's travelling. Rahul and Sunaina greeted her warmly as soon as she entered the house. It was as if she was their long-lost daughter and Angela felt a little uneasy as she remembered the difficult task she had been given by David Fairfax.

"Angela, I'm most delighted to see you again," said Sunaina with obvious enthusiasm in perfect English, "It must be nearly two years now."

"Yes, that's right. Quite frankly I never thought I'd be coming back to India. As you know I enjoy travelling very much and rarely go back to a country more than once as there is just so much to see in this world but I suppose these are different circumstances. As you know I'm not here entirely of my own volition."

"Rahul's resignation you mean," Sunaina interrupted with a sad tone to her voice, "I wondered who they'd send. I didn't think for one moment that David Fairfax would have the courage of his convictions and come himself. But I'm glad it's you. I remember the happy times we had and how much we had in common last time you were here. I hope that whatever happens we will remain friends and that things will be civilised between us."

"You can count on it," interjected Rahul, "Angela is the soul of discretion. If I've learnt anything in my dealings with the Fairfax Group it's that she can be trusted where many others employed there cannot."

Angela smiled without making comment but she thought to herself, "If only you knew the truth."

"I have a suggestion," proposed Rahul, "It's obvious that Angela is tired from her journey and I, for one, don't wish to add to her discomfort. My suggestion, therefore, is that we put all thoughts of business out of our minds for tonight and enjoy the meal that Juhi and Smriti have prepared in Angela's honour. After that Angela can get an early night and we will all be fresh in the morning to discuss the situation."

Rahul's suggestion was eagerly taken up by Angela and after a very tasty traditional Indian meal she retired to her room for an early night.

Angela slept like a log in the massive double bed and was awakened just before nine o'clock by Simran who brought her a cup of tea and left it on a bedside table. Simran opened the curtains and the morning sunshine streamed in through the window illuminating the bedroom.

"Malik says to run you a hot bath and give you a massage," Simran said as she disappeared into the en-suite bathroom.

Angela took her time sipping the tea. When Simran left the room she got up and wandered into the bathroom. "Just as I remember it," she said to herself appreciating the grandeur and elegance of the room, "white marble and gold fittings," and she slipped out of her silk pyjamas and slid into the foaming hot bath.

After about half an hour Simran returned and gave Angela a full Indian massage. It was one of the most pleasurable and soothing experiences she had ever enjoyed and put her in a relaxing frame of mind for what could prove to be a difficult day ahead, "Just like Rahul," she thought to herself, "never leaves anything to chance, might as well do all he can to put me at ease."

It was nearly ten-thirty, when Angela wearing a traditional two-piece yellow silk Indian salvar-kameez given to her the night before by Sunaina, joined Rahul and Sunaina in the dining room for breakfast. Always the perfect host and hostess they had not eaten, even though it was long past their normal breakfast time, and they waited until Angela had taken the first bite before they participated in the meal.

Angela ate frugally as she always did and had a breakfast consisting of fresh tropical fruit, cereal and toast. Rahul and Sunaina, being devout Hindus and therefore strict vegetarians, had similar meals. A cooked breakfast in the English style while widely available in Indian hotels would not be proper as part of a Hindu family meal. The breakfast was characterised by an almost total lack of conversation apart from the normal courtesies and pleasantries.

After breakfast the three of them went into the drawing room and made themselves comfortable on the plush armchairs. Angela was the first to speak, "I'll come straight to the point Rahul, Sir David wants you to reconsider your position and rescind your resignation. He was also most upset and offended by your not attending Nick's funeral so I don't need to tell you the mood he was in."

"I'm well aware of his mood. I got a taste of it on the phone. I really did want to go to Nick's funeral. He was the one person in that family who I admired, but I knew that if I did so and met Sir David in person, then we would most certainly have had some sort of a public row. I felt that would be wrong on such an occasion and an insult to Nick's memory. So what is Sir David's ultimatum?"

"Putting it bluntly, Sir David wants you to continue as the head of Fairfax Telecoms' All India Division. He realises Fairfax Telecoms in the UK is now finished but firmly believes the Indian side of the business can remain very profitable."

"Indeed it can," agreed Rahul, "but it doesn't necessarily need me to head it."

"Sir David thinks otherwise. He has great faith in you."

"And if I don't agree to his, how can I put it, request?"

"He says it's a well known fact that everyone, no matter who, has secrets they would prefer to stay hidden. Sir David doesn't want you to think he's putting pressure on you but he has let me into a little secret that if it became known might be very serious for you. I believe the police are still investigating somebody's disappearance."

"That's right, they are. I've been interviewed several times but there's no evidence to connect me to Jagdish

Chopra's disappearance. That all happened over two years ago now."

"But it was most convenient for you, wasn't it?" Angela said sarcastically, "He was the boss and you were his number two. The two of you go on a religious pilgrimage and only you return. What a way to get promotion!"

"It wasn't like that. I'll tell you what I told the police. We had travelled to the Rishikesh area to visit some historic temples and one night he went out and didn't return, that's all there is to it."

"Sir David thinks there's more. He thinks you murdered Jagdish Chopra and disposed of his body."

"I have nothing more to say on the subject," Rahul said emphatically and got up and sat next to Sunaina who gripped his hand tightly.

"Then," said Angela, "I'm afraid you leave me no choice. I take it there is still a police station in this town?"

"Unlike England we do not close our police stations. The Thana, sorry police station, can be found just as you reach the centre of town."

Without further word Angela got up and walked across the room very conscious of Sunaina's eyes following her every footstep. Without even the merest hint of a glance towards her she left the room and made her way outside towards Amrish and Shakti sitting in their little cabins on either side of the bungalow's gates. As Angela approached they immediately jumped up and opened one of the gates and as she walked past they made a point of saluting very positively.

The geography of the area hadn't changed much since Angela's last visit and she quickly remembered the way into town. She easily found the police station and after the briefest of hesitation went inside. It was nearly an hour later that she came out in the company of a police inspector and two constables. The four of them made their way back to 'Shanti Bhavan' in a police jeep and Amrish and Shakti could hardly believe their eyes as the jeep pulled up at the gates.

When Angela and the police officers arrived at the bungalow Rahul was already waiting at the main door. In complete silence he got into the jeep and was driven away. Angela thought this behaviour, accepting the inevitable without complaint, to be very odd but put it down to his beliefs and cultural background as she recalled Sunaina to be of a similar disposition.

Angela went inside the bungalow and made her way to her bedroom. She opened a wardrobe and took out her suitcase and was about to start packing when Sunaina came in and asked her to stop. The two women then made their way to the drawing room.

"I always knew this day would come," Sunaina volunteered, "it was just a matter of time. When you are dealing with the likes of David Fairfax you always have to expect the worst. But I never imagined for one moment that it would be you doing his dirty work."

"Look, I'll be perfectly honest with you," responded a sad looking Angela, "I find all this hard to believe. I know Rahul very well and I don't believe he's capable of murder."

"He isn't, but he is capable of being foolish and naïve," and Sunaina paused before continuing, "He enjoyed working for David Fairfax's Indian operation but he didn't like Jagdish Chopra's methods. The technical and business sides were fine but, as I'm sure you're aware, there was a time when lots of our technicians were smuggled into England illegally to help expand Fairfax Telecoms. Although Rahul had to go along with it he didn't like it one little bit and made his opposition clear to Jagdish.

To cut a long story short, about two years ago Jagdish asked Rahul to accompany him on a pilgrimage to some rather remote Hindu temples and places of worship. Rahul jumped at the idea and the two of them set off on a pilgrimage that should have lasted six weeks."

"It seems an odd sort of thing for two businessmen to do."

"No, not at all, it's very common for people in India to go on pilgrimages. Anyway, everything was all right until they got to Rishikesh and were visiting some ancient temples a few miles away. I don't know how it started but they began arguing over the people smuggling side of the business and Jagdish pushed Rahul who responded by pushing him back. Unfortunately Jagdish lost his footing and fell over the side of the temple and was killed when he hit the ground below.

Rahul should have notified the authorities but he panicked and hid the body under some rocks in an abandoned temple. The next day when others in the group asked, Rahul said Jagdish had gone out the previous evening on his own and hadn't returned to the dharmshala."

Sunaina paused, "I'm sorry, a dharmshala is a type of basic hotel for pilgrims."

"That's not quite the account David Fairfax gave me. He said there was no doubt that Rahul had murdered Jagdish in cold blood."

"Rahul told him exactly what happened so he knows the truth of this matter. The problem now is that when Rahul tells the police where the body is, and he told me he will do just that, it will confirm their suspicions."

Just then the telephone rang. Juhi picked up the receiver and after a few seconds turned to Sunaina, "It's for you, memsahib, Inspector Deshpande," and Juhi handed the telephone to Sunaina.

After a few minutes Sunaina replaced the receiver and turned towards Angela, "As you gathered that was Inspector Deshpande. He says he'll be getting his colleagues in Rishikesh to search the temples but until a body is found he's prepared to release Rahul on bail."

"That's very good news," replied Angela, "how much is the bail and are there any conditions?"

"The amount they want is ten lakh Rupees and the only condition is that Rahul must remain here in 'Shanti Bhavan'."

"I never did understand the Indian way of counting. How much is ten lakh?"

"One million Rupees."

"One million Rupees!" gasped Angela, "Where on earth will you find that amount of money?"

"Don't worry, I'll find it," said Sunaina and she abruptly left the room.

* * * * *

Angela spent the remainder of the day strolling around the small town on her own. She enjoyed wandering in and out of the small shops and never once did she feel under any sort of threat. It was late afternoon when she returned to the bungalow and Sunaina was waiting for her in the drawing room.

"It's all set up. The money will be available tomorrow morning and Rahul will then be released. I'm glad you've decided to stay on for a few days. I'm sure Rahul will take time to give you his side of the story and fill in any details I may have left out."

Rahul arrived home just before lunch the next day and broadly confirmed to Angela what Sunaina had told her about the incident at Rishikesh. Thinking about what both Sir David and Rahul had told her Angela came to the conclusion that she was more inclined to believe Rahul's account of the incident.

Two days later, however, events took a more sinister turn. Angela was walking round the well-tended gardens when a police jeep entered the grounds. She watched as Inspector Deshpande jumped out of the vehicle accompanied by two constables. Angela had always been surprised that while police inspectors in India wore nicely fitting khaki uniforms the constables tended to wear ill-filling blue serge uniforms sometimes with shorts that came down to their knees. She found it hard to imagine police constables in England wearing similar uniforms even in hot weather.

Angela made her way back to the house and was just in time to hear the Inspector bark out in English, presumably for her benefit, "We've found some human remains in the temple-complex you described that may be those of Jagdish Chopra. In these circumstances we have no alternative but to place you under arrest! Come with us!"

Sunaina rushed forward but was roughly pushed back by one of the constables. She turned to Angela who tried to comfort her as best she could.

Rahul turned to face the two women, "Don't worry about me. I'm sure things will turn out for the best. I should have told the police about the argument with Jagdish and his fall from the temple when it happened but I didn't so it's only natural they're suspicious. In this life we have to take the consequences of our actions. I did wrong so I have to accept my punishment. It is written 'that which you can't avoid you should welcome' and that is what I now have to do."

The jeep with Rahul and the police on board left the bungalow in a cloud of dust and Angela and Sunaina stared into the distance long after it had disappeared from view. Angela eventually managed to calm Sunaina down and took her into the drawing room.

Angela decided to leave for England the next day but, just as Vinod was loading her cases into the boot of the car, a convoy of police vehicles entered the grounds of the bungalow. This time they were accompanied by two officials who announced that following Rahul's arrest the accounts of the All-India division of Fairfax Telecoms had been investigated and many irregularities found. In particular there was evidence of bribes being paid to secure contracts and of illegal trading taking place with countries deemed to be hostile to India. As a result the company had been closed down by the authorities and all its assets seized including 'Shanti Bhavan'. Sunaina and the staff had two days in which to vacate the premises.

* * * * *

On the flight back to England Angela reflected on the events in India. Despite her best efforts she had failed to persuade Rahul to rescind his resignation so in accordance with David Fairfax's instructions she had engineered his downfall. "Very curious," she thought to herself, "how David Fairfax is quite prepared to have one of his companies go under just because he couldn't get his own way. He must have tipped off the authorities about those bribes and the illegal trading after I telephoned him about Rahul's arrest." She thought further for a while then sipped another glass of champagne and smiled broadly.

Chapter Forty-four

The demise of Fairfax Telecoms and the arrest of Rahul Dixit soon afterwards on suspicion of murder sent shock waves through the Fairfax Group at all levels. The remaining three managing directors felt distinctly ill at ease as news of the events in India were revealed. It was widely known in the Group that Rahul wanted to resign and that David Fairfax wasn't prepared to countenance his departure. If this was the result of crossing David then they knew what fate awaited them if they were to contemplate a similar move. It appeared that once an employee of David Fairfax, always an employee, there was no easy way out.

David Fairfax himself seemed to accept the loss of both Fairfax Telecoms and the All-India Division with hardly any regret. That was certainly his public face but it was a difficult time for him. The three other divisions were still losing contracts to the Anne Harvey Group and cash flow was becoming an increasing problem.

Because of the on-going police investigations into the deaths of his sons David did not believe he could resurrect any of the Group's former illegal activities. This was particularly ironic in view of the actions of Ken Winter and Craig Bentley, who risked not only discovery by the forces of law and order, but also retaliation from some particularly sinister organisations if they should fail to deliver.

On Angela Hamilton's return from India David made a point of telling her how pleased he was with the outcome of the visit and immediately gave her a large bonus to show his appreciation. Angela told him that it was all part of the job but, nonetheless, she willingly accepted the money.

Security was still very tight at Forest Glade with two of Feb's former SAS colleagues being employed on permanent guard duty in the grounds. Feb himself accompanied David every time he left the safety of the house, whether this was on business to the Fairfax Building in Canary Wharf or any other family or personal reason.

Lucy still firmly refused to leave the house unless it was absolutely necessary and then only in the company of David or Feb. Increasingly, however, she had her circle of like-minded friends visit the house and gradually these gatherings turned into regular social events. On occasions even Susan Rumble and Angela Hamilton participated in these gatherings, but this was more from a desire not to offend David Fairfax than from their fondness for Lucy. David believed it was only a matter of time before Lucy regained her enthusiasm for the high-life she had previously enjoyed so much and would be prepared to leave the house once again.

Callisto was David's chief worry. At first she had willingly consented to being accompanied everywhere whenever she was out of the house. But as the days went by she increasingly either gave her minder the slip or deliberately went out without him. Despite both Feb and David taking her to task in no uncertain manner she refused to relent or change her behaviour.

Inspector Westwood kept David Fairfax up to date with progress on the two murders but had to admit that in the absence of any new leads he didn't hold out much hope of a break-through in the near future. This annoyed David who soon lost faith in the way the inquiry was proceeding but, despite using his parliamentary connections, he had failed to get the Inspector removed from the case.

Inspector Westwood was well aware of how David felt towards him and the actions he had taken to try and get him replaced. This soured the relationship between them so much that Inspector Westwood often sent Sergeant Benson to update David on progress rather than go and talk to him himself.

David Fairfax had a little more respect for James Palmer even though he hadn't yet come up with anything concrete. When he outlined to David the scope of his inquiries, without revealing too much of the detail and his suspicions, David had been satisfied with the direction things were going. This surprised James who was afraid his lack of definite progress might have annoyed him. Imagine James' surprise, or more aptly his shock, when David said he was topping up his fee and sending Feb to his house with another £10,000. Although James was delighted with this bonus Jenny felt a little uneasy.

Chapter Forty-five

"So," said Jenny Palmer with a gleam in her eye, "it's agreed then. I'll drive over to Old Harlow to see what I can find out about Beverley Fairfax, or Jenks should I say if I go back to the days of her maiden name, and you'll go to Ipswich to see what you can find out about Angela Hamilton's car accident."

"If you say so," agreed a rather resigned James, "but I think I've drawn the short straw again. You just have a nice relaxing fifteen or twenty minute drive and I have well over an hour – and along the A12 with all those lorries!"

"Never mind, I'm sure you'll survive," Jenny teased playfully, "and with any luck I'll be back in time for lunch."

"I'll be suitably envious," laughed James as he suddenly leapt forward and snatched the keys to the Focus and jangled them in front of Jenny.

"You beast!" she exclaimed, "I wanted the Focus."

"Sorry, it's the Fiesta for you today," and James ran towards the door closely pursued by Jenny clutching her set of car keys.

After a quick kiss on the doorstep the two of them went their separate ways. Jenny took the narrow lane from North Weald through to Hastingwood and Old Harlow and James took the road towards Ongar that would lead on to Chelmsford and then the A12 to Ipswich.

* * * * *

Jenny soon arrived at Old Harlow and in no time at all she had found the street where Beverley Jenks had grown up and located the house where she used to live.

"What a nice area," she thought to herself, "lovely big old houses standing on large plots of land, and all the gardens nicely manicured too. What a super place to spend your childhood," and looking towards a rather grand house situated right at the end of the cul-de-sac, she exclaimed, "There it is, there's Beverley Jenks' old house!"

After standing and looking at the houses for a few minutes Jenny finally plucked up the courage to knock on some front doors. However, her early enthusiasm was soon dampened. Those few people at home and not at work hadn't lived in the street when Beverley Jenks was living there in the 1960s and 70s. She resisted the temptation to call at Beverley's old house as she reasoned the present occupants wouldn't know anything about her. It was, after all, over 30 years ago that Beverley had lived there.

"Time for 'Plan B'," Jenny said aloud as she made her way to her car, "let's see what the local press had to say about her. If she was as good a horse rider as everyone claims then there should be lots about her in the local press, both from her time at school and afterwards when she competed in various local and national contests. Hopefully she won lots of medals and prizes as they always make good stories for local papers."

Jenny left Old Harlow and turned into First Avenue for the short drive to The High, the centre of Harlow New Town, where she knew she would find the offices of 'The Harlow Courier'.

* * * * *

Unlike his previous journey to Ipswich James found the drive to the County Town of Suffolk uneventful and almost pleasant. There had been a marked absence of heavy lorries on the roads and the bright sunny day had ensured he was in a happy frame of mind. It was obviously his day because when he reached the offices of 'The East Anglian Weekly Times' he found the last remaining parking space with ease.

James knew Anne Harvey and Angela Hamilton had both been at Ipswich Grammar School between 1987 and 1994 so he asked the archivist to make available back numbers of the paper covering the years 1993 to 1995. He reasoned this would give him a window spanning the time just before Angela's seventeenth birthday, the earliest she could have commenced driving legally, and a year or so afterwards. Jenny had failed to ask Mrs Goodenough if Angela was still at school when she had her fatal accident but from what had been said about Anne and Angela's school days Jenny had come to the conclusion that it must have taken place soon after they left school. "I'll have to have a word with Jenny when I get back," James mused, "tell her to pay more attention to detail in the future."

It took quite a while before James found any mention of Angela Hamilton in the newspapers and the first time he came across her name was in connection with a school play. It was a period piece and there she was in costume with Anne Harvey staring up at him from the page, "Pity it's in black and white," sighed James, "still it's true what Mrs Goodenough told Jenny, you can't tell those two apart."

During their final year at school Anne and Angela appeared in a couple more school plays that were reviewed in the local papers but there were no photographs. James continued his search and suddenly there it was, a report about a fatal accident on the A14. He read the report and then read it again. There was no mistaking it was the same Angela Hamilton who had been at Ipswich Grammar School with Anne Harvey. By all accounts it had been a terrifying accident. In driving rain a lorry had braked sharply on a particularly dangerous bend then jack-knifed and crushed the car Angela Hamilton was driving. She was killed instantly.

James paused after reading the account for a third time and then sat back in his chair. He made brief notes of Angela's date of birth and where she had grown up and then realised there were no photographs accompanying the article.

"Perhaps," he thought, "it's because the accident occurred just before the paper went to press," and he thumbed through the pages to the next week's edition. Sure enough, there it was, a photograph of Angela Hamilton taken during her school days illustrating an article that gave more details about the accident.

* * * * *

Jenny was given a huge pile of bound editions of 'The Harlow Courier' covering Beverley Jenks' last two years at secondary school and up to the time she married David Fairfax. She stared at them with a degree of resignation and shrugged her shoulders. She then started the long slog of looking at both the features pages and the sports pages because many local papers give much space to the exploits of local teams and individuals. Her trawling through the sports pages soon yielded results. There were numerous articles spanning a long period where Beverley's prowess at horse riding and show jumping was reported and her success at many equestrian events described in detail.

"Here is someone who loves horses and lives for riding," Jenny mused, "that's most evident from the tone of these articles and the vast amount of trophies and medals she won. She was a good looking young woman too, not like some of them who compete in this sport who look just like their mounts."

Jenny then moved forward to the time when Beverley married David Fairfax and was surprised to find an article about the marriage, "Now that was a grand affair," she couldn't help but exclaim out loud after reading about the number of guests present and how much it was estimated to have cost, "I wonder if all three of David Fairfax's weddings were like that?"

This spurred Jenny into action and she decided to see if she could find out anything about the riding accident Beverley had when she lost the unborn child she was carrying. Once again she was faced with a huge mountain of bound papers to wade through.

Just as she was becoming despondent and thinking she should call it a day, Jenny found what she was looking for, an article entitled 'Top show rider in tragic accident'. Jenny read the article which confirmed what she had already been told. Beverley had been riding one of her horses on her own land when quite unexpectedly she had been thrown. There was nothing in the article to suggest she had lost her baby so Jenny turned to the following week's edition of the paper and there it was 'Double blow to top rider'. This follow-up article gave the tragic news that it had not proved possible to save Beverley's unborn child and doctors had warned she may not be able to conceive in the future.

"Tragic, very tragic," thought Jenny as she went to close the heavy volume but, for some unknown reason, she let the papers fall open to a following week and was more than surprised to discover an interview with Beverley Fairfax herself. Jenny began to read what Beverley had to say and then stopped about half way through the article, "Wow!" she exclaimed, "I must get a photocopy of this. James will never believe me otherwise."

* * * * *

James stared long and hard at the photograph of Angela Hamilton but no matter how hard he tried he couldn't accept that this was the same Angela Hamilton who worked for David Fairfax.

"Even making allowances for the fact that fourteen or fifteen years have passed since this photograph was taken," he thought, "I'm convinced that we're talking about two different people here. But the names," he paused for a moment to think, "the names, just what sort of a coincidence is that?"

James made a few brief notes before returning the bound volumes of newspapers to the archivist. He then put his papers into his briefcase and went to leave the building. However, as he was walking towards the entrance his eyes were attracted to a large display of prominent local business people in the foyer, and one of the people featured was none other than Anne Harvey. Curiosity got the better of him and James went to have a closer look at the display.

The details given about Anne Harvey's background and business activities were largely the same as those he had already obtained from Martin Travers and other sources but there was one additional factor. Much was said about Anne Harvey's phenomenal success over recent years and the fact that this had all been achieved on a part-time basis. According to the article Anne hardly ever made an appearance in the office and most business was done through her Chief Executive Martin Travers or by email. Anne herself was said to be something of a recluse.

"Strange," thought James, "she didn't strike me as a recluse when I bumped into her, quite the opposite I'd say," and he shrugged his shoulders and made his way back to his car.

* * * * *

Once again by the time James returned home an excited Jenny was already there waiting for him. As soon as he came through the door and took his coat off Jenny practically dragged him into the lounge as she was almost unable to curb her enthusiasm.

"Any chance of a cup of tea? I'm parched."

"Tea, *tea*, is that all you can think about?" exclaimed Jenny hardly able to contain herself, "Just wait until you hear what I've found out about Beverley Fairfax's accident," and she changed chairs so that she was sitting directly facing her husband.

"Ok," said James with a look of anticipation on his face, "you go first. What did you find out?"

"Well," replied Jenny hardly able to stop herself, "I went to the street in Old Harlow where Beverley grew up but none of the people living there now had any recollection of her so I went to the newspaper offices at The High to look through some back numbers. As we thought, Beverley was a very skilled horse woman and won absolutely loads of prizes and trophies and the back pages are full of her achievements. I was most envious," and she paused for breath.

"I then skipped forward a few years and found an article on her marriage to David Fairfax. Now that really was a grand affair and I definitely wouldn't have wanted to foot the bill for that. But the really interesting discovery came about a year later when I found reports of her riding accident. As you'd expect the accident made the news for a couple of weeks but the really fascinating thing occurs a few weeks later when Beverley is released from hospital and gives an interview. What do you think she says?"

"I've no idea," replied James with a grin, "but I'm sure you're going to tell me."

"Beverley Fairfax claimed it wasn't an accident at all. She maintained that somebody deliberately spooked her horse."

"Are you sure?"

"No doubt about it at all," said Jenny handing James a photocopy of the article, "See for yourself. Beverley says the horse she was riding was well known for its placid nature and was very used to her riding him. She insists that somebody deliberately made a large bang, such as from a starting pistol or a car exhaust, just as she was about to go over one of the small jumps she used for practice."

"Interesting, very interesting indeed," James said quietly and deliberately as he quickly cast an eye over the photocopied article, "particularly when it's only about a year or so later that she supposedly commits suicide on that cruise ship."

"A cruise ship on which not only David Fairfax, but also his future wife, just happens to be aboard. Sounds very fishy to me, if you'll forgive the pun," Jenny stressed.

"Do you still think David Fairfax murdered Beverley?"

"I think it's a distinct possibility. What's more I wouldn't put it past him to have murdered his first wife, Dawn, as well!"

"Don't like my old school pal, do you?" asked James with a wry smile.

"No, I don't. There's something unpleasant about him. I can see him looking upon those two women as nothing more than providing him with those vital stepping stones he needed to break into business. And once he's got what he wants he gets rid of them and marries his childhood sweetheart. It all makes good sense to me."

"You may well be right, but how do we prove it?"

"Not easily, I'm sure," said Jenny with a tinge of sadness in her voice, "Anyway, how did you get on in Ipswich?"

"Not very well, really," admitted James, "nothing as exciting as your day but I did manage to confirm what Mrs Goodenough told you. Angela Hamilton and Anne Harvey often acted in school plays together and looking at them pictured together in costume it really is hard to tell them apart. She was also right about that accident, Angela Hamilton was killed outright when a lorry jack-knifed and crushed her car. Very tragic indeed, she was only eighteen years old. There was also a photograph of Angela, taken at school I would think, and that shows she looks nothing like the Angela Hamilton who works for David Fairfax. That's about it but I did make a few notes while I was ploughing through all those old newspapers," and James handed his papers to Jenny.

"Oh, and one other thing," volunteered James, "there was a display of prominent local business people at the newspaper offices and Anne Harvey was one of those featured. There was nothing new there really apart from the fact that she hardly ever comes into the office. Apparently she is something of a recluse and does much of her work from home and keeps in touch with the office via email."

"Right," said Jenny appearing most uninterested in what her husband had just said. She looked once more at James' notes and then went into the study without saying a word. A few minutes later she appeared with a very perplexed look on her face.

"You told me the Angela Hamilton who went to school with Anne Harvey is dead. You said you had managed to confirm that what Mrs Goodenough had told me about the car accident was true. You also said a school photograph of Angela Hamilton bears no resemblance to the Angela Hamilton who now works for David Fairfax."

"That's correct," James agreed, "so what are you trying to say?"

"I'm not trying to say anything," responded Jenny, "but if what you say is true how come the Angela Hamilton who died in that car crash and the Angela Hamilton who works for David Fairfax have exactly the same date of birth?"

"What!" shouted James so loudly that Jenny almost dropped the papers she had brought into the room, "Let me see those papers."

Jenny handed her husband the papers she had brought from the study. These were notes written at the beginning of the enquiry by James and largely forgotten by him as events had progressed.

"There you are," smiled a very smug Jenny, "look at those dates! Everything matches, the day, the month and the year. Good job one of us is on the ball and can remember what we've already found out."

"There's no doubt about it," agreed James after looking at his notes once more, "those dates of birth are exactly the same."

"So," said Jenny with a very puzzled look on her face, "just who is the Angela Hamilton who works for David Fairfax?"

Chapter Forty-six

It was Wednesday afternoon and, as had become part of her routine over the last few weeks, Callisto slipped out of her office in the Fairfax Building. She caught the Docklands Light Railway to Stratford where she changed onto the Central Line for the journey back to Theydon Bois. However, she didn't leave the train at Theydon Bois but stayed seated until it reached the end of the line at Epping.

"How nice to be able to walk about with nobody keeping an eye on me telling me what I can and cannot do," she thought to herself as she strolled slowly up the hill from the station to the High Street, "Ah, here we are, 'The Tanning Studio', an oasis of heat and pampering. I do like my twice-weekly sessions here. I can keep my tan all-year round and be the envy of my friends. And the manicure, mustn't neglect my nails, let's go for the lot today. I feel like indulging myself."

Callisto walked up to 'The Tanning Studio' pushed open the heavy glass door and approached the small reception desk.

"Good afternoon madam, what can I do for you today?"

"You're new here aren't you?" enquired Callisto who was expecting to see one of the familiar members of staff who all knew her by name, "And nobody doing the nails today," she added after glancing around the empty salon, "I was after some colourful nail extensions with original designs for a function I'm going to at the weekend. These ones have nearly grown out," and she showed her hands to the assistant.

"Sorry, Neeta who does the nails phoned in sick this morning. She's really put me on the spot. I'm new here and only started on Monday. This is the first time I've been entirely on my own. It's been a busy morning and I could hardly cope but as you can see this afternoon is the exact opposite. You're the first person I've had in here since lunch."

"So I've got the pick of the booths, then?"

"That's right. You can have one of the stand-up booths here at the front of the studio or you can use one of the beds out the back, it's entirely up to you."

"I usually use the stand-up booths for quickness but as I won't be able to get my nails done today I'll take it easy and relax on one of the beds. By the way, are you sure this is your first week here?" Callisto asked trying to peer into the assistant's eyes through the heavy black-rimmed glasses she was wearing and looking closely at this obviously middle-aged lady in her tight-fitting uniform, "It's just that you look familiar. You remind me of someone but I just can't put my finger on it."

"No, I can assure you this is my first week here," the assistant replied with a smile, "Now, how many minutes would you like today?"

"Normally I have 12 minutes in the stand-ups so I'll have 20 minutes on the sun-bed as that's an equivalent amount of time."

"That's fine," and the assistant programmed a 20 minute session into the computer. She then handed Callisto her tanning lotions from a rack to the side of her desk, a pair of goggles, an antiseptic wipe and some tissues, and the two of them went to the rear of the premises.

After the assistant had left the small compartment Callisto undressed and stretched out naked on the sun-bed. She never tanned wearing her swimsuit or bikini as she wished to avoid having any white areas showing when she was away on holiday or sunbathing in the garden of Forest Glade. She settled down on her back and when she was comfortable she closed the top canopy over her prone body and pressed the start button to activate the ultra-violet tanning tubes.

"This is the life," she mused to herself, "lying back in the warmth and soaking up a tan without a care in the world. I wonder if we'll go away this year to somewhere hot. Perhaps not, but I don't mind, I'll still be able to keep my tan if I come here every week during the summer," and she let her thoughts wander free.

Lost in thought and lost in time, lying on her back and soaking up the heat Callisto completely forgot how long she had been on the sun-bed until she began to feel uncomfortably hot.

"Must be nearly time for this session to be over," she reasoned, "I'm getting so very hot under here. Glad I put my lotions on or I may have burned and that would never do."

After a few more minutes as she became increasingly hot and uncomfortable she decided it was time to bring the session to a close. She pressed the button but much to her surprise nothing happened, the heat still poured out unrelentingly onto her now red and very sore body. Callisto panicked and pressed the quick-release button but to her astonishment and anger nothing happened.

"Damn!" she exclaimed out aloud, "What's the matter with this thing? It should pop open at the touch of a button. Anyway, what's happened to the cut-out? I thought these things could only be on for a limited number of minutes before they went off automatically!"

By now Callisto was beginning to panic and tried desperately to force up the top of the cabinet but to no avail. As the heat intensified and her skin began to blister she banged her hands and feet as hard as she could on the sides of the cabinet but it didn't budge. In her blind fervour she started to wriggle from side to side but as the heat was coming from all angles around her body she couldn't escape from it.

"Surely," she thought desperately to herself, "that assistant must know by now that I've been in here well over my time-limit. What's the matter with her, can't she hear my banging? She must know something's wrong. For Christ's sake, I can't take much more of this," and she resumed her frantic banging on the sides of the cabinet in sheer desperation.

But the minutes ticked by relentlessly and suddenly it dawned on Callisto that nobody was going to come to her assistance, "Damn!" she repeated to herself, "Damn! Unless I get out of here soon I'm done for," and then out of the blue the stark realisation hit her, "Damn! This is it! I'm next! Why didn't I listen to dad and Feb? Why didn't I take their advice? Still, I'm not finished yet," and she made one more desperate attempt to free herself. But as she looked up through the tinted top of the cabinet she was aware of the assistant standing there looking down on her and smiling broadly.

Callisto started to see and feel her skin blister and begin to peel off and she began to smell burning flesh. She looked up again and watched in mounting disbelief as the assistant removed her glasses, wig and makeup and a familiar face gazed down at her with a mocking smile.

"You!" Callisto mouthed and tried to speak, but her voice failed her and as her agony increased she lost consciousness.

Once she was sure that Callisto had indeed lost consciousness the assistant unlocked the cabinet and dragged Callisto across the floor towards the one stand-up booth that was not visible from the front of the studio. Safely inside she produced an old-fashioned pink bikini from the 1970s and with some difficulty she put the two pieces of material onto Callisto's almost-lifeless body. She then tied Callisto's hands together above her head and suspended her in front of the bank of tanning tubes from one of the two grab handles screwed into the ceiling.

Satisfied with her work the assistant replaced her wig and glasses and went to the desk at the front of the studio. She then reprogrammed the computer to activate the tubes in the stand-up booth where the lifeless Callisto was hanging. She checked the tubes were pumping out maximum heat, closed the door and placed a small card on the outside of the booth. Finally, as she left the studio she made sure that the sign on the entrance read 'closed' but she didn't lock the door.

Chapter Forty-seven

Susan Rumble stretched out on the bed and let her hair fall loosely across her face and shoulders. She watched as Craig Bentley came into the room and approached the bed with a bottle of champagne in one hand and two glasses balanced precariously on the other.

"Why were you so late?" asked a rather anxious Craig as he carefully placed the champagne and glasses on a bedside table, "I thought you weren't coming. I was beginning to think you'd had enough of our regular Wednesday rendezvous. This afternoon was really beginning to drag until you arrived."

"Not at all," replied Susan eagerly, "I had some urgent work to finish for David Fairfax that I just couldn't leave until tomorrow. Luckily I could do it from home and email it to the office, otherwise I wouldn't have just been late but wouldn't have made it here today at all. Bearing in mind the mood he's been in lately I couldn't not do it, he'd probably have fired me."

"We certainly don't want that, not yet anyway, not until our little scheme has paid off and we've enough money for our, how can I put it, retirement?"

"Precisely!" agreed Susan, "It won't be long before we can bid farewell to Sir David and that corrupt empire of his. Hopefully, once we're gone it'll all collapse around him. I, for one, would willingly shop him after we're far away from here in Spain."

"I'll second that," agreed Craig enthusiastically as he opened the bottle of champagne with hardly a sound. He poured Susan a glass, "Here's to us!" and he filled his own glass and they each took a sip.

"You were about to propose a toast," a playful Susan said.

"To us," said Craig as their two glasses touched.

"When I think of how many people David Fairfax has ripped off in the past I think it's only fitting that he'll soon be getting his just desserts."

"I couldn't agree more and we mustn't forget what Dimitri said about Ken Winter. Who'd have thought it, dear old Ken going into business with the Albanians? Hope he makes a packet at David's expense too," added Craig reaching again for the champagne.

"You can have some more of that later. Right now I want you sober and in full control of what you're doing," and Susan grabbed Craig by his tie and pulled him down on top of her. They frantically began to tear each other's clothes off and just as they were locked together in a firm embrace Craig's mobile rang.

"Leave it," urged Susan, "it can wait!"

"No, I'd better answer it. You never know it might be Sir David himself. Talk about the devil and all that."

Craig put the phone to his ear and listened. After a few seconds he said, "Ok, we'll be there," and he put the phone back into his inside jacket pocket, but his facial expression betrayed his apprehension.

"Who was that? What's the matter?" enquired a worried-looking Susan.

"That was someone from Sir David's office at the Fairfax Building. She says Sir David wants to meet us right now at 'The Tanning Studio' in Epping High Street."

"The Tanning Studio? I think I know where that is, it's almost opposite St. John's Church. We can be there in five or ten minutes."

"That's not the point," said Craig, "how did Sir David know we were together?" and after a moment's thought continued, "And how the hell did he know we were here in Thornwood at The Carpenter's Arms? I thought no-one knew about our little arrangement but it's leaked out somehow. He'll be furious. We'll need to think carefully about what we're going to say to him."

"Don't worry, we'll think of something. Come on, let's make a move. The sooner we get there the sooner we can get it over with and get back here to finish our day in style."

Susan and Craig quickly got ready and drove to Epping. They took Susan's car rather than Craig's Land Cruiser and parked in the car park at the rear of St. John's Church and made their way to 'The Tanning Studio'.

"It looks empty to me and there's a closed sign on the door," Craig observed as they approached the studio.

"Very strange," said Susan but as she grasped the handle the door opened, "It's open, let's go in and see what this is all about," and Craig followed her into the studio.

Craig closed the door behind him and the two of them stood looking into the deserted studio.

"It's terribly hot in here," said Susan loosening her jacket, "I've always wondered what it was like in one of these places."

"It's not only hot but smelly too. What on earth is that smell?"

"There's a light on in one of the booths. I wonder if Sir David is in there," said Susan taking off her jacket and hanging it on the back of a chair.

She and Craig walked across to the booth. They knocked and waited for a few seconds and when they didn't receive any response they opened the door.

"Oh my God!" shrieked Susan, "What on earth is that?" and she turned and buried her head in

Craig's arms as she tried not to retch from the blast of heat and stench that rushed out and enveloped her body.

"That's disgusting! It looks like a body hanging in front of the tubes," said a very nervous Craig trying to suppress a cough, "It looks in a very bad way as if it's been burnt to a cinder. How do you turn these things off?"

"I've no idea. We should leave it. Look, this is serious. Let's get out of here before anyone comes in," and much to Craig's surprise Susan composed herself with remarkable speed.

"You're right, nobody knows we're here. We'll just leave quietly, come on!"

But as they turned round and hurried towards the studio entrance they saw none other than Inspector Westwood and Sergeant Benson coming through the door.

"Going somewhere are we sir, madam?" enquired the Inspector in a very stern voice, "Now why would you be in such a hurry to leave, particularly when it's so nice and warm in here?"

"Inspector, glad you're here, we were about to call you," stammered Craig.

"Is that so?" replied a sceptical Inspector Westwood, "Now why would you be doing that?"

"In there, in that booth, there's a body. Look for yourself."

"If you'd kindly stand over there with Sergeant Benson I'll do just that."

Inspector Westwood walked over to the booth and gingerly opened the door. He placed a handkerchief over his mouth and went inside. He came out almost immediately, coughing and struggling to get his breath, and quickly took out his mobile phone, "Get a scene of crime team to 'The Tanning Studio' in the High Street immediately. Got a particularly nasty one," and he closed the phone and returned it to his pocket.

"I think you've got some explaining to do sir," the Inspector said as he went and stood over by Craig Bentley, "Do you mind telling me what exactly you and, er, it's Susan Rumble isn't it? Do you mind telling me exactly what you and Miss Rumble were doing here?"

"Not at all, Inspector," replied Craig in a faltering voice that betrayed his nervousness, "we were meeting David Fairfax. He called earlier and asked us to meet him here."

"Funny place for a meeting isn't it sir? Business meeting was it?"

"I don't know, he didn't say. Actually it wasn't him that telephoned it was one of his staff."

"That's right," chipped in Susan, "I was with Craig, I mean Mr Bentley, when he took the call."

"And where was that, in your office?"

"No," replied Susan in a distinctly hesitant voice, "we were at The Carpenter's Arms hotel."

"What the hotel in Thornwood? And would this by any chance be another business meeting?"

"No, not exactly, we often meet up for a drink and to discuss business away from the office," suggested Craig.

"So you just met for a quiet drink, nothing else?"

"Look inspector, I'll be honest with you. Susan and I are more than just good friends and have been for sometime but we've kept this from Sir David and the rest of the Managing Directors. We know he would frown on that sort of thing."

"And your wife sir, is she aware of this little, how can I put this, liaison?"

"No, she's not," and Craig hesitated before adding, "and I'd rather she didn't find out."

Just then a small group of scene of crime officers arrived from the nearby police station, all suited up in readiness, and Inspector Westwood pointed them in the direction of the body. Two of them cautiously entered the booth and a third went over to the computer on the reception desk and managed to switch off the tanning tubes. After a couple of minutes one of the officers emerged from the booth carrying a bundle of clothes and a handbag that he passed to Inspector Westwood.

The Inspector quickly looked through the contents of the handbag and looked very surprised at the name he found on the credit cards. He then told Sergeant Benson to ensure that the constable on duty outside the salon didn't let anybody in and he went to view the body again. When he emerged he walked straight over to Susan and Craig.

"I suppose you're going to tell me you don't know who that poor soul is in there strung up like a kipper?"

"That's right Inspector. We arrived just before you did, we saw the body and I suppose we panicked."

"Panicked, sir? You didn't seem to be in much of a panic to me. In my view you looked like you were about to make off from the scene of a crime."

"No," Craig tried in vain to convince the Inspector, "we were about to phone 999 for the police."

"Who is it in there anyway?" Susan asked nervously.

"Don't tell me you don't know!" said the Inspector as he turned and looked her straight in the eyes, "It's Callisto Fairfax!"

"Callisto!" exclaimed Susan in disbelief, "Oh no, not Callisto!" and she buried her head once more in Craig's arms and began to cry.

"Sorry to interrupt, sir," apologised one of the scene of crime officers, "but we found this on the outside of the booth," and he handed the Inspector a small card he had placed in a plastic evidence bag. Inspector Westwood read the card then put it in his pocket without any comment.

"Craig Bentley! Susan Rumble! I'm arresting you on suspicion of the murder of Callisto Fairfax. Sergeant, caution them!"

"But inspector," pleaded Craig, "we didn't do anything, you must believe me!"

"You'll have plenty of time to explain down at the station. Now please, come along now."

Chapter Forty-eight

"Constable!" boomed Inspector Westwood as they entered Epping Police Station, "Take these two to the custody sergeant and have him put them in separate interview rooms." He then turned and spoke in more subdued tones to Sergeant Benson before he went up to the desk, "A spell apart will prevent them concocting a story or agreeing on an alibi. We got there just in time as they were leaving the scene. On the basis they thought they could make a clean get-away they won't have prepared for our interrogation."

"Very good, sir," and Sergeant Benson went to make the arrangements with the custody sergeant. He then went to Inspector Westwood's office where he found the inspector deep in thought.

"Penny for them, sir?"

"Sorry Benson, I was miles away," and after a few seconds he added, "We'll let those two stew for an hour or so before we speak to them. It'll soften them up a bit when they realise they aren't going anywhere."

"Do you think they did it, sir?"

"I'm not sure. There are some aspects of this particular incident that worry me," and he paused again before looking straight at Sergeant Benson and adding, "If you commit two murders and get away from the scene without apparently leaving any clues at all, why would you be so careless in this case? Besides, who was the person who phoned us and told us to go to 'The Tanning Studio'? It just doesn't add up."

"Perhaps you're right," nodded the sergeant in agreement, "the duty constable said the caller was a woman who asked for you by name. She said you were to go to 'The Tanning Studio' immediately if you wanted information about the murders of Tom and Nick Fairfax. The caller then hung-up before he could respond."

"And we got there in the space of two or three minutes. It's all so convenient, as if we were meant to catch them red-handed on the premises."

"You think they were set up?"

"Possibly, or one of them did it and the other one is covering up for them."

"Or one of them did it *unbeknown* to the other one," stressed the sergeant.

"Well done Benson, that's a distinct possibility. We'll make a detective of you yet."

Inspector Westwood looked through the heap of files on his desk and took out his notes concerning the anonymous Christmas presents and cryptic cards received by the Fairfax family on Christmas Day. He then put them in his briefcase and strode towards the door.

"Well come on then! What are you waiting for?"

"Where to, sir?"

"Theydon Bois and David Fairfax of course. Someone's got to break the news to him about his daughter. Unless you want to go and tell him on your own?"

"No, that's all right, sir," stressed a relieved Sergeant Benson, "I'm more than happy to go with you," and he hurried after the inspector who was already half-way down the corridor.

* * * * *

In the early evening twilight the Inspector's car drove through the gates of Forest Glade and made its way along the cypress-lined drive up to the portico. As they walked towards the front door both men were conscious that they were being observed not only by the CCTV system but also by two security guards patrolling the grounds.

Almost immediately after ringing the bell the door was opened by Katie who seemed surprised at the presence of the two policemen.

"We've come to see Sir David," Inspector Westwood said sternly before Katie could say a word and the two men pushed past her into the hallway.

"Sir David's busy in his study. I'll check if he'll see you."

"He'll see us. Tell him it's vital that we speak with him."

"Very good," replied Katie appreciating the gravity in Inspector Westwood's voice, "if you'll wait here in the drawing room I'll get Sir David for you," and she left the room.

A few minutes later Sir David entered with the two cats hard on his heels and sat down in his favourite chair, "Well Inspector, what can I do for you? Are you any nearer to solving the murders?"

"I'm afraid I've got some very bad news, Sir David," and he paused, "It's Callisto, I'm afraid she's been killed!"

"Killed!" shrieked Sir David and he threw Ponsonby off his lap with such force that the cat slid along the carpet on its back before regaining its balance and cowering under a small table, "What do you mean killed? Have you come here to tell me she's been murdered? My precious daughter, murdered! That you've failed her as you failed my two sons?"

"That's not fair, despite my many protestations you refused police protection in favour of your own arrangements. But I'm not here to debate the merits of that decision. I'm here to ask if you knew what Callisto's movements were today and why she was unaccompanied."

"Before all that tell me, how did she die? I must know. Was it quick or was it like the boys? I wouldn't want to think of her suffering."

"I'm not at liberty to divulge that information at the moment sir, but what I can tell you is that she was found at 'The Tanning Studio' in Epping this afternoon."

"I might have known," Sir David ranted, "I told her not to slope off work and go to that damn place on her own."

"Who would have known she was in the habit of going for tanning sessions on her own?"

"Just about anybody who worked at the Fairfax Building – and her mates I suppose, they also go there regularly."

Sergeant Benson looked hesitantly at Inspector Westwood as both men were unsure what to say next but the uneasy silence was broken by Sir David, "Callisto was my favourite you know," and he sobbed, "I loved that girl. I admired her. I lived for that girl. I always fancied that one day she would take the reins once I stepped down but now," and he looked up at the ceiling, "now, there's nothing left. Who'll inherit the business now?" and he buried his face in his hands.

"Oh, and one last thing, Sir David. It appears Callisto was wearing a bikini when she was killed and we also found a small card at the scene. The message reads 'You were warned you'd get your fingers burnt and now you have!'" The Inspector then produced a file from his briefcase and continued, "I'm reminded of the old-fashioned bikini that Callisto received at Christmas and the card containing the warning about getting her fingers burnt. You still have no idea who might have sent those items?"

"No I haven't but believe you me if I find out I'll ..." and his words faded as he thought once again about Callisto.

After a few moments of silence Sir David added, "It's about time you found out who's doing this and arrested them! All these clues must be pointing you somewhere."

"I wasn't going to mention this as it's very early days but we do have a suspect at the station."

"Who is it?" Sir David shouted, "Who is it? Tell me!"

"Afraid we can't do that sir," said Sergeant Benson anticipating the Inspector's reply. "As the Inspector said, it's early days yet and there's a lot of work to do before we can bring any charges or eliminate this person from our enquiries. As soon as we are able to give you any details then we'll do so."

"We'll be going now, Sir David," Inspector Westwood said, "but we'll be in touch tomorrow when we should be able to give you some more information. Meanwhile if anything occurs to you about Callisto's movements then please get in touch. We'll see ourselves out," and the two detectives left the room.

Sitting alone in the drawing room David Fairfax put his head in his hands and thought, "How am I going to break this to Lucy? She'll be devastated!"

* * * * *

On the way back to Epping Police Station as the two detectives discussed the case Inspector Westwood asked, "What did you make of David Fairfax's reaction to the news of Callisto's death?"

"Much more subdued than I thought would be the case. As the realisation gradually sunk in he changed and became almost emotional."

"For him that's quite an achievement. Do you think he did it?"

"Kill his own daughter? No I don't think so. Besides, what would be the motive?"

"I think you're right. I don't think he did it either," and the Inspector continued, "Speaking of motives, I wonder how James Palmer is getting on? He's been doing a lot of digging behind the scenes so I think it's time we had a word with him. When we get back to the station let's invite him over for a little chat. Don't want him to think we're ignoring him that would never do!"

* * * * *

Inspector Westwood and Sergeant Benson interviewed Craig Bentley first.

"So take your time and tell us in your own words everything you did today, from when you got up to when we found you with Callisto's body."

"I don't like that inference, Inspector, I had nothing to do with her death. If you must know I got up early today at about six-thirty as I had to inspect a number of our farms in connection with the receipt of EU subsidies. Normally it's an all-day job but I wanted to finish early so I could get over to The Carpenter's Arms and meet Susan."

"Can anyone vouch for you this morning and give you an alibi?"

"Just about everyone who works on our farms in the Bury St Edmunds area. I chose that area deliberately as it means I only have about an hour and a half's drive over to Thornwood to meet Susan. Here," and Craig handed the Inspector a sheet of paper, "Here's a list of farm managers who will all confirm I visited their farms this morning and should be able to let you have the times as well."

"Thank you. So what time did you arrive at The Carpenter's Arms?"

"About one-thirty. In fact I was a little early as we had arranged to meet there at two o'clock."

"We'll check with the hotel staff. Now what time did Susan Rumble join you?"

"I don't want to drop her in it, you understand, but she didn't arrive until just after three o'clock."

"Was she often late?"

"No, that's the odd thing about it. Normally she looks forward to our, er, meetings, and if anything she's usually a bit early."

"Did she say why she was late?"

"Yes, she said she had some urgent work to do for David Fairfax that simply couldn't wait and had to be done before she could get away."

"So why did you leave the safety of your hotel room and go to 'The Tanning Studio'? Neither of you looks particularly tanned to me!"

"There was a phone call from Sir David asking us to meet him there."

"From Sir David you say?"

"Well actually it was from one of his staff. I didn't catch her name but she said Sir David wanted to see us urgently in 'The Tanning Studio'."

"And you didn't think that was odd? Did he know about you and Susan?"

"We thought it very odd indeed but as it's most unwise to get on the wrong side of him we decided to go there straight away. At the same time we were extremely puzzled and worried that he might have found out about us, he frowns on that sort of thing. Staff have been sacked for less."

"So what happened when you arrived at the Tanning Studio?"

"We went in and looked around but there was nobody there. It was very hot and there was that horrible smell and then we saw the light on in one of the booths. We opened it and looked inside and when we saw the body we decided to make a hasty exit. That was when we turned round and met you coming in the door."

"I see, sir. Well that's all for now. We'll be back to have another word shortly," and the two detectives left the room.

As they left the interview room and were about to enter an adjacent room they met James Palmer walking towards them.

"James," exclaimed Inspector Westwood, "glad you could make it. We won't be long, take a seat in my office," and he and Sergeant Benson entered the interview room where Susan Rumble was seated behind a small table.

"So Miss Rumble, tell me what you did today from when you got up this morning to when we found you with Callisto's body."

"Nothing much to tell really. I had some urgent work to finish for Sir David. Rather than go into the office where I risked all sorts of interruptions and delays I opted to stay and complete the work at home."

"Very convenient, no-one to give you an alibi!"

"It's not convenient, it's the truth."

"So when did you get to The Carpenter's Arms?"

"I was supposed to meet Craig, I mean Mr Bentley, at two o'clock but because the job for Sir David took longer than I thought I didn't get there until about three o'clock. You can check with the hotel staff. I asked them when I arrived if he was still in his room."

"Don't concern yourself about that, we'll be speaking to them in due course. What happened next?"

"I went up to Craig's room and we had a drink and then his mobile phone rang. He said it was a message from Sir David to meet him at 'The Tanning Studio' in Epping."

"Didn't you think that rather strange? Didn't you think Sir David would have wanted to meet you in his office or at his home? After all Forest Glade is only a few minutes' drive from Epping."

"Yes, we both thought it very strange indeed, but when Sir David calls you don't ask questions you just do as he says. We were worried, though, because we thought nobody knew about our meetings. If it had got back to Sir David then we would both have been in trouble."

"So what happened when you got to the Tanning Studio?"

"The place appeared deserted. There was a closed notice on the door but when I tried it the door opened so we went inside. We looked around the studio but there was no-one there. I felt hot and took my jacket off and then we noticed the smell. We saw a light on in one of the booths so we went over and I looked inside. I'll never forget that sight, it was horrible," and Susan began to cry.

"Take your time," said an understanding Inspector Westwood handing her a tissue, "Then what happened?"

"Well," said Susan sobbing uncontrollably, "I was nearly sick and grabbed hold of Craig. He had a quick look inside and we decided to get out straight away before anyone found us there and thought we had done it."

"Why didn't you dial 999 for the police?"

"I don't know. I suppose we panicked. It all happened so quickly. We turned to leave and literally ran into you."

"Lucky we happened to come along. Did you get on well with Callisto Fairfax?"

"Yes of course I did. I'll admit we didn't always see eye-to-eye and she could be very abrasive at times, but I had no reason to harm her. From an accountant's point of view her business methods often sailed very close to the wind but I certainly had no reason to kill her."

"One final question for now," stressed the Inspector, "What size shoes do you take?"

"Shoes? Size 5, why?"

"That's all. We'll be back later with some more questions," and the two detectives left the room.

"Come on Benson back to my office. Let's see what we can get out of James Palmer. He owes me a favour or two after what I've told him about how the investigation is going."

Inspector Westwood greeted James most warmly and came straight to the point, "There's been another murder and this time it's Callisto Fairfax!"

"Oh no!" exclaimed a surprised James, "What can you tell me about it?"

Inspector Westwood went into some detail about how Callisto had been killed in 'The Tanning Studio' and how he had found Craig Bentley and Susan Rumble about to leave the scene. He also told James about his interviews with Craig and Susan and of his suspicions.

"Now," said Inspector Westwood, "I've been very frank with you so it's time for you to bring me up to date with how your investigations have been going. What have you been able to discover."

James Palmer outlined to the Inspector what had emerged from his various visits to East Anglia and what he had found out from John Harwood, Mrs Goodenough and the local papers.

"Most interesting, you've done a thorough job as I knew you would. More to do though and I trust you'll keep me in the picture."

"You can bank on it Ben. As soon as I get anything concrete you'll be the first to know."

James was about to leave when a thought came into his head, "Was 'The Tanning Studio' supposed to be open today or was it closed? I mean, surely somebody knows who should have been on duty there. Have you spoken to the owners?"

"Ahead of you there, Benson's already made enquiries. Apparently someone by the name of Gillian Fish should have been there all day. She's new and has only been employed since Monday. Nobody knows what's happened to her. She was there in the morning but seems to have disappeared."

"Description?" enquired James.

"Middle-aged, long darkish hair, wearing heavy black-rimmed spectacles. A description that could fit lots of people. One more thing, though," added Benson, "she telephoned the manicurist this morning and told her not to come in as there was some sort of a leak and the studio was out of commission for the day. She obviously wanted to be on her own."

"Not really a lead there, then," sighed James.

"The description could fit Susan Rumble and, would you believe, she takes size 5 shoes."

"Size 5 shoes?" asked a puzzled James.

"Remember, at Ongar Park Woods. Whoever killed Nick Fairfax was wearing size 5 shoes."

"It's a bit thin, though, isn't it?"

"It's all we've got at the moment. On the strength of it we've managed to obtain a warrant to search Susan Rumble's house. We're going there now. Want to tag along, unofficially of course?"

"Very much so," replied an enthusiastic James Palmer, "but do you think Craig Bentley is involved as well?"

"Hard to say at the moment. He may have just been used by Susan to provide a sort of an alibi – not cast iron but enough to put us off the scent. We'll hold him as well as her for the time being."

"One thing that does puzzle me, though," said James after a few moments thought, "If Susan Rumble is our murderer then why would she tip you off? Why send you to that tanning studio to catch her in the act, it doesn't make any sense at all."

"As I said earlier, it could be to put us off the scent. Come on, let's go."

Inspector Westwood was about to leave his office when a thought occurred to him, "Benson, I think we should take Susan Rumble with us when we search her house. Let's see her reaction if we find anything significant. Have her cuffed to a WPC."

Inspector Westwood, Sergeant Benson, James Palmer and a team of forensic officers, together with Susan Rumble herself, then left for Susan Rumble's house in Woodford Green.

Chapter Forty-nine

The small convoy of police vehicles arrived at Susan Rumble's house in Woodford Green long after darkness had fallen.

"Looks like a very nice house, sir," Sergeant Benson said sarcastically as he and Inspector Westwood stared at the large detached four-bedroomed property which was illuminated with the help of two nearby street lights, "must be a lot of money in accountancy."

"Or a lot of money in crime!" suggested the Inspector.

"Come on Ben you don't know that," interjected James Palmer.

"I think I do and you do too. You've been digging around in David Fairfax's businesses and I think you've a good idea by now just what sort of a man he is and how he operates. I'm told the fraud boys are investigating his empire and it's just a matter of time before they move against him."

Inspector Westwood and the rest of the police team put on their white all-in-one boiler suits and entered Susan's house and began their search. Susan reluctantly followed them as they made their way around the property, "I keep telling you," she pleaded, "there's nothing here to find," but her words fell on deaf ears.

Nothing of any significance was found on the ground floor but when the forensic team entered Susan's upstairs study they couldn't believe their eyes. In a locked cabinet they found a supply of old style 'DesboroDenim' paper bags and carrier bags. Looking elsewhere in the room they came across a drawer containing a selection of old-fashioned 'DesboroDenim' clothes and underwear.

"I've never seen them before in my life," said a bewildered-looking Susan, "I've no idea how they got here."

"A very convenient lapse of memory, madam," snapped Sergeant Benson.

Moving on into the master-bedroom Inspector Westwood opened one of two large fitted wardrobes and stepped back in amazement. In front of him was a selection of different coloured wigs and other make-up items ranging from face paints to coloured contact lenses.

"I suppose you've never seen these before, either?" he asked sarcastically.

"No, never," answered Susan most emphatically.

Then, just as the Inspector had opened the second wardrobe to reveal a large collection of sexy underwear and kinky PVC clothes, one of the forensic team called him into an adjoining bedroom.

"What do you make of this, sir?"

Inspector Westwood went through the door and found himself looking at a manikin dressed in 'The Tanning Studio' staff uniform complete with a dark-haired wig and heavy black-rimmed spectacles.

"I'd say we've just found the elusive Gillian Fish wouldn't you sergeant? The elusive Gillian Fish who doesn't exist. The elusive Gillian Fish who is none other than Susan Rumble!"

"No!" protested Susan who had followed the Inspector into the room, "I've never seen those things before. Why don't you believe me?"

"All in good time, you'll have your say in due course," and Inspector Westwood moved on into the next bedroom but nothing further was found.

"Look Benson, you stay here with the forensic boys and keep an eye on things, and constable," he said turning to the WPC handcuffed to Susan Rumble, "take Miss Rumble back to the nick and make her comfortable for the night."

"But inspector, I keep telling you I've never seen any of these things before. They're nothing to do with me! Somebody must have planted them here!"

"No signs of a forced entry. Take her away constable," and turning to James Palmer he added, "I think we should pay a visit to David Fairfax on our way back to Epping and bring him up to date on the investigation. Want to come along?"

"I wouldn't miss it for the world," said James and the two men left the house deep in conversation.

Chapter Fifty

"To wake me at this time of night you must have something important to tell me," said David Fairfax in subdued tones, "I'd appreciate it if you kept your voice down as Lucy has taken this very badly and has only just managed to get off to sleep."

"Certainly, Sir David. When I left you earlier this evening I said we had a suspect. Well things have moved much faster than I could have hoped and we are now holding someone on suspicion of the murders of Tom, Nick and Callisto," announced Inspector Westwood proudly, "and I assumed you'd want to know this as soon as possible."

"Well spit it out man! Who is it?"

"It's Susan Rumble."

"Susan Rumble! Is this some sort of a joke? She's one of my key employees. Why do you think it's her?"

"She was apprehended at the scene of Callisto's murder and a search of her house has revealed a number of items that link her to the crimes."

"And what are these items exactly?"

"Sorry, can't say at the moment, but they're significant and directly link her to all three murders."

"Susan Rumble, who would have thought it?" mused David Fairfax, "But why would she do this?"

"Hopefully we'll find that out during the course of her interrogation. It's possible she had an accomplice and you should know we're also holding Craig Bentley."

"Craig Bentley! Now you're getting ridiculous. Craig's been with me for over ten years. What would he hope to gain by killing my children?"

"There's something else you may not be aware of, Sir David. It appears Susan Rumble and Craig Bentley have been having an affair for some considerable time and ..."

"What!" fumed Sir David interrupting the Inspector, "Are you sure? They've been having an affair under my very nose! How dare they? They'll pay for this!"

Inspector Westwood didn't respond to Sir David's outburst and ignored the implied threat but added after a suitable interval, "We're not sure just what Craig Bentley's involvement is in this matter. If we can't get any evidence against him we may have to release him."

"Release him! You'd better be sure he had nothing to do with any of this before you let him go!" he said menacingly.

414

Inspector Westwood once again ignored the threat from Sir David and concluded by saying, "Sorry to have intruded. We've taken up enough of your time, we'll be going now," and Inspector Westwood and James Palmer went to leave.

"Thank you inspector, sorry I was a little abrupt at first," Sir David apologised and as the two men approached the door he added in more conciliatory tones, "James, could I have a word with you, won't keep you long."

After Inspector Westwood had left and the sound of his departing car could be heard on the gravel outside, David Fairfax sat down in his favourite armchair and looked directly at James, "This is a complete disaster. I paid you good money to find out who was behind all this and that Inspector beats you to it. I should demand my money back. No bonus for you now I'm afraid, you can kiss that one goodbye."

"I'm not so sure Susan Rumble was behind the murders. I've seen the evidence and it's true, it is very convincing, but there's something about it that doesn't seem quite right to me."

"If Inspector Westwood and the forces of law and order think she's guilty then that's good enough for me. You can go your work for me is finished!"

"If that's what you want then I'll willingly go, but I really do think there are loose ends to tie up and they point to someone else being responsible."

"Who?"

"I don't know, but I think I'm getting close to finding out."

"Look, I'm inclined to believe the Inspector so the matter's over as far as I'm concerned. If you want to carry on digging the dirt then that's up to you but don't expect any more money from me."

"Right enough!" said an indignant James, "I will carry on and I'll prove you and that inspector wrong!" and he stormed out of the room.

As soon as he heard the front door close David Fairfax picked up his mobile phone and punched in a number, "That you Feb? Good! I've got a little job for you and the boys. In the morning get down to Epping Police Station and wait outside. When Craig Bentley is released I want you to take him to 'The Shop', I have a score to settle with him!" and he put the phone down and made his way back to bed.

Chapter Fifty-one

"I still can't believe it," said Jenny stretching across the breakfast table to pick up a slice of toast, "Sacked! David Fairfax actually had the gall to sack you!"

"That's right," replied James between mouthfuls, "he told me in no uncertain terms that by hiring me to investigate on his behalf he'd wasted his money. He said he should have left it to the police all along. I tried to tell him Susan Rumble may not be the murderer but he wouldn't listen. He wouldn't even let me explain why I thought it might be someone else."

"If it isn't Susan then who do you think it might be?"

"If Susan was the culprit then surely she'd have taken precautions to make sure there was nothing incriminating in her own house. All three of those murders were most meticulously planned, nothing was left to chance. I can't believe that someone who could plan in such detail would be so careless as to leave a whole house-full of damning evidence virtually on show for anyone to find. Besides, there's that phone call to Epping Police Station and the message for Inspector Westwood. Why shop yourself? It just doesn't add up!"

"It does seem a little odd," agreed Jenny, "and the more I think about it the more I'm inclined to agree with you. Let's look where we've got to so far. None of our enquiries have led us anywhere near Susan, quite the contrary in fact. Either she's been very clever at misleading us and throwing us off the scent, or she's innocent and somebody has set her up."

"Precisely, that's it in a nutshell. My money's on the latter."

"So," enquired Jenny as she finished the last of her toast, "where do we go from here? Throw in the towel on this one or carry on digging to see what we can unearth?"

"Well we've done very nicely out of David Fairfax so far and haven't spent much of the money he's given us, so why don't we follow up the leads we've got and see where they take us?"

"Agreed," said a very pleased Jenny hugging her husband and causing him to spill his cup of tea on the floor, "after all the effort we've put into this case it would be a pity to just abandon it."

"Abandon, no! Postpone, yes!"

"What do you mean?" said Jenny giving a cloth to James so he could mop up his spilt tea, "What do you mean postpone?"

"Why don't we spend some of David's money? Let's go away for a couple of weeks. I think we deserve it after all the time and effort we've put into this case over the last few months. We can come back refreshed and see how things are, whether Susan is still in custody and whether any other incidents have occurred in the meantime."

What a great idea! Where do you want to go? You know I'll go anywhere so long as it's hot."

"I've no idea but let's make it somewhere special this time, somewhere exotic. Come on, let's get changed and go down to the travel agents right now."

"Best thing you've said in ages," said Jenny and she and James raced each other up the stairs.

* * * * *

Feb and two of 'the boys' waited across the road from Epping Police Station keeping a close watch on the entrance and scrutinising all those who went in and out. They passed the time by reading newspapers and making rude comments about passers by but as the morning dragged on they started to become agitated and bored. All of a sudden Feb spoke up, "Look! There he is now!" and the three of them began to cross the road as Craig Bentley appeared on the steps of the Police Station in the company of Inspector Westwood.

"Leave him to me, boys," snapped Feb as they reached the centre of the road, "I'll grab him as soon as the Inspector goes back inside and Craig is on his own."

But as the three of them watched no sooner had Inspector Westwood gone into the building then two other obvious plain-clothed policemen approached Craig and escorted him back into the Police Station.

"What the hell's all that about?" thought Feb, "I'd better phone Sir David," and he took out his mobile phone.

"Ok Feb, thanks for letting me know. You come back here but leave one of the lads in town to keep an eye on things just in case they let Craig out later. We wouldn't want to miss him now would we?"

* * * * *

Back in Forest Glade David Fairfax was a worried man as all manner of thoughts streamed through his mind, "Why would they let Craig go just to take him back inside again. Who were those other detectives anyway? It didn't appear they had anything to do with Inspector Westwood and his investigations," and he sat down in his study to think and lost all track of time as he gazed out of the window. He was brought back to reality by the sound of a car pulling up on the driveway, "That's quick! Feb must have driven here at a fair old rate of knots."

A few minutes later there was a knock on his study door and a nervous looking Katie peered into the room, "Excuse me Sir David, but there are two gentlemen to see you, an Inspector Beedham and Malcolm Caddick from the immigration service."

"That's all right, Katie, tell them I'll join them shortly in the drawing room," and a look of deep apprehension and foreboding appeared on David Fairfax's face as he rocked to and fro in his chair.

After a minute or two Sir David strode into the drawing room, "Good morning gentlemen, I'm David Fairfax, what can I do for you?"

"Good morning Sir David, this is Malcolm Caddick from the immigration service and I'm Inspector Beedham from the serious crimes squad."

"I'll come straight to the point," said Malcolm Caddick in a stern tone of voice, "Do you know a Dimitri Komarov by any chance?"

"Dimitri Komarov?" Sir David looked up at the ceiling as if in deep thought, "No, I don't think I do. What has he to do with me?"

"Dimitri Komarov is well-known in east-European circles as a people trafficker and he's also an illegal immigrant in this country. We've been after him for a couple of years now but he always manages to be just one step ahead of us."

"I'd like to help you Mr Caddick but as I said, I've never heard of him."

"That's very strange because earlier today we arrested him and most of his gang on one of your Norfolk farms. We also found nearly a hundred illegal immigrants from former Communist Bloc countries working there without the necessary work permits and official approval. At this very moment we have teams searching your other farms in the area and I'm reliably informed that more illegal workers have already been found."

"I, I, don't know what to say," stammered Sir David, "this is news to me. I would never sanction that sort of thing. I've always prided myself on abiding strictly by the law in all my business ventures. I've no knowledge of this at all."

"That may well be the case, sir," interjected Inspector Beedham, "but we think otherwise. I'd be obliged, therefore, if you could accompany us to the station."

"What now!" exclaimed Sir David, "Just like that?"

"If you wouldn't mind, sir," and Inspector Beedham indicated they should leave at once.

As the three of them made their way to the front door Lucy came out of the kitchen. She saw her husband in the grip of one of the men but before she could utter a word Sir David shouted to her, "Phone Julius! Tell him I'm being taken to Epping Police Station and tell him to get there as soon as he can."

"But David," sobbed Lucy in bewilderment as her husband was led away, "what's happening?"

"A simple misunderstanding that's all," replied Sir David in a bid to reassure his wife, "but tell Julius to get there as soon as he can."

Lucy watched in amazement as Sir David was bundled into the back of the Inspector's car and driven off. She hurriedly went inside and telephoned the family's solicitor to tell him what had happened.

* * * * *

David Fairfax steadfastly refused to answer any questions until he had had an opportunity to speak to his solicitor. Julius Rosenberg had a reputation for being a very sharp lawyer and was famed for his ability to get his clients freed on the merest of technicalities. In the past there had been numerous occasions when Sir David had made use of his services in connection with his business empire but he never envisaged that he would need him on a personal basis.

"At last we can begin," said an exasperated Inspector Beedham, "Sir David, how do you explain the presence of illegal immigrants and workers on your farms in Norfolk?"

"My client categorically denies all knowledge of any illegal workers. He has not taken a direct interest in the farming side of his business for some months now and has been content to leave the day-to-day running of that side of things to his Managing Director."

"Oh really!" said Inspector Beedham, "I was under the impression that one of your well-known company slogans referred to you as being in full command all the time!"

"That's correct," replied Julius, "but that was when Sir David personally oversaw all aspects of his businesses. I would remind you that he is a Member of Parliament and until earlier this year was also a Minister of the Crown when he was required to relinquish all connections to the businesses. Since then, as I'm sure you are more than aware, he has had to live with all three of his children being murdered in the most brutal of ways including his daughter only yesterday. He is still in a most distressed condition and his mind has been concentrated on personal and family matters and he hasn't been able to devote any of his time to business affairs. The running of the various elements has been left in the hands of his three managing directors."

"So you're asking me to believe that Sir David was unaware of what was going on under his very nose on his own farms!"

"Totally unaware! He was completely ignorant of these matters and it has come as a complete shock to him. He is devastated by the news and still finds it hard to accept."

"It seems to me that this is all so very convenient!"

"My client takes great offence at that remark. I would remind you that his daughter was killed only yesterday! Convenient is hardly the word he would use!"

"I'm sorry. I don't want to appear insensitive but Sir David is the head of Fairfax Farms."

"I'm not disputing that fact but he hasn't had any active involvement in the day-to-day running of those farms for many months now. As I said earlier you should be speaking to Craig Bentley about this matter. He's the person in charge and responsible for what has taken place."

"Very well Mr Rosenberg, we will be speaking to Mr Bentley about his involvement with Dimitri Komarov and I would ask that you wait here with your client until we return."

"My client willingly agrees to this but I would remind you that in the absence of any criminal charges I'll be expecting my client to be released at the earliest opportunity."

Inspector Beedham and Malcolm Caddick left the room and a constable came and stood inside the door of the locked interview room. Julius Rosenberg and Sir David leant towards each other and exchanged a few words in little more than a whisper, "Don't worry Sir David, they haven't got any evidence to link you to any of this. They're bluffing. I think they know Craig Bentley is involved with that Dimitri Komarov character and they're just trying to net a bigger fish."

It was nearly an hour before Inspector Beedham and Malcolm Caddick returned to the interview room.

"Sorry to have kept you waiting, gentlemen," announced Inspector Beedham as soon as he entered the room, "but we had enquiries to complete. As a result of further investigations we expect to be charging Craig Bentley with a number of offences in connection with the trafficking of illegal immigrants and employing illegal workers. He has made a full confession and also implicated Dimitri Komarov."

"However," Malcolm Caddick stressed, "it isn't that simple, the matter doesn't end there. Under current legislation we are entitled to confiscate any assets and property that have been gained through criminal or illegal activity. We have, therefore, applied to take possession of all assets including the farms themselves. The business has, therefore, effectively been closed down."

"That's outrageous!" shouted an indignant Julius, "My client knows nothing about this matter! If you want to confiscate anybody's assets then it should be those belonging to Craig Bentley. My client will contest this arbitrary decision vigorously through the courts, to the European Courts if necessary."

"That's his prerogative but case law and precedent dictate that he is most unlikely to be successful."

"We shall see. Is my client now free to go?" enquired Julius Rosenberg regaining his composure and suppressing his outrage, "If you have no further questions then we'll ..."

"For the time-being," interrupted the Inspector, "Sir David is indeed free to go but our enquiries are not yet complete and we may need to speak to him further.

CHAPTER FIFTY-ONE

I trust Sir David has no foreign holidays planned in the near future!"

"Thank you, Inspector," replied Julius and he and Sir David quickly left the interview room and made their way outside to Julius' car.

"Come back to the house," proposed Sir David as he and Julius drove back to Forest Glade but Julius declined the invitation.

"Some other time," he replied, "I had to leave an important briefing to come here but if anything crops up in the future don't hesitate to contact me."

David Fairfax was seething with anger when Katie answered the front door and let him in, "Where's Lucy?" he roared, "I want to speak to her!"

"She's in the lounge, sir."

David stormed into the lounge and sat opposite Lucy. The cats sensed his mood and took the opportunity to escape and ran off to another room.

"Would you believe it?" he shouted almost deafening Lucy, "That bastard Craig Bentley has been in league with some east-European gangster and running an illegal immigration racket and employing illegal workers on my farms! *On my farms*! What's more the immigration people say they're going to seize all the assets. I'll get him for this!"

"But what about the police? Haven't they got him?"

"Yes, they've arrested him but when he gets out I'll," and David paused before ordering his thoughts and adding, "You know this spells the end for Fairfax Farms. Julius was upbeat about fighting the seizure but I don't think we stand much of a chance. This is a disaster, a bloody great disaster. If I get my hands on him!"

Lucy remained silent. Past experience had taught her to be quiet and David would eventually calm down.

"It's all because of my not paying sufficient attention to the day-to-day running of the businesses. Those Managing Directors have taken advantage of my absence. Look at Susan Rumble! An affair, who would have thought that of 'the spinster'? Last person I'd have thought would do anything like that – and with Craig Bentley as well! Still, they're both going to get their just desserts now. That reminds me, I wonder if Craig's wife knows about his little bit on the side?"

"I doubt it dear. If none of us knew then why should she?"

"I'll soon see to that! Tomorrow I'll get Angela to phone and put her fully in the picture. She must know by now about Craig's arrest but let's add to her discomfort by telling her about his affair with Susan."

"If it'll make you feel better."

"It certainly will," and David sat in his chair and tried to calm down by pouring himself a drink. He didn't think to offer Lucy one.

"And one other thing," he added after emptying his glass with a single gulp, "If this sort of thing can happen in one area then it's possible it can happen elsewhere. I'm going to get Angela to do a bit of investigating to see if those other two, Ken Winter and Alan Box, have been up to anything behind my back. God help them if they have!"

"Good idea," agreed Lucy hoping this would satisfy her husband.

"I'm back in charge! And nobody's going to be left in any doubt about that," and David helped himself to another drink and sat back in his armchair with a determined look on his face.

Chapter Fifty-two

The taxi reversed onto the road and sped away from the house. A weary James Palmer carried the two very heavy suitcases into the hall closely followed by Jenny who was carrying their two shoulder bags.

"I'd like to say I'm glad to be back," exclaimed Jenny as she followed her husband into the lounge and almost threw the shoulder bags onto the floor, "but I'm not."

"Neither am I," replied James abandoning the cases and slumping down into one of the armchairs, "holidays are all well and good but the journey home!"

"Yes, bit of a long haul, almost makes you want another break doesn't it?"

"It certainly does. That cruise was just fantastic. I'm glad I persuaded you to book it."

"What a cheek, it was my idea!" said an indignant James.

"Ok, if you insist. Still, just think, three weeks sailing around Borneo and Malaysia. We've visited places I never thought we'd ever get to see."

"Yes. I liked the jungles and beaches of course and that mountain, what was its name again?"

"Mount Kinabalu."

"That's the one, most impressive!"

"I also liked the shopping," said Jenny, "I never realised that Singapore and Kuala Lumpur were full of such wonderful places to shop. All those designer labels, and so cheap!"

"You would if you had to carry the cases!" retorted James.

"A small price to pay for my new wardrobe."

"And they were so high-tech as well. I was most impressed with how the modern skyscrapers blended in so well with the Moorish buildings and colonial architecture in Kuala Lumpur."

"Well it's back to reality now. I wonder if those two children of ours kept an eye on the house or if they just came over this morning and tidied up?"

"Let's find out," and James got up and went to the kitchen. After a moment's hesitation Jenny followed him.

"Good old Matt, he's done a good job here," said James thumbing through three neat piles of mail that had been sorted into priority order, "Do you think Vickie came round while we were away?"

"Yes," replied Jenny looking in the fridge, "she's filled this up for us. Even put a couple of beers in here for you too. I must have a word with her about spoiling you," and after checking to see what was in the freezer she added, "One of them has even sorted out the newspapers into date order for us."

"Very thoughtful," said James, "Tell you what, why don't you make a cup of tea and then we can sit down and see what's been going on while we've been away."

"Just because you've been waited-on hand-and-foot for the last few weeks don't think you're going to get the same service here," and Jenny thrust the pile of newspapers into James' hands and pushed him out of the kitchen.

The Palmers spent the next hour or so sifting through the newspapers. Most of them reported that Susan Rumble had been charged with the murders of Tom, Nick and Callisto Fairfax and had been remanded in custody pending her trial at the beginning of September. There were also reports of Callisto's funeral which had been restricted to just close family and friends. The most surprising news, however, was that David Fairfax had resigned as a Member of Parliament and a date for the resulting by-election had already been set.

"Who would have thought it?" said Jenny, "David Fairfax resigning his seat."

"I imagine the Prime Minister put pressure on him. He was most probably becoming a little too embarrassing for the party what with the recent deaths of his children and talk of dodgy business dealings and the like, so he had to go. A ruthless business politics."

"So where does that leave us? Do we just forget about all the time and effort we've put into this case or do we carry on?"

"The easy option is just to walk away from it," pondered James, "but I'm not so sure that Susan Rumble is the guilty party. As we discussed before we went away it's all so very convenient."

"So we soldier on then?" Jenny said expectantly.

"From reading the newspapers nothing untoward seems to have happened to the Fairfax family or the Fairfax business empire in the last three or four weeks so it seems as if it's all over. But I'm not entirely convinced and I think it's worth spending a little more time on the case."

"I'd agree with that," said a delighted Jenny, "but where do we go from here?"

"Dinner then an early night," replied James with a grin on his face.

"You'll be lucky! I've no intention of cooking tonight," and Jenny switched the television on.

"Just in time," said James smugly, "the news is about to start."

James and Jenny settled down on the settee together and watched in disbelief as the newsreader announced, "Earlier today armed response units from Essex Police were called to a warehouse complex in Witham, near Chelmsford, where two rival gangs of Albanian gangsters were involved in fierce fighting. It appears the dispute centred on which of the gangs should have control of a racket that is thought to have led to millions of pounds worth of illegal alcohol and cigarettes being smuggled into the United Kingdom. A fierce gun battle was already in progress when the response unit arrived and several members of the rival gangs are known to have been killed.

The warehouses at the centre of this incident are owned by Fairfax Forwarding a company owned by Sir David Fairfax who recently resigned his Parliamentary seat. It is believed that Ken Winter, the Managing Director of Fairfax Forwarding, has been shot and is now in Broomfield Hospital in Chelmsford. As yet there is no word on his condition but it is not thought to be life-threatening. We will give you more on this story later in the bulletin when we hope to bring you a live interview with the Chief Constable of Essex who is at the scene."

"What do you make of that then?" said an excited Jenny, "Not a dull moment where that old school chum of yours is concerned."

"I'd say Ken Winter's been indulging in a bit of private enterprise unbeknown to David Fairfax. I'd say he's taken advantage of David loosening his grip of late to go into business on his own and it's all gone horribly wrong. I've heard these Albanian gangs can be quite ruthless and have no qualms about gunning down anyone who gets in their way."

"A nasty business then. I wonder how David Fairfax has taken the news?"

* * * * *

In the Fairfax building at the heart of Canary Wharf David Fairfax finished work for the day and telephoned Feb to say he was ready to be driven home. As he closed his briefcase and got up from his chair there was a knock on his office door and Angela Hamilton rushed into the room, "Sir David, switch the television on, now!"

Sir David placed his briefcase on the desk and quickly pressed a button on the remote-control. The television instantly flickered to life and he sat back in his chair as details of the shooting unfolded before him and he listened intently to the interview with the Chief Constable of Essex. The more he heard the more he began to fume. As his face turned from red to purple Angela decided it was prudent to leave the room.

"Where the hell do you think you're going?" he boomed, "Sit down!"

Angela nervously sat down as far away from Sir David as she physically could.

"This is outrageous!" he ranted out aloud, "Albanian gangsters – and at my warehouses! If Ken Winter has a hand in this he'll wish he'd never been born!"

Sir David switched off the television set and threw the remote-control down on the desk with such force that the battery compartment sprang open and the batteries rolled out across the desk and onto the floor. He picked up his briefcase and stormed out of the office without saying a further word. Angela remained alone and rather bemused in the empty office.

Sir David took his personal lift to the ground floor and left the building. He deliberately ignored the fawning commissionaire who received a scowl rather than his customary 'goodnight Wilson'. Feb, sensing something was wrong, immediately jumped out of the car and opened one of the rear doors for his boss. He then drove Sir David away.

"Step on it, Feb," said Sir David in a menacing tone of voice and Feb, always the diplomat, decided to remain silent for the drive home to Theydon Bois and thereby not risk incurring the wrath of his boss.

* * * * *

Lucy had already seen the news and was waiting for her husband's return with more than a degree of trepidation. The two of them barely had time to discuss the matter when there was the sound of a car pulling up on the gravel drive and voices could be heard as two men approached the house. A few minutes later a rather flustered Katie entered the room and announced that Inspector Westwood had arrived in the company of Inspector Beedham.

"Show them into the study," said Sir David, "and tell them I'll join them shortly."

After a few minutes Sir David entered the study, "Good evening gentlemen, I think I know why you're here."

"We thought that might be the case, sir," Inspector Westwood said in a sarcastic tone of voice.

"This concerns the incident at your warehouses in Witham this morning," added Inspector Beedham almost immediately, "You seem to be making a habit of breaking the law."

"Now look here," retorted an angry Sir David, "the first I knew about this matter was when I saw it on the television a few minutes before I left the office. I don't like your tone and what you're implying."

"We take a very dim view indeed of gun crime, sir, and we have to ask you a few questions," said Inspector Westwood in a much quieter tone of voice in an attempt to calm the situation.

"Well I want my solicitor here," snapped Sir David, "before I answer any of your questions.

"That's your prerogative of course," replied Inspector Beedham calmly, "but we do only want to ask you some questions. If you prefer to have your solicitor present then we can do this down at the station. On the other hand if you're prepared to answer our questions now then we can conclude this matter right here, in the comfort of your own home."

"Very well, then," said a resigned Sir David, "what do you want to know?"

"What exactly is your involvement with these Albanian smugglers and how long have you done business with them."

"I'll make this crystal clear," stressed Sir David struggling to contain his temper, "I've never conducted any business whatsoever with Albanian or any other sort of smugglers, this is all news to me. As I said during our last conversation at Epping Police Station I haven't been involved with the day-to-day running of any of my companies for some months. As a matter of fact now that I'm no longer a Member of Parliament I'm about to take a more active role again."

"It seems that might be a bit late now, Sir David," Inspector Beedham said before asking, "How long has Ken Winter worked for you?"

"I really am so very disappointed with Ken. He's been with me now for over 20 years. I've always considered him to be one of my more able managing directors. He's always been so reliable. I find it hard to believe he would be involved in this sort of thing."

"From what we've been able to gather so far it looks like he was involved in a big way with these people. The problem appears to be that he was caught up in a rather vicious turf-war between rival gangs and it came to a head this morning. By the time our armed response units arrived on the scene a fierce gun battle was in progress and several members of both factions were already dead. Ken Winter himself was wounded in the exchange of fire."

"How is he? They said on the news that his injury wasn't life-threatening."

"That's right, it's not. At the moment he's under armed guard in Broomfield Hospital but as soon as he's fit to be discharged he'll be helping us with our enquiries. We may need to speak to you again," stressed Inspector Westwood and he began to walk towards the door.

"Oh one last thing, sir," added Inspector Beedham who from his tone of voice was making no secret of his dislike for Sir David, "this does mean that the assets at your warehouses will be seized under the Proceeds of Crime legislation by the Assets Recovery Agency. The premises will be sealed and you shouldn't try to enter them or attempt to remove any items from them."

"I note what you say but I will be taking advice on the matter."

"That's entirely up to you. Now, we must be going. Good evening and thanks for your time."

David Fairfax sat in silence fuming as the two Inspectors left the room. He made no attempt to get up from his chair until he heard their car make its way along the driveway.

Lucy finally plucked up the courage to join her husband and sat next to him on the settee. After a few minutes of silence she looked him straight in the eyes and said, "This is bad for us isn't it?"

"It certainly is, and it couldn't have come at a worse time. I never thought Ken would do this to me, nor Craig for that matter. This is what comes of taking my eye off the ball. I should never have taken that damn ministerial post. We made a lot of money out of it but that's small beer to what we've lost over the last few weeks. I should have remained more visible at the helm and none of this would have happened or, if it did, I'd have had only myself to blame. I still can't believe it, in the space of a month both Fairfax Farms and Fairfax Forwarding have gone."

"You've still got the 'DesboroDenim' group, you've not lost everything," said Lucy trying to console her husband, but then she remembered her children and broke down in an inconsolable bout of crying.

"Yes, we've still got the 'DesboroDenim' group but what's the point? There's nobody left to build it up for, nobody left to inherit it!" said David as the realisation that all his children were now dead flooded back into his mind.

Sir David and Lucy sat hugging each other in silence, neither of them knowing what to say for fear of upsetting the other. They remained this way until Katie knocked on the door. Getting no answer she gingerly looked into the room, "Sorry to trouble you, Sir David," she said in a faltering voice, "but I've got Alan Box on the telephone. He says he's been trying to reach you on your mobile. He says it's urgent he speaks to you."

"Tell him I'll contact him later as soon as I'm free."

"Very good, Sir David," and Katie left the room.

Later that night after he and Lucy had eaten a late supper and his wife had gone to bed Sir David telephoned Alan Box.

"Alan, what can I do for you?"

"David, thanks for getting back to me. It's bad news I'm afraid!"

"Bad news? Are you talking about that incident at Witham this morning?"

"No I'm not, and I was very sorry to hear about that. I take it the police have been to see you?"

"Yes they have. I knew nothing at all about what was going on there but I don't know if the police believe me or not. I suppose I'll find out soon enough. Now, what was it you wanted to tell me?"

"I don't really know how to put this and it might be best if we meet soon to discuss it in detail. Over the last

few months we've not only lost contracts to the Anne
Harvey Group but we've also seen a marked tailing off
in both orders and sales. From a cash-flow point of view
we're heading for serious trouble. With Susan Rumble
no longer around I've had one of her team, Cliff Hall,
go through the accounts and he says we'll be lucky to
survive more than a few weeks if things don't improve.
I thought you would wish to know this now at an early
stage so we can decide what to do and put together an
action plan. Cliff thinks we're very vulnerable to being
taken over by our competitors."

"Yes, yes, I hear what you say," Sir David replied
clearly becoming angrier by the minute, "This is
becoming an absolute disaster. I'll expect a full report
from you tomorrow, is that clear? I know tomorrow's
Saturday but I want you and Cliff to come here, to
Forest Glade, so we can go through the papers together."

"But that's not enough time to ..."

"Just do it," barked Sir David cutting Alan Box off in
mid-sentence and he hung up the telephone.

Chapter Fifty-three

Saturday morning and Lucy Fairfax got into her red sports car and roared off through the narrow forest roads towards Epping. Following Susan Rumble's arrest her self-confidence had quickly returned. Although the deaths of her children still weighed heavily on her mind she had made a conscious effort to break free of her cycle of self-pity and force herself to get out into the wider world once more.

Lucy drove along the narrow twisting forest road and her mind wandered to the new shoes she hoped to buy from a small designer boutique in the High Street. As she rounded a particularly sharp bend on the brow of a small hill she was quickly brought back to reality as she almost collided head-on with a pedestrian walking on her side of the road.

"Bloody nuisance these people who insist on walking in the road!" Lucy said angrily to herself as she swerved to the centre of the winding road. She then glanced in her mirror to see if the pedestrian was all right.

"No, it can't be," she gasped as she glimpsed the figure and immediately brought the car to a halt. Once stationary she looked back along the road but she couldn't see any sign of the person she had so narrowly managed to avoid.

Lucy sat trembling in the parked car for a few minutes to recover her composure. She then reversed the vehicle to where the pedestrian had been walking but there was no sign of anybody.

"Must have been my imagination but it certainly looked like Callisto. No, it couldn't have been," and after a moment's reflection she started the car and continued her journey.

Epping is always a very busy town on Saturdays and Lucy had trouble finding a parking space, so in desperation she parked at the rear of 'The Shop'. She knew it was where David often conducted business and met people he would rather not be seen with in public but she was ignorant of its other more sinister function. She locked the car and walked round the side of the building towards the High Street when her attention was drawn to the driver of a passing car.

"No!" she exclaimed as the car sped past her, "Not again!" and she hurried to the end of the road to try and get a better view of the driver but the car had disappeared in the heavy High Street traffic. She began to feel weak at the knees but managed to walk around the corner and into The Upper Crust Restaurant.

"Good morning Lady Lucy, this is indeed an honour," said a surprised Colin Rust as Lucy almost fell through the open doors of the restaurant, "let me find you a table."

"Thank you, Colin. Can you get me a coffee, black with lots of sugar."

"Certainly, are you all right?"

"I'm just a little flustered that's all. I'll be fine after a drink."

Colin hurried to the kitchen. He didn't want to risk upsetting the wife of one of his best customers.

Lucy tried to calm down and looked sheepishly around the restaurant. "Only two other tables occupied, how does he make a profit? I suppose it's still quite early for lunch."

In no time at all Colin returned with a cup of black coffee and a plate of cream biscuits, "I thought you might like these as well," he explained, "on the house of course," and he went back to his small desk just inside the door.

Lucy quickly drank the coffee and ate a couple of the biscuits. She looked round the restaurant once more then glanced through the large plate-glass windows. As she did so, she saw someone walk past that sent a shiver through her entire body.

"No!" she screamed at the top of her voice, "This can't be happening!" and she stood up as if in a panic and rushed straight out of the restaurant much to the amazement of Colin Rust and the other customers.

* * * * *

"I knew it was a mistake coming into town today," said James Palmer as he drove round the car park searching in vain for a space in which to park, "It's not fair every time you drive here you find a space straightaway."

"There! Over there!" Jenny almost shouted as she saw a car reversing out of a space, "If you're quick you'll get in that space over there!"

James parked the car and the two of them made their way past St. John's Church and up into the High Street.

"Where to first?" asked James, "I'll just follow you and carry the bags shall I?" and he ducked as Jenny aimed a playful punch at him.

"That was uncalled for. I only want a few things but first I want to go to ..."

Jenny's sentence was cut short as she and James saw a flustered looking Lucy Fairfax rush out of The Upper Crust Restaurant and collide with an electric buggy being driven on the pavement by an elderly woman. They quickly crossed the road and helped her to her feet.

"Lucy!" exclaimed James, "Are you all right? What's the matter?"

"I'm fine," she replied, and then noticed the blood running down her legs and leant on James for support.

"But you're hurt," added Jenny, "let me take a look."

"I'm terribly sorry," said the woman in the buggy who appeared somewhat shaken by the incident, "but I didn't see you coming out of the restaurant."

"That's all right," replied Lucy, "it was entirely my fault. I wasn't looking where I was going. I'll be fine, don't worry, you carry on."

After a moment's hesitation the woman reluctantly drove the buggy away and James turned to Lucy and said, "Are you sure you're ok? You look as if you've seen a ghost. Why were you in such a hurry?"

"Didn't you see her? Didn't you see Callisto? She was right here – walked past the restaurant. That's why I came running out – but she's gone," and Lucy looked frantically up and down the street but to no avail.

"Callisto!" exclaimed James and Jenny in unison, "It can't have been."

"But it was! I'm telling you it was!"

"Look, we'd better get you home," said Jenny, "how do you feel now?"

"A little queasy actually. Matter of fact I don't feel very well at all and my legs are beginning to hurt now."

"That settles it then," James reassured her, "Jenny will take you home in our car and I'll follow in yours."

"But," Lucy began.

"No buts," Jenny insisted, "we'll take you home. Now where's your car?"

* * * * *

At Forest Glade in David Fairfax's study a heated meeting was in progress.

"How the hell did we get into this mess?" David Fairfax barked, "And why wasn't I informed earlier?"

"It all started after we lost that first round of tenders to the Anne Harvey Group," replied Alan Box nervously, "after that our factories were operating at well below half capacity and at the same time there was a marked slow-down in our retail sales. It was almost as if the Anne Harvey Group was getting to know our new lines and not only beating us to the high street but also undercutting us substantially."

"Well, now that Susan Rumble is behind bars where she belongs we should notice an improvement."

"It's not quite that easy, Sir David," said a very reticent Cliff Hall, "there have been knock-on effects."

"What do you mean, knock-on effects?"

"Many of our regular customers, including several large wholesalers who normally take lots of our stock, have not renewed their contracts."

CHAPTER FIFTY-THREE

"So," boomed Sir David, "find some more to take their place!"

"But that's not all," hesitated Cliff, "there are other consequences now that DesboroDenim is the only remaining part of the Group. Most of the front-line staff of the three former parts of the business have gone and we're also in the process of making redundancies at the Fairfax Building. Soon that building will be more than three-quarters empty. Perhaps we should think of moving to a smaller building or renting out some of the surplus office space."

"Never!" roared Sir David jumping up from his chair and towering menacingly over Cliff, "I've worked all my life to aspire to a building like that, I'd rather leave it half-empty than let other people use it."

"But we can't afford to keep it, the business just won't sustain it for very much longer," argued Cliff.

"We're also very vulnerable to being bought-out or taken over," added Alan, "as our cash-flow situation is critical."

At this revelation Sir David almost exploded, "So once again I'm being let down by my own people. You've got to have faith in the business. We can succeed if we all work hard and pull together. I built up all four of my businesses from scratch and if I can do it once then I'm more than capable of doing it again."

"But Sir David," Alan interrupted him, "things are different this time. Someone out there is determined to bring you down. We're in a desperate situation. It seems obvious that the Anne Harvey Group is determined to force us to go under or take us over."

"Be that as it may, I'm not going to take this lying down."

Just then the sound of two cars pulling up in front of the house was heard and Sir David went to the window. He was most surprised to see James Palmer get out of Lucy's sports car and even more surprised when Jenny helped Lucy out of the other car and supported her as she limped towards the house.

"Meeting over, gentlemen!" Sir David announced in a most perfunctory way, "You can leave now," and he strode out of the room without even a single backward glance at the bemused Alan and Cliff who remained in their seats.

"What is it darling?" David asked anxiously as he followed Lucy and the Palmers into the drawing room, "What's happened?"

"It's nothing," insisted Lucy, "I walked into one of those buggy things that the elderly and disabled ride on the pavement, that's all."

"But James, Jenny, how come you're with Lucy?"

"Quite by chance, really," explained James, "we were crossing the road and saw Lucy leave the Upper Crust Restaurant and collide with a buggy."

James decided to play the diplomat and not mention what Lucy had told him and Jenny about seeing Callisto.

"We saw her legs were bleeding and felt she shouldn't drive home on her own," Jenny added taking a cue from her husband not to mention what Lucy had told them.

"I'm most grateful to you both," David said in a relieved tone of voice, "can I get you anything to eat or drink?"

"No, thanks all the same," replied James, "we must be going. Jenny has some serious shopping to do. You know how it is."

"That's right," added Jenny, "we must be going. Nice to see you again."

"Yes," replied David, "but you'll have to come over one evening for a drink. I'll be in touch in a few days."

"That'll be nice," said James and he and Jenny took their leave.

As soon as they had left the room Lucy told David about seeing Callisto but he was unconvinced.

"Callisto's dead," he said rather coldly, "and we've just got to accept that fact. You probably saw someone who looked like her or reminded you of her."

"Perhaps, but I'm not so sure," and Lucy looked up at David and said in a trembling voice, "I'm scared."

* * * * *

James drove slowly through the forest back towards Epping and he and Jenny discussed the incident with Lucy.

"What do you think?" asked Jenny.

"I don't know what to think at the moment," James replied, "it could just be someone who looked like Callisto or there could be more to it. It's a difficult one to get my head around."

"Or," said a thoughtful Jenny, "Lucy imagined the whole thing. Perhaps she saw what she wanted to see."

"Maybe," responded James, "but what this incident does is to firm up my resolve to undertake a bit more work on this case. I'm sure there's something out there we've missed."

"So," said a contented looking Jenny, "we're going to do a bit more digging and see if we can unearth something."

"That's correct," emphasised James, "and we'll start with Anne Harvey's family and any links we can uncover to David Fairfax."

"And Angela Hamilton, don't forget Angela Hamilton," stressed Jenny, "I'm sure there's more to her than meets the eye. I want to know just who she is!"

The car approached Epping High Street and much to James' astonishment Jenny announced she had changed her mind and didn't want to go shopping after all. James refrained from making any sarcastic remarks and the two of them were soon deep in conversation reliving their holiday for the remainder of the journey home.

Chapter Fifty-four

Martin Travers walked boldly into the Fairfax Building and made his way to the reception desk, "John Smith," he announced, "I'd like to see Alan Box. I haven't got an appointment but I'm sure he'll see me. Tell him it's about some new contracts."

"One moment, Mr Smith," the receptionist replied, "I'll see if he's available."

A few minutes later she gave Martin Travers a visitor's pass and ushered him towards the lifts.

"Good morning, Alan," beamed Martin as he entered Alan's office.

"What on earth are you doing here?" exclaimed a very surprised and very nervous looking Alan, "If David Fairfax finds out he'll go spare!"

"Don't worry about him. Have you thought any more about my proposition?"

"Yes I have. I've hardly thought of anything else over the last few days," and after a moment's hesitation while he wiped the sweat from his forehead, he continued, "Yes, I'll do it. I'll accept your offer."

* * * * *

James and Jenny Palmer were sitting in the lounge discussing their plans for the day over a cup of tea.

"So," said James, "it's agreed. I'll go to Companies House to see if there is any mention of what happened to those companies which bought that old DesboroDenim stock all those years ago. Hopefully I'll find out if they just went out of business or if they were taken over by other companies. I'll also see if I can find out anything of interest about Chris Harvey's old companies."

"Great," replied Jenny, "and I'll go and see an old friend who works in the National Health Service's records section. I'm sure she'll have no objection to me trawling through a few old files. After all, the people I hope to find are all dead."

"Or should be!" exclaimed James.

Jenny smiled broadly, "We can take the tube together as far as Liverpool Street before we have to go our separate ways. Do you want to meet up afterwards for a meal or a drink or something, or would you prefer that we make our way home separately?"

"We'll make a day of it. That's why I decided to visit Companies House in person rather than search on-line.

Whoever finishes first can phone the other one and agree a time to meet."

"That's fine with me," Jenny said enthusiastically, "a good meal in a little restaurant would be an excellent way to round off the day."

"Let's be going then," responded James most eagerly before getting up and fetching his car keys from a hook in the kitchen, "The sooner we drive to Epping to pick up the Central Line the sooner we can get started."

"And the sooner we can have that nice intimate little meal, just the two of us," Jenny stressed as she snatched the keys from her husband and made her way to the front door, "I'll do the driving!"

* * * * *

"What are you waiting for?" asked Martin Travers, "It's time to go, time for you to leave this building and never return."

"I know," and Alan hesitated, screwing up his small weasel-like face as if he were in great pain, "but it is still a big step for me. I've been with David Fairfax for over 20 years."

"And now that he's well on the road to ruin it's time for you to make a well-timed exit. If you've any doubts just think about our offer. We buy your house, give you a villa in Malta and also throw in a lump sum equal to a year's salary. I'd say that's very tempting."

"It's very tempting indeed," and Alan Box looked round his office one last time before standing up and announcing, "Come on, it's now or never."

Martin Travers and Alan Box strode through the reception area and got into Martin's car and drove away.

* * * * *

At the National Health Service's records' section Jenny finished her researches and phoned her husband, "Hello James, I've just finished here and you'll never guess what I've found out, something really interesting. I'll save it for later though – when you're buying me that expensive candle-lit meal. I just wondered how much longer you expect to be. How's it going?"

"Fine, I've unearthed something as well. About another hour or hour-and-a-half should do it, I shouldn't be any longer than that."

"Good, I'll meet you in two hours' time outside our favourite restaurant in Covent Garden. By the way don't bother hurrying on my account there's plenty of shops around there to keep me out of mischief!"

"Keep you *in mischief*, you mean."

"There's no such expression and you know it."

"That's true, but I also know your track record when you're let loose around the Covent Garden area, you just can't resist all those bargains."

CHAPTER FIFTY-FOUR

"You've got no worries today. I'll just be looking, promise. See you later."

* * * * *

"What!" rasped David Fairfax as Angela gave him the news, "Alan Box has gone! Without a word! After all these years! How could he? The traitor!"

"Apparently he left the building in the company of Martin Travers about an hour ago."

"Martin Travers? From the Anne Harvey Group? The bastard! I'll get him for this. What's Feb's number? No, on second thoughts let him go. I'm better off without him. I'll show him how to run this company. I'll build it up again to its former standing. I don't need him or anybody else."

* * * * *

"Sorry I'm late darling," said a breathless James as he ran up to Jenny standing outside the restaurant and kissed her on the cheek, "but the tubes all seem to be up the creek this evening."

"Never mind, but I have to admit I've only just got here myself so no harm done. Come on let's go inside, I'm starving."

"Me too," agreed James and he and Jenny went into the restaurant hand-in-hand and made their way to their favourite secluded alcove.

* * * * *

"That was a fabulous meal, darling," said Jenny emptying her glass of wine and looking across the table at James.

"Another bottle then?" enquired James as he tried in vain to attract the waiter's attention.

"No, I've had enough and besides when we get to Epping one of us has to drive home. Let's have a coffee."

"Good idea," agreed James and he ordered two coffees.

"So," said Jenny, "shall I go first?"

"If you insist."

"As a matter of fact I didn't get all that far but I did manage to confirm what John Harwood told you. Chris and Elaine Harvey's family doctor for many years was none other than Dr Greg Smith. He did refer them to the Ipswich Fertility Clinic but most records for that clinic are missing as the facility closed and transferred to a regional unit in Bury St Edmunds a few years ago. Not to worry, however, as my contact has promised to let me have anything she is able to find out from the clinic's old records in the next few days."

"It's a start," acknowledged James, "and I had some success too. One of those companies that bought a substantial amount of old DesboroDenim stock was East Anglian Designs and that company was bought-out a few months later by none other than Chris Harvey. He took over their premises just up the coast at North Deben. So once again we have a connection, I admit a rather tenuous one, between Chris Harvey and David Fairfax. As before, though, there's nothing concrete to link them in any direct way."

"Yes, we keep getting so tantalisingly close. Oh," said Jenny suddenly recalling something she had meant to tell her husband earlier, "I almost forgot! I looked up the National Insurance number of Angela Hamilton, the Angela Hamilton who went to school with Anne Harvey. As Mrs Goodenough didn't mention any form of further education I reasoned she must have left school and started work rather than gone to university. This means that before she had her accident she would have been given an NI number."

"Very good," said James playing with the candle at the centre of the table, "but what does that tell us?"

"It tells us a great deal," said Jenny rather smugly, "because I also looked up the NI number of the Angela Hamilton who works for David Fairfax and guess what? They are the same!"

"The same!" exclaimed James.

"That's right, it looks like whoever is working for David Fairfax," and Jenny leaned forward and whispered in a most dramatic way to give full emphasis to her remarks, "isn't Angela Hamilton at all, but an impostor who has assumed her identity!"

Chapter Fifty-five

The sudden departure of Alan Box from the DesboroDenim Fashion Group was given prominence in the trade press by an anonymous leak from inside the Anne Harvey Group. This rapidly led to a severe loss of orders and a sudden decline in business which triggered a crisis of confidence in the organisation.

David Fairfax tried desperately to postpone the inevitable but the Group was on the verge of collapse. He finally had no alternative but to sell the DesboroDenim Fashion Group to the highest bidder or, in this case, the only bidder, the Anne Harvey Group. This was a terrific blow to him and his pride. The first and most successful of his businesses had now slipped from his grasp and fallen into the hands of his bitter rival. The final humiliation was when Anne Harvey refused to meet him in person to sign the necessary papers and sent Martin Travers to be the signatory on her behalf.

The Fairfax Building was now almost empty but David Fairfax refused to sell it or even lease it to other organisations despite receiving some very lucrative offers. People began to think he was cracking up under the strain of losing his children and his business empire as, for no apparent reason, he often took to wandering around the empty building looking deep in thought.

With all his staff now made redundant the inevitable had to come and David Fairfax called Feb into his study.

It was with a very heavy heart that he said, "I'm sorry Feb but it's time for us to part and go our separate ways. I've placed a great deal on your shoulders over the past few years and you've been one of my most loyal and trusted employees. I only wish there had been more like you and then perhaps I wouldn't be in the position I'm in today."

"That's all right, Sir David, I know this state of affairs isn't of your making."

"Perhaps it is in a way, perhaps I should have seen it coming. Still, no use harping on the past, everything changes and we must move on with it. As a sign of my appreciation for what you've done for me I'd like you to accept this cheque for two years' salary, it's the least I can do. I would keep you on but the way things are at present I just can't afford it."

"Thank you, Sir David, that's much appreciated."

"Do you think you will have much difficulty in finding other employment?"

"No, I don't think so. There's always a market out there for people like me in security and, how can I say this, 'protection'. I should be fine."

"Good!" replied Sir David and he and Feb shook hands warmly before Feb took his leave and left Forest Glade for the final time.

David Fairfax was not looking forward to his next task, the departure of Angela Hamilton. He had always thought most highly of her and her work. He was very reluctant to see her leave but he had no alternative as there was now so very little for her to do. Most of his work was now concerned with private and personal matters and as such there was no longer a place for her.

Angela walked into the drawing room and Sir David slowly let his eyes wander over her body from head to toe and back again. She was dressed in a most expensive dark-blue pin stripe suit with knee-length skirt and matching blue shoes. Her unbuttoned jacket revealed a white almost transparent blouse which tantalised him as he struggled not to make it too obvious that he couldn't take his eyes off what lay beneath. She sat opposite him and much to Sir David's delight deliberately let the jacket fall open to reveal her more than ample figure that seemed to be struggling to escape the confines of the tightly-fitting blouse.

Sir David picked up Vienna and slowly stroked the cat until it was purring deeply and almost asleep. It was with genuine difficulty that he started to speak, "Angela, I don't know quite how to say this but you're more than aware of how things have gone of late and the state of the business and my finances so I've got no choice but to ..."

"To sack me," interrupted Angela cutting him off in mid-sentence, "to dispense with my services?"

"After all we've been through these past three or so years you make it sound so cold. I've come to regard you as much more than a personal assistant. More of a friend, a confidante if you like, someone whom I could rely on and trust, when all around me were plotting my downfall," and his eyes once again focussed on Angela's blouse.

"Thank you, Sir David, I've always tried to please," she replied deliberately crossing her legs and rearranging her skirt.

"And you have," he replied enthusiastically trying to stop his eyes staring at her legs, "you have. But the time has come for us to part and I see no point in prolonging matters."

"I couldn't agree more," Angela replied playing with the buttons of her jacket.

"To show my appreciation for all you've done for me and the business I've arranged for the equivalent of two years' salary to be paid into your bank account. I very much regret having to let you go, I really do, but there's no alternative. I hope you don't have too much difficulty in finding another job. I'm sure someone of your calibre and with your talents should easily find something suitable."

"I've enjoyed working with you. I feel I've achieved a lot that should stand me in good stead for the future and for the unfinished aims and ambitions I still have in life."

"Thank you Angela for being so understanding and for taking it so calmly. Some people wouldn't have taken their dismissal with quite so much dignity."

"I've believed for some time that this day was inevitable and you were keeping me on for as long as you were able, so there's no hard feelings," and Angela stood up ready to leave.

Sir David also stood up and unthinking dropped Vienna on the floor. He had hoped that on this occasion he would get the chance to kiss Angela, even if it was only goodbye, but his hopes were dashed. She held out a hand and after a rather weak handshake she left the room without even the briefest of backward glances.

Chapter Fifty-six

"Why do you keep insisting on going to that place? Why not stay at home a bit more with me?" pleaded Lucy as her husband picked up some papers and stuffed them forcibly into his briefcase, "The place is almost empty, there's no one there any more."

"I know," replied David, "but there's work to be done. I know I can start again, I just know it!"

"But wandering round the Fairfax Building isn't going to get you anywhere. People are beginning to think you're obsessed with that building."

"I am, in a way I am. That building represents all I have strived for in life. It's the pinnacle of my business career and I just can't abandon it without a fight. It may be empty now but I'm confident I can find a niche market somewhere and build up another business."

"But why? We have more than enough money to carry on with our present lifestyle. Why not just accept the way things have turned out and relax, take it easy for once in your life. After all, we only have the two of us now and time is getting precious," said a very sad

Lucy as she reflected on the loss of the children and shed a tear.

"I understand, darling," David reassured her with a hug, "this has been a most terrible time and you want something permanent to cling to, but I want to cling to something as well and that something is the Fairfax Building. Apart from you and the children that building represented my life. I know there's still a small mortgage on it but I shall try my utmost not to sell it unless I can't meet the bills and absolutely have to."

"Well I don't know what you do there all day. It's bad enough here at home nowadays with Feb and the lads no longer around and Katie, well she's just part-time now, and it gets very lonely here on my own."

"But I thought you were having your friends over today for lunch around the pool and all that."

"I am, but it's not the same as having you here. This is a big house for one person when you're away," and after a moment's thought Lucy added, "Perhaps we should sell it and move to a smaller house."

"Never!" rasped David, "I worked hard and struggled for years to get a place like this and I have no intention whatsoever of moving."

Lucy knew from past experience that it was no good arguing with him so she kissed David goodbye and watched from a window as he drove his car slowly along the drive. Surprisingly, unlike her he was not known for his speeding.

Lucy had invited about a dozen of her like-minded friends over for lunch and to spend time in the pool afterwards. Luckily it was a very hot autumn day and they could alternate between swimming in the pool and sunbathing on one of the lawns. She had also arranged for Colin Rust and one of his staff to come over and cook an outside barbeque so she could enjoy the day without any worries.

The first of her guests turned up soon after midday and within the next hour they had all arrived and were eating outside on the lawn. The afternoon was a great success and in many ways Lucy began to think that perhaps she could once again embrace her former lifestyle.

It was a little after five o'clock. The last of Lucy's guests had left and after Katie had tidied up and put the garden furniture away she also took her leave. Katie no longer lived in Forest Glade with the Fairfax family but had returned to live with her parents in Epping.

Lucy locked the outside doors and wandered through the house. She knew David wouldn't be back until seven o'clock at the earliest so thought she would have another swim and perhaps round off the day in the sauna. However, as she reached the pool she hesitated as she thought she heard a noise.

"Who's there?" she called out nervously, but there was no reply.

She walked hesitantly all round the pool and looked in the changing rooms but there was nobody there. "Must be my imagination," she thought to herself with some relief, "I think I'll forego that swim and just have a sauna, it's been quite a tiring day," and she opened the door to the sauna and made her way inside.

No sooner had Lucy stepped inside the cabin than a hand reached out from behind the door and held a thick pad firmly across her nose and mouth. She tried to break free but all her efforts were in vain. After a few seconds she lost consciousness. When she came round she found she was lying beside the pool, face up, with her hands and feet securely tied behind her back. She looked round and saw a figure dressed entirely in black sitting on one of the pool-side chairs smiling at her and rocking to and fro.

"Who the hell are you? What's this all about?" Lucy shrieked struggling to break free from her bonds, "What do you want? These cords are biting into my skin. I'm in agony here!"

The figure stood up and very slowly came towards Lucy who was writhing on the floor trying to free herself, "My husband will be back soon so you'd better get out of here!"

"I don't think so," said the figure breaking her silence, "he'll still be in that empty castle of his in Canary Wharf wondering where it all went wrong. He won't be back here for at least a couple of hours. That gives us plenty of time to talk."

"I've nothing to say to you!" replied Lucy, "Let me go! Do you hear me? Let me go now!"

"You know I can't do that," said the figure in a soft but very menacing tone as she bent over Lucy, "You and me need to talk."

"It was you in the forest wasn't it? It was you who forced me off the road!"

The figure remained silent.

"Well say something!" Lucy shouted, "Say something, damn you! Why did you do it? Why did you do it and why are you here?"

"It was a sort of test for me. I needed to prove to myself that I could actually go through with it. If I could do that to you in the forest then I could do what had to follow," replied the figure breaking her silence, "and I found I could. I had the nerve and the guts to carry it through. Do you know it was surprisingly easy once I had started."

"So it was you," realised a horrified Lucy still struggling to break free, "it was you who killed my children and for no reason at all."

"There was a reason. Believe me there was a very good reason and your husband, *Sir David Fairfax*, will soon find out just what it was. But now it's your turn to talk."

"I don't understand," said Lucy trying to comprehend the situation, "talk about what? I don't know what it is you want from me."

"I want information, or should I say confirmation, about the events that took place on a certain cruise ship in 1980 that culminated in the death of Beverley Fairfax, your husband's second wife," and the figure pushed Lucy close to the edge of the pool and flipped her over onto her stomach.

"She was very depressed and committed suicide. You can confirm that from the inquest if you're that interested," blurted out Lucy.

"I've read the inquest papers but the coroner didn't know what I know," and the figure paused before continuing, "that you were present on that ship and that you murdered Beverley Fairfax."

"That's not true," screamed Lucy, "I wasn't on board the ..." but her words were cut short as the figure grabbed hold of Lucy's head and held it under the water for about thirty seconds before roughly pulling it out again.

"I wasn't there! You must believe me!" cried Lucy struggling for breath.

"Not good enough! Try again!" and the figure thrust Lucy's head under the water once again and held it there for nearly a minute before pulling it out.

As soon as her head was out of the water Lucy started coughing and fighting for breath, "All right, I admit I was on the cruise but what does that prove? I was there in case David needed any help. I'd known him since our secondary school days and knew he was finding it difficult to cope with Beverley and her moods and depression. I was as surprised as David when Beverley threw herself over the ship's side."

"Still not good enough!" and the figure thrust Lucy's head under the water for a third time and held it there for well over a minute.

Lucy emerged coughing up water and barely able to catch her breath, "All right, all right, I'll tell you but it was all David's idea."

"That's better. Why put yourself through all this unnecessary pain? Tell it from the beginning just as it all happened."

"You must understand I didn't really want any part of this but David was so ambitious, he wouldn't listen to me. He forced me, it was all his plan," and Lucy paused to get her breath, "his plan to gain control of Beverley's company and take it over.

One night at dinner he put something in her drink to give her a headache. Later, during the meal, when Beverley was in obvious pain David suggested she go back to her cabin for some rest and then go up on deck for some fresh air when she felt a little better. This she did and while she was leaning on the rail looking out to sea I was supposed to come up behind her and grab her legs and tip her into the water. But I couldn't do it. I just froze and stood there motionless behind her. Then as if from nowhere David suddenly arrived. He simply walked up to her and pushed her over the rail. It was so easy and all over in a second or two. You must believe me. As soon as I realised the full gravity of what he'd done I was mortified but it was too late there was nothing I could do."

"And the scarf! Whose idea was that?"

"That was also David's idea. He said it would look like she had stood there and thought about the full implications of what she was doing before taking that final fatal step."

"And who put it there?"

"That was me. David gave it to me the night before when he came to my cabin to tell me about the plan. You must believe me! I was under the impression when he asked me to come on the cruise that he just wanted me there to help him out, I had no idea he had murder in mind."

"But you agreed to his plan. You as good as murdered Beverley Fairfax yourself and deliberately left a scarf at the scene," and pausing to dangle a scarf in front of Lucy the figure continued, "A scarf just like this one!"

"Oh no!" gasped Lucy as she realised the full implications of the predicament she was in and what her impending fate was going to be and she started to sob hysterically.

"Too late now," said the figure as she casually dropped the scarf by the side of the pool and grabbed hold of Lucy's head, "let's recreate the scene on the ship, only this time you can be Beverley and I'll be that husband of yours."

"No!" shrieked Lucy, "At least tell me who you are!"

The figure loosened her grip on Lucy's head and slowly removed her face mask. Lucy turned her head and looked up into a grinning face she had seen so many times before. Shocked, she began to sob uncontrollably.

"So it was you all along," sobbed a disconsolate Lucy, "but why? What have we ever done to you?"

"That you'll never know because it's now time for you to be reunited with your husband's first two wives," and the figure once again sat astride Lucy. Without a further word she held her head under the water with gloved hands until all struggling had ceased and there were no signs of life. She then pushed the lifeless body into the pool and watched as it slowly sank to the bottom before, after ten or twelve minutes, it gradually floated to the surface again.

The figure carefully folded and draped the scarf over the back of one of the plastic pool-side chairs. She reached into an inside pocket and took out a small card which she also placed on the chair.

The figure then went inside the house and removed a tape from the CCTV system before returning to the pool area to ensure all traces of her presence had been eradicated. The figure then crossed the adjacent lawn and made her way to a secluded corner of the grounds. She nimbly climbed over the boundary wall and dropped down into the forest on the other side. She then ran through the trees to a small track where her car was parked and drove off.

Chapter Fifty-seven

David Fairfax pressed a button on the dashboard of his car and the electronic gates slid silently open as if by magic. He drove through and glanced in his mirror to make sure they were closing behind him. He then continued to his front door and parked his car adjacent to the portico.

"That's strange," he thought to himself as he walked towards the front door, "it's getting dark and there are no lights on anywhere in the house. Perhaps Lucy's gone out with her friends. I would've thought though she'd have phoned me to let me know."

David let himself in and switched on the lights in the hall. He stood and listened for a moment but couldn't hear any sound, the house appeared deserted. Suddenly he heard a scratching noise coming from the drawing room. He opened the door and both Vienna and Ponsonby leapt out of the room and jumped up at him miaowing loudly.

"What's the matter?" he said, taking Vienna in his arms, "You two look hungry. Has that naughty wife of mine been neglecting you?" and he put Vienna back on the floor. The two cats immediately raced him into the kitchen almost tripping him up in their eagerness to have something to eat. David searched the cupboards and despite being a virtual stranger in the kitchen he eventually managed to find their food. Once the cats were happily munching away he decided to have a look round to confirm that he was indeed alone in the house.

David wandered round the apparently deserted house, switching lights on and off as he went in and out of the numerous rooms, and finally decided to have a look in the pool area. He went down the stairs and through the double doors and turned on the ceiling lights. He immediately froze in terror as his eyes were drawn to a body floating in the middle of the pool. He quickly pulled himself together and raced to the poolside. As he looked at the body he realised in horror that it was Lucy. He sank to his knees and tried to prevent the tears forming in his eyes but without success.

"No! Not Lucy!" he blurted out, "Not my Lucy!" and he looked closely at the body hoping in vain that it was somebody else but finally he had to admit it was indeed his wife. He endeavoured to stem his emotions. Trying hard to fight back the tears he took his mobile phone from his pocket and called Inspector Westwood.

* * * * *

Inspector Westwood and Sergeant Benson were on the scene at Forest Glade in less than fifteen minutes and were accompanied by a full forensic team. The first thing they did was to cordon off the house and take David upstairs to the drawing room.

"I'm sorry, Sir David, I'm really sorry about Lucy," said Inspector Westwood, "but I must ask you some questions. What time did you arrive home this evening?"

"It was about 15 minutes before I called you. I was surprised to find the house in darkness and thought Lucy had gone out somewhere without telling me. I knew she had some of her lady friends over today for a barbeque lunch on the lawn and a swim in the pool. When I couldn't find her in the house I thought she'd decided to spend the evening in town with the girls."

"Then what did you do?"

"I fed the cats as they were very hungry then wandered around the house looking in the rooms. I didn't find Lucy so decided to go to the pool and that's where I found her," and David broke down sobbing with his face buried in his hands.

"Lucy was my life. I worshipped her. We'd known each other since I was 12 years old. I can't imagine life without her. First the children and now this," and he stared silently into space seemingly oblivious to the Inspector.

"I really am most sorry, Sir David, but I do need to ask you some more questions," and Inspector Westwood paused before adding, "Do you know who came to the house today? Can you tell me their names?"

"Yes," replied David, and he gave the Inspector the names of those he could remember who were invited,

"Oh, and I mustn't forget Colin Rust he came along to prepare the barbeque."

"Thank you, I'll get someone to interview them all as a matter of urgency to see if anyone noticed anything that may help in our enquiry."

Just then Sergeant Benson looked furtively around the door. He motioned to Inspector Westwood who promptly left the room.

"What is it Benson?"

"Look at these, sir," and Benson held up two plastic evidence bags, one containing a scarf and one holding a small card.

"Where were they found?"

"The scarf was found draped over a plastic chair by the side of the pool and the card was placed near it. The card reads 'I told you not to go overboard, not to get wet', and looks similar to the others we found when the children were murdered."

Inspector Westwood stared intently at the card and then produced his notebook, "Yes, just like the others," and he read out aloud what was on the card Lucy received at Christmas, "This will look good around your neck. But don't go overboard. Don't get it wet."

"Could this be the same as the others, sir?"

"I don't know! I need to think about this. Let's get back to Sir David," and the two detectives returned to the study and told him about the findings. They were taken completely by surprise and totally unprepared for the resulting outburst.

"You told me you had arrested the person who murdered my children! And now my wife's been murdered! You told me I had nothing more to worry about. Now you're telling me that a card, just like all the others, has been found by the pool, *by my pool*!" shouted Sir David almost uncontrollably. He got up from his chair and paced round the room, "How is this possible if the person responsible is behind bars?"

"Please calm down, Sir David," Inspector Westwood said slowly as he tried to reassure him, "All the evidence to date does point to Susan Rumble being the murderer but it's possible someone else has found out about the cards and has carried out a copy-cat murder."

"Yes," responded Sir David sarcastically, "*it is possible* but nobody knew what was written on those cards received at Christmas. That information has never been made public. Only what was written on the cards found at the scene of the murders has been reported. Are you sure you've got the murderer behind bars?"

"I am, but we can't rule anything out. There are two possibilities here. The first is that we've got the murderer in custody and this is a copy-cat crime or, secondly, we haven't got the murderer and he or she is still at large."

"So what are you going to do?" boomed Sir David.

"For now we do nothing in haste. Susan Rumble will remain behind bars while we investigate your wife's death. The Scene of Crime Officers and the forensic boys will be here for sometime, certainly overnight and most of tomorrow. After that I'll make sure there are more patrols in the area."

"You think I could be in danger then?"

"It looks very much like it. I would suggest for your own safety that you don't go out anywhere alone particularly after dark."

"Don't worry Inspector, I've no intention of doing anything foolish that could put me at risk."

"Glad to hear it," replied Inspector Westwood, "Have you anywhere you could stay for a couple of days?"

"No, not really, I'd prefer to stay here."

"That shouldn't be a problem. My officers will be concentrating on the pool area, of course, but they'll also be examining other rooms in the house and the grounds. That reminds me," said Inspector Westwood suddenly remembering the CCTV cameras situated at key vantage points around the property, "we ought to start with the tape from the CCTV cameras, that may tell us who was here and when they left."

Inspector Westwood and Sergeant Benson accompanied David Fairfax to the small security room. A bank of monitors was showing pictures of the grounds from a number of angles but when the video recorder was opened there was no tape inside.

"It was worth a try. If the murderer had left in a hurry then it's something that could easily have been overlooked," admitted the Inspector.

"Well we're obviously dealing with someone who knows their way around the property," added Sergeant Benson, "because this room is quite well concealed from casual view and it's unlikely you'd come across it by chance."

"From the beginning these murders and the leaking of sensitive tender information have pointed to an inside job. That's why Susan Rumble was such an obvious suspect and the things found in her house seemed to confirm it," said a very thoughtful Inspector Westwood.

The two policemen then took their leave of Sir David but returned after about 30 minutes to inform him that the murderer had left the property by scaling the perimeter wall and making off into the forest. It was possible a car had been hidden in the trees nearby but the recent dry weather meant there were no footprints or tyre marks to offer any clues as to identity.

David Fairfax sat alone in the almost-dark drawing room that was illuminated by a solitary low-wattage table lamp and listened to the sound of heavy boots moving through the house. He didn't even attempt to go to bed but sat in the study throughout the night reflecting on his life, his career, his family and his wife, wondering how and why it had all gone so horribly wrong.

"Who?" thought Sir David as he buried his head in his hands once again, "Who could hate me this much, and why?"

Chapter Fifty-eight

James and Jenny Palmer had been to a late night show in London. They hadn't returned to North Weald until well after midnight so were totally unaware of Lucy Fairfax's death. When they heard details on the morning news bulletin while having a late breakfast they were shocked. But they were doubly shocked soon afterwards when James received a phone call from David asking them both to come and see him as soon as possible.

"And you agreed to go and see him, just like that!" said an angry Jenny, "After how he treated you!"

"That's right," replied James with a broad smile, "so we can tell him just how wrong he's been."

"But you can't," said a worried-looking Jenny, "not now Lucy's been killed. It wouldn't be right, the poor man must be in a terrible state."

"You've soon changed your tune. One minute you don't want us to go there and the next, when I say I'll go and see what he wants, you don't want me to do that either!"

"Perhaps I wasn't thinking straight," admitted Jenny after finishing her tea and calming down, "It would be churlish not to go and see him, particularly at this dreadful time for him."

"And don't forget," added James, "when we took Lucy to Forest Glade after that accident with the buggy David did seem genuinely grateful. Let's give him the benefit of the doubt and see what he wants."

"Very well," agreed Jenny rather reluctantly.

* * * * *

It was nearly an hour later when James and Jenny arrived at Forest Glade. As they pulled up outside the gates to the house they were confronted by a police cordon. After explaining who they were and that they had been asked over by David Fairfax they were admitted to the grounds once permission had been given by Inspector Westwood.

Before being allowed access to Sir David, however, it was made clear that Inspector Westwood wished to speak to them and they were ushered into the lounge.

"James! Jenny!" exclaimed Inspector Westwood as they entered the room, "It's good to see you both again but I never thought it would be under these circumstances. I understand Sir David has called you over but I thought it prudent to have a word with you beforehand to put you in the picture."

"That would be useful," replied James as he and Jenny sat down opposite the Inspector, "All we know so far is what we've heard on the news this morning."

"A sad business," said the Inspector, "From what we've been able to piece together it looks as if Lady Lucy was drowned in the pool sometime between five and six o'clock yesterday afternoon. We've already spoken to all those who were here, including Colin Rust and his assistant, but none of them can shed any light on the matter. They all seem to have left at the same time around five o'clock. So it looks like the murderer must have managed to get into the house and hide until all the guests had gone."

"Easy enough, I suppose," responded James, "particularly if they know the layout of the place. It's a big house and with Sir David out of the way there would be nobody around to discover you."

"Was there anything about Lucy's death that wasn't made public?" asked Jenny determined not to be left out of the conversation.

"She was drowned," replied the Inspector, "but her hands and feet were tied and it looks like she may have been tortured ..."

"Tortured!" exclaimed James cutting short the Inspector's sentence.

"Yes, it appears from a number of marks and blood found at the poolside that she was pulled in and out of the pool a few times before she was finally held under the water."

"As if somebody wanted to obtain some information?"

"Correct," confirmed Inspector Westwood, "but what that information was I doubt we'll ever know."

"Anything else of interest?"

"Yes," replied the Inspector and he handed James the two plastic evidence bags, "Look at these! The scarf was found draped over a chair by the pool and the card was placed nearby."

"Just like the others," said James sadly after reading the card, "So are you still convinced Susan Rumble murdered Sir David's children?"

"It's a difficult one. All the evidence clearly points to it but I can't say for certain anymore."

"Right from the start I've had my doubts about that evidence at Susan Rumble's house. It was all so very convenient, as if it was put there for the police to find," replied James shaking his head.

"So how's Sir David taken it?" Jenny enquired.

"Much harder than I ever imagined he would. He's broken down several times and is still in a state of shock. When I heard he'd asked you two over I was a bit reluctant to agree at first but on reflection I felt it might be beneficial. After all he did involve you at an early stage and, if I may say so, we have worked well together so far."

"If he says anything of interest then we'll certainly let you know," said James, and he and Jenny made their way to the study where Sir David was still sitting in semi-darkness with the curtains closed staring at photographs of his wife and children.

"James, I'm so pleased you agreed to come over, and you too Jenny," said Sir David rising to his feet as the husband and wife team entered the room, "I didn't know who else to turn to," and he beckoned them to sit down.

"We were very sorry to hear about Lucy," said Jenny, "I just don't know what to say. If there's anything we can do."

"As a matter of fact there is," David immediately replied, "When we parted you said you didn't believe Susan Rumble was guilty. Well I've been thinking a lot about that too. Does that remain your view? The police still think she did it – at least they're not going to let her go, but I have my doubts."

"I think they're beginning to have their doubts too," replied James, "but if she didn't do it then who did?"

"I don't know," said an exasperated Sir David, "I've wracked my brains trying to think who and why?"

"We're following up a number of leads at the moment, actually," piped up Jenny, "that might take us somewhere."

"Really," said a puzzled Sir David, "then you didn't abandon the case?"

"No," replied Jenny, "we'd invested too much time and effort to just give up on our enquiries."

"I'm very pleased indeed!" said a surprised Sir David, "I'd be most grateful if you could stick with it and try and get to the bottom of this for me. I might have lost my businesses but I'm still a very wealthy man and will certainly make it worth your while. What can you tell me that the police don't know?"

"Our lines of enquiry," said James putting on his former police voice, "lead us to Anne Harvey and Angela Hamilton. Somehow those two are connected to you and your family but as yet we haven't been able to establish any direct link. You're certain that you never had any sort of contact with Chris Harvey, Anne's father?"

"No, none whatsoever."

"There's definitely something that triggered Anne Harvey to pit her group against yours and we're determined to find out just what it was."

"And Angela, you said she might be involved somehow."

"That's right. It's early days but she might not be who she says she is. We've discovered that Anne Harvey went to school with an Angela Hamilton but she was killed soon after leaving school in a road traffic accident. There may well, of course, be two Angela Hamiltons and the name is just a coincidence but it does seem most unlikely."

"Really," said a very surprised Sir David, "but Angela was one of my most valuable and trusted employees. She was my right hand and I was most reluctant to let her go."

"As I said, David, it's early days yet. Would you by any chance still have Angela's personal file? It would be most useful if we could have a look at it."

"Yes, as a matter of fact I have. I brought it here when I asked her over to tell her I had to dispense with her services. Just a minute," and David got up and walked across the room and unlocked a large filing cabinet. He took out a slim red folder and handed it to James, "Here, hold onto it for as long as you like."

"Thanks, we'll get back to you once we find out anything more," and James and Jenny got up to leave.

"James," said Sir David with a touch of genuine sincerity in his voice which hadn't been noticeable before, "I really appreciate this."

James looked at David for a second then, without further word, he and Jenny left the room and made their way back to their car.

Chapter Fifty-nine

Jenny Palmer woke up with a start and opened her eyes. Much to her surprise James wasn't in the bed beside her. She looked over at the clock and saw the time was just after seven o'clock.

"Where on earth is he at this time in the morning?" she thought to herself as she lay back on her pillow, "It's not often he gets up early since he left the force."

Before she could muse further on the matter the bedroom door opened and James entered carrying a cup of tea.

"For you, darling," he said with a broad smile on his face, "I thought you'd be awake by now."

"Thank you," Jenny replied somewhat puzzled, "I must say this is a most unexpected surprise, tea in bed is something of a rarity nowadays."

"All part of the service."

"Well, are you going to tell me or shall I ask?"

"Ask what?"

"Why you're up and about so early," and Jenny playfully threw a pillow at James who ducked just in time.

"I've been doing some research, some comparisons if you like. I've been comparing what we've learned from the inquests into the deaths of David Fairfax's first two wives, from people like John Harwood and Mrs Goodenough, and piecing it together with information we know about Anne Harvey and Angela Hamilton. It makes fascinating reading particularly when read in conjunction with Angela's staff file."

"I'll come down then."

"That's a very good idea. I've made breakfast and it's ready and waiting for you on the kitchen table," said an animated James, "Once we've eaten I'll show you what I've found out."

James steadfastly refused to tell Jenny what he had discovered while she was eating so she ate breakfast as quickly as she could and the two of them then went into the lounge.

"Goodness me!" exclaimed Jenny when she saw the papers spread all over the lounge floor, "You have been busy. Hope you're going to clear this lot up!"

"No problem," said James, "Now, where shall I start?" and he paused for a few seconds before continuing, "It was the information in Angela's staff file that set me on the trail that at last began to make sense of everything that's happened so far.

In Angela Hamilton's staff file her date of birth, school attendance and history up to the time she left school, are exactly the same as given to you by Mrs Goodenough. The certificates and letters all look genuine too. However, according to the staff file she then went to Cambridge, to the same college as Anne Harvey and, would you believe, left with exactly the same qualifications. I have no means of confirming this but I suspect the certificates copied onto that file are forgeries, but very good ones mind you.

I've also looked at the information Martin Travers gave us about the company and it appears Anne Harvey returned to East Deben to look after her father when he became ill with cancer. Soon after he died she took over his business empire but it's only in the last year or so that she's made concerted efforts to outbid the Fairfax Group.

In the meantime Angela Hamilton joined the Fairfax Group as David Fairfax's personal assistant. She became much more valuable to him in business terms than that job description would imply if David is to be believed. It was when she had been there for about two years that the Fairfax Group began to experience its difficulties."

"So you think these two women are linked in some way?" Jenny said thinking about what she had just heard.

"I certainly do. I think Anne Harvey supplied Angela Hamilton, or someone who calls herself Angela Hamilton, with a credible past with the specific intention of getting one of her own people on the inside of the Fairfax Group. And once Angela had become a trusted member of that organisation she could start to feed information to Anne to enable her to undercut the Fairfax Group and start to ruin them."

"It certainly makes sense," added a thoughtful Jenny thumbing through the papers, "but what about the murders?"

"I think Angela Hamilton could be behind them too. Remember, Chris Harvey bought out East Anglian Designs so Anne could have inherited a lot of unsold DesboroDenim stock from the 1970s. And that stock could have been used for the Christmas presents and also left at the scene of the murders."

"That's possible, but why?" asked Jenny, "Why would Anne Harvey want to murder everyone in the Fairfax family? And even if she did could she really employ a woman to do it for her?"

"There are plenty of 'hit-men' in the business, so why not some 'hit-women'? I met all sorts while I was in the force so nothing would surprise me."

"It's perfectly possible and it all makes sense, but I'm still not sure of a motive. There must be a reason for the murders and the particularly nasty way they've been carried out."

"My view entirely," agreed James, "That's why I thought we'd pay a visit to Angela Hamilton and ask her."

CHAPTER FIFTY-NINE

"Ask her! Just like that?"

"That's right, her address is right here in the staff file. She lives in a house called 'King's Raven' just on the edge of Brentwood. I thought we could go over and pay her a visit later this morning."

"Brentwood?" queried Jenny, "It's an ideal location. If she is working for Anne Harvey then not only is it on the main line to Liverpool Street and convenient to get to the Fairfax Building in Canary Wharf but, at the same time, it's close to the A12 for an easy drive to Ipswich to report back to Anne herself."

* * * * *

Soon after breakfast, James and Jenny drove over to Brentwood and quickly found the road where 'King's Raven' was located.

"This is impressive," said Jenny glancing down the narrow road, "a few old grand-looking houses bunched together in this rather isolated corner of the town. Now which one is Angela's?"

"Here it is!" exclaimed James, but his joy was short-lived as both he and Jenny saw the estate agent's 'Sold' board nailed to the gate, "I hope we're not too late to catch her in. Let's go and see."

James opened the front gate for Jenny and they walked up to the house and peered through the windows, "Empty!" said a despondent Jenny, "We're too late after all. There's not a single piece of furniture in there."

"She's not here," said a voice from over the hedge in a heavy rural Essex accent, "she's gone but even when she lived here you'd hardly ever find her at home. I never spoke more than a few words to her in the last three years. She made it quite clear she didn't want anything to do with us round here. Good riddance if you ask me," and without waiting for a reply the elderly neighbour turned and went back inside his house.

"That tells us a lot," said Jenny sarcastically, "so where to now?"

"Brentwood and the estate agent. Let's see what we can find out there."

* * * * *

James and Jenny found the estate agent's premises in Brentwood High Street and went inside.

"We've come about 'King's Raven'," said Jenny.

"Afraid that one's sold," said a member of staff, "but we've got some similar properties that should interest you."

"No thank you," replied Jenny, "we're interested in the owner, Angela Hamilton, and would like to contact her."

"I'm afraid we can't release names and addresses of our clients, madam. But I think you've made a mistake the owner of 'King's Raven' isn't Angela Hamilton but is someone called Anne Harvey."

"Anne Harvey! Are you sure?" exclaimed James.

"That's correct, but as I said, I can't let you have her address."

"That's all right. We know Anne Harvey and where to find her," replied James and he and Jenny quickly left the premises.

As they made their way back to the car Jenny clung to her husband's arm and said tantalisingly, "This would seem to confirm your theory that Angela was working for Anne. Now that the job is done Angela can disappear and the last trace of Angela's whereabouts, the house where she lived for the past three years, can be disposed of. What a clever detective you are!"

"Thank you. It's all very neat but I'm sure we're missing something – there's got to be something more," said James thinking out aloud, "The murders, why did the murders take place? And why sell up now? Is it all over?"

"It could be," replied Jenny, "but what about David Fairfax himself? Was he intended to be a victim too? It's just as well the police are keeping an eye on him."

"For the time being but if nothing happens for a few weeks then they'll gradually relax the surveillance."

* * * * *

It was mid-afternoon when James and Jenny returned home. They were sitting together relaxing in the lounge talking through the morning's events when Jenny's mobile phone sounded. She put the phone to her ear and listened. After a few minutes she said, "Are you sure? Are you certain?" and listened again for several minutes more before switching off the phone. She sat silently looking at James with a strange look on her face.

"Well," he said unable to bear the silence and the suspense any longer, "who was it and what did they want?"

"That, my dear, was my contact in the National Health Service Records' Department. You may find this hard to believe because I certainly did and had to ask her to double check just to make sure."

"Make sure of what," exclaimed James almost running out of patience, "what did she say?"

"She said that Elaine Harvey, *Anne Harvey's mother*, was unable to have children. Extensive tests carried out by the fertility clinic at Ipswich Hospital all confirm this. Despite many years of treatment she was judged to be infertile and unable to conceive! What is curious, though, is that the family doctor's records, those maintained by Dr Greg Smith, are silent on this matter."

"What a turn up for the books," said James excitedly, "So who are Anne Harvey's parents? I suppose her father, Chris Harvey, could have had a child by another woman and his wife agreed to look after it, that sort of thing has often been known in the past."

"Hardly likely," replied Jenny, "it would seem totally out of character from what we know about him."

James sat back in his chair and let his mind wander for a while then he leaned towards Jenny and said, "Let's think the unthinkable. Let's imagine the following scenario ..." and he outlined to Jenny a sequence of events that could, in his opinion, explain all the happenings of the last few years.

When he had finished Jenny remained silent thinking over the implications of what she had just heard before adding, "If that is indeed the case then David Fairfax is in great danger."

"That's correct. I think we should speak to Inspector Westwood as soon as possible."

Chapter Sixty

"Hello, is that the duty sergeant?" asked James Palmer as his call to Epping Police Station was answered, "Can you put me through to Inspector Westwood? It's vital I speak to him as soon as possible!"

"Sorry sir, Inspector Westwood is busy right now. I'll ask him to call you back. Who shall I say called?"

"Tell him it's James Palmer and stress it really is urgent that he gets in touch with me right away."

"Not available I take it," said Jenny as James replaced the receiver, "Do you think we should try and contact David and warn him?"

"It's worth a try but I doubt he'll believe us. We'll have to confront him face-to-face. After all, if what we believe happened is true, then this places him not only in danger but also under suspicion of murder."

* * * * *

David Fairfax was in a sombre and reflective mood. He was relaxing in the safety of his own home, secure behind locked gates and high boundary walls with their

CCTV surveillance cameras, but he was bored. He needed something to occupy his mind. He wasn't a person to just sit around and do nothing. He had just begun to think about how his business empire could be rebuilt when the telephone rang.

"Hello, David Fairfax," and he suddenly perked up as he listened to the voice of someone he never thought he would hear from again.

"No, no I don't mind you getting in touch at all. As a matter of fact I'm rather glad you did. It will be nice to see you again. It's agreed then, I'll meet you there in about an hour and a half and we'll discuss your proposal in detail," and he hung up the phone.

"Fancy that," he thought, "Who'd have believed it? Better hurry, it wouldn't do to be late," and he rushed into the bedroom and changed into one of his more expensive business suits.

As he was leaving the house he met Katie, "Glad I've bumped into you. Look, something's come up and I've got to go out. You've worked hard today so why not take the rest of the day off. Don't forget to lock up when you leave."

"Very good, Sir David, that's very kind of you," and Katie watched as Sir David's Mercedes made its way along the drive and through the gates. She quickly finished the job in hand and left the premises, remembering to lock up and ensure the electronic gates were closed after her departure.

* * * * *

James tried telephoning both the house at Theydon Bois and David's mobile phone but got no reply.

"That's very strange," said James, "I was under the impression he was staying indoors at Forest Glade. Inspector Westwood felt it would be safer just in case he was the next intended victim."

"There's not much we can do then," replied Jenny trying to calm her husband's increasing frustration, "until Inspector Westwood gets in touch."

It was nearly an hour after his call to Epping Police Station that Inspector Westwood got back to James Palmer, "What can I do for you James?" said the Inspector.

"I think it's more a case of what I can do for you," replied a very happy-sounding James, "I think I've solved the case!"

"What case is that?"

"Don't play the innocent with me. The Fairfax murders. I know who did it and why!"

"That's certainly very welcome news indeed. I take it you don't believe Susan Rumble to be our murderer then?"

"No I don't. I never did if the truth be told and you'll never guess who it is," and before Inspector Westwood could reply James whispered a name into the phone.

"I hope you've got evidence to back up that assertion," said the Inspector, "Tell you what, why not come over to the station and we'll talk it through."

"But what about Sir David, I think he's in danger."

"He'll be all right. He's under strict orders not to go out anywhere or to let anybody in. If what you say is true then once I'm satisfied we'll go round and tell him."

"Ok," sighed a reluctant James, "we'll come into the station now."

"He doesn't believe you then," said a perceptive Jenny, "He'll take some convincing but I'm sure he'll agree once you outline the sequence of events."

"I hope you're right. Come on, let's get started. The sooner we get there the sooner we can finalise this case," and they made their way outside and got into James' car.

* * * * *

David Fairfax curbed his enthusiasm and managed to drive to the Fairfax Building by just keeping within the speed limits. As he approached the building he looked along the road but couldn't see the person he was expecting, "I must have got here first," he mused.

He pulled up outside what should have been a deserted building but noticed straight away that there was a light on in one of the offices.

"What's that all about?" he thought, "Why's that light on in my office? My office! There shouldn't be anybody there. I'll soon sort this out," and he marched up to the entrance determined to get an explanation.

He unlocked the door and was careful to lock it again once he was inside the building. He almost ran to his personal lift but much to his annoyance found it was stuck on a higher floor and wouldn't come down when called.

"Damn!" he shouted out aloud and made his way across the reception hall to the general lifts. He went inside one and pressed the button. The lift ascended almost silently to the third floor. David then walked along the corridor to his office but found it locked.

He unlocked the door and stepped inside. As he did so he failed to notice a trip wire and went crashing to the floor. He struggled to get up but a figure stepped out from behind the door and viciously coshed him over the head and he slumped back onto the floor.

* * * * *

It took James Palmer nearly 45 minutes to explain his theory to Inspector Westwood and Sergeant Benson. But it was readily apparent from their manner that they were very sceptical about it.

"I hear what you say, James," said a very doubtful sounding Inspector Westwood, "but there's so little proof to back any of it up. I admit it's very plausible but so much of it is conjecture. More concrete evidence will be needed for it to stand up in court and I don't think you can get it, not after all these years."

"Unless we can obtain a confession from Anne Harvey," responded James.

"Or a confession from Sir David," retorted Jenny.

"At least take it seriously," said James, "it's worth following up. Surely you'll at least speak to them both."

"No harm in that, sir," piped up Sergeant Benson not wishing to be left out of the conversation."

"All right then," agreed the Inspector, "let's go over to Theydon Bois and see what Sir David has to say about all of this. But mark my words, if he goes off at the deep end you've only got yourself to blame. I'm going to make it crystal clear from the start that this is all your idea."

"We'll go in my car," said Sergeant Benson and the four of them made their way to the car park at the rear of the police station.

* * * * *

David Fairfax regained consciousness. Not only was he suffering from a dreadful headache and cuts to his face but found he was also tied very tightly to his office chair. He looked around but there was nobody in the office. He tried his utmost to break free from the cords securing him to the chair but no matter how hard he struggled he couldn't loosen them.

"Get me out of here!" he shouted, "Untie me this instant! Let me out of here now! Whoever you are let me go now or else you'll regret this."

"You can shout as loud as you like but nobody will hear you. We're three floors up, double-glazed and soundproofed. Shout to your heart's content."

"Who the hell are you?" rasped Sir David angrily as he surveyed the masked figure dressed all in black who had silently glided into the office.

"Think of me as your Nemesis, your comeuppance, your death!"

"I don't understand! What the hell do you want?"

"I've already said what I want, *your death*!"

"What's this all about? Who are you? Show yourself damn it!"

The figure hesitated for a moment then slowly removed her face mask.

"Angela!" gasped David, "But why?"

"Because you ruined my life and destroyed everything I believed in and held dear."

"I treated you almost as one of the family," David blurted out still unable to fully comprehend the situation.

"Almost as one of the family," repeated Angela slowly, one syllable at a time and in a voice betraying more that a hint of sarcasm, "How ironic. You simply don't understand do you? I am one of the family, a family you chose to destroy. Just as you destroyed my family and everything I lived for, so I've destroyed your family and now it's your turn."

David Fairfax suddenly realised the gravity of the situation, "Then it was you who murdered Lucy and the children!" he stammered, "But why?" and once again he struggled violently to break free but to no avail.

"I spent a very happy childhood growing up in East Deben. In many respects it really was the happiest days of my life. During my teens my mother died but my father was a tower of strength and encouraged me to study. I went to Cambridge where I received a first class honours degree and several post-graduate qualifications. Then a few years ago my father became seriously ill with cancer. It soon became clear he had only a few months to live so I gave up my academic life and returned to live in East Deben.

My father's wish was for me to take over the business. It had grown into a thriving concern by then and I readily agreed. I had always thought I would inherit it one day but that day came a little sooner than I had anticipated. Then just a few days before he died my father told me about my true origins. And when he did my world fell apart. It was at that point I swore revenge on you and your family. I knew nothing about you but I made it my mission to find out as much as possible and to use that knowledge to destroy you and everything you held dear."

* * * * *

Sergeant Benson drove through the narrow forest roads as if there was no tomorrow and arrived at Forest Glade less that 10 minutes after leaving the police station in Epping.

"Looks secure enough to me," said Inspector Westwood punching in a number on his mobile phone, "but still no answer from Sir David. Benson, sound the horn a few times then perhaps he'll open the gates for us."

Benson sounded the car's horn repeatedly but there was no response.

"Ok Benson, over you go," ordered the Inspector.

"Over where, sir?"

"The gate, man, the gate! There's a control box on the other side."

"Very good, sir," and after some initial difficulty Benson managed to scale the gate and open it from within. The car entered the grounds and quickly made its way along the drive to the front door.

"No lights on and no sign of life," remarked the Inspector, "Perhaps you're right after all James, perhaps Sir David is in danger. Benson! Do your stuff. I'll look the other way."

Without a word Benson produced a bunch of skeleton keys from his pocket and skilfully opened the door in a matter of seconds. All four of them rushed into the house and began a thorough search, including the pool area, but there was no sign whatsoever of Sir David.

"Nobody here," said James stating the obvious, "I wonder where Sir David has gone. Katie may know."

"Good idea," replied Inspector Westwood, "Do you know her phone number?"

"No, but she lives in a road called Princess Close near Epping Station. We could be there in a few minutes."

"What are we waiting for then?" exclaimed the Inspector and all four ran back to the car for the return journey to Epping.

* * * * *

"My father told me about a night in March 1976. It was a night when one of the worst storms on record was battering the east-coast and a night when you murdered your first wife, Dawn Desborough."

"That's not true," pleaded David, "it was an accident. If you don't believe me look at the coroner's report."

"I have and I don't believe a word of it. In fact I know it's a complete travesty, nothing more than a pack of lies. You took Dawn onto the cliffs and deliberately pushed her over the edge onto the rocks and into a raging sea. You knew she didn't stand a chance of survival. But what you couldn't know was that you were seen. Just for an instant a flash of lightning illuminated that cliff-top scene and the occupants of a small fishing boat struggling to return to port saw what appeared to be a body falling into the sea.

You didn't notice that boat because it had been fishing illegally and wasn't showing any navigation lights. You made your way back to 'The Bull Hotel' unseen and concocted your story about Dawn going out on her own. But what about that boat? What did the crew on board that boat do?

There were two good men in that boat who despite the obvious danger to themselves decided to take a look. And they pulled a body from the water. Well not a body but a young dying woman who begged them to listen to her story. She told them what a monster you were and how you pushed her over the cliffs onto the rocks. Fortunately she survived the impact and was washed out to sea. Her condition, however, was grave. She had lots of broken bones and many internal injuries and knew she wasn't long for this world.

Your wife, Dawn Desborough, was dying. But she was also in the eighth month of pregnancy, as you were well aware, and her last wish was for her baby to be saved. Luckily one of the crew members was a doctor.

He managed with the crudest of instruments that were normally reserved for gutting fish to perform a caesarean and give life to that baby. And that baby was me!

Just think!" shouted Angela almost dementedly as she grabbed hold of David Fairfax's chin and roughly turned his head to force him to look into her eyes, "Just think of the agony and torment that poor woman went through as she gave birth to me and, at the same time, realised that her own life was ebbing away and she would shortly be dead. She embraced me for a mere moment knowing full well that she would soon likewise be embraced, not by life as I was, but for all eternity by death itself!"

"I don't believe a word of it," hissed David Fairfax, "you're making it all up."

"Dawn barely had time to hold me in her arms before she died. But with her dying breath she implored those two men on that boat to keep my birth a secret from you. She was terrified of what would happen to me if I were to be given to you. This placed them in a terrible dilemma but one where there was a way out.

Chris Harvey, the other person on that boat had been married for many years but despite undergoing various fertility treatments his wife had been unable to conceive. In a flash, therefore, an instant solution to two problems was found. I would be the baby they had so desperately wanted for so many years.

When the boat eventually made its way back to port I was concealed in a fish basket and given secretly to

Elaine Harvey. When she learned of the circumstances of my birth she immediately agreed to bring me up as her own child. To be on the safe side and to avoid any possible connection, my birth was announced about a week after your wife's body was found on the beach at North Deben."

"Very touching, I'm sure. But what about the post-mortem examination, you can't fake that!" snarled David.

"You forget about Dr Greg Smith. He was also the local police surgeon and the person who carried out the autopsy. Chris Harvey and Dr Smith knew the local tides and how long a body would take to make its way from East Deben to be washed up on the beach at North Deben. So two days later they placed the body of your wife on the beach and they were the ones who reported its discovery to the police. It was a simple matter for Dr Smith to make out his report and, naturally, he made sure he included a mention of Dawn's unborn child being dead in the womb.

From that moment I was brought up by Chris and Elaine Harvey and always considered them to be my natural parents, I had no reason to suspect otherwise. You can imagine my shock, therefore, when on his death bed my father revealed my true origins. I was devastated but once I'd reconciled myself to the full circumstances of my birth I resolved to take revenge on you and your family."

"I still don't believe it. You don't look anything like me at all," David said contemptuously.

Angela stood in front of Sir David and very slowly and deliberately removed her dark-rimmed spectacles, a set of prosthetic dentures, her green contact lens and her dark brown wig to reveal blue eyes and blonde hair.

David gasped, "Callisto, you look the spitting image of Callisto!"

* * * * *

"So you don't know who telephoned Sir David or where he went?" Inspector Westwood asked Katie.

"Sorry sir, he didn't say. All I know is that he was dressed in one of his best suits and was obviously looking forward to meeting someone. I got the impression it was an important business meeting."

"Thank you anyway," and the Inspector turned to leave.

"I don't know if this is relevant" volunteered Katie, "but I got the feeling he may have been meeting someone at the Fairfax Building. That's certainly where he's spent most of his time recently."

"Of course," interjected James Palmer, "that's the one place he would go to. It's also the one place that could be used as perfect bait to lure him into a trap."

"You may be right," said Inspector Westwood and he turned to Sergeant Benson, "Benson, put the blue light and the siren on, and get us to the Fairfax Building as quickly as you can. Step on it man!"

* * * * *

"Ok, so I admit you could be my daughter. But what now?" said a very dejected David Fairfax fearing the worst, "Where do we go from here?"

"I complete my mission," and Anne Harvey, no longer in the guise of Angela Hamilton, struggled to push David's chair towards the open lift shaft.

"The doors are open but the lift's not there," exclaimed David in terror as Anne pushed the chair near to the edge and he stared down the empty lift shaft. Once again he attempted to break free from his bonds but was reluctant to struggle and rock the chair too much in case it tipped over the edge.

"How observant, the lift's on the floor above. But look down that shaft and tell me what you see."

"The lift machinery and some water. It looks flooded down there."

"That's because I turned the sprinklers on in the basement for a short while. I've calculated that a fall from up here on the third floor won't kill you but it will leave you badly injured with many broken bones. Tied to this chair you'll land face down and drown choking in the water as you struggle to breathe.

Just think about it, we're recreating Dawn's death, only this time I'll be you and you can be Dawn. The lift shaft is the cliffs, the machinery below is the rocks and the water is the sea. Very appropriate, this whole saga will end as it begun," and Anne laughed out aloud and pushed David's chair to the very edge of the lift shaft and rocked it violently. He panicked and the sweat began to stream down his face.

"You're mad! You're completely insane! You've just said we're family. Surely you wouldn't kill your own father?" implored David desperate to find some way out of the situation.

"You were quite prepared to kill me. You were quite prepared to kill a child you didn't want. That's why I killed your children, in revenge for what their father tried to do to me.

I know exactly what your game was. From the very beginning you planned to take control of both Dawn Desborough and Beverley Jenks' businesses. That's why you didn't want any children from your first two marriages. You had planned from the very start that your heirs would all be from your third marriage to your childhood sweetheart, Lucy Murray. It was all most meticulously planned.

I know you spooked the horse Beverley was riding when she lost her child and I know you murdered her on that cruise ship. You thought you'd got away with it, and you would have too if it hadn't been for Chris Harvey telling me how I was brought into this world. From that moment I knew my mission in life was to track you down and destroy you. And do you know what? It's proved far easier than I ever thought it would be."

"I'm sure we can talk this through," pleaded a terrified David Fairfax peering down the lift shaft and sweating profusely. "I'm still a very wealthy man and you could share that wealth."

"Money! I don't want your money. Money's the solution for everything as far as you're concerned. I've got more money than you can imagine. Unlike your businesses mine are thriving."

Anne paused and slowly pushed David's chair closer to the edge. One leg slipped over the void and the chair lurched forward but didn't quite tip over. David was sitting absolutely still and rigid. He was scared to make even the slightest of movements in case he hastened his own demise. Once again Anne pushed the chair forward and it hovered on the brink.

"Please," implored David, "I'll do anything, but not this! Please!"

"Too late! Prepare to meet your maker and go to hell where you belong! Good riddance!" and Anne pushed the chair forward as slowly as she was able until it finally lost its balance and tipped over into the lift shaft. The chair plunged swiftly to the bottom of the shaft and a last scream from David Fairfax echoed up the void and reverberated round his office before silence once more engulfed the room.

Anne made her way to the basement and waded through the ankle-deep water until she stood at the bottom of the lift shaft where the water was nearly two feet deep. She watched and listened for several minutes as David choked and fought for breath. When she was satisfied that he was dead she returned to his office and removed all traces of her presence. She then opened a small case and took out a number of packages and scattered them around the room. After placing a card on the middle of his desk she jauntily skipped down the stairs and made her way out of a rear exit of the Fairfax Building.

"Dangerous things, rocks!" she said to herself as she turned a corner and walked towards her parked car, "Dangerous things, rocks!"

Chapter Sixty-one

With flashing blue light and siren blazing Sergeant Benson drove at breakneck pace and arrived at the Fairfax Building in record time. The car screeched to a halt but there was no sign of life within.

"The place looks in complete darkness," said Inspector Westwood.

"Yes, but isn't that Sir David's car parked just along the road?" asked a worried-looking Jenny.

"It certainly is," replied James, "that means he could be inside the building."

"Benson, the door!" Inspector Westwood said in a voice that betrayed his anxiety.

Sergeant Benson produced his well-worn skeleton keys and quickly gained entry. Once inside he took out a pocket torch. After much searching he eventually found a switch and turned the lights on.

"Nobody down here," observed the Inspector, "let's try upstairs."

"Yes," replied James running towards the lifts, "if I remember correctly David's office is on the third floor."

All four took the lift to the third floor and crossed the corridor to David Fairfax's office. The room was in complete darkness but Benson soon found the light switch just inside the door.

"What on earth's happened here?" exclaimed Inspector Westwood looking at the packets of underwear strewn about the office.

"More DesboroDenim fashions from the 1970s I would think," said Jenny bending down and examining one of the small still-sealed packets, "There are lots of them thrown about everywhere. But where is Sir David?"

Inspector Westwood made his way to Sir David's desk and found a card placed exactly in the centre of the blotter, "I think we're too late it's the murderer's calling card," and he handed the card to James.

James read out aloud what was written on the card, 'I said pride comes before a fall and it did. Now it's all over'.

Inspector Westwood reached into an inside pocket. He took out his notebook and read what was on the card David Fairfax had received at Christmas, 'Just as betrayal comes before a fall so does pride'. He shook his head in disbelief.

James looked round the office and then his eyes glanced into the adjoining room and he saw the open lift shaft.

"The lift!" he shouted, "The lift shaft is open!" and he ran towards the lift closely followed by Inspector Westwood, Sergeant Benson and Jenny who struggled to get up from the floor and keep up with the others. All four peered down the shaft. At the bottom they saw an upturned chair with a person tied to it. The chair had fallen with the body underneath face-down so they could only see the bound arms and legs and couldn't make out who it was.

"That's horrible," gasped Jenny in sheer disbelief at what she had seen, "Who would do such a thing?" and she turned away in disgust trying her utmost not to retch.

"Come on Benson," urged Inspector Westwood, "don't just stand there gawping let's get down there and see who it is," and the two detectives rushed out of the office and made their way to the basement.

"Aren't you going down there, James?" enquired Jenny, "I think I'd rather stay up here if that's all right with you."

"I'm not in that much of a hurry. There's no doubt in my mind that the person under that chair is David Fairfax," and James walked slowly out of the room and down the stairs to the basement. Jenny sat down on a seat in the corridor outside Sir David's office and buried her head in her hands.

By the time James reached the bottom of the lift shaft Sergeant Benson and Inspector Westwood had managed to pull the chair out of the lift machinery and stand it upright. David Fairfax's badly mutilated face was clearly recognisable despite the injuries caused from falling onto the cogs and wheels that helped power the lift.

"Poor sod," commented Inspector Westwood looking closely at the horrific injuries and searching for a non-existent pulse to confirm death, "nobody deserves to end up like this! Benson, get onto the local nick and arrange for a forensics team to come over here straightaway."

"Very good, sir," replied Benson and he took out his mobile phone.

"Well, James," said an exasperated Inspector Westwood, "it looks like you were right after all but we were too late. It's difficult to say when David was killed due to the body being partially submerged in that cold water but I wouldn't think it was all that long ago. We must have missed the murderer by a matter of minutes."

"So where to now?" asked James, "Speak to Anne Harvey?"

"Yes, but not now. If she's hired Angela Hamilton, or whoever this person calls themselves, to murder David Fairfax then no doubt she'll also have a cast-iron alibi. We'll wait until tomorrow morning before we go and speak to the illusive Anne Harvey."

"Fine with me," agreed James and then he added, "I don't suppose you'll have any objection to me and Jenny coming along."

"It's most irregular as you know but bearing in mind your background and the help you've given me on this case I'm prepared to let you tag along. No word about this to the 'Super' though or I'll be for it! I'll meet you at ten o'clock tomorrow morning in Ipswich outside the headquarters of the Anne Harvey Group."

"That's fine," said a very relieved James who feared he might have been left out of what could be the final chapter of this investigation, "I suppose I'd better go and find Jenny. She seemed a bit upset when she saw David's body at the bottom of the lift shaft."

James made his way back up to the third floor. He found Jenny still sitting in the corridor outside David Fairfax's office trying to stop trembling.

"Come on," he said, "let's get you back home," and then added after realizing, "We'll have to take the tube. I almost forgot we came here in Sergeant Benson's car."

"Never mind," responded Jenny, "I think the walk will do me good. I need some fresh air. It was quite a shock seeing that body down the lift shaft."

James and Jenny Palmer left the building. As they walked hand-in-hand towards the tube station they heard the wailing of sirens as a fleet of police vehicles descended on the Fairfax Building.

* * * * *

The next morning Jenny was still feeling a bit queasy but insisted on going to Ipswich with James. On this occasion, however, she was more than willing for James to drive her there.

James and Jenny parked the car and made their way to the Anne Harvey Group's headquarters. They were a few minutes early but Inspector Westwood and Sergeant Benson were already standing outside awaiting their arrival. The four of them entered the building and walked across to the reception desk.

Inspector Westwood showed his warrant card to the receptionist and said he wished to see Anne Harvey. A few minutes after the receptionist had made a telephone call Anne's personal assistant Nikki arrived and escorted them up to Anne's office.

"Come in, please take a seat," said Anne Harvey in a most welcoming voice, "What can I do for you?"

"You already know James Palmer, I believe," said Inspector Westwood, "but this is Jenny Palmer, James' wife, Sergeant Benson and I'm Chief Inspector Westwood."

"Pleased to meet you," replied Anne appearing somewhat bemused by the presence of these four people, "Can I offer you some refreshment?"

"No thank you," said the Inspector rather curtly, "we're here on official business. We're making inquiries into the death of David Fairfax and believe you can help us in those enquiries."

"I heard about Sir David's death on the news this morning. I couldn't believe it, especially coming so soon after his wife was killed, a nasty business indeed," and Anne Harvey's voice faltered with emotion, "If there's anything I can do to help in your enquiries then of course I will be more than pleased to do so. But as I'm sure you're aware I've never met the man. Admittedly we were business rivals but I'm not in the habit of murdering my opponents, I prefer to get the better of them by using my business acumen."

"Ms Harvey do you know ..."

"Miss!" insisted Anne abruptly cutting off the Inspector in mid sentence, "I prefer to be addressed as Miss."

"Very well, *Miss Harvey*," stressed an openly annoyed Inspector, "do you know an Angela Hamilton?"

"No," replied Anne, "I did go to school with someone of that name but she was killed in a car accident many years ago."

"We have reason to believe you hired someone called Angela Hamilton to work for David Fairfax in order to glean inside information about future tenders and undercut him. We also believe you hired this very same person to murder all members of the Fairfax family."

"That's complete nonsense, a fantasy. What reason could I possibly have for murdering that family? As I said before, I've never met David Fairfax or any other members of his family."

"What if David Fairfax was your father?" asked James unable to contain himself any longer.

"Then surely that would be even less reason for me to have him murdered. Sorry to disappoint you Mr Palmer but I had my own mother and father, Elaine and Chris Harvey. They idolised me and I was devoted to them. In fact I had a very happy childhood."

"But what if your parents, or the people you thought were your parents, had been unable to have children? What if when someone was pushed over the cliffs at East Deben she was pregnant and although it was impossible to save her it was possible to save her unborn child? What if that child was saved and given to a childless couple to bring up as their own? What if that child was you?"

"I'd say you have a very vivid imagination," replied Anne Harvey with a smile, "but I'm sure the inquest into that person's death would say whether or not her unborn child died with her."

"It does," said James, "it says the baby died in the womb. I suspect you already know that but I still think my theory is correct."

"Sorry to disappoint you," responded Anne, "but I fear it will have to remain just that, simply a theory."

"Miss Harvey," interjected Inspector Westwood sternly, "do you mind telling me where you were yesterday and also on these dates," and he gave Anne a list of dates on which members of the Fairfax family had been murdered.

"Nikki," said Anne speaking into the intercom on her desk, "bring in my appointment books for the last two years."

Almost immediately Nikki brought in three appointment books and gave them to Anne.

"Here you are Inspector, help yourself," and Anne handed the books to the Inspector who quickly checked on the dates. Unbeknown to Anne he also looked at what she was doing when attacks had been carried out on property belonging to the Fairfax Group. However, on each of these dates, Anne was in meetings where there were plenty of people present.

"Very convenient, very convenient indeed!" exclaimed Inspector Westwood, "On all these dates you were attending board meetings in this very building or at a hotel miles away from the murder scenes." He purposely didn't mention the other incidents he had checked upon.

"That's correct, and on each occasion there are at least a dozen people who can vouch for me. I believe Martin Travers was present at every one of those meetings and he can confirm my attendance. I can call him if you wish. But surely, inspector, if you think this Angela Hamilton person was behind the murders you should be looking for her and not trying to implicate me."

"I may speak to Martin Travers in due course but I'm still not convinced that you don't know Angela Hamilton or the person who calls herself Angela Hamilton. I may be in touch again," and the Inspector stood up.

"If I can be of any further assistance please feel free to come and speak to me again. Nikki will see you all out," and Anne pressed a button on the intercom to summon her personal assistant.

* * * * *

Outside the building Inspector Westwood spoke to James Palmer, "It was a good theory and I think Anne Harvey may be involved somehow but there is just no way we can prove it. From the minutes of those board meetings it appears Anne Harvey herself is in the clear. Even on last New Year's Eve and New Year's Day she was hosting a special meeting for Board Members followed by a party at a hotel in Felixstowe.

If Anne Harvey denies knowing Angela Hamilton and we can't prove any kind of a link between the two of them then I'm afraid we're going to have to call it a day, unless of course we can find this Angela Hamilton."

"What about Susan Rumble?" asked Jenny, "What are you going to do about her? It looks like she's in the clear."

"I think you're right. The more I think about it," admitted the Inspector, "the more I think she was set up. Finding all those things in her house certainly made us lower our guard and become almost complacent and, I suppose, paved the way for the murders of Lucy and David Fairfax."

"Yes, it was all so very clever, not just the murders but also the framing of Susan Rumble," said Sergeant Benson joining in the conversation.

"So you'll be letting her go," said Jenny.

"I think so," replied Inspector Westwood, "there's no reason to hold her now. Anyway," he said after a short pause, "it was nice working with you and James," and the Inspector shook hands warmly with both Jenny and James before he and Sergeant Benson made their way back to their car.

"Come on," said James, "let's get back home. Tell you what, why don't we stop off somewhere on the way back for lunch."

"What a good idea," responded Jenny enthusiastically, "and you can pay!"

Chapter Sixty-two

The next day James and Jenny Palmer were sitting quietly in their kitchen having breakfast and reading the morning papers.

"Look here, James," said Jenny between mouthfuls of toast, "there are some fabulous new shows in town. Why don't we make a day of it at the weekend? See a show and have a meal out?"

"What was that, darling?" replied James as he looked up from his newspaper.

"I said there are some fabulous new shows in the West End. You know, up town, in London."

"What a fool I've been!" exclaimed James suddenly without responding to Jenny, "Not London, but 'The London', the hotel!"

"What on earth are you rambling on about?"

"The London! Remember when I went and spoke to the manager there and that receptionist, Maria! Whose photograph did Maria say looked like the woman who walked past her desk that New Year's Eve when Tom Fairfax was murdered?"

"Callisto, but we now know that she couldn't possibly have done it," replied a very puzzled-looking Jenny, "What are you trying to say?"

"I'm trying to say we've missed the obvious. What if my theory about Anne Harvey hiring someone called Angela Hamilton to infiltrate the Fairfax empire and murder the family was only partially correct? What if it wasn't Angela Hamilton but Anne Harvey herself all along?"

"I don't follow you?" questioned Jenny putting down both her toast and newspaper and staring directly at her husband, "But knowing you I'm sure you're going to enlighten me!"

"If Anne Harvey is David Fairfax's daughter then it's not beyond the bounds of possibility that she looks like him or Callisto. Don't forget, with the exception of Lucy all the family members were blue-eyed blondes. And the prophecy by that holy man in India that so upset Nick predicted he'd be killed by his sister. Perhaps the sister in question was a half-sister he didn't know he had."

"But we've met Anne Harvey and she's not blonde at all and she hasn't got blue eyes. And as for a prophecy by a so-called holy man well now you are getting just a little bit ridiculous," said a disbelieving Jenny.

"It's not quite as far-fetched as you might think. Let's look at what we know. We know from your conversation with Mrs Goodenough that Anne Harvey was skilled in the art of make-up. We know that Dawn Fairfax's unborn child probably survived and could have been brought up by Chris and Elaine Harvey as their own. We know that Anne Harvey could have inherited lots of old 1970s DesboroDenim stock from her father. We know it was only after Chris Harvey's death that Anne Harvey took over the business and that soon afterwards an Angela Hamilton started to work for David Fairfax. We know that Anne Harvey is something of a recluse and doesn't often make appearances in the office. We know that a couple of years after Angela Hamilton begun working for David Fairfax things started to go wrong for him. Why, therefore, is it beyond the bounds of possibility to suppose that Angela Hamilton is none other than Anne Harvey herself!"

Jenny sat silently for a while contemplating the full significance of what she had just heard before asking, "Even if what you say is true how can you prove any of it? You saw what happened yesterday. There's no way you can prove it, Anne Harvey is a very clever and resourceful woman. If she did commit those murders, and I must say it does seem highly plausible, then I'm sure she's covered her tracks very well. Let's face it she's got a cast-iron alibi for all the murders and Inspector Westwood appeared most reluctant to pursue the matter any further."

"Those alibis are sufficient reason in themselves to indicate her guilt. They are so good, so watertight and just so readily available that they must be false. She knew we'd be paying her a visit and she was ready for us."

"So what are you going to do, speak again to Inspector Westwood?"

"No, that would be a complete waste of time! I'm going back to Ipswich to have another word with Anne Harvey. Want to come?"

"If you don't mind I think I'll stay out of this one but you go by all means. I've a feeling that if there's anything more to be gleaned by speaking to Anne Harvey again then you'll have more luck on your own. You'll be better off without me."

"Fine," said James and he prepared to drive down to Ipswich for what he hoped would be one final time.

* * * * *

James Palmer walked through the revolving doors and over to the reception desk, "Good morning, I'm James Palmer and I wish to speak to Anne Harvey as a matter of urgency."

"That's fine, Mr Palmer. Miss Harvey is expecting you and left instructions for you to go straight up to her office."

James was somewhat taken aback by this revelation but he managed to retain his composure and strode purposefully over to the lifts almost thinking aloud, "How could she know I'd be coming here today? I only made up my mind over the breakfast table!"

Nikki greeted James and quickly showed him to Anne's inner office. James walked briskly inside and then stopped dead in his tracks. Sitting directly in front of him behind her impressive oak desk was Anne Harvey but not the Anne Harvey he knew. This Anne Harvey was no longer a brunette with hazel-brown eyes but a blonde with blue eyes. He stood there momentarily speechless.

"James, nice to see you again," said a very happy-looking Anne, "Of all those here yesterday I knew it would only be you who came back. Only you would have something more to say to me. Please, don't stand on ceremony, take a seat over here in front of my desk," and she gestured for him to come forward.

"Thank you," he replied quickly pulling himself together, "that's most kind."

"Not at all," said a gentle-sounding Anne, "Now tell me, what can I do for you?"

"I'll come straight to the point. I think I got it wrong yesterday. I don't think you hired anyone to murder David Fairfax and his family, I think it was you all along. You were Angela Hamilton and you destroyed his business empire and murdered his family!"

"That's quite an accusation. Glad there's just the two of us in this office or else I might have to seek redress through the courts."

"I don't think you'd do that. You'd have far too much to lose. I know you're skilled at makeup and prosthetics and could quite easily take on another identity. I suspect, although I can't prove it, that Dawn Fairfax's child survived that fall from the cliffs and was brought up by Chris and Elaine Harvey as their own. I also suspect it was soon after Chris Harvey told you the truth about your origins that you decided to embark on your trail of revenge and destroy the Fairfax empire and murder the Fairfax family."

"It all makes for a fascinating tale, but can you prove any of it?"

Before James could reply Nikki knocked on the door. Without waiting for a response she entered the room carrying a tray with two cups of tea and a plate of biscuits. She placed the tray on Anne's desk and left the room. Without a word Anne placed one of the cups in front of James, a cup of black tea with no milk or sugar, and gestured with a smile for him to continue.

"No, I don't think I can prove it. I don't think I can prove a single word of it. What I would like to know, though, is why you've changed your appearance? You look the spitting image of Callisto with your blonde hair and blue eyes, almost a *chip off the old Fairfax block*! Angela wore spectacles and had green eyes and dark brown hair whereas you, until yesterday, had brown eyes and were a brunette."

"James, what can I say? I have simply reverted to my natural colour as I often do. This theory of yours is quite fascinating but I'm afraid it will have to remain just that, a theory and a figment of your imagination. If there was any prospect of the good Inspector Westwood believing this story of yours then I'm sure you would have brought him along with you this morning, but you didn't. I have to conclude, therefore, that this matter is now closed."

"I regret to say I have reluctantly to agree with you. I can't condone what you've done in the slightest but I think I can understand why you did it. If I was wearing my former policeman's hat then I might now be taking things further with a view to arresting you on suspicion of the murders of five members of the Fairfax family. But wearing my private investigator's hat I have to admit defeat and say that I'll be taking no further action whatsoever."

"I'm glad to hear it," smiled Anne who paused briefly and then took out a small brown envelope from her desk, "Here, I believe this is yours."

"Mine!" replied a startled James putting his teacup on the desk and at a loss to think of how anything of his could possibly have found its way into Anne Harvey's desk.

"Take it," insisted Anne almost thrusting it into his hands.

James reluctantly accepted the small envelope. He peered inside and took out a cheque. To his astonishment he saw it was for a sum of £50,000 made payable to him by David Fairfax.

"This cheque," he began, but Anne cut him off in mid-sentence.

"Isn't it strange what you find when you take over a company. I found this in a pile of David Fairfax's DesboroDenim fashion papers. He must have forgotten to give it to you," said Anne with a gleam in her eye, "If I were you I'd cash it as soon as possible before his administrators take steps to freeze his assets and bank accounts."

"You found it in a pile of David Fairfax's old papers?" questioned James, "I don't believe a word of it. It would make more sense if you had been Angela Hamilton and just taken it with you when you left his employ."

"Well you'll just have to take my word for it then," and Anne smiled gently once again.

James got up as if to leave but Anne stopped him, "Don't forget this!"

"What is it?" asked James as Anne handed him a thick A4 sized envelope that was on one side of her desk, "Not another cheque I trust?"

"No," replied Anne, "it's something much more valuable than that. Open it and find out!"

James opened the envelope with more than a degree of trepidation and pulled out a wad of papers. The papers made reference to the investigation he had undertaken into a meat-packaging firm based in Chelmsford. What he didn't know at the time was that the firm was in the process of being acquired by the Fairfax Group.

James sat down again and flicked through the papers hardly believing what he was reading. It was clear that none other than David Fairfax himself had deliberately bribed workers at the plant to make corruption allegations against him. This had not only resulted in him being taken off the case but having to leave the police force under ignominious circumstances.

"David Fairfax," muttered James barely audibly, "David Fairfax. It never occurred to me that he could have been behind those corruption allegations."

"I'm sure deep-down you know what sort of a man, what sort of a monster, he really was. No point in dwelling on the past, you can take those papers and clear your name."

"Thank you, thank you very much. I'm most grateful to you. I'll certainly speak to the Chief Constable and get the record put straight but I've no intention of going back into the police force. I'm really too old for all that now and besides I like working for myself as a private detective," and looking straight into Anne Harvey's eyes he added, "You meet much more interesting people, much more interesting people indeed," and he got up and left the office without even the slightest suggestion of a backward glance.

Anne Harvey smiled and watched him go in silent admiration, "He was the only one who got to the truth and who could have been a danger to me," she thought to herself. Then spinning slowly on her swivel chair she added with a chuckle, "In the end it's as if I cheated death before I was born; from the grave to the cradle, so to speak! From the grave to the cradle!"

Epilogue

About six months' later James and Jenny Palmer are having a late breakfast, after an evening show in London the night before, when there is a loud thud as the postman pushes a large heavy envelope through the letter box in the hall.

"I'll go," said Jenny, quickly placing her cup on the table, "but I don't think we're expecting any mail."

"Probably just junk mail, nothing to get excited about," added James.

"I'm not so certain," replied a curious Jenny a few moments later, "look at this! A large envelope addressed to both of us in embossed silver lettering. It could be something important."

"Better use the letter opener then, just in case," responded a sarcastic James.

"You'll never believe this," said an excited and animated Jenny as she stared intently at the silver embossed card she had plucked from the envelope, "it's a wedding invitation."

"A wedding invitation?" questioned James.

"Yes, and you'll never guess who it's from. It's from Anne Harvey, she's marrying Martin Travers, her Chief Executive, and we are invited to their wedding."

"Well, that's out of the question. We can't possibly go. Think about what she has done!"

"Can't go!" stressed Jenny ignoring the remark from her husband, "This invitation is not only to the wedding on a private island in the Caribbean but includes a two-week stay at a luxury five-star hotel on the island, first class air tickets and a chauffeur driven car to the airport and back!"

"I still think it would be most inappropriate."

"Inappropriate! I'll need a new dress for the wedding, of course, and a complete new wardrobe. I can't wait!"

THE END

About the Author

Keith Plummer was born on the Suffolk Coast, moved to Essex as a child and, some years after early retirement, relocated to a converted Grade II listed barn in a very small Leicestershire village, where he is able to indulge his passion for long country walks. Other interests range from studying the ancient world to modern-day cosmology, a love of travel (he has been to 99 different countries) and the natural world, modern technology and Indian cinema - an interest he enjoys when staying in his second home in Jaipur. He modestly claims to "get by" in Hindi. One other pastime is researching and writing biographies of family members - both past and present. He is married with one daughter and two grandsons. Until November 2021 when he published "Tales of the *Completely* Unexpected", a collection of short stories in the style of Roald Dahl, his previous writings had all been of a non-fiction nature in the scientific press, so "From the Grave to the Cradle" is his first long-overdue full-length novel.

CPSIA information can be obtained
at www.ICGtesting.com
Printed in the USA
LVHW110443170522
718911LV00004B/47